COUNTER ATTACK

BOOKS BY PATRICIA BRADLEY

LOGAN POINT SERIES
Shadows of the Past
A Promise to Protect
Gone Without a Trace
Silence in the Dark

MEMPHIS COLD CASE NOVELS
Justice Delayed
Justice Buried
Justice Betrayed
Justice Delivered

NATCHEZ TRACE PARK RANGERS
Standoff
Obsession
Crosshairs
Deception

PEARL RIVER
Counter Attack

COUNTER ATTACK

PATRICIA BRADLEY

Revell

a division of Baker Publishing Group
Grand Rapids, Michigan

© 2023 by Patricia Bradley

Published by Revell
a division of Baker Publishing Group
Grand Rapids, Michigan
www.revellbooks.com

Printed in the United States of America

Library of Congress Cataloging-in-Publication Data
Names: Bradley, Patricia, 1945– author.
Title: Counter attack / Patricia Bradley.
Description: Grand Rapids, MI : Revell, a division of Baker Publishing Group, [2023] |
    Series: Pearl River ; 1
Identifiers: LCCN 2022035648 | ISBN 9780800741624 (paperback) | ISBN
    9780800743093 (casebound) | ISBN 9781493441259 (ebook)
Subjects: LCGFT: Detective and mystery fiction. | Novels.
Classification: LCC PS3602.R34275 C68 2023 | DDC 813/.6—dc23/eng/20220728
LC record available at https://lccn.loc.gov/2022035648

This book is a work of fiction. Names, characters, places, and incidents are the product of the author's imagination or are used fictitiously. Any resemblance to actual events, locales, or persons, living or dead, is coincidental.

Baker Publishing Group publications use paper produced from sustainable forestry practices and post-consumer waste whenever possible.

23   24   25   26   27   28   29   7   6   5   4   3   2   1

To my sister, Barbara,
who journeyed with me 1,120 feet below the earth
so I could see what being in a cave felt like.

And to Bryan and Carole,
who never complain about my deadlines . . .
at least not to my face.

But most of all,
to my Lord and Savior, Jesus.
Thank you.

Phame fingered the White pawn and opened the Tor browser from a USB drive. It took a minute to scroll through the sites before finding the right one on the dark web.

Good. So far over five thousand gamers had played the new video game. Half a mil in cryptocurrency . . . None of the other video games had ever brought in this much money. But then none of the other games were like this one. The murders had been a stroke of genius. And focusing on similar victims killed two birds with one stone.

Phame shuddered at the cliché. Phillip had hated clichés.

"Still, you'd be proud of me." The words dropped into the quiet room held a catch.

Revenge for Phillip's death was sweet, but it'd always been about the money. The potential to make millions of dollars relied on new victims. Retribution for Phillip's death made the choice of victims easier.

Minutes later, new additions to the game that would bring in even more money were up and running. That so many would pay to be a killer, even vicariously . . . Phame had to laugh.

Getting away with the first murder had brought such a

sense of power that outsmarting the police had become very addictive. Soon, everyone would know about Phame, and one police officer in particular. The officer would pay—not by her own death but knowing her actions had caused the deaths of many.

2

Undercover detective Alex Stone twirled a strand of hair around her finger. Her spidey sense tingled from the back of her neck to the small of her back, where a bellyband secured her small backup pistol.

Someone was watching her, hopefully the person the media had dubbed the Queen's Gambit Killer. She clenched her jaw. Leave it to the media to link a killer to a TV program because a White pawn had been found in the hand of each of the five victims. She'd give anything to know who leaked that information to the public.

Her neck prickled again. Was the killer watching her every move?

Alex swiveled the barstool, casually scanning the Lemon Tree Bar and Lounge and making brief eye contact with a man who nursed a drink at the other end of the bar. One of the two Chattanooga, Tennessee, police detectives covering her in case the killer took the bait. The other officer sat at a nearby table.

Alex smoothed the short skirt that revealed way more leg than she liked. But the style was similar to what the victims had worn to the bar. She glanced down at the red three-inch heels. What she wouldn't give to slip on her running shoes.

When homicide requested her for the undercover operation, she'd insisted on Detectives Watkins and Parker as her backup. She trusted them, and the three of them were a team, one that she would hate to break up if her request to transfer to homicide came through. Homicide was the only department in the Special Investigation Division she hadn't worked in. If she was able to lure the killer into a trap and he was captured, that would surely help the transfer to go through.

She sipped a nonalcoholic Tom Collins—fizzy water with a wedge of lemon—as her gaze shifted to the stage, where a lanky kid with peach fuzz on his chin crooned of lost love in the smoky haze. Then she watched a young waitress as she wove around the tables delivering orders. Kayla. That's what she'd said her name was when Alex ordered her drink. The girl didn't look old enough to be admitted to the bar, much less serve patrons.

Alex continued her scan of the room, and a man caught her eye. He raised his glass as if inviting her to drink with him. Should she take him up on his offer? Although he was the right age, Alex doubted he was the killer—the FBI profile indicated the killer was an introvert, and this man seemed anything but. She decided to ignore him for now.

He was the third man to hit on her. Alex wasn't sure exactly what she was looking for—maybe someone showing interest but not in a way that drew attention to himself.

She realized Kayla had stopped by her barstool and was speaking to her. Alex leaned toward her. "I didn't catch what you said."

"Ready for another drink?"

Alex glanced at her almost-empty glass. "Oh, sure."

"Tom Collins mocktail again?"

Alex nodded, and the girl disappeared. She'd been watching her work the crowd off and on all night, and when Kayla returned, she handed the girl a twenty and took the glass. "Keep the change." A broad smile made the waitress look even younger. "Are you in college?"

The smile dampened. "No. My dad died a while back, and between his hospital bills and my mom losing her job, there was no money. I had to drop out with only half my credits toward a degree in social work." Then she smiled brightly. "But I'm not letting that stop me. My financial aid advisor is helping me find grant money, but it probably won't be this semester. Next year for sure, though."

Even though she'd just met Kayla, Alex had no doubts about the waitress getting her degree. She seemed the type to not let anything stand in her way.

"You haven't worked here long, have you?" Alex didn't remember seeing Kayla's name in any of the case reports.

"Off and on for five years next month."

Alex blinked. A person had to be eighteen to work in a bar, so the girl was a lot older than she seemed. Had she been working at the Lemon Tree during the times of the murders and slipped through the cracks? Or was she not working there at the time of the murders? "Did you know Trinity Collins?"

"The woman who was murdered after she left the bar?" Kayla shook her head. "That was so sad, but I was working the afternoon crowd back then, and she never came in during that time."

That explained why there was no statement from Kayla in Trinity's file.

"Was she your friend or something?" the waitress asked.

"Something like that."

Victims four and five, Maria Brooks and Trinity Collins, had been at the bar earlier on the nights they were killed, and Alex had almost made the fatal mistake of sounding like a cop. And now she didn't dare ask if Kayla knew Maria Brooks.

Kayla jumped as someone called her name, and Alex followed her gaze to the same man who'd raised his glass to Alex earlier. "Houdini probably wants another scotch and water," she said with a shudder.

"Houdini?" She was surprised Kayla even knew who the dead magician was.

The girl giggled. "Yeah. He comes for a while then he disappears for a month or so."

"Get it," Alex said. "And I'll take it to him."

"You don't mind? He gives me the willies, but I have to be nice to him since he's a friend of the owner."

"I don't mind at all." Houdini was sounding more interesting by the minute.

Alex slid a hose-clad leg from the barstool and stood, straightening the leather skirt while she covertly checked the small Sig at her back. Normally she wore it attached to her sports bra, but the low-cut blouse ruled out that option. At least the top hung loosely past her waist. She glanced down, making one last check to verify the top didn't reveal too much cleavage.

With a pasted-on smile, she took the drink Kayla handed her and walked toward Houdini's table. There was a small chance he was the person she was looking for.

3

Well, well," Houdini said as he took the drink she offered. "I thought you weren't interested."

"Maybe I am, and maybe I'm not. What's your name, handsome?" She couldn't very well call him Houdini. And he was good-looking in a movie-star kind of way. Perfectly styled hair, icy blue eyes, rugged face, and pearly white teeth. His clothes looked as though he'd had them tailor-made.

"Reggie. And yours?"

A fake name if she'd ever heard one. "Lexie." It was one of the nicknames she'd been given over the years. Alex glanced at his ring finger.

"Nope, not married."

At least he was sharp. "Maybe you've never worn a wedding band."

"Believe me, honey, if I'd ever gotten married, I would've worn one."

"So, Reggie, what do you do?"

"Would you believe me if I said I was a preacher?"

She eyed the drink in his hand.

"Hey! Some preachers drink."

"Not in the Bible Belt." At least she didn't know of any.

"Guess I forgot where I was." Then he winked. "Reckon I blew that one."

"You blew that one when you walked in the door."

"You're funny. You want to cut to the chase or play the dating game?"

"I'm not going home with you, if that's what you're hinting at."

His eyes turned cold as he raised the scotch to his lips. "Then don't waste my time."

Alex shivered at how fast he'd gone from warm and inviting to ice cold. "I'm not going to say it was nice talking to you."

She hoped one of her colleagues snapped a photo of him because he'd just gone to the top of her list of possibilities. As an undercover cop, she'd seen the worst of the worst. Rarely did they come packaged as nicely as "Reggie."

No one had taken her seat at the bar and she reclaimed it, almost tempted to take a sip of the drink she'd left behind. She knew better, though; someone could have slipped something in it, and she needed a clear head in case the killer was trolling for his next victim. His pattern was a kill every three months, and it'd been almost three months since the last murder.

None of the victims had lived to tell how they made contact with their murderer, but for the first three, who were prostitutes, contact probably had been easy. For the last two, the connection to the bar was strong. According to a statement given by the Lemon Tree bartender, who was a lot more helpful than the owner, on the nights the women were murdered, each woman had shown up at the bar without an escort, and they'd left alone. Perhaps they'd encountered Reggie and turned him down, and he hadn't liked that.

The medical examiner had placed the time of death for those two women between 11:00 p.m. and 1:00 a.m. The killer could've followed the victims home and forced his way in . . . except none of the murder sites showed forcible entry.

Did he catch up to each victim as she arrived home and use the weapon he eventually committed the murder with to force them to open the door? Or perhaps, remembering him from the bar, had they invited him in?

Alex checked her watch. Eleven. Unless someone followed her from the bar, tonight was a bust and she might as well leave. Since the Lemon Tree was the only connection the homicide detectives had found between the last two women, she'd be back tomorrow night. And the next, hoping the killer made a move on her.

She texted the two undercover officers shadowing her that she was leaving.

Give me five minutes before following.

Too long.

She gritted her teeth. Parker and Watkins were being too protective.

No, it isn't. And don't leave together.

Their killer wasn't stupid. He had to figure the police had made the connection to the bar, and if he'd chosen her as his next victim, he would wait to make sure she wasn't bait. Two men leaving at the same time screamed they were cops and that it was a setup.

She slipped her phone into her bag and climbed off the barstool just as a man bumped into her.

"I'm so sorry," he said.

"No problem." She looked up in the dimly lit room, and the smile on her face froze as her past stood in front of her.

"Alexis?" The man stared wide-eyed at her.

For a second the years fell away as she stared into the blue eyes that belonged to her high school crush. Alex worked to keep her expression from matching Nathan Landry's dropped jaw. Several thoughts ran through her mind, the main one being she couldn't let him blow her cover. "You must have me confused with someone else," she said, her voice blunt.

His gaze swept her from head to foot, and she tugged the hem of the short skirt, acutely aware of how she must look in clothes she'd never be caught dead wearing back home.

Slowly Nathan nodded. "Yes, I guess I do have you confused with someone else." He tipped his head. "Have a good evening, ma'am."

She frowned as Nathan picked up the drink he'd ordered and walked toward the tables at the back of the bar. Alex had never known him to drink alcoholic beverages. What was he doing in Chattanooga, in this bar, tonight of all nights? Why wasn't the Pearl Springs chief of police watching after its citizens? Not that the small Tennessee town had much crime. And "ma'am"? Really?

She stepped away from the bar stool, her gaze following him. Evidently, Nathan was alone. And he looked as good as ever. Fit and extremely sexy with a five o'clock shadow covering his strong jaw.

He looked her way. Busted. She quickly shifted her gaze to the other side of the room. What was wrong with her, anyway? Why was she even taking notice of how he looked after the way they'd ended things? Alex clenched her jaw, remembering how he'd cheated her out of capturing the honor of valedictorian their senior year of high school.

She lifted her chin. There were more important things to think about than a silly romance she'd had as a teenager, even if it had broken her heart. Like finding justice for the five women who'd been murdered.

Alex gave a slight nod to the officer at the end of the bar as she reached for her purse. Then she sauntered out the door.

If she walked slow enough—which wouldn't be hard in three-inch heels—Watkins and Parker would soon catch up with her. She wanted to live long enough to enjoy the promotion to homicide she expected to receive any day now.

At the last minute, she glanced back to see where Nathan was. She frowned. He was sitting at Reggie's table, except there was no sign of Reggie.

4

Nathan sipped the Arnold Palmer he'd ordered and set it down in front of him. From the way Alexis had jerked her head in a different direction when he'd turned to look back at her, it was apparent she'd watched him walk to his table. Was it possible she still felt something for him? Something other than contempt? In his dreams.

He'd quickly caught on that she was working undercover, because he'd never known Alexis Stone to dress in anything so revealing. Of course, maybe she'd changed over the years—he rarely saw her, and the only news he heard about his high school sweetheart came from her grandparents. Nathan winced. Her grandmother would have a fit if she saw the outfit Alexis wore tonight.

He studied her as she scanned the other side of the bar. Working undercover was basically lying, and the girl he'd known in high school couldn't lie. It just wasn't in her. Everything was mostly black or white with precious little gray in between.

So, what had happened to make her compromise her values?

Nathan and Alexis—he'd never been able to call her Alex like most of her friends—had taken different routes to become police officers. She'd wanted to get out of Russell County and Pearl Springs and jumped at the chance to study criminal justice at the University of Cincinnati. It'd been far enough away for Alexis to be independent, but close enough to check on the grandparents who raised her. And Cincinnati was way more exciting than Pearl Springs.

It'd surprised him when he heard she took a job with the Chattanooga police department. He'd figured she'd land in Cincinnati or even Nashville, but with her grandparents getting older, Chattanooga was probably a compromise. He'd watched her grandfather struggle with disappointment when she chose Chattanooga over working for him as a Russell County deputy.

Nathan sipped the drink again and noted his confidential informant in the corner of the room, talking to a woman. He looked up and his head moved in an almost imperceptible nod, Nathan's cue to rendezvous in five minutes. He noted the time on his watch.

The CI had asked to meet at the Lemon Tree, and Nathan had agreed once he learned the CI had information on who was behind the supply of heroin coming into Pearl Springs.

Three overdoses at the high school in the past week, and if it hadn't been for Narcan, three teens would have died. Nathan glanced toward the door in time to see a hefty bouncer-type leave the bar—Alexis's backup. Nathan had made the cop as soon as he saw him. And as backup, he should have left the minute she walked out the door.

He scanned the room again and recognized Ken Parker sitting at the end of the bar. He knew the detective from the shooting range. Parker worked vice and was more than likely another backup.

Too bad Nathan didn't have a delete button to get rid of the image of Alexis in that outfit. Her shapely legs looked as fit as when they'd dated back in high school. He'd almost not recognized her with the blood-red lipstick and dark eyeshadow and fake eyelashes. At least he didn't remember her lashes being that thick and long.

Worry gnawed at his gut. He knew, courtesy of her grandparents, that Alexis lived only a few blocks from the Lemon Tree. If she decided to walk home, it'd be more than a little nippy in that outfit. But the temps weren't what worried him.

He'd been keeping up with news articles on the Queen's Gambit Killer and knew two of the victims were associated with the Lemon Tree. It didn't take a rocket scientist to know Chattanooga's homicide department was using Alexis as bait to draw the killer out.

Another check of his watch. Five minutes were up. Seconds later, J. R. stood and walked to the restroom. Another minute and Nathan made his way to the restroom as well. When he reached the hallway, it was empty as he expected. The men's room door opened, and his informant stepped into the hall. He looked both ways then walked toward Nathan, bumping into him.

"Watch where you're going," Nathan snapped.

"Sorry, man." J. R. held up his hand. "Didn't see you come in," he said, lowering his voice as he kept walking.

Nathan felt his coat pocket. Like before, his CI had slipped an envelope there in the exchange. This was the third time they'd met like this, and each time the brief exchange for information had been worth the trip into Chattanooga.

When Nathan returned to his table, his drink was gone and a couple had taken over the table. Just as well. He had what he came for. He'd wait until he got into his pickup to look at the contents of the envelope. And then maybe drive by Alexis's house on his way out of town to make sure she made it home okay.

A few minutes later, Nathan let the motor idle while he read the slip of paper. Four names. One wasn't a surprise—a known drug dealer—and Nathan recognized the other three as boys who occasionally attended his church's youth group, mostly to check out the girls. The ringleader was the son of Pearl Springs's top defense lawyer. He'd have to have more than a name on a paper to even interview the boy and the other two as well.

When he pulled out of the parking lot, he turned toward the street Alexis lived on. She would be furious if she saw him, but something in his gut said he needed to check on her.

5

A lex hadn't walked far before pain shot through her feet. Three-inch spiked heels were not made for walking.

What was that? She stopped and cocked an ear. Alex would have sworn it was footsteps, but when she looked over her shoulder, the sidewalk was empty.

Even for almost midnight, the neighborhood had an eerie quiet about it. She took another step, and her feet protested. Maybe she'd take off her shoes and walk barefoot. She shuddered. Not a chance with all the germs crawling on the sidewalk.

Alex pushed the pain to the back of her mind and kept walking. Again, a noise behind her sent her heart into overdrive. She looked over her shoulder, but again, nothing stirred. The creepy sensation of someone watching lingered. Three more blocks, and she would be home. But would she be safe?

Safer than now—at least once she was home Watkins and Parker would be nearby her house keeping watch. Where were they, anyway? Usually by now they would've made a pass by her. Up ahead a bus stop beckoned like a glass of water in the desert. She hobbled toward the bench, texting her backup that she'd stopped for a minute to rest her feet.

A silver Mazda pulled to the curb and parked before she reached the bus stop. The driver's door opened and a woman climbed out. Kayla?

Before she could call out to the waitress, cold steel pressed into Alex's side and a man's arm snaked around her waist, holding her tight.

Where had he come from? She should have been paying more attention to her surroundings instead of focusing on her feet.

"Don't do nothing stupid unless you want to die here."

She wasn't dying period and tried to jerk away, but his grip held strong.

"One more move like that, and I'll kill the girl," he said as Kayla walked toward them.

She had no doubt he would. The sour odor emanating from the man indicated he was stressed to the max. The slightest thing could set him off. Alex couldn't let him hurt Kayla.

"Keep walking," he whispered. "If you say anything to warn her, I promise, I'll kill her. Got it?"

Alex nodded.

"Need a ride home, Lexie?" Kayla asked, eyeing the man at Alex's side.

The gun pressed harder into her side.

"No, I'm good, Houdini, but thanks." Maybe calling Kayla by the nickname of the rude man at the Lemon Tree would be enough for Kayla to realize Alex was in trouble and call 911.

Kayla gave her a thumbs-up, then turned back to her car. "My low-tire light came on. I need to check it out." Kayla squatted beside her car.

The waitress hadn't understood, and Alex held her breath as the man prodded her past the car. In her peripheral vision, there was a flash of black as Kayla sprang from beside the car.

There was a thud and the man screamed, loosening his hold

on her. Alex jerked free. The sharp crack of a bullet exploded the quiet into a thousand shards.

Alex stumbled forward, pain burning her side. She caught herself and turned toward the man. He pointed his gun at Kayla.

The world spun out of control, darkness creeping over her as she fumbled for the Sig at her back.

Stop! Police! The words didn't make it past her lips.

She had to stop him. Alex swung her pistol toward the man, the gun heavy in her hand. He fired, and the gunshot echoed in her ears. Kayla dropped to the ground and rolled.

Alex fought the dimness as he aimed at the girl once more. The last thing she remembered was pulling the trigger.

6

Nathan turned the corner two blocks from the street where Alexis lived, and the scene unfolding in front of him almost stopped his heart. The woman he'd never stopped loving fell to the sidewalk. A man with a baseball cap pulled low clutched his chest and pitched forward. Like lightning, a girl dressed in black kicked away the gun he'd dropped and knelt beside him.

Nathan slammed on his brakes and threw the car into park. He jumped out with his service revolver in his hand.

"Keep your hands where I can see them," he yelled at the girl.

She raised her hands and turned to face him, tears streaming down her face. "I can't find my phone. Thought he might have one. Call 911. He shot her. Then he tried to shoot me, but Lexie saved my life. I . . . I think he's dead."

Nathan knelt beside Alexis while he kept his gun trained on the other two. The girl could be telling the truth, or she could have been a partner in the crime.

Dark red circled the thin blouse Alexis wore, but it didn't look as though the wound was pumping blood. Didn't mean internal bleeding wasn't going on, though.

A faint pulse fluttered on her wrist, and he yanked his phone from his belt, thumb-punching 911. When the operator answered, he identified himself and gave their location. "I have a female victim with a gunshot wound to the right side and a man who appears unresponsive. Need first responders dispatched ASAP. And the police."

The operator instructed him to stay on the line, and Nathan punched the speaker on and laid his phone on the sidewalk as he felt for Alexis's pulse again.

The girl knelt beside them. "Is she alive?"

He nodded. Up close, she seemed older than she first appeared. "Who are you?"

"Kayla Jackson." Her voice hitched. "I work at the Lemon Tree. That's where I met Lexi."

She must mean Alexis. The girl seemed harmless enough, and Nathan had a vague recollection of her from the bar. "What happened here?"

Kayla hugged her arms to her waist. "I was checking my tire and they walked by, but he didn't seem like someone she'd be with, you know what I mean? Then she called me Houdini, and I knew something was wrong. That's when I drop-kicked him. But when I did, the gun went off, and now she might d-die." Kayla burst into tears again.

"She's not going to die." She couldn't. He wouldn't let her. Nathan jerked his head toward the man on the ground. "How'd he end up dead?"

"Lexi shot him. She saved my life." A fresh round of tears rolled down Kayla's face. "Why'd she have a gun?" Then she gasped. "Is she a cop?"

Nathan didn't want to blow her cover if Alexis was indeed working undercover. "Do you know him?"

Kayla glanced toward the man. She started to shake her

head, then she frowned. "Maybe . . . I've seen him in the bar a few times, but not tonight."

Nathan was sure all of this would make sense later. He glanced over his shoulder. Where was that ambulance? And where were the guys who were supposed to be protecting Alexis?

He no sooner had the last thought than a gray Malibu skidded to a stop behind his truck, and two plainclothes officers piled out of the car with their guns pulled. The two he'd seen at the Lemon Tree earlier. Parker and the shorter "bouncer type."

"Drop your weapon," Parker shouted. "And make sure I see your hands at all times."

Kayla raised her hands, and Nathan laid his gun on the sidewalk and turned to face the detectives. "It's me, Parker—Nathan Landry, Pearl Springs chief of police. Badge is in my jacket."

A long moment passed as Parker squinted at Nathan. "He's okay, Al," he said, but the detective didn't holster his gun as his partner knelt beside Alexis. "What are you doing in Chattanooga?"

"Taking care of a little business. The girl's name is Kayla Jackson. She may have saved Alexis's life."

Parker holstered his gun. "Al Watkins and I are part of Alex's team."

Alexis groaned, and Nathan leaned closer to her.

"Hang on. An ambulance is on the way." He should've followed her home when his gut first said so. If she didn't make it, he would never forgive himself. He looked up as Watkins felt her wrist.

"When I took her pulse, it was faint but steady." Nathan pulled off his jacket and put it over her. "Do you have a blanket in your car? The ground is cold. Don't want her going into shock."

"Should be something we can use." Watkins stood and jogged to their Malibu while Parker approached the gunman.

"Kayla thought he was dead." Nathan looked around for her. She'd walked to the bus stop bench and sat hunched over.

Parker felt the shooter's wrist. "She was right. Do you know what happened?"

"Not really. Kayla can tell you more than I can." Nathan pinned a hard stare on the detective as sirens approached from a few blocks away. "Where were you guys?"

Parker blanched. "Standard practice with Alex is not to follow too closely, so we made a trip around the block."

"And I took a wrong turn," Watkins said as he handed Nathan a corner of the blanket and helped him spread it over Alexis. The detective jerked his hand toward the subdivision they'd come from. "It's a maze in there."

Before Nathan could tell them what he thought, Alexis's eyes fluttered open. "Nathan?" she whispered.

"I'm here."

She turned toward his voice, and her intoxicating blue eyes locked onto his. "Somehow . . . I knew you would be."

His heart stuttered in his chest as she looked at him the way she had years ago. He gently cradled her hand in his. "You're going to be all right."

"Kayla . . . is she . . ."

"She's fine."

"Saved my life." She closed her eyes. "I'm so cold."

It was hard to hear over the approaching sirens, and he leaned closer to her ear. "Hang on, help is here."

Her eyes flew open. "The man . . . did you get him?"

"He's not going anywhere. Paramedics are here, and I'm gonna have to move, but I'll see you at the hospital."

"Don't call Gramps . . . it's late. Wait till morning."

"Alexis, you know—"

She gripped his hand. "Promise me you won't call him tonight."

"You'll have to move out of the way." The paramedic's voice was firm as he handed Nathan the jacket.

"Promise . . ."

"Okay." He reluctantly let go of her hand and let the paramedics take over.

Nathan rubbed his neck. His former boss would chew him up and spit him out if he didn't call and let him know what was going on. But he'd promised Alexis he wouldn't call the Russell County sheriff until morning. Kayla approached him, her arms still wrapped around her waist.

"Is she going to be okay?"

"I think so." He'd seen worse gunshot wounds, but they hadn't involved Alexis. Nathan slipped his jacket over Kayla's shoulders.

"Thanks."

"I appreciate what you did, but it was awfully dangerous."

"I was afraid if he took her away, he'd kill her for sure. Is she your friend?"

"Something like that."

Nathan stayed close to the scene as the paramedics treated Alexis. Best he could tell, she was going to make it. She had to. Once they had her loaded into the ambulance, he asked the lead paramedic what her condition was.

"I'm not a doctor," the paramedic said.

"You know if she's stable or not."

"She's stable, now let me get her to the hospital." Without another word, he hopped in the back of the ambulance.

Alexis had to be all right. It would break the Stones' hearts if something happened to their only grandchild after losing their son to a landmine in Iraq years ago. Not to mention Nathan's heart.

If tonight had done nothing else, it had shown him he'd never stopped loving Alexis, and that he wanted a second chance with her.

7

The ambulance sped away with flashing red and white strobe lights, taking Nathan's heart with it. Alexis would immediately go into surgery, and he wanted to be there. Instead, duty held him to the crime scene. Parker and Watkins needed his statement, and Nathan needed Kayla Jackson's and the answers to a few questions he had.

He looked for Kayla. She'd returned to the transit bench. Nathan had seen her talking to Parker and was pretty sure she'd given her statement. So, why hadn't she left? He walked to the bench. "You okay?" he asked when she looked up.

Kayla shivered as she pulled his jacket closer. "Not really."

"I want to thank you for what you did. Pretty sure you saved my friend's life."

"I wish I could've kept her from getting shot."

"The paramedics believe she'll make it." He rubbed the side of his face. "You're probably tired of repeating what happened, but do you think you could go over it one more time for me?"

"You're a cop, aren't you?"

Nathan showed her his badge.

Her eyes widened. "Wow! A chief of police."

"Yeah. Pearl Springs is small, so the job isn't as impressive as it sounds." He hooked the badge on his belt. "Do you mind answering a couple of questions?"

"But this didn't happen in Pearl Springs."

"I know, but Alexis and I go way back. Her grandfather will want to know what happened, so anything you can tell me will help."

She cocked her head and quirked her mouth. "If you'll tell me why you acted like you didn't know her at the bar."

So she'd seen their exchange. When he didn't respond right away, Kayla said, "Lexi is a cop, isn't she?"

He hesitated. "What makes you say that?"

While she didn't roll her eyes at him, she might as well have. "Those two, for one thing." Kayla nodded toward Parker and Watkins. "And it was obvious to me that she didn't belong at the bar—she ordered a Tom Collins mocktail, and I know people come to bars and don't drink alcoholic beverages, but she kept trying to make her skirt longer. I just had a feeling."

He'd noticed that about the skirt, and Nathan had ordered a gin-free Tom Collins more than once when he'd needed to fit in to the bar scene. "Do you think anyone else came to the same conclusion?"

She shook her head. "I only noticed because I study people, and she didn't fit the profile of what I call a 'regular.' That's what Lexi was passing herself off as, but I didn't suspect she was a cop until she pulled the gun hidden in her waistband."

"What were you doing here?"

"My low-tire light came on when I turned the corner, and I pulled over." She rubbed her fingers on her black pants. "Then I saw Lexi and that man, and I just had the feeling that something was wrong."

"Why not just call the police?"

"I don't know. Maybe I thought he'd hurt her before the

police got here. Then she called me Houdini, and I knew she was in trouble."

"Why did she call you that?"

"It was an inside joke. Once I realized there *was* trouble, I had to help her. I'm fairly proficient in karate and caught the guy by surprise with a dropkick."

Nathan figured she was more than fairly proficient.

Footsteps drew close and Nathan looked around as Parker approached, a notepad in his hand. He was eyeing Kayla.

"You've given me your statement, so you're free to leave whenever you'd like."

"Thank you, Detective Parker. I believe I'll do just that." She turned to Nathan. "Would you let me know how she is tomorrow?"

"Sure. Give me your number, and I'll call you." He put the number she gave him into his contacts along with her name. Then he walked her to the car.

"Thank you," she said.

As Kayla pulled away from the curb, his gut said there was more to her story than she'd told him. He turned as Parker approached.

"How did you happen to show up here tonight?"

Nathan pulled his attention back to the detective. "I ran into Alexis at the Lemon Tree. Figured she was working a case from the way she was dressed, and when I saw you two, it confirmed it. When I concluded my business at the bar, I decided to swing by her house, see if she made it home okay."

The detective raised an eyebrow. "You two an item?"

Nathan laughed. "Not in this lifetime. Sheriff Stone in Russell County is her grandfather. He would expect me to make sure she made it home okay."

"Stone's a good man. Didn't know he was Alex's grandfather, though." His heavy eyebrows raised expectantly.

What could he say? Alexis was a very private person, and if she hadn't told Parker that Stone was her grandfather, Nathan had already said too much. "I don't think she broadcasts it."

"Stone's getting up there in years. You used to be his deputy—you gonna run for sheriff when he retires?"

It seemed a hundred years ago that he was Carson Stone's deputy, even though it'd only been four years. "Stone retire? That'll be the day."

"Yeah, but what is he, eighty?"

"He's not that old." Seventy-five, maybe. Running for the office did cross Nathan's mind every now and then. "Not sure I want to go from managing nine officers to twenty-nine *and* the corrections facility."

Parker laughed with Nathan. "So what *were* you doing in this part of town? The Lemon Tree doesn't strike me as your normal hangout."

"It's not. Had a meeting with someone."

"Care to give me a name?"

"Can't. I could tell you the name I was given, but I doubt it'd do you any good."

"A confidential informant?"

Nathan nodded. "The Queen's Gambit Killer—is that who you were trying to catch tonight?"

The slight hesitance in Parker had Nathan holding his breath, then the detective shrugged. "We're on the task force trying to crack the case, so I don't see why homicide would care if I discussed it with you—it's not like we're overrun with answers."

"I'd appreciate it."

"How much do you know?"

"Only what I read in the newspaper and see on TV. Five victims?"

Parker nodded. "The first murder occurred a year and a half ago—a prostitute. Homicide had no idea it was a serial killer until the second murder three months later. The victim, another prostitute, clutched a White pawn in her hand, just like the first one."

The detective opened his mouth as though to say something more but instead slipped his hand into his pocket and withdrew an amber-colored bottle holding toothpicks. Parker chose one and stuck it in his mouth, then held the bottle out to Nathan. "Toothpick? It's cinnamon."

"Thanks, but no."

The toothpick bobbed up and down as Parker chewed on it. Nathan waited. After a long minute, the detective cleared his throat. "If you've been following the news, then you know the first victims were prostitutes—I personally think that was for practice. The last two were nine-to-fivers and valued employees, according to their bosses.

"Each of the women were about the same build as Alex and each had a shade of red hair similar to Alex's." He moved the toothpick to the other side of his mouth. "She also knew the second victim, had counseled her at a women's shelter."

Nathan didn't like hearing that Alexis had a personal connection to one of the victims.

He turned back to the crime scene. More police cars had arrived, and yellow crime scene tape stretched across the sidewalk on either side of the body as the medical examiner knelt beside it. Three evidence markers pinpointed shell casings. Based on their location, one belonged to Alexis, which meant the dead man had fired twice.

A photographer snapped pictures, and several officers had left to canvass the neighborhood. One officer approached Parker and handed him a plastic bag with a wallet.

"Who is he?" Nathan asked.

Parker held up the bag. "Driver's license says George Smith."

"Think he could be the serial killer?"

"I don't think so. We're looking for an organized killer, and trying to take Alex here where so much could go wrong doesn't fit what we know about the Queen's Gambit Killer."

Nathan scanned the area around the fallen man and frowned as a crime scene tech picked up a small knapsack near the body. "Reckon that contains his tools of the trade?"

"We'll know in a minute."

The tech removed items from the bag—zip ties, tape. The last thing she brought out was a small, black velvet pouch. Nathan and Parker stepped closer as the crime scene tech emptied it. Nathan caught his breath. "Is that what I think it is?"

The crime scene tech lifted a White pawn. "Gentlemen, I do believe we may have caught the Queen's Gambit Killer."

8

Alex drifted closer to the surface, away from whatever was holding her back. So thirsty. She took a deep breath and suppressed a groan. Why did it hurt to breathe?

Disoriented, she lay still as unfamiliar noises prodded her fully awake. Something creaked as it rolled past wherever she was. Murmurings. She strained to understand and gave up.

Her neck hurt . . . and the pillow didn't feel like hers. The fresh cotton scent didn't come from any detergent she used, either . . . and that disinfectant. When she moved, pain shot through her side, and she gasped.

"She's waking up, Carson."

Alex would know that voice anywhere. "Gram?" she asked, her voice croaking. She blinked her eyes open. Her grandmother leaned over the bed and brushed a strand of hair from Alex's face.

"We're here, honey. You're going to be all right."

All right? Why wouldn't she be? Where was she, anyway? Not in her house, that was for sure. Or at her grandparents'.

A memory floated just out of reach, then the event came flooding back. Kayla. The man pressing a gun to her side. The gunshot. "Kayla," she whispered. "Is she okay?"

"She's fine."

"Gramps?"

"I'm here, baby."

Alex must be pretty bad for her grandfather to call her that. She had a vague memory of Nathan promising not to call him until morning. Should've known she couldn't trust her old boyfriend.

He squeezed her hand. "It might take a while to recover, but you're going to be all right."

"How did you know?"

"Nathan called this morning." From her grandfather's gruff tone, he wasn't happy with Nathan. "That boy's in trouble for not calling me last night."

For some reason that pleased her. She shoved the thought away. Alex wasn't sure why, but she didn't want anything Nathan Landry did to please her.

She took stock of her body. Fingers worked. Alex moved her legs then wiggled her toes, thankful she wasn't paralyzed. She tried to take another deep breath, but pain stopped her with a whimper. Wincing, she looked up at her grandfather. "How bad . . . ?"

"The bullet went through soft tissue, didn't hit any major organs other than nicking your lung. That's why it hurts to breathe." He squeezed her hand. "How much do you remember?"

Her grandfather, the sheriff. Alex would laugh if it didn't hurt so much. "Let me think."

"Take your time."

"Carson Stone, she'll have plenty of time to remember when she's better. You let this girl rest."

Her grandmother was the only person Alex knew who could tell Gramps what to do. "It's okay, Gram."

"No, it's not. It's not his investigation, and besides, there's a young man who wants to see you. Okay to let Nathan in?"

Nathan? Here? Alex's heart warmed at the thought, but she quickly brushed it away. "I suppose."

Her grandmother rose and went to the door. Seconds later Alex was looking into Nathan's blue eyes.

He smiled at her. "You had me worried."

"Kayla . . . is she really okay?"

"She's fine."

Relief poured through Alex. "The man . . . ?"

"Dead."

Once more Alex struggled to breathe. Most cops worked their entire career without killing anyone. Why did she have to be the exception? Not once, but twice.

"You had no choice," Nathan said softly. "He would've killed Kayla and then you."

The back of her throat tightened, and she blinked back tears. "Who was he?"

Nathan glanced at her grandfather. It was almost like he was asking permission to tell her. Alex raised the head of her bed. "What are you not telling me?"

Her grandfather gave a slight nod, and Nathan said, "He dropped a bag. Inside were zip ties and tape. And a White pawn."

She stared at him, not comprehending his words.

Nathan nodded. "You got him, Alexis. The Queen's Gambit Killer."

"Are you certain?"

"The zip ties were like the ones used to restrain the other women. He had the pawn with him . . . evidently, you were his next victim."

Alex let the words sink in. She'd taken out a serial killer. Why didn't that make her feel better?

Her grandfather planted himself beside her bed. "You know from the last time this happened, you'll need therapy, and that will help. But like before, you'll have to learn to deal with the shooting."

Gramps always could tell what she was thinking, and he probably knew exactly what she was feeling. As sheriff, her grandfather had been forced to kill two people that she knew of, one in self-defense and the other to keep a child from being stabbed. "The police department has a psychologist—"

He shook his head. "When you're released from the hospital, you'll be coming home."

Go home to Pearl Springs? No. She loved her life in Chattanooga . . . well, at least *liked* it. Living in a big city hadn't been exactly what she'd thought it would be. But tucking tail and running home . . .

After a sharp rap on the door, it swung open and an older man with a clipboard and a stethoscope hanging around his neck entered and glanced around the room before he approached the bed.

"Well, how's my patient doing?"

"You tell me."

He stared at her for a long minute, then his lips curved into a smile. "Fair enough. I'm Dr. Moore, the surgeon who removed the bullet lodged between two of your ribs." He looked at the clipboard. "While the projectile missed your major organs, its path perforated your lung, causing a pneumothorax. That's why there's a thoracic catheter inserted into the pleural space on your right side. It drains—"

"Whoa." Alex held up her hand, and the doctor paused and peered at her over his glasses. "Could you say that again, in English?"

"Sorry. I just came from dictating my notes on your case. Plain and simple—the bullet punctured your lung, and air escaped into the space between it and the chest wall, causing the lobe to collapse. The tube lessens the pressure and allows the lung to reinflate."

"Thank you. How long will I be here?"

"It depends on how long it takes your lung to return to normal, but barring complications, I'd say you're looking at five to seven days."

She processed the information. "And after that, when can I return to work?"

"Every case is different—it'll depend on how fast you heal."

Her grandfather cleared his throat. "Don't forget, you returned fire and the man died, so I imagine it'll be up to your department's psychologist when they'll clear you for work."

That could take months, especially since this was the second time she'd had to use deadly force. Both times were in self-defense, but that didn't mitigate the fact that someone died. She still had nightmares from being forced to kill a man two and a half years ago. Some cops never recovered from taking a life. To this day she didn't know why the man she killed raised an unloaded gun and pointed it at her. She'd fired, hitting him in the center of his chest.

And now it'd happened again—except this time the gun pointing at her had been loaded.

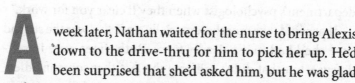

9

A week later, Nathan waited for the nurse to bring Alexis down to the drive-thru for him to pick her up. He'd been surprised that she'd asked him, but he was glad to do it.

In between following up on the information his confidential informant had given him, he'd managed to visit her at least every other day. The days he hadn't come, he'd talked to her on the phone.

His heart rate spiked when she was wheeled through the doors. *Don't go there.* Even so, he couldn't help noticing the way her dark red hair shone. The aide must have helped her shampoo it. He couldn't stop himself from jumping out and setting a small stool on the pavement so it would be easier for her to get into his truck. The smile she gave him reminded Nathan of years ago when things were different.

"Thanks for doing this. Gram didn't want me to ask Gramps. Something about him not feeling up to par. And she doesn't drive in Chattanooga."

"Glad to do it." He handed her a small pillow to put between her shoulder and the seat belt before he fastened it. A clean floral scent teased his senses.

"After you take me by my house to pick up a few things, would you mind making one more stop at a cemetery?"

"Not at all. Anyone I know?"

She shook her head. "Rebecca Daniels."

The second victim of the Queen's Gambit Killer. "Is that the one you knew personally?"

She nodded. "We connected when I volunteered at the women's shelter. I met Rebecca—she liked to be called Becky—not long after the first victim was killed. A group from the women's shelter was handing out coffee near 23rd and Main Street and I gave her a cup of coffee on a cold November night. Becky wanted off the streets, and I talked her into going to the shelter. We met at least once a week for a couple of months. The last time I saw her alive, I took her to my hair stylist—she had a job interview the next day and wanted her hair cut and styled like mine. A couple of weeks later I heard she was working the streets again."

"And then she was killed."

Alexis turned and stared out the passenger window. "Yeah."

A few minutes later Nathan parked in front of the small house Alexis rented. He turned to her and tensed at how tired she looked already. "Are you sure you feel up to this? I can drive your grandmother here—she'll be happy to gather what you need."

"Are you kidding me? Judith Stone would have a stroke if she saw some of the outfits I wear for undercover work."

Since Alexis was dead serious, Nathan coughed to cover a laugh. "You're probably right there."

"Besides, she'd clean my house out, thinking I'm going to stay in Pearl Springs."

Alexis had made it perfectly clear she'd be returning to Chattanooga. "You might change your mind once you get home."

"This is home." She nodded toward the house.

"What do you have against Pearl Springs?"

"It's not that I have anything against Pearl Springs—it was a great place to grow up . . . but once you're an adult, everyone wants to know your business. And then there's grannies like Mrs. Jones trying to fix me up with her grandson . . ."

"What's wrong with Teddy?"

Alexis pinched the bridge of her nose. "Nothing, but he's already dating someone. At least that's what he told me the last time I was in Pearl Springs and stopped by the drugstore to pick up medicine for Gram."

"Then why is she trying to fix you two up?"

Alexis palmed her hands. "I don't know. And Mrs. Jones isn't the only matchmaker in town. Besides, there's nothing to do in Pearl Springs except watch TV."

"Well, we do have the state fair coming up, and besides, peace and quiet isn't a bad thing," he said. "And in my line of work, everyone watching out for their neighbor keeps my workload down."

"Are you telling me you enjoy all those little old ladies try-ing to fix you up with their granddaughters and great-nieces?" She unsnapped the seat belt, and the small pillow he'd placed between her chest and the belt tumbled to the floor.

"At least they care. How many of your neighbors have even checked on you while you've been in the hospital?"

Nathan waited for an answer as she fumbled with the door handle.

"Okay, so I haven't exactly gotten to know my neighbors, but I've been so busy . . ."

"Outside of work, how many friends do you have?"

For an answer, she pushed the door open and swung her legs around.

"Hold on. Let me help you." For a second, he thought she was going to plow ahead, then her shoulders sagged.

"Sure."

Nathan jogged around to her side of the pickup before she could change her mind. "I know you have long legs, but not that long. Do you want to use the step, or would you let me pick you up and set you on the ground?"

"Step."

He set it in place, and Alexis slid her foot to the side bar, then leaned on his arm as she put her feet on it then the ground. She stood still a minute as sweat beaded her face.

"I don't think leaving the hospital this soon was a good idea," he said. It'd been a week since the shooting, and while the doctor had released her, it was only because Alexis had threatened to check herself out if he didn't.

"I can sleep at Gram's. That's all I was doing at the hospital, and besides, sleeping won't get my strength back."

"Just don't rush it." He waited while Alexis took her key from her pocket and unlocked the wooden door. "Can I help?"

She shook her head. "I won't be long."

He took in the tiny living room of the older house while he waited. Several boxes sat along one wall. A photo of her grandparents sat on a table that held her TV. When a thud sounded from the bedroom, he rushed down the hall to find her putting clothes in a suitcase on the floor.

"Are you okay?"

"Yes. I was just getting my suitcase down."

"You could've let me get it."

"And here I thought you'd be proud of me for not trying to lift it."

Nathan stared at her. Was that a tiny smile? "You get points for that."

He glanced at the closet as she tossed in a pair of sneakers. Except for a small section of what looked like skimpy dresses and short skirts—tools of her trade, so to speak—it was empty. Had she put every piece of clothing she owned in one suitcase? Maybe there was another closet. "Get everything you need?"

"Not quite. I'd like to put a few personal items in. I'll call you when I need you."

Nathan gave her a thumbs-up. "I'll be right outside the door."

A few minutes later, he pulled the suitcase toward the living room. "How long have you lived here?"

"Is next week the first of October?"

Nathan frowned. "You don't know?"

An exasperated breath came from Alexis. "I've been in the hospital for what seems like a month. I lost track of time."

He could see how that could happen. "It's just past the middle of September—the twenty-third, so yes, next week is the first."

"Then I've lived here almost a year."

"And you haven't had time to decorate?" He pointed toward the boxes. "Or unpack?"

"I . . ." Alexis stopped and put her hand on the back of the sofa while she glanced around the room, a frown on her face. Then she turned toward him and shrugged. "I don't spend a lot of time here."

"Where do you spend your time?"

"Work. The gym. I mostly only sleep here."

Judging from the way she'd looked in the skimpy outfit she'd worn at the bar, she worked out a lot. "So you don't attend all those cultural events you would miss if you lived in Pearl Springs?"

Her lips twitched. "No. But the opportunity is there if I want to catch one. Are you ready to take me to your precious town?"

Nathan stiffened. The sarcasm he'd witnessed the past week hadn't been part of Alexis's personality in the past.

46

Then her shoulders slumped, and she pressed her hand to her forehead. "I'm sorry. That was totally uncalled for."

Alexis swayed, and he jumped to steady her. "Let me help you to the sofa."

Once she was seated, she leaned her head against the back and closed her eyes. He'd like to know what was going on in that stubborn head of hers. Or maybe not, given their conversations lately.

"Don't say it." Defeat rang in her voice.

"Say what?"

"I told you so—I know you're thinking it."

"Nope."

She raised her head and stared at him. "Nope you're not thinking it, or nope you're not saying it?"

He grinned.

She sighed and leaned back on the sofa again. "Probably should've stayed in the hospital another day."

"I will agree on that." Nathan studied her a minute. The tough aura she projected was gone. "What's with this GI Jane thing you have going on?"

"You have to ask?"

No, he supposed he didn't. While law enforcement had come a long way in embracing female officers, there was still a bias in many departments.

"Do you know how hard I've had to work to gain the trust of the male detectives in the department? If I show any softness, it's perceived as weakness. It's one reason I've stayed in vice as long as I have. I work undercover with Watkins and Parker as *my* backup, and not the other way around. It's been easier that way."

Nathan hadn't given a lot of thought to how difficult a female officer might have it, mainly because he didn't have any female officers. Maybe that needed to change. "So why do you do it?"

"I like punishment, I guess." Alexis chuckled, then sobered. "No, I like a challenge and want to make a difference, especially for women coming up in the department. It's one reason I'm shooting for the commissioner's job."

"You want to head up the Chattanooga police department?"

"Don't sound so surprised. Even in high school, you know I always had a game plan."

True. No matter what Alexis had been involved in, she'd had a strategy, usually written out. "And that's why you want to stay in Chattanooga?"

She nodded. "And for the record, I don't hate Pearl Springs. I deal with a lot of guilt for not being there for my grandparents, but if I want to be commissioner, some things have to be sacrificed."

Guilt was probably one of the reasons she jumped bad when he brought up living in Pearl Springs.

Alexis took a deep breath. "And if you're ready to take me there, I'm ready to go."

"You sure?"

"After our stop at the cemetery. I won't take long there since I'm sure you have a lot to do besides nursemaid me." She stood. "I do appreciate everything you've done this past week."

"Glad to be of service." Nathan bowed and then walked to the door and opened it. "Your carriage awaits."

Alexis stayed put long enough for him to stow her suitcase, then Nathan helped her up into the cab of the truck and fastened her seat belt. As he placed the small pillow between her chest and the seat belt, once again the scent of her hair shot him back to a time when—

He stopped himself. What was he thinking? They'd taken different paths.

"How's that?" he asked as Alexis leaned her head against the seat, her eyes closed.

"Good." She took a breath and opened her eyes. "Thanks again."

For a second, their gaze locked. Her lips were kissable close. Briefly he thought about claiming them before he jerked back, bumping his head on the steel frame. Nathan quickly closed the truck door. The puzzled look on her face reflected the feeling in his heart.

He jogged around to the driver's side, mentally chiding himself. He could not let his heart go there with her. Pearl Springs would never be home to her. And he never wanted to leave.

10

I f she'd still been hooked up to a monitor, Alex's heart would have broadcast how she felt when Nathan almost kissed her. And he'd definitely been about to kiss her. Now she kept her eyes closed and processed her emotions as Nathan followed her directions to the nearby cemetery.

"We're here," he said. "Where is her grave?"

She opened her eyes and sat up. "It's to the right, in the back corner of the cemetery." Heaviness weighed on her heart as they wove around to the section where Rebecca was buried. She pointed to a small tombstone in the middle of the row. "It's right there."

He parked as close to the marker as he could, and for a second, Alex didn't move, just stared at it.

"The ground is kind of rough. Can I walk with you?" he asked.

"I'd rather be alone."

But before she could open the door, he hopped out and jogged around to her side of the truck. "At least let me help you get out."

It was a long step to the ground. "Thanks."

"The ground isn't even, so I won't use the step. We'll try this instead," he said, slipping his hands on either side of her waist to help her out of the truck.

Alex did not like it one bit the way her heart reacted. Again. Sure, she'd thought she was in love with Nathan Landry when they dated their senior year in high school. But that was then and this is now, and a romantic relationship wasn't in her plans.

She turned toward the marker and wobbled as she took a step in the thick grass. Nathan steadied her before she could fall.

"Let me help you to the gravesite, and then I'll come back to the truck. You can wave when you're ready."

She glanced up at him. When had he gotten so . . . so intuitive? Alex smiled her thanks and leaned on his arm as they made their way to Rebecca's grave. Just like he promised, he left her at the site and returned to the truck.

She looked at the granite marker and blinked back tears. The day Becky was buried, Alex had stood in this very spot and vowed to find her killer. But now that she was here, she couldn't find the words to tell her friend that the person who'd killed her would never hurt anyone else.

At least she had peace about where Becky was. Alex had told her about Jesus, and she'd accepted him in her heart. They'd even worked through a short Bible study together. It was one reason Alex had been so hurt when she learned Becky had returned to the streets.

She felt her pockets for a tissue and came up empty. She knuckled the tears away. Maybe if Alex had tried harder to find Becky after she left the shelter . . .

Pain stabbed her side from the bullet wound. Time to go, and she patted the headstone again before turning and waving to Nathan. Seconds later he was at her side, pressing a tissue into her hand.

"Thank you." She blotted her eyes and then leaned heavily

on his arm until they were at the truck. He helped her into the seat and reached for the seat belt. "I can get it," she said.

"Sure."

A few minutes later they were back in Chattanooga traffic. "Feel better?" he asked.

"Not really. I wanted to tell her I'd caught the scumbag who killed her, but I . . . I don't know why but I couldn't."

"You don't think George Smith is the Queen's Gambit Killer?"

"I don't know what I think, just that something doesn't feel right. I guess it could be the aftermath of getting shot."

Alex swayed as Nathan made a sharp turn, and she glanced around. "You're not taking 27?"

"They're repaving it. This is longer but probably won't take as long."

"Understood." The state was always working on the roads around here. She leaned back against the seat again. "Sorry I'm not good company."

He chuckled. "If I'd been shot and left with a collapsed lung, I wouldn't be good company either."

She'd missed the sound of his chuckle and the way he always put a positive spin on everything.

Briefly Nathan shifted his gaze from the road to her. "Your folks will be glad to see you."

"How many texts have you gotten from Gram?"

"Oh, maybe three or four."

"Or five or six," she said dryly. She glanced out the window as they left the rolling valley of Chattanooga behind and climbed a ridge of the Cumberland Mountains that would take them to Russell County.

It wasn't long before they topped the ridge, and she looked across the valley below. It'd be another month before the maples and hickory changed colors, but the poplar trees stood out against the dense green foliage like yellow butterflies. "Wow! I need to get out of Chattanooga more often."

She'd gotten so used to seeing the mountains surrounding Chattanooga, it took seeing them from a different perspective to realize how beautiful they were. "I didn't know the trees were already turning."

"Just the poplar. But come mid to late October, the other hardwoods will turn and we'll get all the traffic from sightseers."

"Maybe I'll get to see the colors this year."

"Only if you make time for it."

She gritted her teeth instead of snapping back at him. Nathan was only trying to make conversation, not criticizing her. Or maybe he was, but it pleased her that she hadn't jumped to the bait. Surely she could refrain from being churlish for a couple of weeks until she could get back to her job and Chattanooga. After all, he'd been nothing but helpful since she was shot. And she needed to remember that.

They entered a stretch of highway that had deep drop-offs with little or no shoulder. Alex kept her gaze straight ahead and forced herself to breathe in and out. *Think of something else.* "You still go caving?"

"Sometimes," he said. "Where'd that come from?"

"I don't know." Maybe she'd caught a glimpse of a cave. There were enough in Russell County, which probably had more caves than any of the counties surrounding it. Whatever the reason, yearning for those carefree days before responsibility took over stirred Alex.

"You know if my parents and your grandparents had known we were exploring the caves, they would've grounded us for life."

"You better know it. We were lucky we didn't kill ourselves."

Nathan tapped his fingers on the steering wheel. "How long do you think you'll stay at your grandparents'?"

"A week, tops." His laughter startled her, then she laughed along with him. "Okay, maybe Gram will let me go after two weeks."

"How about your job? Any word when you can go back to work?"

Another sore spot. "The department psychologist came by while I was in the hospital. I guess I didn't answer some of her questions the way she wanted—she let me know it wouldn't be anytime soon. She wants me to call and set up an appointment with her once I get back on my feet."

"It's probably better if you don't rush it."

They rounded a curve in the highway, and she caught her breath as the afternoon sun lit up the trees. It was after dark most of the times she drove this route or the one on US 27 to check on her grandparents and usually just as dark when she returned home. "I definitely need to get out of town more often while it's daylight."

"Yeah, Carson said you usually arrived late and left late." Nathan glanced over at her. "Maybe now that you'll be here longer, you can go to church with them."

Guilt stabbed her. Again. The weekends she visited, Alex usually managed to convince her grandparents she needed to sleep in, and that might work for this Sunday. But once Gram thought she was well enough . . . "I'll go with them before I return home, but not this Sunday—right now there'd be too many questions from the LOL at church."

"What? LOL?" He shot a frown at her.

"Little old ladies I told you about."

He grinned. "Gotcha."

A few miles down the road, he tapped the steering wheel. "When was the last time you did something for fun? And I'm not talking about visiting your grandparents."

"I don't know—haven't given it much thought." Who had

time for fun, anyway? After making detective by the time she was twenty-six, she'd spent the last eight years working her way through the different departments. Her goal was to become lieutenant by the time she was thirty-seven—in three years. Then captain and finally police commissioner while she was still young enough to enjoy the job.

As they crossed the Pearl River, she stared up the river that divided Russell County in half. Wouldn't be long until they were in Pearl Springs.

"Once you're feeling stronger, would you consider a trip to Ruby Falls with me?"

She turned and stared at him. Then she touched her chest before she pointed at him. "You want us, as in you and me, to go to Ruby Falls. Together?"

He nodded. "When you're stronger, of course."

Thoughts of their near-kiss flooded her mind. Surely he didn't mean . . . "As in a date?"

"I think it's time we buried the hatchet. I don't even remember what broke us up."

"You *are* kidding—right?"

He shook his head. "Why would I do that?"

"Nathan Aaron Landry! If you hadn't cheated, I would have been valedictorian of our graduating class in high school. That—"

"Cheat? Me? You're crazy. My GPA was half a point higher than yours. So how do you figure I cheated?"

"It was only higher because you took shortcuts and easy subjects our senior year. I took chemistry and physics while you took health and PE." Valedictorian of Pearl Springs High School would have looked good on her resume and might have swayed the powers-that-be at Irvine to accept her application.

"I took physics in the tenth grade. And I worked my rear off taking extra classes. So don't tell me I cheated."

No way did he take physics as a sophomore. Even though they hadn't started dating until their senior year, surely she would have remembered that. When she looked up, his jaw was set, and all his face needed to burst into flame was a lighter.

"Are you telling me that you broke up with me because I beat you out for valedictorian?"

The hard edge of his voice scraped her heart. "No." It wasn't a total lie. "We were going in different directions. And it was for the best. You ended up being content to stay in Russell County and work for my grandfather before you took the Pearl Springs chief job, and I want something bigger."

Why had she brought up something that happened almost twenty years ago, anyway? And if he took physics before their senior year, that meant she'd been totally off base all these years. "Did you really take physics in the tenth grade?" Even to her own ears, her voice sounded small.

"Have I ever lied to you?"

"No." How could she have gotten it so wrong? She flinched at the answer her conscience gave her—she'd wanted the honor of being valedictorian. Whether or not she got it had nothing to do with not being accepted at UC Irvine. That had been on her and no one else. "Let's talk about something else."

"No. I want to know why you're still mad about me being valedictorian."

She sighed. "I'm not mad, I promise . . . it's just that Dad dying that year and then losing out to you and not getting into the university I wanted was all mixed up in my head."

"Your senior year was tough." His voice was softer. "But you went to a great criminal justice school, maybe the best there is now. And it sure worked out better for you to be near your grandparents."

"I know."

Nathan stopped, and with a jolt, Alex realized they were at

Pearl Springs' one traffic light. She glanced to the left and could just barely see the roof of the high school they'd just discussed.

"Are you hungry?" Nathan nodded toward the building to his left. "The lunch rush is over at the diner, if you'd like a burger."

He'd never been one to hold a grudge. Her mouth watered. After a week of hospital food, one of Pete Harrel's thick, juicy hamburgers sounded like heaven. She told him so, and he turned left and parked at the Corner Diner.

"You sure you feel up to going in?"

"I'll be fine. Pete's burgers don't taste as good unless you're there."

Nathan came around and opened her door. She took his arm when he offered it. "Thanks. And I'm sorry about earlier. I know you weren't the reason I didn't make the cut for Irvine."

11

Alexis leaned on Nathan's arm, her gait measured as they approached Pete Harrel's Corner Diner. He couldn't believe she'd thought he'd cheated all those years ago. At least maybe now she realized he hadn't. Nathan grabbed the door and held it open for her. Once inside, the harsh fluorescent lighting highlighted the dark rings under her eyes and the pasty color of her skin.

She wasn't up to this. "You okay?" he asked softly.

"No, but point me toward the nearest booth." She took a breath and winced. "I am not giving in to this."

He half supported Alexis and guided her to a red booth, where she eased onto the cracked vinyl seat and rested her head against the back. After a minute, she sat up straighter and looked around. "Oh my. This place hasn't changed since . . ."

"Before we were born?"

"Yeah." She caught her breath. "Ethel is still working? She has to be past seventy."

Nathan looked up in time to see Pete's wife scurrying toward them. He chuckled. "Couldn't tell it by me."

The older lady took out her pad. "The usual for my favorite

police chief? Hamburger, medium well, mustard, pickles, and onion, and no fries?"

"Yes, ma'am."

Then she turned to Alexis. "And you, Miss—" Her eyes widened behind the lavender frames. "Alexis Stone! Is that really you?"

"Yes, ma'am."

"Honey, you don't look too good. How about I bring you a strong cup of Pete's coffee?"

Alexis gave a quick shake of her head. "I'm not that far gone. I'll have what Nathan's having and a Diet Pepsi."

"Don't have it."

A frown crossed Alexis's face. "Don't have what?"

"Diet Pepsi. Pete figures anybody eating his burgers don't worry about their calories. Regular?"

"Sure."

"Good. How's Judith? She took you getting shot pretty hard."

Alexis flinched. Nathan wished he knew how to turn Ethel off. "We all did. And now she needs food to get her strength back," he said pointedly.

Ethel looked from Alexis to Nathan, then slowly nodded. "Right. Don't know what got into me, talking about you getting shot and all. Imagine you're wanting to forget that. I'll get Pete to working on this and have it to you in a jiffy."

"Sorry about that," he said when Ethel scurried away. He could only imagine the conversation going on in the kitchen.

"I might as well get used to it. I'm not in Kansas anymore." Her cell phone rang, and she fished it out of her pocket and glanced at it before punching the answer button. "Hi, Gram. We're at Pete's." She listened for a minute. "It sounds great, but could we have that for supper? . . . Good. We should be to the house in about thirty minutes . . . Okay, see you then."

"She wasn't happy we stopped at Pete's?"

"No. Seems she's cooked all my favorites. Roast beef and gravy, potatoes, chocolate cake—you get the picture."

"I'm sorry. Guess we should've called her first."

"She was good with waiting. Gramps is out on a search and rescue call. Did you know Russell County has a SAR dog?"

"Gem. She's also trained for explosives and drugs. Mark Lassiter is her handler. You might remember him. He was a couple of years behind us. Kind of laid-back, bends the rules sometimes, but he's a good detective. Not someone you'd enjoy working with, though."

"What's that supposed to mean?"

"Nothing . . . except you're so by the book, you two would have a little friction." He shook his head. "I don't know how I got off on that subject since you're not the sheriff and don't have to work with him."

"I still don't understand what you're getting at."

When would he learn to keep his mouth shut? Probably never. "Let's just say I *was* surprised to see you working undercover at the Lemon Tree."

He chanced a peek at Alexis. Her lips were tightly pursed, but at least he'd gotten a little color in her cheeks.

"I have no idea what you're talking about."

The way she shifted in her seat told a different story, and he lifted an eyebrow. "Can you honestly say you're comfortable using deception to get information? I mean, the girl I remember couldn't even lie if one of her friends asked if their outfit made them look fat."

"At least my friends knew that I'd tell them the truth." She lifted her chin. "But if they'd already bought the outfit, I kept my mouth shut. Besides, that was a long time ago, and criminals are fair game."

Nathan started to respond and decided he'd better stop

while he was ahead. Thankfully, Ethel appeared with their burgers and drinks.

"Y'all enjoy."

Nathan was glad she didn't hang around to talk, especially since Alexis was eyeing her burger like it was a mountain. "Just eat half of it."

"Good idea. I had forgotten how big they are. Glad we didn't get fries too." She cut the hamburger in half and took a bite and sighed after she swallowed. "This is so good."

He chomped down on his and nodded. "Pete still has the touch."

It wasn't long before Alexis set her uneaten portion on the plate. "That's about all I can do for now."

He half rose. "I'll get you a to-go box."

"Not just yet. I want to talk to you about something. Two things, actually."

He sat back down and waited for Alexis to continue.

"First, I want to thank you for everything you've done. I know Pearl Springs probably doesn't have a lot of crime, but I'm sure you have plenty on your plate without nursemaiding me."

"We do have crime, but you haven't kept me from working on it."

"Which is?"

"Drugs."

"You're kidding. I'd hoped Pearl Springs was immune to that problem."

"Hardly." Nathan wrestled with how much to tell her. He leaned forward. "That's why I was at the Lemon Tree the night we ran into each other."

"I don't understand."

"I was getting information about the dealers in town."

She nodded slowly. "You were meeting with a confidential

informant. Do you know who the dealers are? Maybe it's a spillover from the drug dealers in Chattanooga."

"It's possible. I have a lead on the locals, and we're keeping them under observation."

"You didn't arrest them?"

"I want the ones selling to them," he said. A comfortable silence fell between them. "You said two things?"

She pressed her lips together and glanced around at the diner, finally bringing her gaze back to him. "I've thought more about George Smith since you asked me earlier. I'm not sure he's the Queen's Gambit Killer."

"What makes you think that?" Nathan had dropped by the Chattanooga PD and talked with Parker two days ago. The detective was more than happy to have the case wrapped up.

"I don't know . . . with his background, Smith doesn't strike me as someone who could commit five murders and leave no trace evidence behind."

Nathan had gotten hung up on her knowing Smith's background and almost missed the rest of what she'd said. "How did you—"

"I was going crazy, lying in that bed, so I called Al Watkins a couple of days ago and asked him to drop the case file off at the hospital."

"And he did?" Alexis was nowhere near well enough to deal with reading that file. And because she'd shot Smith, she was automatically on administrative leave until the shooting was cleared by Internal Affairs. Not to mention the department psychologist would have to release her back to active duty. Watkins should have known better.

"No, but he came by and pretty well told me everything that was in it. I think he felt a little guilty that he got lost and allowed Smith to practically kidnap me."

"What makes you think Smith isn't the serial killer? He had a White pawn in the bag on his belt."

"Copycat, maybe?" She looked toward the window. "I don't know . . . I just have this feeling we're not done with the Queen's Gambit Killer."

12

T wenty minutes. Alex slowed the treadmill to a stand-still and wiped sweat from her face. She'd come a long way in three weeks. Usually, she walked twice a day on the treadmill Nathan had moved into her bedroom, but she'd probably skip the second workout later today.

He'd been a lot of help since Alex opted to stay in Pearl Springs after Gram threw a fit when she wanted to return to her house in Chattanooga. Today they were combining a trip into Chattanooga for her to check on her house and a short scenic tour on a steam engine. Nathan's idea of her doing something "fun." It wasn't Ruby Falls, but she wasn't up to the amount of walking that trip would take. The scenic tour would be just enough that she wouldn't need another treadmill session.

Alex picked up her Yeti and sipped the protein shake she'd made earlier—much to Gram's chagrin. Every morning, it was always the same song. *"You need a good, hot breakfast for your body to heal."*

"Gram, I need protein, not biscuits and gravy."

If she ate everything her grandmother cooked, she'd spend her day working off calories instead of getting stronger. Not that a stronger body would get her back to active duty anytime soon. While Alex had been cleared by Internal Affairs, she still had the department psychologist to contend with.

She'd driven into Chattanooga yesterday to see Dr. Hudson, expecting a one-and-done deal, but the doctor pointed out this was Alex's second shooting-related death in two years. She wanted Alex to come in once a week for the next month before she would even think about releasing her to active duty.

She understood Dr. Hudson's insistence that she go through the sessions—the weight of taking a life, even to keep the other person from harming someone, weighed heavily on her. Even now Alex struggled with Phillip Denton's death. It'd been suicide-by-cop.

Briefly she closed her eyes, the memory of pleading with Denton to put his gun down as fresh as yesterday. Instead, he'd raised his gun, that turned out to be unloaded, and pointed it at Alex as she dropped to the ground and fired.

There was a light tap at her bedroom door before her grandmother opened it and came into the room.

"Good. You're done." Gram's tone indicated Alex was spending way too much time working out.

Alex made sure her hand didn't shake as she set the empty Yeti on her dresser. "Yes, ma'am. Everything okay?"

Gram didn't normally visit her room; instead, she waited for Alex to find her in the kitchen or her sewing room.

"I suppose." She frowned. "Have you noticed that your grandfather . . ."

"Hasn't been feeling up to par?" Alex finished for her. "I have. Has he been to the doctor?"

"The old fool won't admit anything is wrong, so of course he hasn't made an appointment with his doctor. I thought maybe if you said something to him, he'd go see the doc."

"I'll see what I can do, but anytime I ask if he's feeling okay, his standard reply is 'I'm fine.'"

"Asking him to make an appointment with Doc won't hurt. What time is Nathan picking you up for your date?" Gram wiggled her eyebrows.

"It's not that kind of date—I'm mostly going because I want to test my strength." The outing that would take up most of the afternoon should let her know where she stood in her rehab. "Besides, we're just friends, and it's never going to be anything more."

"Be careful what you say never to," Gram said. "You don't know what God has in store."

"I seriously doubt God has given much thought to my dating life."

"Alexis Judith Stone, you know better than that. God cares about every aspect of our lives."

"I know." Alex hugged her grandmother. "But it's just that the few men I've dated since college didn't quite measure up."

"Maybe because you were comparing them to Nathan," she said with a knowing grin. "And regardless of what kind of date it is, I've made a snack to take with you."

"Thank you." She kissed her grandmother's cheek. "That was so sweet of you, and Nathan will be very happy about it, especially if you included those brownies he loves."

"You sure know a lot about him."

"Gram." Alex made the name two syllables. "It's bad enough that your friends at church are trying to play matchmaker, don't you join them."

"You never said what time Nathan was picking you up."

"Noonish. We have to be at the railroad station by two and it takes about an hour to get there, but we have to park and all that good stuff."

"So you'll eat lunch before you leave?"

Alex checked her watch. Ten thirty. She wouldn't be hungry but knew better than to try to get out of the house without eating something. "I'll eat a scoop of your chicken salad on lettuce before I leave."

"I'll fix it for you."

Alex bit back an exasperated sigh. Her grandmother was hovering, her way of expressing love. Alexis didn't necessarily want her to change, but sometimes it smothered her. "Sure. I'll come to the kitchen as soon as I shower and dress."

Gram smoothed a strand of hair behind Alex's ear, then hugged her. "I'm glad to see you improving, and I hope we can keep you in Pearl Springs another month, at least."

Not happening. But she kept that to herself as Gram shut the bedroom door behind her. Alex went in the bathroom and turned on the shower. She'd have to admit, Pearl Springs was growing on her. It was kind of nice to see someone on the street and get a wave, to know them by their first name and who their kids and parents were.

After dressing, Alex made her way to the kitchen as her grandmother set a salad plate with a huge scoop of chicken salad on a bed of lettuce on the island. "I heard Gramps say something about coming home for lunch?"

"Yep. Probably about the time you leave." Gram set a similar plate across from Alex's. "He won't be happy that he's getting the same thing."

"How'd you do that? He's eaten lunch at Pete's for as long as I can remember."

"And that's why he's put on twenty pounds in the last ten years. Pete will have to get someone else to advertise his burgers."

Alex ate about half the chicken salad and put her fork down. "I can't eat all of this."

"You can and will. It's only half a cup—I measured it."

Her grandmother must have a big half cup. Alex was still trying to finish hers when a knock came at the back door. Gramps wouldn't knock, so it had to be Nathan.

"Door's unlocked," Gram called out.

Nathan opened the door and stepped inside the kitchen, his presence filling the room. And when he smiled at Alex, it sent her heart into high gear. Gram broke the spell when she asked if he'd eaten.

"Peanut butter and crackers."

"Then sit yourself down, and you can have what we're having."

He checked his watch. "Maybe just a tiny bit."

"Gram doesn't know the meaning of 'tiny bit,'" Alex said dryly.

"Hush, girl." She set another plate at the end of the island and heaped a healthy scoop of salad onto it.

"See what I mean?"

All three of them stared at his plate then burst out laughing. "Okay," Gram said and used her spoon to remove part of the chicken salad before she pushed a plate of crackers toward Nathan.

A few minutes later, Alex's phone dinged. Before she could fish her phone from her back pocket, Gram's rang.

She exchanged a puzzled glance with Nathan, then as her grandmother answered her phone, Alex read her text from her grandfather's chief deputy. She covered her mouth with her hand. *No!*

Gramps had collapsed with a heart attack and was being airlifted to Erlanger Hospital in Chattanooga.

13

By the time Nathan got Judith and Alexis to the hospital in Chattanooga, Judith had given verbal permission for the surgeon to do whatever it took to save her husband's life, and the sheriff was in surgery. Since the artery supplying blood to the heart muscle hadn't been totally blocked, the surgeon hoped to stent it instead of opening his chest.

Both women sat where they could watch the doors to the ICU. Judith rested her chin on her thumbs with her fingers pressed together. Praying, he assumed. Alexis watched the doors, stiffening every time they opened.

At least they hadn't been taken to the small chapel where families learned their loved one hadn't made it. That's what happened when Nathan's dad died. He stood and walked to the window and stared out at the turning fall foliage set against the backdrop of the blue October sky. He'd hoped a change of scenery would take his mind off the antiseptic smell smothering him.

How did bad things happen on such a beautiful day? Nathan forced himself to breathe evenly to calm his anxious thoughts. In spite of that, he jumped when the ICU doors opened, and a man in green scrubs and a surgical cap approached Judith.

Both women started to stand, but the doctor motioned

for them to remain seated. Nathan joined them as the doctor dragged a metal chair closer to them and sat in it.

"How is he, Dr. Holley?"

"Stable." He glanced at Alexis and Nathan.

Judith quickly introduced them. "You can talk about his condition in front of them."

The doctor nodded. "I was able to stent the left anterior descending artery as well as two smaller ones . . ."

"That's good, isn't it?" Judith said.

"Yes, but your husband had a heart attack prior to arriving at the hospital. He sustained damage to his heart muscle."

"Will he be all right?" Alexis asked.

"Barring complications, he'll live, but we won't know how much damage occurred for a day or two." He turned to Judith. "Has he exhibited any signs he was having heart problems, like chest pain, shortness of breath, or being more tired than usual?"

"Only the last one," Judith said. "But when I asked him to make an appointment with you, he said he was fine."

"No surprise there," the doctor said with a chuckle.

"When can we see him?" Alexis asked.

"You can go in now, but don't stay over five minutes. He's very tired, drifting in and out of sleep."

Memories of his father hit Nathan. Much like Carson, Paul Landry had loved Pete's burgers, been overweight, and never exercised. In Nathan's last memories of him, he was hooked to wires and tubes after bypass surgery. Surgery he didn't recover from.

Surgery Nathan talked him into having.

"I'll stay here." He didn't want images of Carson hooked to equipment embedded in his mind.

"No," Judith said. "You're like a grandson to us both, and he'll want to see you."

There wasn't much way to say no to that. The Stones were the grandparents he'd never had, and Nathan couldn't disappoint them. He brought up the rear as they followed the doctor through the ICU doors.

The antiseptic smell was stronger in the ICU than the waiting room, and there was no beautiful scenery to distract him. Only critically ill patients. *Please, Lord, don't let Carson die today.*

The doctor paused at Carson's room.

"I have other patients to see, but don't stay over five minutes," Dr. Holley cautioned once again.

Judith pushed the door open, and Alexis followed her into the room. Nathan reluctantly walked in behind them. A monitor beeped a steady rhythm, not like the erratic beat he remembered with his dad.

"Carson," Judith said, taking her husband's hand. "Are you awake?"

"Of course I'm awake. Raise me up so I can see."

Nathan relaxed slightly at the sheriff's crusty tone. Maybe he was okay. He ventured a glance toward the older man. No tubes. Just the IV and oxygen.

Judith searched for the button to elevate the head of the bed, and Nathan stopped her. "He's just had a stent, and they may want him to lay flat."

"Ignore him," Carson growled.

"I don't know what I was thinking." She turned to her husband. "We're only allowed in here for five minutes, so let's not use it arguing."

"I know Nathan's here, but is Alexis?"

Alexis stepped up to the bed and squeezed his hand. "You need to behave."

"That'll be the day," Judith muttered.

"Since we don't have but a minute, I need you to do something."

"Anything, Gramps."

"Good. Remember that, 'cause you're not going to like it." He closed his eyes briefly.

Alexis turned toward Nathan, her eyes questioning, and he nodded. "Maybe we better come back later," Nathan said.

"No." Carson blinked his eyes open. "I haven't been feeling well for a while now, and this heart attack confirms what I need to do . . ." He gripped his granddaughter's hand. "I want to hire you as my chief deputy."

Alexis opened her mouth to say something, then closed it and stared at her grandfather. She shook her head. "Did I hear—"

"You heard me right." Carson gave her a gentle smile. "I need you, Alexis. I can't handle the job anymore on my own, especially after this."

Alexis lost what little color she had. "Nathan would be a much better choice if you retire."

"Pearl Springs needs him as police chief. Besides, I'm not retiring. Not yet, anyway. Probably would if you could step into my job, but since you haven't lived in Russell County for a year, I can't get you appointed as sheriff.

"What I can do is hire you and make you my chief deputy. You'll be running the office—in other words, you'll be the sheriff in everything but the title."

"What about the chief deputy you already have? Harvey Morgan," Alexis said.

Carson shook his head. "Harvey isn't the man for the job. I think he'll be happy if I move him to chief of staff."

Wise move on Carson's part. Nathan liked the chief deputy, but Harvey tended to let things slide. And maybe he wouldn't think being moved to chief of staff was a demotion, depending on the way Carson handled it. No need to worry about that— the sheriff had been handling touchy situations for years.

14

Alex stared at her grandfather. He couldn't do this to her. Before she could protest, a nurse hurried into the room. "I'm afraid you'll have to leave for now. Mr. Stone needs to rest. You can come back during regular visiting hours at five."

Her grandfather grasped her wrist. "Stay." Then he turned to the nurse. "You have to let me talk to her."

The nurse eyed her patient. "Two minutes. And just you," she said, pointing at Alex.

Once they were alone, Gramps loosened his grip. "I know you don't want to stay in Pearl Springs, but I need you to do this."

Her heart sank. How could she refuse to do what he asked? "But I have a job in Chattanooga. Why can't your chief deputy take over until you're better?"

"Like I said, Harvey's not right for the job." He rested a minute then squeezed her hand. "I need you, Alex."

Her heart hitched. Gramps rarely called her that, usually preferring Alexis—like Nathan.

"I hear they're putting you behind a desk in Chattanooga for a while. I think you'd like being my chief deputy a whole lot better than riding a desk."

"But the psychologist won't release me to work out in the field."

"She's in Hamilton County and has no authority here."

He'd thought it through. But when? Alex glanced up at the monitor. His pulse had jumped to a hundred. "Let me think about it."

A slow smile broke the tension in his face. "I'll take that as a yes."

"I didn't say that." But she knew in her heart she couldn't turn him down. She owed him too much. "I better get out of here before your nurse gets back."

"Yeah . . ." He sounded drowsy.

Alex bent over and kissed his cheek. "We'll talk later."

He was snoring softly by the time she reached the door. She looked back. His age had crept up on her, and for the first time ever, he looked every bit his seventy-five years and more. The thought of losing him paralyzed her. Alex brushed the thought away. It wasn't happening today.

When she joined Gram and Nathan in the waiting room, her grandmother handed her a cup of coffee. "I figured you might need it."

Alex shot her a wry grin. "Did you know he wanted to hire me?"

"When you live with someone as long as I've lived with your grandfather, you know things you don't voice. And he might have mentioned in the last few days that he was getting too old for the job. It's one reason I was worried about his health—couldn't see him saying that unless he felt he couldn't do the job. I didn't know he planned to ask you to be his chief deputy, but it's a sound idea."

She turned to Nathan. "How about you? Did you know?"

"I'm as surprised as you are."

Was that disappointment etching his face? Maybe Nathan

thought he'd have a shot at the sheriff's job when her grandfather stepped down. "Why didn't he choose you? You're more
qualified, knowing the county the way you do."

"I can tell you why," Gram said. Both of them turned to her.
"It's because Nathan's done such a good job being police chief."

"But that would be all the more reason—"

"Hear me out." Her grandmother smiled gently. "Carson
thinks he's too valuable to the town."

"So he's done too good of a job to be sheriff?"

"Sort of. Nathan here has whipped the Pearl Springs police
department into something it's never been, and I'm not just
talking about the way he's got them exercising.

"His officers are highly visible now instead of spending half
their time at Pete Harrel's restaurant and the coffee shop . . .
or the hardware store. And Nathan's always available. He goes
into the schools, he's started an afternoon program for the
teenagers, and he gives talks at the senior citizen center about
phone scams and gun safety. And—"

Nathan laughed. "I need to hire you to do PR for the department."

"Carson is very proud of the job you've done," Gram said.
"And with the mayor's new initiative to promote the lakes and
waterways around here, Carson figures the town and county
will get an influx of visitors, maybe even new residents. We'll
need a good man as police chief if that happens."

Nathan shook his head. "Heaven help us if the mayor is
successful. More people means more crime, and neither the
police department nor the sheriff's office have enough manpower as it is."

Alex had always heard life could turn on a dime but until
now hadn't known exactly what that meant. She had her life
planned out. If she did what her grandfather wanted, it could
possibly change everything—especially if he wanted her to

run for sheriff if he retired. She blew out a breath. No need to cross that bridge until she came to it.

She turned to her grandmother. "You do think this is only temporary, right? Once he's feeling better, he'll go back to being sheriff? I mean, he's only seventy-five and, until now, in good shape."

"It'll depend on how much damage the heart attack did."

But the uncertainty on her grandmother's face told her all she needed to know.

"You'll do this for him, won't you, Alexis?" Gram's eyes pleaded with her.

Did she have a choice? They'd given up a lot for her. If it hadn't been for her grandparents, there was no telling where Alex might've ended up after her mother died in a car wreck when Alex was six. Her father had been stationed in the Middle East, and Gramps and Gram had taken her in. They were all she had.

"You know I will." She chewed her thumbnail. "But what if Dr. Hudson won't release me?"

"You don't need her release to take the job," Nathan said.

"I know, but taking the job while under the care of a psychologist might come back to bite us. I'd rather get her to release me."

"Good point," he said.

Gram took both her hands. "I'd like for you to tell Carson you'll take the job when we go in to see him at five. Why don't you call and see if you can see the doctor this afternoon?" Gram said. "Nathan, you'll take her, won't you?"

Gramps had nothing on his wife when it came to getting people to do what she wanted. Alex turned to him. "Do you have time?"

"Yep. I'd already arranged for Jared to cover for me this afternoon while we were in Chattanooga."

Jared Westbrook was Nathan's second-in-command. While she remembered that, Alex had totally forgotten their afternoon outing. "Thanks. Let me check and see if I can see her."

She dialed Dr. Hudson's number, and after Alex explained how important it was to see the doctor, the receptionist put her in as Dr. Hudson's last patient of the day, provided she could be there in the next half hour. Alex relayed the information to her grandmother and Nathan.

"I'm ready," he said.

Nathan drove her the short distance across town to Dr. Hudson's office that was located next to the Chattanooga police department. She opened the truck door. "Thanks. This shouldn't take long."

"Text me when you're ready. I'm going to drop in and see Ken Parker."

She cocked her head. "Any particular reason?"

"Just want to know if he has any new information on Smith."

"You don't think he's the Queen's Gambit Killer either, do you?"

"I don't know, and that's why I want to talk to Parker. Smith certainly doesn't fit the profile."

"I'm glad I'm not the only one with a gut feeling about it, but I guess time will tell."

A few minutes later, she stepped off the elevator on the sixth floor and walked a short distance to the first door. Once inside, she approached the receptionist. "Checking in, Gail," she said.

The slender blond gave her a dazzling smile. "Dr. Hudson had a cancellation, and she instructed me to take you to room three as soon as you arrived."

She followed the receptionist down the hall to the room painted in a soft, dusty blue. Light streamed in through the bank of windows facing west. Alex chose one end of the leather sofa.

A side door opened, and Dr. Hudson stepped into the room and sat in the chair facing her. "Alex," she said, nodding. "I'm surprised to see you back so soon."

"You and me both."

"So, what can I do for you today?"

Alex explained what her grandfather wanted of her. "I'd like you to release me. I'd feel better about taking the job if you did."

The doctor nodded. "How do you feel about his request?"

Always the psychologist. Alex took a minute to organize her thoughts. "While Gramps isn't laying a guilt trip on me, I think I'm laying one on myself."

"What do you mean?"

"They were in their late forties when my mother died, and they took me in. I'm sure raising their granddaughter wasn't on their list of things to do with the rest of their life, especially since they'd never been around me."

Dr. Hudson cocked her head. "Why's that?"

"My mom and Gram didn't get along."

The doctor was quiet a minute. "Did you ever feel like they didn't want you?"

Alex didn't even have to think about that question. "Of course not."

"How about your dad? Was he in the picture?"

"Peripherally. He was in the Army, gone a lot, and didn't want to be saddled with a child, and my grandparents stepped up. He was killed in Iraq my senior year in high school."

"I'm sorry." Dr. Hudson wrote something on her notepad. "What was your life like before you went to live with them?"

Alex didn't like to revisit that part of her life and rarely talked about it with anyone.

When she didn't answer, the doctor said, "When you think of that time, what do you remember?"

She searched her memory bank. "I don't have a lot of memories . . . Yelling. My mom and dad fighting—when he was around."

"Do you know what they fought about?"

"Me." That she was sure of.

"How do you know?"

She tried to pinpoint why she believed that, but nothing surfaced. "I—I'm not sure."

"Children often believe they are the cause of their parents' problems, like divorce, when in fact, they aren't. Any other memories come to mind?"

She picked at her cuticle. "The storm. I have recurring nightmares about the night my mom died."

"I thought she died in a wreck."

"She did, but wind and driving rain swept her off the road."

"Tell me about that night."

She did not come here to relive her childhood, and normally Alex would simply clam up like the last time Dr. Hudson tried to dig into her past. But this was a special circumstance. She pressed her fingers to her temples as she dredged up the memory. "They'd been fighting again, and Mom stormed out of the house. If it hadn't been for me, Dad probably would've gone after her. There were tornado watches and warnings out, but we hadn't heard any of the reports. It was pitch black, and she drove right into a storm."

"Is that when you went to live with your grandparents?"

"Yes, right after the funeral." She shook her head, trying to clear it. "What does all this have to do with you releasing me? Not that I have to have the release to take the chief deputy job, but I'd feel better about taking the position if you were on board."

"Nothing . . . and everything. When you came to see me after the Denton shooting, I couldn't get past your walls. You've told me more today than all those sessions put together."

It was true that when she was here before she'd been reluctant to talk about her past, but that's what it was—her past. What difference did it make that her mother hadn't gotten on well with Alex's grandparents, or that she'd had little contact with them and was virtually a stranger when they took her in when she was six? That hadn't stopped Gram and Gramps from opening their hearts to Alex. All of that had nothing to do with her job as a police officer.

"Will you sign a release?" If she was taking the job, Alex didn't want anyone to question whether or not she was mentally fit. "It's not a dangerous job, at least it hasn't been. Russell County is a small, peaceful place. Shouldn't be the level of pressure I have as a Chattanooga detective."

"Will you be satisfied with that?"

"I'll have to be if I want to help my grandfather. It's like my grandmother always says—be satisfied in whatever condition you find yourself."

"Philippians four-twelve."

Alex nodded. "Is it a go?"

The doctor looked at her notes and jotted something down, then she leaned forward. "You don't need my permission to take the job. But I want to caution you—if you start exhibiting signs of post-traumatic stress, come see me."

"Don't worry. I will."

Dr. Hudson put her notes down. "You will of course be resigning from the Chattanooga police department, right?"

Alex's heart sank. She hadn't had time to think that far ahead. Resigning would stall her plan to become the first female chief of the Chattanooga Police Department.

On the other hand, how could she disappoint the man who had raised her?

15

Phame inserted a USB drive into the computer and thought about Alex Stone while waiting for the dark web to boot up. It had taken a while to track Stone to Pearl Springs in the Cumberland Plateau north of Chattanooga.

It'd been totally unexpected that she would leave the Chattanooga police department, especially after the way the second victim talked about Stone and how she wanted to be the top police official. A rather lofty goal for a woman. So why leave Chattanooga for Pearl Springs? To recover, most likely from George Smith's bullet.

"Copycat." Smith had tried to cash in on the Queen's Gambit killings. If Stone hadn't shot and killed Smith, Phame would have tracked him down and done the job.

The dark web filled the computer screen. With a click, the video game appeared, and Phame uploaded new photos of the victims and revised the game slightly, making it more difficult for the players to get through the twists and turns where gunmen lay in wait to ambush them. Only the best players made it to the top where the prize was a video of the latest victim's death.

Phame had thought about killing Stone's grandparents, her

only living relatives, but the deaths of two old people wouldn't be interesting to the players of the video game. They wanted mystery and young victims who looked like Stone. Playing with her mind was half the fun of the killings.

The early killings had been retribution for Phillip's death, but now it was more about the game—the video game, of course, but also the game of outsmarting the police . . . particularly Alex Stone.

Perhaps a Queen's Gambit victim should show up in Pearl Springs . . .

16

athan's phone buzzed, and he checked it. Alexis was walking over to the police department and would meet him out front. He texted back.

Why don't I pick you up?

No. I need to build my strength.

Stubborn woman. He stood and offered his hand to Parker. "Thanks for filling me in on George Smith. The more I learn about him, the less I believe he's the serial killer."

"Time will tell," the detective said. "How is Alex?"

"Healing. Her grandparents are happy to have her home."

"She's missed around here, for sure, but we were losing her anyway."

"What do you mean?"

"The captain said her transfer to homicide came in."

He hoped that didn't make a difference in whether Alexis took the chief deputy job. He gave Parker a thumbs-up and walked out of his office.

He wasn't sure how he felt about Carson offering Alexis the job instead of him. For as long as Nathan could remember, he'd wanted to run for sheriff of Russell County when his friend retired, and Carson knew that. The chief deputy position was the position to be in in advance of that run.

Reason nudged Nathan. Carson was looking at the big picture, and Nathan was doing a good job as police chief with the changes he'd implemented. He'd seen to it that Pearl Springs was a safe place to live, and if the town was safe, it made the county safer as well.

Besides, Nathan understood why Carson wanted Alexis to take the interim job. She was capable and would do things the way he wanted them done, and he'd still have control of the office. He would also have his granddaughter home doing a job that was nowhere as dangerous as working the streets of Chattanooga as a detective, especially an undercover detective.

Nathan exited the front door of the building and frowned. Alexis stood near the American flag talking with someone. As he drew closer, he recognized Kayla Jackson, the woman who'd probably saved Alexis's life that night . . . or caused her to get shot—he hadn't decided which yet. They both turned as he approached.

Alexis nodded toward the woman. "You remember Kayla, don't you? The captain wanted to talk to her about the shooting again."

Nathan dipped his head toward Kayla. The last time he saw her, she'd worn dark eye shadow and eyelashes that made him wonder how she kept her eyes open. Today her hair was in a ponytail, and if she had on any makeup, he couldn't tell it. She looked like a teenager or a college student, which she probably was. "Not much fun having to relive that again."

"It wasn't, but I really didn't mind. He wanted to know if I'd noticed the bag on the assailant's belt, and I hadn't, not until that cop found it."

Nathan hadn't noticed it either—he'd been too busy worrying about Alexis. Like now. He didn't like the dark circles under her eyes. "You ready?"

"Yeah. Gram texted. The nurse said Gramps was resting well and all vital signs were good."

Alarm lit Kayla's eyes. "Is your grandfather sick?"

"He had a heart attack."

"Oh, I'm so sorry. I hope he gets better quick. Can I do anything?"

"No," Alexis said. "But it is sweet of you to offer. Are you still working at the Lemon Tree?"

"No. I got tired of men like Houdini and quit last week."

"Houdini?" Nathan remembered Kayla mentioning that name the night Alexis was shot.

"Houdini is a name we tagged this creep with at the bar," Alexis said.

"I don't understand."

Kayla laughed. "You had to be there." Then she sobered. "Don't suppose either of you know of any job openings? I'd like something part-time so I can go back to college."

"My part-time dispatcher is quitting at the end of the month." As soon as he said the words, Nathan questioned if it was the right move.

Kayla's eyes widened. "Are you serious?"

He supposed he was. Peggy, his office manager, had told him just this morning he needed to fill the spot before Jimmy Arnold left so he could train someone. "The job *is* in Pearl Springs."

"Not a problem. From where I live, that'd only be a forty-five-minute commute, and who knows, I might even move there since I don't have anything holding me in Chattanooga."

"Good. Fill out an application, and we'll do a background check."

Kayla frowned. "That might be a problem since I don't have

much background to check. I've only ever had part-time jobs. Would that affect my chances?"

"You have college transcripts, right?"

"Absolutely."

"List that and your past residences." He rubbed his chin. "And since you don't have much background to check, send your high school transcripts as well. If you don't mind."

"Not a problem. Where do I apply?"

"At the Pearl Springs police department—it's located right across from the courthouse on Washington Street." He took a card from his wallet, wrote a note on the back, and then handed it to Kayla. "Give this to Peggy Armstrong, and she'll get you set up."

For a second, he thought Kayla was going to hug him, but then she grinned. "I promise, you won't regret it!"

He turned to Alexis. "Why don't you wait here while I get my truck."

"I think I will."

He jogged to where he'd parked, and after he picked up Alexis, he pointed the truck toward Erlanger.

"That was a nice thing to do for Kayla."

Nathan shrugged. "She needs a job and I need a part-time dispatcher. Seems providential." He glanced at Alexis. "How well do you know her?"

She laughed. "That night at the Lemon Tree was the first time I'd ever seen her. But we just sort of clicked. I do know she was working and saving her money to go back to college."

He felt better about his impulsive move. "Do you know what she's studying?"

"She mentioned social work."

He would have figured something in criminal justice, considering how she reacted when she realized Alexis was being forced to accompany George Smith. Using her martial arts training to disarm the man was quick thinking on her part. "Maybe you can talk her into being your deputy." If Alexis was still in Pearl Springs when that time came.

Alexis laughed. "Let's see if she follows through first."

"So, what did the psychologist say?" he asked.

She blew out a long breath. "She raised a point I hadn't even thought about. If I do what Gramps wants, I'll have to resign from the Chattanooga PD."

"This opportunity has come at you fast," he said. "You have a few days to decide."

"Not really—Gramps will want an answer today, and I don't see how I can disappoint him," she said. "I wonder if I can use my accrued vacation time. That would give him enough time to recover."

"How much time are you talking about?"

"Six months."

He stopped for a traffic light and turned and stared at her. "Six months? Have you never taken your vacation time?"

"I thought I had, at least that first year."

He'd known she was focused, but not to the point of never taking time off. "I wouldn't get my hopes up about that—I doubt Chattanooga PD would give you that much time off, especially to work another job."

"You're probably right," she said. "Did you learn anything from Ken Parker?"

"Not really. He did tell me something you need to know before you decide about quitting. Your transfer to homicide has been approved, pending your return to work."

Alexis sat perfectly still. "I can't believe it," she finally said.

"I wish there was something I could say to help you decide."

Neither of them spoke until Nathan turned into the drive-thru at Erlanger and stopped in front of the door. "Don't wait for me—parking lot looks full. No telling how long it'll take me to find a space."

"Sure." She unbuckled the seat belt and climbed out of the truck. He found a spot on the back row and parked, then checked in with Peggy.

"Everything is fine here," she said. "How's Sheriff Stone?"

"Word travels fast," Nathan said.

"The head of the church prayer committee called, requesting prayers."

He should've known. "The doctor was able to stent the blocked artery, and the sheriff was resting comfortably when I left him earlier."

"Good."

"By the way, a young lady will be coming by to fill out the paperwork for the dispatcher job."

"So my reminder got you on the ball?"

"Yep, and now we have a couple of weeks until Jimmy leaves for him to train her if she checks out okay."

"I'll take care of it."

Nathan walked through the automatic doors at the hospital. "Thanks. I'll be here at the hospital if you need me."

He pocketed his phone and started toward the elevators when he noticed Alexis standing by the information desk.

"I decided to wait on you," she said when he reached her.

He nodded. "Elevator or stairs?"

"Elevator. Not quite ready for the stairs yet."

He took her arm as they walked toward the elevators. "You want to go down to the cafeteria first? It's been a while since we ate."

"That might be a good idea."

The cafeteria was practically deserted when they walked through the doors. Nathan nodded toward a table. "Why don't you sit there while I get you something."

"Thanks."

When he returned with a Pepsi and a package of peanuts, she smiled. "You remembered."

He had. In high school she'd buy a Pepsi from the vending machine and pour peanuts into the bottle. "You still do that?"

"Not so much, but it's comfort food, and right now that's just what I need." She unscrewed the top on the drink and dumped the nuts in. Neither of them spoke for a minute, then she looked up. "I want to ask you something."

"Okay. Shoot."

"You know if I take this job, I can kiss the transfer to homicide goodbye, because it won't wait for me. What would you do?"

"I thought you'd pretty well decided to do what your grandfather wanted."

She swirled the drink, stirring the peanuts. "I had until I learned the transfer came through. I've wanted to work in homicide since day one."

"I probably shouldn't have told you, especially since it isn't official yet."

"If Parker knows, it's official. What do you think I should do?"

"I don't know. I can't make that decision for you. But I can help you look at the pros and cons."

She took a sip of Pepsi. "Okay, start helping."

"Well, what do you see as the pros?"

"I'd make my grandparents happy."

"Is that the only benefit you see?"

Alexis shrugged. "What do you think the pros are?"

"I see several. The chief deputy acts as the sheriff when he's out of commission, so you'll basically be in charge of the department. It isn't running the Chattanooga PD, but it'd be close.

"Second, you're right that you'd be helping your grandfather, and that would make you feel good.

"Third, it doesn't have to be permanent. See what the job is like. If you don't like it, I'm betting your department head will be happy to have you back. But who knows, you might even like it and want to run for sheriff when the time comes."

She was quiet a moment, and he could tell she was at least considering what he'd said. "How about you? Are you disappointed Gramps didn't pick you?"

That was a question he didn't want to answer just yet, and he hoped she didn't press him for an answer.

17

Alex had seen the hurt in Nathan's face when her grandfather asked her to take the chief deputy position, and it was there now. If he really wanted the job, she didn't want to stand in his way.

Nathan stood. "I need a cup of coffee. Be right back."

That pretty well said it all. He wanted the job. They'd been friends since elementary school. When he returned, Alex would tell him she wasn't taking the job, that he could have it—if he wanted it.

A minute later, Nathan returned and set the cup on the table. "I want—"

"I'm not—"

She motioned with her hand. "You go first."

"I want to make something clear. God has a plan for both our lives. And right now, I think his plan is for me to finish what I started in the Pearl Springs police department. And with you as chief deputy and basically the sheriff, maybe we can work together on some of the changes I want to implement for the county as a whole. Changes I haven't brought to Carson because . . . he's old school, and I wasn't sure he would want to expend the energy to see the projects through—not everyone likes change." He smiled. "Your turn now."

Alex didn't know what to say. She'd been prepared to relinquish the job to him. And why did she have to notice how blue his eyes were right now? If they married, would they have blue-eyed babies?

Babies? Where in the world did that come from? What was wrong with her? Besides, Nathan was fly-by-the-seat-of-his-pants, and she lived by rules and liked structure and organization and following procedures.

"Are you okay?"

Alex knew better than to look into those eyes again. They would be full of compassion. Because that was Nathan. Instead, she nodded and took another sip of soda.

"Well . . ." Nathan leaned closer. "What were you going to say earlier?"

"We haven't talked about the cons."

He laughed. "What do you think they are?"

She held up her finger. "One, I'd have to leave Chattanooga and keep living with my grandparents, at least for a while. Two, what if his deputies resent me? Three, what if I'm no good at managing people . . ."

"Stop worrying. You'll be great at the job," he said. "I won't sugarcoat it though. Some of the deputies might resent that he went out of the county to fill the job, but I know you'll win them over."

What if she didn't? That wasn't a bridge she had to cross today. She took a deep breath. "Then I guess we better go tell my grandparents I'll be needing my room a little longer."

Grinning, he tipped his cup at her. "Let me be the first to congratulate you."

"You may want to wait until all the i's get dotted and the t's crossed. Somebody might kick up that the sheriff is hiring his granddaughter as his chief deputy."

"That's one of the nice things about being sheriff, especially sheriff of a small county—he pretty well can hire anyone he wants to, and if he wants to hire you, there's nothing anyone can do about it as long as you aren't a felon."

"You don't think Harvey Morgan will be upset?"

"Knowing your grandfather, by the time he finishes talking to Harvey, he'll think it was his idea to transfer to chief of staff. And I don't think you'll have any trouble about it with the other deputies—they all know Harvey was chief deputy because he's been with the department the longest. Mark Lassiter is the only other deputy who might resent Carson hiring you, but both men like and respect your grandfather. I believe they'll give you a chance."

She stared at the floor. Now that she'd agreed to do what her grandfather asked, all kinds of questions bombarded her. What if some of the deputies resigned because Gramps hired her? It would stress her grandfather at a time he didn't need stress.

"Look at me."

She raised her gaze.

"Stop worrying. It's not going to be that complicated."

18

Twelve days later on a Monday morning at nine o'clock, her grandmother and Nathan looked on as Alex lifted her right hand and her grandfather swore her in as his chief deputy.

Her head swirled with how quickly everything moved once she said yes. Even resigning from the Chattanooga PD wasn't as painful as Alex had expected. Her lieutenant had wished her well and indicated there would be a place for her if she ever wanted to return.

After her grandparents congratulated her, Kayla hugged her. Alex had been surprised to see her at the brief ceremony. Kayla had started working for Nathan a couple of days ago and had even found a place to live in Pearl Springs.

"Congratulations, if this is what you want," Kayla said.

"Thanks. Stick around—I think my grandmother brought refreshments."

"I gotta run or I'll be late for work," Kayla said as the Pearl Springs's mayor stepped next to Alex and held out his hand.

"Thanks for coming," she called to Kayla's retreating form before she turned to the mayor and shook his hand as he congratulated her.

"I look forward to working with you."

Alex was surprised that he showed up at the swearing in. "Gramps told me you have plans for the area. I'd like to hear about them sometime." She glanced over his shoulder at Nathan. "Thank you for coming."

"Sounds good. I believe you're just what the county needs."

When the mayor moved on to shake hands with her grandfather, Nathan stepped beside her.

"You look good in green."

"Thanks." The uniform, a dark green polo and khakis, had arrived Friday, just in time for her swearing in. She held out her hand.

He didn't settle for a handshake, instead enveloped her in a hug. "I'm proud of you."

Before she could respond, the photographer motioned her over to pose for photos with her grandfather, who refused to be photographed in the wheelchair he'd come in, then with Nathan, the mayor, and grandfather for the local newspaper. Last of all, Alex stood with the US flag and the Tennessee state flag as backdrops for her official chief deputy photo that would be placed where Harvey's photo had been on the wall identifying the command staff. Harvey's new photo would be on the other side of her grandfather's.

When the photos were finished and practically everyone had left, she leaned over to her grandfather. "Want to show me around?"

"Good idea."

Alex glanced at Nathan. "You want to tag along?"

He grinned. "If you don't care—a tour might be as close as I'll ever get to the office."

Her grandfather's head jerked up. "Nathan Landry! You know I didn't offer you the job because you're needed where you are."

Nathan palmed his hand. "I know. And I'm happy in my job."

"Good." Her grandfather swept his arm around the room. "While I'm recovering, you'll take over this office. If I return, we'll share it."

He was no longer saying *when* he returned. That saddened and frightened her. While he tired easily, which was the reason for the wheelchair, his recovery from the heart attack had gone much smoother than even the doctors expected, but the threat of another one hung over them all. She glanced around the room where she'd be spending most of her time.

Heavy red curtains covered the windows, and earlier she'd flipped on a light that revealed pale blue walls. "You're free to do whatever you want to the office," he said.

"Does that include replacing those?" She pointed at the curtains.

He grinned. "Depends on how much you want to spend. There's only so much in the budget for that sort of thing, and it isn't much."

Blinds for three windows shouldn't be that costly, especially if she hung them herself. His cherry desk was tidy and it would stay that way—the apple certainly hadn't fallen far from the tree. She smiled, remembering playing under the desk when she was a child. It was no wonder she became a police officer, the way she hung around the jail all the time.

"Don't worry about money," Gram said. "I've been saving up to do something with this office for years, but old 'Don't Change Anything' here never would let me."

Nathan pointed to a blank wall. "Your awards would look good there."

Alex was both proud and embarrassed of the awards. It didn't seem right that she would get recognition for simply doing her job.

She sat behind the desk like she had a hundred times in the past, but it felt different now that it would be "her" office. Alex glanced down, suppressing a grin. The initials she'd carved into the wood drawer years ago were still there. Even though she'd been disciplined, it pleased her that her grandfather hadn't had the drawer refinished.

Alex sat back in the swivel chair. The side door opened, and she swung around as the new chief of staff stepped into the room. He'd been conspicuously absent from the swearing in. She stood. "Harvey."

He nodded. "Sorry I missed the swearing in, but my wife had a reaction to her medicine."

"Is she all right?"

"Yeah."

"Good." He was no longer the trim young deputy who'd often found her under her grandfather's desk and escorted her out of the office. Now he carried an additional forty pounds or more. Perhaps she would institute some of Nathan's exercise programs for her deputies. But not anytime soon. For now, she wanted things to run as they were.

"Miss Alex . . . uh." He scratched his head. "What am I going to call you, anyway?"

The name he'd called her when she was a child wouldn't do now. Before she could answer him, her grandfather folded his arms over his chest. "How about Chief Deputy Stone?"

She shook her head. "I like just plain Alex better. That good with you?"

"Kind of what I was thinking." Harvey stood a little straighter. "Most of the deputies are here, if you'd like to speak to them."

Showtime. A sudden attack of nerves had her hands sweaty and her heart in overdrive. "Thank you, Harvey."

At least her voice didn't give her away. Alex stood and wiped the palms of her hands on her slacks. She was about to find out how many of the deputies resented being overlooked for this position in favor of a woman. Especially a woman who wasn't one of them. Would they view her hiring as nepotism, even though the sheriff was free to hire whomever he wanted? Or that she was more than qualified?

Her grandfather pushed himself out of the wheelchair. "Mind if I introduce you?"

That should help. She pointed at the wheelchair. "Only if you use that."

He stood straighter and squared his shoulders. "I will not appear before my officers in that contraption."

With his jaw set, he walked ramrod straight through the door. She didn't know where he got the strength, but she was right on his heels to catch him if he fell.

Every officer stood and clapped, then saluted.

Her grandfather returned their salute, then cleared his throat as he held up his hand. When the room quieted down, he said, "Sorry I haven't been here much lately, and I'm not going to lie to you. I have no idea when I'll be back.

"But I'm leaving you in good hands with your new chief deputy, Alex Stone, my granddaughter. For the past twelve years, she's been a decorated Chattanooga police officer, starting out at the bottom in patrol, and then the last eight years as a detective. As chief deputy, she's more than qualified to take the reins of the Russell County sheriff's department until I can get strong enough to return, and I need you to respect her authority just like you would mine. I know you will. Thank you."

He turned and slowly walked to his office, his back as straight as it'd been when he walked into the room. She swallowed down the lump in her throat and almost followed him to make sure he was all right, but Gram and Nathan were there. Alex needed to follow through on his introduction.

The room grew quiet as she stepped forward. "First, I want

to thank each of you for serving my grandfather so well. I know that will continue. I already know a few of you and look forward to getting to know the rest."

She paused long enough to scan the room, making eye contact with each deputy, most of whom were male. Adding more female deputies was something she definitely wanted to accomplish. "I want you to know the door to the chief deputy's office will always be open for anything you want to discuss. I hope you'll take advantage of the opportunity—I can't fix a problem if I don't know what's wrong. I look forward to working with each of you. In the meantime, everything will run the same way it's been running, since Sheriff Stone will be overseeing everything. He'd be the first to say, 'If it ain't broke, don't fix it.'"

A ripple of laughter spread across the room, then an officer stepped forward, followed by his dog beside him. Mark Lassiter. Gramps had said if anyone might question her authority, it'd be him.

"Chief Deputy Stone."

"Call me Alex, please."

"Yes, ma'am."

From his tone, she couldn't tell if this was going to be the first test. She focused briefly on the trim German shepherd at his feet. "Yes, Mark?"

He seemed surprised she knew his name. "This is Gem," he said, nodding toward the dog. "I think I speak for everyone here"—he looked around at the men behind him—"when I say we want you to know we're here for you. You need something, just let us know."

The other deputies nodded in agreement.

The words sounded good, but there was something about Lassiter's tone. Like maybe he expected her to mess up and they could rescue her. Or maybe she was looking for trouble where none existed.

"Thank you. I appreciate your offer," Alex said as a phone rang in the background. She waited briefly in case anyone else had something to say. When no one spoke up, she said, "If there's nothing else, I'll go check on my grandfather."

The door to her office opened, and Nathan barreled out just as the dispatcher called her name.

Alex turned toward the dispatcher. "Yes, Marge?"

"There's a hysterical teenager on the line. Said she found a body at one of Tom Weaver's rental houses. Kid's pretty sure she's dead, but the kicker is"—Marge swallowed hard—"the victim is holding a White pawn."

19

Nathan pocketed his phone and burst from Carson's office in time to hear Marge's statement. In his bones he'd known George Smith wasn't the Queen's Gambit Killer, and the phone call he'd gotten from his sergeant, Jared Westbrook, confirmed it.

Alexis quickly dispatched her deputies, then turned to him with her fists clenched. "Do you think it's a copycat? Or do you think . . ."

"The killer followed you here? We both had doubts about George Smith." Even though he'd wanted Smith to be the serial killer.

"I know. I need to get there. If you'll excuse me."

"Hold on a minute. Tom Weaver's place is in the Pearl Springs city limits."

She frowned. "And Pearl Springs is in Russell County."

"Just letting you know I won't be shut out." The sheriff's department might have more resources than Nathan, but he had a vested interest in keeping a killer out of his town. "Do you have wheels yet? If not, you can ride with me."

"I have Gramps's SUV." Then she grimaced. "But Gram is taking him home in it. I'll find something."

"Come on, it'll be quicker for you to ride with me."

"Oh . . . okay."

Probably agreed so she could chew him out. But they might as well establish expectations and boundaries right now. Might save hurt feelings in the future.

Instead of chewing him out, Alexis was on the phone, directing Marge to locate the two crime scene investigators and send them to the Weaver house. Nathan turned on the dead-end road just inside the city limits and pulled parallel to the house.

To his left, a female county deputy talked with a teenage girl Nathan recognized from the youth group at church. Mary Beth Meyers. She must be the hysterical teen Marge said had called in the crime. To his right, two other deputies hung crime scene tape around the yard while Nathan's sergeant strung tape across the front porch.

He'd inherited Jared when he took on the police chief job. If Jared minded being passed over, the sergeant had never shown it. He looked up now. "I cleared the house. The victim is the only one there, and I didn't find anything useful."

Shorthand for no obvious evidence pointing to a suspect. "This is the Russell County chief deputy, Alexis Stone," he said, nodding toward her. "Take us through what you do know."

Alexis took out her phone. "Do you mind if I record your comments?"

Jared questioned him with his eyes.

"Good idea." Nathan took out his own phone.

The lanky officer pointed toward the house. "Mary Beth Meyers, Robert and Jean Meyers's daughter, found the deceased in the kitchen. The woman's—"

"What was Mary Beth doing here?" Nathan asked.

The sergeant glanced toward the teen, then pinched his right forefinger and thumb together and brought them to his pursed lips. "She tried to get rid of the reefer when I pulled in, but she couldn't hide the skunky smell."

Nathan's stomach turned. Smoking pot? Not Mary Beth. He glanced toward the girl who stood with her arms wrapped around her waist, looking everywhere but at him. "What else have you found out?"

"I called Tom Weaver, and the woman's name is Gina Norman. She paid cash for the first and last month's rent two weeks ago, but she hadn't moved in yet. According to Mary Beth, the kids around here had been using the house as a regular meeting place. She didn't know someone was moving in. It looks like this Norman woman was cleaning up, getting the house ready."

"So Mary Beth goes in and discovers the body." Alexis's question was more like a statement.

Jared nodded. "She called 911. I was the first to arrive, and I ascertained the victim was deceased. Then I got out of there before I disturbed any more of the crime scene."

Nathan nodded approval. "Did you recognize her?"

"Never seen her before."

"What can you tell me about the victim?" Nathan asked.

His sergeant took out a top-bound spiral notebook and flipped it open. "The deceased, Gina Norman, is Caucasian with dark reddish-brown hair in a ponytail." He glanced briefly at Alexis. "Kinda looks like the chief deputy—slender build, maybe five-seven, same color hair. Appears to be in her mid-twenties."

He checked his notebook again. "She was faceup when I found her. Gunshot wound to the right side of the chest, and she was holding a White pawn." He looked up. "Appears the Queen's Gambit Killer has moved to Pearl Springs."

Or, like Alexis had mentioned, a copycat. "Has the medical examiner been notified?"

"Yes, and Doc Williams notified the Forensic Center in Hamilton County to be expecting a body."

"Good." The Russell County medical examiner was a great family practitioner who knew his limits. Any time Richard Williams had to make a determination in what was obviously a murder case, the doctor passed the case on to the Southeast Tennessee Regional Forensic Center in Hamilton County.

"There's also a note pinned to her shirt."

"What?" He and Alexis turned to Jared. "And you're just now telling us?" Nathan said. "What does it say? Never mind, I'll see for myself."

He started for the porch and stopped. He didn't want to go in like Bigfoot and destroy evidence. What was wrong with him? The note could wait until the crime scene techs checked for footprints.

He'd almost committed a rookie mistake. It wasn't like he hadn't worked murder cases before, but they were usually what he'd call in-county—both the perpetrator and victim were from Pearl Springs and Russell County and were acquainted with each other. Often it was a drunken brawl that got out of hand.

He clenched his jaw. This was entirely different—a serial killer may have come into his town and randomly murdered an innocent victim. Nathan turned to Alexis. "Shouldn't your crime scene techs be here by now?"

"They're on the way."

She'd no sooner spoken than her techs arrived. Nathan recognized the red-haired Dylan Wells right off, but it took him a minute to place the female with purple streaks in her blond hair. Her name came to him just as he was about to ask. Taylor Owens. Both were good at their job.

Alexis conferred with them, and before they began processing the porch, they checked Jared's shoe prints, then the teenager's. She rejoined Nathan when they began with the front porch. After a few minutes, Taylor shook her head.

"No prints," she said. "We'll check the entryway and kitchen and then you can go in."

Twenty minutes later, a white van with a Russell County Medical Examiner logo on the side rolled to a stop behind Nathan's truck. Dr. Richard Williams climbed out of the vehicle and grabbed a satchel from the passenger's seat before joining them. Assuming Alexis didn't know the ME, Nathan started to introduce them.

"We've met. He visited Gramps last week," Alexis said as a text chimed on her phone. "Good to see you again, Doc. Sorry it's under these conditions."

"How's Carson?" Williams asked.

Of course. Sheriff Stone would be one of the doctor's patients. Williams had probably even come to the house to check on him. With only five regional forensic centers in the state with forensic medical examiners and pathologists, each county had at least one local medical examiner who was usually a practicing doctor.

She checked her phone, then looked up. "Gramps isn't being a particularly good patient—wanting to do more than Gram thinks he should. Otherwise, he seems to be improving."

"I should've known he'd push it when he said his cardiologist told him to do what he felt like doing. I'll have a talk with him . . . or call his cardiologist and have him talk to him." The doctor nodded toward the door. "Are your techs done?"

"They just let me know they've finished checking for footprints in the kitchen, so we can go in."

"Then I guess it's time for me to do my job."

"Did they find any shoe prints?" Nathan asked Alexis after the doctor went inside.

"No. Evidently Gina Norman had recently mopped the floors. They're still checking for fingerprints."

With Alexis behind him, he walked up the wooden steps and inside the house, dread filling him, knowing what they would find. A victim who was someone's daughter, maybe a sister, possibly a mother . . . Nathan paused in the kitchen doorway. He would find whoever did this.

Gina Norman lay on her back, her arms extended cactus-like with a White pawn in her right hand. Except . . .

For a split second, Nathan thought he was looking at Alexis, and his knees threatened to buckle. When his sergeant said the victim looked like Alexis, Nathan hadn't expected to think it *was* Alexis, even briefly. Then reason took over. She was standing beside him.

Nathan tried to swallow, but his mouth was cotton-dry. *Shake it off.* He shifted his gaze to the note pinned on the victim's shirt that made no sense. Just numbers, and his mind returned to the resemblance to Alexis. Even though Parker said the other victims bore a resemblence to Alexis, he hadn't been prepared for the reality. "She could be your younger sister," he said softly.

She was focused on the note and didn't answer.

"Alexis?" He raised his voice. "What is it?"

20

The unique way of printing was the same as the notes with the victims in Chattanooga, but this time there were only numbers, no letters. 0-0-0.

A chess term Alex had seen before in her limited research, but the meaning eluded her now. She knelt beside the victim. Gina Norman was so young. Sadness and a sense of failure weighed on her heart that another victim had died a senseless death. She snapped a picture of the note with her phone. "It's not a copycat."

"Why do you say that?"

She felt Nathan's gaze on her and stood. "The note. It's the same ink and handwriting as the others. Since we haven't released that bit of information, it's something only the killer would know."

"Is there any other information I need to know about?"

"No." Alex stared at the body. She'd been hoping against hope . . .

Dylan unpinned the note and bagged it. "There's something on the back," he said, handing it to Alex.

She turned the note over and froze.

"Welcome to Russell County. Phame."

After taking a breath, she read the note again. Questions bombarded her mind, the first being why had the killer followed her here? And who or what was a Phame? "Can someone explain this signature for me?"

Dylan turned toward her. "In the computer world, it's a code name," he said. "Could have started out a hacker name, but I'd put my money on this person being a gamer. Names like Fame or Fate or even Freak spelled with a p-h were popular back in the 1980s, and it hasn't gone away in some circles, like gamers."

Oh, great. It wouldn't be so bad if the person was a gamer, but if they were dealing with a hacker, it would be someone who understood and preyed on weaknesses. "But if this person was around in the eighties, that would put our killer in their fifties now."

"Maybe not," Nathan said. "How popular are these names now?"

Dylan shrugged. "Pretty popular on the dark web or dark net as some people call it. Practically everyone uses an alias there."

Alex pointed to Dylan. "You sound familiar with it, so I need you to research the dark web and discover all you can about this Phame person."

"There's probably more than one user with that name," Dylan said.

"I expect that." She tilted her head. "What name do you use?"

Dylan clamped his lips together and shifted his gaze toward the mounds of rock and gravel. She should've waited until they were alone to ask him that question.

"It's not Phame," he said.

"I didn't think it was."

Alex took a step back as the doctor began his preliminary examination. "We'll go into the living area, out of your way."

The doctor nodded, and they moved to the front room. It looked as though Gina Norman had cleaned this part of the house as well. Alex wanted to pick Nathan's brain about the notes. "Do you play chess?"

"It's been a few years, but I was pretty good at it." He cocked his head to the side. "Oh," he said, making two syllables of the word.

"Yeah. That was a chess move. I'm glad to know you played the game since I know practically nothing about it. Although I did buy a book that I've been studying."

The corners of his mouth quirked up even though he obviously was trying not to laugh. "Do you know how long it takes to master chess? A lifetime unless you're a Bobby Fischer."

"So I gathered from the first chapter. And a prodigy I am not—I need a shortcut."

"Tell me more about these notes," he said. "Were they all pinned to the victim's shirt?"

"No. They were usually in a pocket—coat or pants—not like this." She held out her phone with photos of the notes on it. "Some of the notes had lettering with the numbers, but I don't remember one like this."

"I assume homicide consulted chess experts?"

She nodded. "And none of them found a connection. They all agreed—they're just random opening moves."

"Tell me about the other victims."

It'd been over a month since she'd viewed their files. "Except for the second victim, Rebecca Daniels, I've only seen their photos, but they all had long, dark reddish hair like mine and similar build. It was why I was chosen to go undercover at the Lemon Tree. Gina fits the profile too." She glanced toward the kitchen. "I wonder if Rebecca would still be alive if she hadn't dyed her hair and had it styled like mine."

"It doesn't do any good to think like that."

"I know, still—"

"Alex!" Dylan yelled from the kitchen. "There's something else you need to see."

What now? She whirled around and hurried to the kitchen with Nathan on her heels. "What is it?"

"This was in her coat pocket." Her CSI held up a newspaper clipping from the *Chattanooga Times Free Press*. He bagged it and handed it to her, and she quickly read the article about a mentally ill man who had pulled a gun on a police officer, and the officer fired, killing him. It turned out the civilian's gun was not loaded.

In the clipping the reporter had used the words *suicide by cop*, and someone, the killer presumably, had marked out the word *suicide* and printed *execution*.

Alex's stomach churned. She remembered this particular clipping about Phillip Denton's death because it was one of the first. She pressed her lips together to ward off the bile rising in her throat. Alex would not throw up in front of her officers.

"Here," Nathan said, quietly slipping a bottle of cold water into her hand.

Where in the world had he gotten it? Probably in his Kevlar vest. She quickly took a sip, praying for the cold liquid to stay down and to cool her stomach. So far, so good, and Alex took another sip while Nathan read the newspaper clipping again. "What do you think the clipping has to do with the murders?"

Once again, Alex felt blood drain from her face. "Maybe everything," she said softly.

"You want to explain? Who is the killer referring to?"

"It doesn't name him, so it had to be written before his name was released, but it has to be Phillip Denton, the man I shot two and a half years ago." Alex chewed her bottom lip. "It makes me think the killer is connected to Denton. The thing is, he had a fake identity, and when detectives searched for relatives and friends, of course they didn't find any."

"How about his neighbors?"

"I haven't read the detective's report, but I remember hearing the investigator didn't have any luck with them, even though he'd lived there five years."

"Who was the investigator?"

"Todd Madden."

"Any other similarities of this death to the others?"

"Other than she resembles me?" Alex rubbed the back of her neck as she tried to recall what was in the files. The details evaded her. Being put to sleep for the gunshot wound had done a number on her memory. "I'll get Chattanooga PD to share their files on the case."

He nodded. "I wonder if they'd let me look at the evidence. And I'd like to drive into Chattanooga and take a look at the actual notes. Physically laying eyes on them helps me more than looking at photos. And maybe talk to Madden."

"I agree. Let me text the captain that you're coming." She started to text, then decided it was too much to do on her phone. She stepped to a corner of the kitchen and dialed her former captain. When he answered, she explained what had happened and requested the files.

"The files are digital," he said. "You want me to email them to you?"

"Yes, but Chief Landry and I will be driving in. Could we see the actual evidence? Clothes, notes with the chess notations, anything else you might have?" She'd thought about it and decided she needed to see everything for herself as well. "And I need to see Todd Madden."

"None of it's a problem, except for Madden—he's in court all day."

She really needed to compare notes with Madden. "I'll call

him tomorrow. Could you go ahead and send me the digital files?"

"Sure."

She disconnected and returned to where Nathan stood. "Madden's in court all day, but the captain is emailing the files. You can look at everything on the way to Chattanooga."

"Good. Something might jump out at me."

Alex hoped so, because she had nothing. She turned her attention back to the victim. It appeared that, like the others, she hadn't been sexually assaulted. But why this victim? Really, why any of them? Alex simply couldn't get into the killer's head. And what were the chess pieces supposed to mean?

She noticed Nathan was looking at the note again. "Do you recognize the chess move?"

He nodded. "It's a notation for queenside castling."

"That tells me nothing." Why hadn't she learned chess as a kid?

"If it's the White king, he moves two spaces to the left—the queenside—and the rook jumps over him and ends up on the other side," he explained, his voice patient. "If it's the Black king, the same thing happens, only to the right."

Alex furrowed her brow as she concentrated on picturing the chessboard. "But what does it mean?"

"That and the welcome means the killer is telling you he's made a shift," Nathan said quietly.

A knot formed in her stomach. "Like moved from Chattanooga to Pearl Springs."

"I'm afraid so. I may know more when I see the other notes left by the killer."

Her phone dinged with a text. Gram.

We're home if you want to pick up the SUV.
Your grandfather is resting.

Alex quickly texted her back.

> Thanks. I'll get someone to run me by there.
> Leave the keys on the kitchen island and take
> a nap.

She signed off with a smiley face then turned toward Nathan. "My grandparents are home. Do you have time to run me by to pick up the SUV?"

"Sure. My sergeant has this covered. Let me tell him I'm leaving."

She followed him outside and spotted Harvey. In a sheriff's department as small as Russell County's, being chief of staff didn't relieve him of investigating. When Alex reached him, she said, "Glad you're here. I need to go into Chattanooga. Would you take over the investigation?"

His eye twitched. "That's what I'm here for."

"Thanks. Make sure we get fingerprints on the victim."

"I know how to run an investigation, Alex."

"Didn't mean to step on your toes, but you could've thought I'd already asked the ME to take them." She smiled, knowing it didn't reach her eyes. "I see Mark, and I need to have a word with him before I leave."

Nathan was still talking with his sergeant as she made her way to the K-9 handler. "Find anything that might help with the case?"

"Not really. It's the last house on the street and looks like more than one person has turned around in the driveway." He jerked his head toward the back of the property. "There's a path back there that leads to the next street over. Appears to have been used a lot."

"Probably the kids coming here to do whatever it is they were doing. Did you talk with the girl?"

"Mary Beth? This was a hangout to smoke dope and—"

"You got that out of her?"

He grinned. "Gem is a real good icebreaker. Mary Beth remembered her from when I went to the high school to talk about drugs and alcohol. And she might have gotten the idea I didn't hold it against her if she was doing a little marijuana."

"Don't do that again."

He looked puzzled. "What?"

"You're not their buddy. And it's lying to them—it's not okay for them to do drugs."

"I know that. But it helped to get her talking."

"Find another way. There's no gray area on kids doing drugs." Mark took a breath, probably to protest, but she cut him off. "Use Gem to charm your way into their confidence."

"Yes, ma'am."

She swallowed back the retort on the tip of her tongue to his use of ma'am in addressing her. To protest it would make her seem thin-skinned. And it wasn't the word, per se, it was his tone. But this wasn't the hill to die on.

21

When they reached his truck, Nathan bit back a smile when Alexis didn't wait for him to open her door. Probably a good idea that he didn't attempt what he considered a gentlemanly action—besides, he wouldn't have opened the door for Sheriff Stone. Except his mama had raised him to say "yes ma'am" and "no ma'am" and to open doors for women. And Alexis wouldn't appreciate either.

He slid across the seat and started the motor. "Do you mind stopping by the police department before we pick up your wheels? I'd like to check on Kayla before we head into Chattanooga since this is her first solo day."

"We had lunch together Friday," Alexis said. "How's she working out?"

"Really good. She's smart—I'm trying to talk her into taking some criminal justice classes."

"She's definitely cool under pressure and handles herself very well. If it weren't for her, I could've been dead."

He agreed with that assessment, although Nathan believed if Kayla hadn't happened along, Alexis would've taken George Smith down before they reached her house. And maybe without being shot. But he kept his thoughts to himself.

He turned onto Washington Street and parked his pickup in

front of the two-story brick building across from the Russell County Courthouse.

Alexis opened her door. "I think I'll pop in and say hello."

Nathan led the way through the double glass doors and down the hall to the police department. They shared the building with Pearl Springs City Hall on one side and his department on the other. Nathan held the door open for Alexis. Even though he'd been police chief for four years, he never tired of seeing his name when he entered.

Kayla looked up from her computer. "Hey, boss. Checking up on me?"

"Just making sure you haven't had any problems," he said.

"Everything is quiet here." She grinned when Alexis stepped around him. "Seeing you twice in one day has to be some kind of record. How does being chief deputy feel?"

"With a murder on my first day, like a ton of bricks hit me," Alexis said. "Did you find a place to live?"

"I did. Ethel at the Corner Diner told me to talk to Tom Weaver, and I rented a furnished duplex on Maple that he had. It's on the east side of the high school."

The hair on the back of Nathan's neck raised at the mention she'd rented a place from Tom. What if she'd been the one who rented the house they'd just left? That house was south of the high school. Kayla could have been the victim. He eyed her sternly. "Be sure to keep your door locked at all times."

"You don't have to worry about that. I will say I thought coming to Pearl Springs would be a change of pace from Chattanooga."

"Crime is everywhere," Alexis said. "I hear Nathan is trying to talk you into being a cop."

Kayla frowned, then her brow smoothed out. "Oh, the criminal justice class. I haven't signed up for it yet. Not sure that's my calling."

"From what I know about the night Alexis was shot, you have the instincts to make a good cop," Nathan said. "I stopped by to let you know I'm headed into Chattanooga. If anything comes up, call my sergeant, Jared Westbrook—he'll know if I need to be in the loop."

She saluted. "Aye, aye, sir."

"Oh, and we haven't received your high school transcripts yet." Kayla's other references had checked out, but she'd had such a brief work record, he'd wanted to see those records as well.

"Really?" She cocked her head. "That's odd. I'll call them. You did receive my college transcripts?"

"Yes. Pretty impressive."

"I try hard."

With a 4.0 GPA, he would agree. Nathan turned to Alexis. "I'm ready if you are."

A few minutes later, he backed out of his parking space while Alexis checked her messages on her phone. Instead of heading toward her grandparents' house, he said, "You sure you want to drive? We can go in my truck, and I can drop you off when we return."

She pointed to the tablet mounted in the cupholder. "The case files came in, and I just emailed them to you. I'd rather drive and let you read over them."

He nodded and then said, "Why don't you drive my truck?"

"You'd trust me with your pickup?"

"You're a good driver, aren't you? I mean, no reckless driving tickets or anything like that?"

"I have a perfect driving record." Then she laughed. "Any speeding went undetected."

He laughed with her, glad they'd slipped into an easy relationship. So much different from a few weeks ago.

She changed places with him, and ten minutes later they

crossed the Pearl River and he'd settled into the passenger seat reviewing the files she'd emailed him. He'd gotten as far as George Smith's file when they reached police headquarters on Amnicola Highway in Chattanooga. He grabbed his tablet and followed Alexis inside.

"Been missing you, Alex," the guard said when they approached the sign-in desk. "You doing better?"

"I'm up and going again, Ralph." She introduced Nathan. "We need passes."

Ralph handed them a clipboard. "Sign here." Then he turned to Alexis. "Hope Russell County doesn't steal you forever."

Her face turned a bright shade of red. "I think my grandfather is on the other side of that fence."

As was Nathan. They signed where the guard indicated and took the passes. He hoped Alexis staying in Russell County was a done deal.

They encountered several people who spoke to her as they walked to the evidence room, most of them expressing the sentiments of the guard. "You're well liked around here."

She shrugged off his comment. "I've always kept my head down and done my job."

Inside the evidence room, Alexis requested the items in the murders, and both she and Nathan signed for them. "We don't want to take them out of the room and will use the table over there." She nodded toward the wall.

The officer brought out six boxes and set them on the scuffed table. "I have to observe to keep the chain of command in place."

"Of course," Alexis said.

Nathan had expected nothing less.

She turned to him. "Start with the first one?"

He nodded and opened an app on his tablet, one that would work with his pen. "That way we can see the pattern."

He quickly made a page for each of the victims and then

returned to the first page and wrote Courtney Johnson at the top along with her age of twenty-five. She'd been killed almost two years ago right before Christmas. The thought of the Christmas her family had experienced made his heart heavy.

Neither of them spoke as they focused on the articles in the bin. Black leather miniskirt and vest, white silk blouse, red purse, and four-inch red stilettos. Clothes of the trade. He glanced at the shoes again. How in the world women walked in those things, he'd never know. The purse held her driver's license, lipstick, and a small package of tissues. And a weighted, almost-White pawn.

The pawn was a wooden piece that probably came from a chess shop. "Why would the killer use this pawn? Unless it's a knockoff, it's a Staunton chess piece, and the set could cost anywhere from a hundred bucks to two hundred. Why not use pawns from a ten-dollar set like you can get at any big box store?"

"It's a real Staunton chess piece," Alexis said. "Although I hadn't heard the detectives mention it might cost that much."

"Has anyone checked the chess stores around here? There are only a couple of places I can think of that might carry a set like this."

"Yes, but her death happened around Christmas, and the stores sold quite a few sets due to the popularity of that Netflix series. Unless the customer made the purchase with a credit card, the game stores didn't have a record of the sale. Do you seriously think the killer would risk buying the chess set from a business that could very well remember him? Don't you think the set was bought online?"

Nathan shrugged. "The killer has a very high opinion of himself and likes taking risks, so it's possible he bought it locally."

He set the pawn back in the bin and picked up a clear plastic bag containing an index card. "Just one move—queen's White pawn to line d, column 4."

She nodded. "I'd just moved to vice and wasn't part of the investigation yet, but of course I heard about the note. One of the homicide detectives told me it was a common opening move. When the second murder occurred, it was evident the killer was letting us know the 'game' had started."

Alexis picked up the second box marked "Rebecca Daniels." She turned to him, a question on her face.

"What?"

"D4. How did you know it was a pawn? It doesn't have a letter in front of it like the other pieces. You know, K for king, Q for queen," she said. "I wanted to ask Madden, but I didn't want him to know I was that ignorant of the game. And it wasn't in any of the research I did."

He smiled. "I don't know why it doesn't use the letter—that's just the way it is. I never questioned it."

"Most people probably wouldn't, but when you start out not knowing anything about the game . . ." She shrugged and then took out a clear plastic bag containing another small index card and handed it to Nathan.

He stared at the neat lettering of the algebraic notation. *Fool's mate.* "Here the killer is saying you're incompetent because in the very first move, White puts himself in check."

"I got that much from what Madden said. Then I looked it up and learned it means that White made a stupid move, and that it rarely happens even with rank beginners."

Nathan chewed the inside ridge of his cheek. "Our killer is playing Black in this note, but in the note left on Gina Norman's body, he's playing White. Does he switch sides in any of the other notes?"

"Good question, one I don't have the answer to, but maybe you can tell me." She opened the third box and handed him the note. "At the end of the notation, he calls us *patzers*, German for 'blunderers.'"

"It's a slightly different variation of the fool's mate. But by calling you patzers, he's calling you amateurs."

"It doesn't get any better with Maria Brooks and Trinity Collins, the two victims who frequented the Lemon Tree." She handed him the bags with their notes. "They're identical. Madden called this move the scholar's mate, and then the killer added some names to indicate what he thinks of us."

Duffers and wood-pushers meant the same thing as patzers, and Nathan didn't have to picture the chessboard to know this notation was checkmate in four moves. Was the killer using the moves to give clues to the next victim? Or simply taunting the police? He looked through the property boxes of the other women, leaving George Smith for last.

"Homicide ran the cases through NCIC."

The National Crime Information Center database. "Any hits?"

"No. Because the pawns were present in the second murder, homicide thought we might be dealing with a serial killer, so they requested a profile from the FBI's Behavioral Analysis Unit."

The Chattanooga detectives had done everything Nathan would have. "Have you received the profile yet?"

She nodded. "But, as you can see, it hasn't helped. The BAU indicated the murders were premeditated and well thought out. The profile indicated the killer is someone in their mid-twenties to midthirties with a higher-than-average IQ, possibly outgoing but more than likely an introvert and very organized. Other than the pawn in each woman's hand and the note, the killer left nothing behind. The report also validated our detectives' belief that the first three victims were practice. Each murder the killer gets away with increases his sense of power."

"How about ethnicity?"

"Probably white, and probably male."

He frowned. "Probably male?"

She shrugged. "The world is changing. There're a lot of angry women out there."

"Maybe so, but chess is a male-dominated sport, and the killer has chosen it to taunt us."

"Either way, we're dealing with a real sicko, for sure," Alexis said.

Nathan opened the box labeled "George Smith" and took out the baggie with the pawn in it. It appeared to be the same style. "Has your crime lab been able to tell if it's from the same set?"

"They're still working on it, but they were able to determine it's like the others and a Staunton pawn. It's why they thought he was the killer."

"But considering Gina Norman's pawn and the note, he can't be."

She took the chess piece from him and returned it to the box. "Which means George Smith was trying to execute a copycat crime. Either that or he was an accomplice."

Was George an accomplice? And why had the killer moved to Pearl Springs? If they could discover those two things, they would be two steps closer to the killer.

22

At 4:45 Alex received a text from Marge that reporters were hounding the office for information. She turned to Nathan. "I need to call Marge. Be back in a minute."

He nodded, and she slipped out the door and called the office manager. "What's going on?"

"We've had a deluge of calls from as far away as Memphis and Cincinnati, asking for information on the murder."

"How'd it get out so fast?"

Marge huffed. "You know how quickly bad news travels. Evidently Mary Beth posted about it on TikTok, and one of the news media picked it up. You'll have to hold a press conference. Want me to set it up for tomorrow morning?"

"Make it tomorrow afternoon at four."

"I'll take care of it."

Alex stared at the phone briefly after she ended the call. She'd never held a press conference—just what she needed her second day on the job. Talk about being thrown into the deep end to learn how to swim.

Her captain always managed to keep his cool when he went before reporters. She could ask him for advice. No. While he'd given her his blessing, he hadn't been over the moon that she was leaving, and she didn't want him to see that she might already be in trouble.

Her grandfather—he'd held his share of press conferences in the past. But he wasn't fond of them either, and she didn't want to stress him out. That left Nathan.

As she turned to reenter the property room, another text popped up on her phone. She read it and grinned. Gram telling her to invite Nathan for supper, that she was cooking his favorites. Perfect. She popped back into the property room and joined him where he was busy making notes on his iPad.

A lock of his dark blond hair had dropped over his forehead, reminding her of a much younger Nathan. The impulse to brush it back like she had in the past startled her. He looked up, and their gazes locked, his blue eyes holding her captive. Alex swallowed hard, breaking the spell. "Uh, are you ready to leave?"

"Yeah."

His husky voice let her know he'd been under the spell as well, and it surprised her how much that pleased her.

23

As they walked out the door, Nathan nodded to the property clerk. "I think we're done here. Thanks for your help."

"Anytime. Did I hear right that there was a murder like these in Pearl Springs today?"

"Unfortunately," Alexis said.

"I hope you catch him."

He did too. And soon. He checked his watch as he held the door for her and frowned. They were going to be in the middle of the five-o'clock rush hour. "Stairs or elevator?"

"I'm beat. How about the elevator?" she said.

"Sounds good." They walked to the end of the hall, and he punched the down button.

She hesitated as the elevator doors silently opened. He was relieved to see it was empty, and they stepped inside.

Alexis punched the first-floor button then seemed to hold her breath as they plummeted six floors—at least that's what it felt like to him. "Breathe," he said, doing the same.

"I hate these things," she muttered.

"Me too, especially fast ones like this one." He was glad to see the doors open. "The phone call to Marge. Anything new happen?"

"She's been getting calls from media outlets all over the country, so she's setting up a press conference for tomorrow afternoon. Can you be there?"

He held the outside door open. "Not my favorite thing, but I won't let you face it alone."

"Good. I hope you'll give me a few pointers on the drive home."

"Your first?"

She nodded. "That always fell to someone else."

Nathan grinned. "Welcome to the real world," he said as they approached his truck. He opened the passenger door and then jogged around to his side and climbed in. "How did the media learn about the murder?"

"Social media—TikTok in particular."

"Mary Beth." Nathan pulled out of the parking lot and re-traced their earlier drive from Pearl Springs. Traffic was as bad as he'd feared, and neither of them spoke until he was out of Chattanooga.

Alexis was the first to break the silence. "I need a favor."

That was a new wrinkle. Alexis never needed anything. "Your wish is my command."

"You better wait until you hear what I want."

"Can't be that bad."

"We'll see. I need to understand that chess move. Do you have time to tutor me tonight? And by the way, Gram texted that I can bribe you with supper—country-fried steak, creamed potatoes, and English peas. And homemade biscuits and apple pie."

His stomach growled, and Nathan realized he hadn't eaten since breakfast and bet Alexis hadn't either. "There's no way I would turn that down."

"Good, because we need to work out our strategy for this case, and I'm hoping Gramps will have some suggestions. Do you think that would be too much for him?"

He barely heard anything past "we need to work." She wanted the two of them to work together? Miracles still happened. His good mood continued as they neared Pearl Springs. He handed her his phone. "We need an update before we discuss strategy. Would you call Jared and see if he's learned anything? And put it on speaker," he said. "That way we both can hear."

"I will and then we'll do the same thing with Harvey and Mark."

What new information Nathan's sergeant and the two Russell County deputies discovered would fill a small paragraph in a report. The only prints they found in the house belonged to Gina Norman and Tom Weaver.

The three had canvassed the neighborhood, but none of the neighbors had seen anything unusual. Most had no idea that someone had rented the house. Any activity the neighbors saw had been attributed to the teens who normally hung out there. By the time Alexis disconnected from Mark, they'd arrived at her grandparents' house, and he parked behind the sheriff's SUV.

Nathan unfastened his seat belt. "Guess you know this is going to be a hard case to crack."

"Yeah." A strand of her dark red hair had dropped across her face, and she blew it away. "The killer is smart, and so far he hasn't made any mistakes."

"Maybe brainstorming with your grandfather will help."

"So you don't think it will be too much for him?"

"I think it'll do him a world of good. He's used to being in the thick of things, and even though he's confident of your abilities, I'm sure he misses the action."

She sighed. "I needed to hear that."

Nathan climbed out of his truck and followed Alexis to the back door, where the aroma of bread baking had his mouth watering. "Something smells so good."

She inhaled deeply. "Gram's biscuits—I can make a meal on those alone."

Her grandmother turned as they entered the kitchen. She was taking a black skillet filled with hot biscuits from the oven. "Supper is ready to be put on the table." Then she nodded at Alexis. "Your grandfather is in the den. He's been a little shaky since we returned home, so would you make sure he gets in here okay?"

"Why don't I go?" Nathan asked. If Carson was shaky, he stood a better chance of keeping him on his feet than Alexis.

When no one objected, he walked to the den. Carson stood at the window looking out, his walker and wheelchair ten feet away from him by the sofa.

"Sir," Nathan said, "I've been sent to tell you supper is ready."

Carson slowly turned to him, and the look on his face broke Nathan's heart. Carson took a halting step, and Nathan felt he should offer to help him, but somehow he couldn't.

"Don't ever get old, son." Then without another word, Carson steadied himself, holding on to the furniture as he shuffled to his walker. He rolled the walker around, then stood straighter and shot Nathan a look reminiscent of the old Carson Stone. "Don't tell them I was standing at the window without this confounded thing."

"Don't worry, and you will get stronger—it takes time to recover from a heart attack."

"If you ever do," Carson muttered. "The thing I can't stand is the hovering. *'Carson, don't do that. Carson, don't forget your walker. Carson, take your medicine . . .'* I had a heart attack, not a mental breakdown."

Nathan turned his head so the sheriff wouldn't see his grin.

128

"Do you think you're up to helping us plan strategy on this murder case?"

"Of course I'm up to it." Energy infused his voice. "How soon can we get started?"

"After supper." Nathan didn't want to incur Judith Stone's wrath. "The note the killer left with Gina Norman referred to castling, and I've promised to show Alexis what that is on the chessboard."

"I haven't played chess in years, but I used to be pretty good at it."

"Maybe you can help us get into the killer's head."

24

A lex pushed the English peas around her plate.

Her grandmother cleared her throat. "Something wrong with those peas?"

With a start she looked up and did a mental shake to clear her head. "No, ma'am. I'm just tired. And can't quit thinking about what Mark told me about that poor woman killed this morning."

He'd called with background information on Gina Norman just before she sat down.

"You want to talk about it?" Gramps asked.

Nathan put his fork down. "I'd like to know what he found out too."

Maybe it would help, except her grandmother had a firm rule of not talking business at the supper table. She glanced at Gram. "Do you mind?"

"No, go ahead, child." She raised her eyebrows. "Only this once, though."

Alex took a deep breath. "She was single, with no children, but does have a mother in Chicago. Mrs. Norman told Mark she hadn't talked to her in a couple of months—evidently they're not close. She mentioned something about a broken engagement, and that she thought her daughter moved to Pearl Springs to teach at the high school. When Mark checked, that turned out not to be true."

Nathan cut a piece of the country-fried steak. "Did the mother have a name or a phone number for the fiancé?"

She nodded. "Keith Sanders, but when Mark called him, he was in Oregon. Been there two weeks."

"With the pawn found in her possession and the note, the fiancé wasn't our number one suspect anyway."

"No." Alex stared at her plate. "I just can't get out of my mind why someone would want to kill these victims. And how does George Smith figure into it? Was it a coincidence that Smith attacked me? Or was he planning a copycat murder with me as the victim?"

"I think he was a copycat," Gramps said.

Alex turned to him. "Why?"

He pointed with his fork. "When you were in the hospital, one of your colleagues came by, and we talked about it. Just seemed strange that he picked you that particular night."

"Maybe because Alexis was hanging out at the Lemon Tree—"

"And if it was a copycat, he would have wanted to stay as close to the facts that he knew." She turned to Nathan. "Do you think George Smith is his real name?"

"I didn't see a background report in the files that Chattanooga PD sent over."

Alex pushed away from the table. "It's been almost a month. I'm going to make a call, if you will excuse me."

She took out her phone and scrolled through her contacts as she walked to the living room. When she came to the homicide detective in charge of the Chattanooga investigation, she pressed call. It was a little after eight, and Todd Madden would probably not want to talk to her after being in court all day, but she needed an answer tonight. He picked up on the second ring.

"Madden."

"Todd, do you have a minute to talk about George Smith?"

"Not really, but I will. What do you need?"

Todd Madden's usual "I'm superior to you" tone grated on her nerves, and she clenched her jaw to keep from spitting out a retort. *Think of still waters. A lake* . . .

"I read the report on him," she said calmly. "And since I know how thorough you are, I wondered if you hadn't gotten around to adding in the background report on him."

"Hold on a sec." There was dead silence on the other end, then she heard papers being shuffled.

She watched the second hand on her grandmother's clock sweep around. Ninety seconds later, he came on the line.

"Here it is." Todd didn't sound quite so arrogant. "Except for a few DUIs in the past, George Smith has a clean record. His prints don't return any criminal hits like burglary or robbery. Haven't found any next of kin yet, but we're still looking."

"I appreciate you sharing the information you have. If we learn anything, I'll return the favor."

"Who have you made mad?" Madden asked.

"What?"

"Part of the profile we received from the FBI indicated the killer had a fixation on a woman who resembled his victims— five-sixish, reddish hair, blue eyes, slim build, midtwenties to midthirties—it all fits you."

"And?" She already knew this—it was the reason she was picked to go undercover.

"As far as I'm concerned, the killer moving to your area and killing someone on the very day you're sworn in as Russell County's chief deputy—congratulations, by the way— confirms my conviction you're connected to the killings."

Madden was making her feel worse than she already did. Had she brought the killer to Russell County? "Anything else?"

"We're still looking at all your cases."

"My cases?"

"Yeah. We pulled them after the second victim—the one you were mentoring. I thought I might find a connection, especially with the Denton shooting."

"What did you come up with?"

"Not a lot other than the shooting wasn't your fault."

"Internal Affairs cleared me of any wrongdoing."

"I know. But we had to look at it with fresh eyes. As far as Phillip Denton, we hit a dead end—couldn't find any relatives or even friends."

Nothing new there, but why hadn't Madden told her they were reviewing her cases? Because that was Madden. Secretive. "How about his background? Did he always live in Chattanooga?"

Since she was the officer involved, Alex hadn't been allowed to participate in the investigation, and she'd never seen the final report. But that was about to change.

"We have no way of knowing," Madden said. "The background on his job resume turned out to be fake."

There were plenty of sites to buy fake IDs on the dark web, and a good hacker could manipulate records to authenticate the IDs.

"We were able to trace back to his first Tennessee driver's license five years ago," Madden said. "No idea where he lived before that or if he had any family. He paid for everything in cash or check and was such a loner that none of his neighbors or coworkers could tell us anything except that he was odd."

Denton's strangeness was the reason a neighbor had turned him in after someone planted a bomb at the mall. "I'd like to see the interviews with his neighbors."

"Sure. I'll have copies made for you, but there's not much to send. Want me to email them to you?"

"That'd be great." She gave him her new email address. "Send the whole file, if you don't mind."

Reading it would probably trigger more nightmares. Not that she didn't relive the shooting at least once a day anyway.

Alex had been so proud of being assigned to the task force investigating the bombing, and while her supervisor hadn't put much credence in the tip from Denton's neighbor, every call had to be checked out. She'd been given that job.

When Denton came to the door and discovered she was police, he went ballistic and she'd been forced to kill him in self-defense, only to learn after the fact that Denton's gun wasn't loaded.

"By the way, in case I never told you, that was good detective work on finding out he was the mall bomber."

"Thanks." She managed to keep the surprise out of her voice.

"I never got a chance to ask you, but how did you figure it out?"

Never got a chance? She worked one floor below him. *Play nice. You might be working with him one day.*

"Some of it was luck," she said. After Denton's shooting, she'd been cleared to return to work after two weeks, but she hadn't returned to the task force. "A month after what went down at the condo, I was working burglary and caught a case involving a construction company and missing laptops. When I took the report and the secretary described the computers, I remembered looking around Phillip Denton's condo while I waited for the medical examiner and seeing three laptops like she described.

"I asked if he ever worked there, and it snowballed from there when she confided that he had and that laptops weren't the only thing missing—they'd just discovered C-4, wiring, and detonators were missing as well. You guys took over then."

"Yeah. The crime scene techs went over the apartment. Never found any of that stuff, but we didn't have a bomb detection dog then. They did find a few pieces of wiring in his spare bedroom that matched the wiring in the mall bomb. I just hope you never lost any sleep over the shooting."

Her fellow officers, superiors, Dr. Hudson, Gramps . . . everyone told her she'd had no choice. But none of that helped when the nightmares came and she was left with replaying her actions that day.

25

Alex disconnected from the call to Madden as Nathan entered the living room.

"Learn anything about George Smith?"

She repeated what Madden had told her. "I don't get it. The man doesn't have a criminal record, so why start now?"

"That's a good question. Chattanooga PD needs to keep digging into his past. Did Madden have anything else to say?"

"He agreed to give us the files on the interviews with Denton's neighbors." She crossed her arms. "Tonight was the first time Todd Madden opened up about the Queen's Gambit murders. Before when I asked anything about the investigation, he'd be so tightlipped that I wondered if his lips were sewn together. I also found out that they're looking at all my cases and even the people I know."

He rubbed his jaw. "When I looked at the photos of the victims today, *I* knew there was a connection to you. All of the women are about your height and build. Same color red hair as yours. The second victim, Rebecca Daniels, even had the same style."

Because Alex had taken the girl to her stylist. She'd only

wanted to help Becky. A heavy weight settled in Alex's chest, and when Nathan pulled her into his arms, she didn't resist.

His gentle touch as he stroked her back calmed her racing thoughts, and she relaxed against the steady beat of his heart. Suddenly she stiffened.

"What?" Nathan pulled back and looked down at her.

"We have a press conference tomorrow afternoon, and I really need you to help me understand the castling move."

"You sure? You look pretty beat."

"I'm not going into that press conference unprepared. I'll get the chessboard and set it up on the kitchen table."

A few minutes later, with Gramps looking on, Alex had all the pieces in place. She didn't know enough about the game to play well, so Nathan played both Black and White pieces and explained each of the moves, going over them until she grasped the concept.

She stared at the board. "I think I have it. One more question—can you castle anytime?"

"No," her grandfather and Nathan said in unison.

Carson smiled at him. "You explain it."

Nathan nodded. "You can only castle when neither the king nor the rook has moved. That's the case here. With nothing between the White king and rook, I can move the king two squares to the left and the rook will move in place to protect his king."

She looked at her grandfather. "Why didn't you teach me how to play?"

"I tried, but you weren't interested."

Well, she was interested now. Alex reached to move the White rook, and Nathan stayed her hand, his fingertips brushing hers. His touch was like electricity jolting through her. She looked up, and his blue eyes held hers. She dropped her gaze to his lips, and briefly the memory of a long-ago kiss sent her heart racing.

"Always move the king first."

His words shook the memory away. She ducked her head and nodded. "Of course, I knew that."

Whatever this feeling for Nathan was, Alex was beginning to like it. And that posed a problem.

26

lexis had felt the electric shock when their hands touched. It showed on her face. Nathan shook off the attraction he felt for her and forced his attention to the chessboard.

In chess a player had to think a certain number of moves ahead and picture the outcome. It wasn't lost on him that he better think about what would happen if he pursued these feelings he had for Alexis.

He wasn't handing over his heart again to have her break it.

But Nathan couldn't ignore that he'd been battling his feelings for Alexis ever since he saw her lying on the sidewalk that night in Chattanooga.

Alexis moved her king over two spaces and then set the rook on the other side of it. "Do you see how your other pieces are defending your king?" he asked.

She nodded.

"Let's say I'm the killer and have just castled queenside. When you counterattack, you're telling the killer you're coming after his king. That's what you want to slip in at the press conference—that you're coming after the killer."

A light bulb went off on her face. "Okay, I get it. Let's say it's my move . . ." She moved her queen. "I believe that's check."

He stared at the board. Her queen had a clear diagonal shot to his king. "I believe you are getting it."

She beamed at him. "Probably just a bit of luck, but I think I'll be ready for the media tomorrow."

His phone buzzed, and he looked at the screen. His CI. "I need to take this." Nathan stood and walked out into the Stones' backyard. "What's happening?"

"There's a big drug meeting going down at the high school tonight."

Nathan gripped the phone. "Are you sure?"

"Yeah."

"What time is it happening?"

"Around ten."

"Thanks." Nathan pocketed his phone and returned to the kitchen. Judith and Carson Stone were nowhere to be seen. "I need to leave. Thank your grandmother for me—supper was great."

"What's wrong?"

He hesitated. If he told her, would she want to take over the case? With Carson out, as chief deputy Alexis was the top law enforcement official in the county. On the other hand, if he didn't tell her, it would affect their working relationship. "There's a meeting of drug dealers at the high school," he said.

"I'm going with you."

He eyed her. Before he could say anything, she held up her hand.

"I'm not taking over your case—I have problems enough with the Queen's Gambit Killer. Just trying to be helpful— you've certainly been here for me."

Okay, maybe it would work. "My truck?"

"Why don't I follow you? That way I'll have my own wheels

and you won't have to bring me home." She took her phone out. "How many deputies do you think we'll need?"

He wanted to say none because he hadn't had enough time to plan a raid, but that would be foolish. "I have no idea what the situation will be, so have three of your deputies arrive in silent mode and then hang back until I can assess the situation. Might not need them tonight at all."

"Sounds like a plan."

He found her grandparents and thanked them for the meal and then hurried out the back door with Alexis on his heels. He wanted to get in place soon in case the drug dealers showed up early. Once Nathan was in his pickup, he contacted his two officers on duty tonight, Eric Malone and Kelsey James, by phone instead of using the radio—he didn't want to risk someone hearing a transmission. He explained what was going on and that tonight was reconnaissance but to be nearby in case things went south. Like the Russell County deputies, they were to arrive in silent mode and stay out of sight unless he needed them.

Nathan glanced in the rearview mirror and frowned. Why was Alexis all over the road?

27

An alert came in that Stone's Tahoe was moving. Phame booted up the screen on the small laptop and opened the directory that would allow the computer to access the Tahoe's Controller Area Network or CAN. Much like a human's brain, CAN sent messages to every part of the car—brakes, steering, gas—you name it, CAN controlled it.

It'd been a simple matter to hack the locks on the SUV and plug Phame's own network device into the proper port while Stone was in Chattanooga. And now, with a few clicks, the Tahoe was completely under Phame's control.

One click disabled the brakes. Another click took control of the steering, and the vehicle crossed the center line and back. Oh, to be able to see Alex Stone's face right about now. Her fear had to be palpable as Phame guided the SUV across the center line.

Phame glanced at the video that reflected real-time activity. Headlights meant an oncoming car. It would be so easy to end Stone's life. Just hold the SUV on the wrong side of the road until BAM! But it wasn't time for Stone to die.

A couple of clicks later, and Stone was back on her side of the road. For the next minute or so, Phame played with the

SUV's controls, stopping it, lurching it backward, speeding it up then stopping it again and reversing direction. This was fun. But time to return control . . . Another couple of seconds and the Tahoe was back in Stone's command.

Tonight had been to show the chief deputy she wasn't in charge, Phame was.

lex fell in behind Nathan's pickup, but a mile down the road had her rubbing her eyes. She hadn't realized she was so tired. And Gram's carb-laden supper made it hard to fight the lethargy seeping into her mind.

Shaking her head cleared it somewhat. She frowned as they turned onto the road to the high school. Alex had never driven the Chevy SUV, but she hadn't expected the steering to be so stiff and hard to turn.

The vehicle jerked to the left, crossing the center line. *No!* She slammed on the brakes.

No response! Her stomach knotted as she fought the wheel. Seconds later, the Tahoe returned to the right side of the road. She released a tight breath only to catch it again when the Tahoe steered crossed the center line again.

Twin beams appeared in the road ahead. Alex wrestled with the wheel, fighting for control. The SUV continued on its deadly path.

The lights drew nearer. Her heart jackhammered in her chest. She jerked the steering wheel, and it suddenly freed up, overcorrecting. The top-heavy SUV rocked, threatening to flip as she held on to the steering wheel.

Still weaving, the SUV surged forward, dangerously close to Nathan's pickup. Alex slammed on the brakes. Nothing.

She tried killing the motor, but it wouldn't die. The SUV hurtled toward a bridge abutment. Jump out? It was her only choice. She fumbled for the seat belt. Why wouldn't it release?

In desperation, Alex slammed on the brakes and jerked the wheel to the left again. This time the brakes held, sending the SUV spinning in a 360-degree circle. When it came to a rocking stop, she couldn't move, not even to release the death grip she had on the steering wheel.

Nathan banged on the window. "Put it in park."

She stared at him. What was he saying?

"The gear—shift it into park!"

She tried and it wouldn't budge. Alex turned to Nathan. She was at her last nerve. "It won't let me!"

"Then unlock the door."

She pressed the button for the doors. Nothing. Alex gritted her teeth to keep from screaming. Suddenly the SUV shot backwards, the mirror almost hitting Nathan as it continued running in reverse.

She had to get out, but the door still wouldn't unlock. *The emergency brake.* Maybe engaging it would stop the car. She pressed the far-left pedal as well as the brake. The car slowed only slightly, and soon the odor of burnt rubber stung her eyes.

A car approached from behind her. She sent up a prayer. *Please let them get out of the way.* At the last second, the car pulled over to the opposite shoulder of the road, and the driver jumped out.

Just as suddenly as the trouble began, it ended. With her foot still pressing on the brake, the SUV lurched to a stop. Nathan reached her and jerked open the door before she could get her seat belt unbuckled.

"Are you okay? What happened?"

Her hand shook as she fumbled with the seat belt. As soon as she had it unfastened, she scrambled out of the SUV on shaky legs. Nathan caught her before she hit the ground.

"I have you. Just relax."

No way could she relax with adrenaline pumping through her the way it was. Except none of it was getting to her legs. "Help me stand a minute."

"Do you want to sit in the Tahoe?"

"No! That thing is crazy."

Nathan half carried her back to his pickup and lifted her up in the seat. "What do you think happened?"

"I . . . I don't know. It's . . . it's like the car had a mind of its own."

He blew out a breath. "You scared me to death."

"Well, I didn't do it on purpose."

A blur appeared in her peripheral vision. Kayla.

"Are you all right?"

"I'm alive."

"I thought you were going to plow into that car for sure."

"What are you doing here?"

"My duplex is on the other side of the school. I was going home from work."

Oh yeah. She remembered now.

Alex tried to swallow, but her mouth felt like it was stuffed with cotton. "Anyone have a bottle of water?"

Nathan reached into a cooler in the back seat of his truck. "Here you go. But drink it slowly. You don't want to get sick."

Once she'd calmed, Nathan said, "Tell me exactly what happened."

Alex pressed her fist to her mouth and collected herself. Then she took a deep breath. "Everything was fine until we turned on this road. Then it was like someone else took over the SUV. I couldn't get it to stop, or turn, or anything."

He stared at her for a couple of seconds and then glanced at Kayla. "Can you stay with her a minute?"

"Sure."

Nathan turned back to Alex. "I'll be right back."

She pulled his visor mirror down and watched as he jogged to her Tahoe and opened the driver door.

Kayla patted her hand. "You scared me to death. Are you sure you're all right? Do you need to go to the ER?"

Alex forced her attention from the mirror to the young woman. "I'm not injured. No reason to go to the hospital."

She glanced up at the mirror again. Nathan stomped toward them, his face steely and something white in his hand.

Alex stared at the small blue box he'd wrapped in his handkerchief. "What is it?"

"It's a device that allows a computer to communicate with the operating system in the Tahoe."

She stared wide-eyed at him. "Are you saying someone hacked into the vehicle? How?"

"I don't know. I assumed you'd want someone to investigate ASAP so I called your CSI team."

That's exactly what she would have done, but why didn't he wait? It was her call to make.

"I made the call because this happened in the Pearl Springs city limits. Technically, it's my case, but your CSI agents are better equipped."

Once again it was like he'd read her mind.

"Oh, wow!" Kayla said. "Can someone, like, really hack into a car?"

"Evidently," Alex muttered. "I appreciate you stopping, but you don't have to wait around with me. I'm sure you have things to do."

Kayla blinked. "Not really, but if you don't want me to hang around, I'll leave." She turned and started to her little car.

Alex felt a little guilty and called after her. "Kayla, listen, I really appreciate what you did in Chattanooga. But I can take care of myself."

Kayla shot her a doubtful look, then she shrugged. "Okay. Call me if you need anything."

"I will, I promise. And thanks again." Alex had hurt the girl's feelings, but she had things she wanted to discuss with Nathan in private. Once Kayla drove away, Alex turned to Nathan. "Don't miss your chance to catch those drug dealers. The CSI team will be here soon—I'll be fine."

His jaw jutted. "Someone just tried to kill you. They hacked into your vehicle and took control of it. If you'd been on Highway 14 when this happened, it could've been an entirely different story."

His words sent a cold chill over Alex. Highway 14 had two-hundred-foot drop-offs on the side of the road. Why was someone doing this to her? "Do you think it's the killer?"

"Who else would it be?" he said, his voice grim.

"How did they get access to the SUV? It's been sitting in my grandparents' carport since ten o'clock this morning."

"The carport is detached and not really close to the house. Anyone could have slipped through the woods that run along your grandparents' property line and broken into it."

"But it was locked."

He held up the blue box. "Anyone who has something this sophisticated would not have any trouble getting past door locks. In the future, you have to check every electronic port to make sure you can't be hacked."

Alex didn't know where to even look for an electronic device much less know where all the electronic ports were.

But she would learn.

29

Nathan stayed with Alexis until her CSI team arrived, and when she tried to smother a yawn, he said, "Come on, I'm taking you home."

She shook her head. "I'm not leaving until they process my SUV, and then I'm driving it home. You"—she tapped his chest—"need to get to the high school and be ready to spy on some drug dealers when they arrive."

Stubborn woman. "You sure you'll be okay?"

"Nathan, I'm a sworn officer of the law with twelve years' training." She eyed him with a pointed look. "I can handle this."

"I know you can." Somewhere down deep, he wanted her to need him, but she never had and probably never would.

"I would come with you, but—"

"No—you're needed here. I hope they can find a fingerprint . . . or something that will give us a clue to whoever did this."

Alexis glanced toward the SUV. "I wouldn't count on it. This person is too slick to make that kind of mistake. And it's most likely the person who's been killing those poor women."

His phone chimed with a text. His CI, letting him know the dealers were on their way. Nathan texted back a thumbs-up.

"Your confidential informant?"

He nodded.

"Then go. You might not get another chance to get information like this."

Still he hesitated. He hated leaving her, not knowing whether there was another interface on her SUV. He opened the screen on his phone and tapped on an icon. "Download the app I just sent you, then accept the invite to share your location with me. That way I'll know you made it home safely without bothering you. Or at least that your phone made it home."

For a second he thought she was going to refuse. "Will it allow me to know where *you* are?"

"Yes."

"Okay, then." She grinned. "That might be useful information to have."

Her phone chimed with the name of the app. She downloaded it, then accepted his invite to share her location with him, and he reciprocated.

"I'll check the app later to see that you made it home okay."

"Thanks. And you be careful."

"I will." Dealing with drug dealers tended to make a person careful. Nathan checked the time. Nine fifteen. Time to get in place. He jogged to his pickup and a few minutes later approached the rendezvous point. His headlights flashed across a Ford Mustang backed into an alley between the gymnasium and school building.

He idled his motor while the lanky J. R. Whittaker unfolded from the car. It never ceased to amaze Nathan when a man well over six foot drove a car the size of the Mustang.

"Where you been?" J. R.'s deep baritone quizzed him as he climbed into the pickup.

"Had a little trouble on another case. Have you seen any action yet?"

"Nah, but I don't expect anyone until closer to ten. They're meeting outside the field house. Probably be a good idea to park your truck nearby and walk to the railroad track and hide on the other side."

"I thought everything was locked up at night."

J. R. shook his head. "I'm sure it is, but there's no gate on the road to the field house."

Nathan pictured the area. The railroad track was built up higher than the surrounding land and ran parallel to the field house road. Less than fifty feet separated the two. The other side of it would be a good place to hide, and they'd be able to see who came and hear what was said.

Nathan sandwiched his truck between two school buses and grabbed his camera before he climbed out. His phone was good for some pictures, but this late, he'd need his telephoto lens. Just as he walked out from the buses, headlights turned in to the school.

It was too late to step back into the shadows. He unsnapped the retention strap on his holster and pulled his Glock just as the SUV rolled to a stop. The passenger door opened, and Alexis stepped out and walked toward him. She'd put her hair in a ponytail and wore a Russell County sheriff's department cap.

"You almost gave me a heart attack." He folded his arms over his chest. "What are you doing here?"

First she waved the driver of the SUV on, then turned to him with a grin as she held up her phone. "Just checking to see if that app works, and it does."

"I thought you were staying with your SUV while they checked it out."

"Dylan wanted to take it in to the garage where they could take their time going over it. Instead of taking me home, I had him drop me here."

"Good." He looked over her shoulder as J. R. stepped out of the shadows and walked toward them. "Meet J. R., my contact," Nathan said.

Alexis turned and stiffened. Then she turned to him and scowled. "*This* is your informant?" she asked, loud enough for J. R. to hear.

"Yes." He looked from her to J. R., who was approaching and looked as puzzled as Nathan felt. "Hold up a minute," he said to J. R. "Alexis and I need to discuss something." He pulled her a few feet away. "What's wrong?"

"That's Houdini," she hissed under her breath.

"Hou—the man at the bar?"

"Yes. Reggie."

Hoo-boy. Nathan tried to recall exactly what Kayla and Alexis had said about him. Something about him being a creep. But that had nothing to do with the here and now. "I need you to work with him. He has information I need."

She pressed her lips together and gave him a curt nod. Nathan motioned for J. R. to join them. "I think you two know each other? Maybe under different names, so let me make the introduction. J. R. Whittaker, Alexis Stone. She's chief deputy to the sheriff here. Prior to that she worked undercover in Chattanooga, and I believe you two met at the Lemon Tree."

J. R. stared at Alexis, then his eyes widened and he snapped his fingers. "Short leather skirt, low-cut top, red stilettos. You certainly look different now."

She narrowed her eyes. "Well, you don't, Reggie. I knew that wasn't your name."

"Au contraire. J. R.—James Reginald Whittaker."

Nathan eyed Alexis. "Can you two work together?"

"Of course I can work with him. It'll be no different than doing undercover work."

"Same here," J. R. said.

"Good. Then mute your phones and let's go. We need to get on the other side of the football field."

J. R. tipped his head. "Lead the way."

He led the way toward the railroad track, glancing around in the pale light of the full moon. Nathan felt exposed and veered farther away from the field house, keeping in the shadows of the buildings, then the trees that lined the railroad track. Finally they crossed it and scrambled down the embankment. They were a good thousand feet up the track from where they needed to be, and quietly made their way to a spot straight across from the field house.

"I wish we could get inside the field house," he said.

"Too risky," J. R. said. "Do you plan to arrest them tonight?"

"No. I want to see who the players are, get a few photos so we can identify them. Then we'll make a plan on the best way to shut them down."

Half an hour later they watched from their lair on the other side of the railroad tracks as a car entered the gravel drive to the field house. A Jeep Cherokee. Probably the lawyer's kid. He snapped photos of the vehicle, then zoomed in on the license plate. It had mud smeared over it. He took a picture anyway.

Three teenage boys spilled out of the car, and J. R. nudged him. Ethan Kennedy, Cole McNeil, and Mason Garrett—the boys J. R. named in the note a month ago. Nathan had been right about who the Jeep belonged to—the lawyer's son was the driver. Nathan quickly snapped their photos.

A few minutes later, another vehicle, a dark Escalade, entered the drive and inched toward the field house. Probably the dealers. Boy, he wished there were a light at the field house. At least the full moon helped.

Nathan didn't recognize the three men who climbed out of the SUV. Two of them wore suits that were tailored to fit muscular men. The third man was lean and stood a head taller than the other two. Probably the leader and the other two were security.

He zoomed in on their faces and snapped more photos. All three were Caucasian and hard-looking. J. R. had said in his phone call that they were Russian, and they had an eastern European look to them.

Another person exited the SUV, and Nathan caught his breath. It was the fourth person Reggie had listed on the note.

"Do you know him?" Alexis asked, keeping her voice low.

"Trevor Martin, a known drug dealer around here," Nathan whispered, gripping the camera. He wished it was the dealer's neck. How did the teens get mixed up with the likes of him?

The group's voices reached them, and Nathan pointed the camera at the one he thought was the leader and pressed the button, snapping several shots individually and then all the players together. He was anxious to see what the boys' parents would have to say about their kids' activities.

"Are you crazy?" The leader's voice carried in the night air. There was barely a hint of a European accent. "This is a setup waiting to happen."

"Hardly. This is the perfect place to meet—isolated, and I've made sure we won't be disturbed." The local drug dealer rubbed his thumb and fingers together. "Besides, it's not like I can bring them to you."

So the dealer was the one who set up the meeting. Nathan would like to know who he was paying off to look the other way. Beside him, Alexis took in a quick breath. "What?" he whispered. She was looking over her shoulder and he followed her gaze.

Kayla?

30

A lex gritted her teeth. It would be a miracle if Kayla didn't get them caught. "What are you doing here?" Alex whispered. "I thought you were going home."

"I was, but I was worried about you so I followed you. What are you doing here?"

Alex looked over her shoulder to see if there'd been any change at the field house. The drug dealers were still talking. "It's a long story. Just try to stay out of sight and be quiet."

A car door slammed, and they all turned toward the field house. The SUV circled and drove toward the main road while the Jeep stayed behind. Alex watched while Nathan snapped several more photos as the drug dealer held out his hand, and whatever he said was lost.

It was evident what he'd said when each of the teens counted out cash in his hand. He turned to go and called over his shoulder, "Meet me here tomorrow night at ten to pick up your next supply."

"You sure there won't be no cops?"

Nathan leaned closer to Alex. "The kid is Jonathan Kennedy's son."

"The attorney?"

He nodded grimly.

"You don't have to worry about any cops. I've got that taken care of."

Another of the boys spoke up. "Want us to drop you off somewhere?"

He shook his head. "Somebody's picking me up in a few minutes. You boys better get home before you're grounded—it's a school night."

The teens left first, and once they were out of sight, the drug dealer walked toward the main drag. A few minutes later, a white Lexus picked him up. Alex strained to see the driver. "Can you tell who's in the Lexus?"

"No, but maybe the camera can."

Alex released a sigh of relief as she unmuted her phone. "We pulled it off."

"What did we pull off?" Then Kayla frowned and pointed at J. R. "What's *he* doing here?"

"It's a long story," Alex said.

Nathan crossed his arms. "And you shouldn't have followed us. You're not trained to investigate."

"I didn't mean to investigate. Like I told Alex, I was worried about her, and when she got out at the school, I don't know, I wanted to know what was going on."

Nathan sighed, and before he could say anything else, Alex held up her hand. "Don't do it again. If those men had seen you or heard you, it would have blown it for us as well."

J. R. cleared his throat. "Think I'll head back to my car. If I hear anything you need to know, I'll give you a call."

"Thanks for the information." Nathan tilted his head toward Kayla. "Can we drop you off? My truck is parked over by the buses."

"I'm good. My car is parked that way at the railroad crossing." She pointed down the track.

"See you in the morning," Nathan called after her. Without looking back, she gave him a thumbs-up.

He shook his head. "That girl has way too much self-confidence."

"Yeah, but if she does apply to the academy, the instructors there will take her down a notch or two. Then she'll make a great detective."

He smiled. "She reminds me of you."

"I was never that cocky."

This time he laughed out loud. "Yeah, right. Come on, let's go."

Nathan took her hand as they climbed the steep hill to the tracks, then they walked single file until they reached the place to cut over to his truck. A sense of peace settled in her heart. They worked well together as a team, something that wasn't easy for her.

After her mom died and her dad dumped her on her grandparents, she'd created barriers to keep people out. Even in middle school, she'd kept her nose buried in a book so people wouldn't approach her. As a cop, she'd been a team player at work, but Alex had never joined the others at the coffeeshop-slash-diner where they hung out.

She'd even found herself trying to withdraw from her grandparents since she'd returned home, especially after Gramps had the heart attack. She couldn't bear the thought of losing him or Gram.

Nathan stopped walking and turned toward her. "You okay?"

She glanced down at their entwined hands then slowly raised her gaze to find him staring at her. The moonlight bathed him in a soft glow, and when he pulled her toward him, his embrace was so inviting. Funny how she remembered that she fit so well in his arms. And that he was just the right height that she could rest her head on his chest and feel his heart beat in time with her own.

Alex ignored the voice in her head yelling for her to move out of his arms. She was too tired.

"I've missed our friendship," Nathan said softly.

"Me too." Friendship. That was all she wanted. Right? So why did his words hurt? Before she could dig deeper into her feelings, her phone rang, shattering the quiet.

He dropped his arms from around her. "You better answer that."

With a fortifying breath, she stepped back and fished her phone out of her back pocket. Dylan Wells. He wouldn't be calling unless it was important.

"Stone," she answered and put the call on speaker.

"Alex, thought you might need to know that we discovered a photo with writing on the back. It was under the driver seat of your SUV, and I'm assuming it's from Gina Norman's killer since a pawn is taped to it."

Nathan tensed beside her as icy fingers gripped Alex's stomach. How had the killer even known the vehicle she would be driving? "What's in the photo?"

"It looks like a chessboard with the White king on its side. There's an O minus written across the top."

Alex didn't have to understand chess to know the killer meant the note as a taunt, indicating she'd lost the game. She lifted her chin. The killer may have meant the note to intimidate her, but for Alex, it was a challenge. She would just have to prove the killer wrong. "Anything else on the photo?"

"There's something written on the back."

"Read it."

Dylan cleared his throat and started reading. "*This was to let you know I can find you anytime I want to.*"

Alex swallowed the bile that rose in her throat. A mind

game. That's all it was. She couldn't let the killer get into her head. "Anything else?"

There was a hesitation. She cringed, waiting for more bad news, and beside her, Nathan leaned closer to the phone, intensity radiating off him.

"Taylor found a tracking device under the back bumper."

Alex shouldn't have been surprised. "Get rid of it. Whoever put it there would expect our CSI team to find it."

"Done," Dylan said. "It'll be in the property room with the other evidence."

She disconnected the call and turned to Nathan. "Now all we have to do is find out who had access to my SUV."

"Yes, but I keep coming back to why would anyone want to kill you in the first place."

31

Nathan and Alexis were both quiet as he drove to her grandparents' house. Although his mind formulated a plan for tomorrow night based on what they'd seen and heard at the field house, the memory of almost losing Alexis when her SUV wove all over the road kept intruding. If the SUV had crashed and seriously injured or killed her . . .

Alexis getting shot last month had reawakened his feelings for her like Mount Vesuvius erupting, but it had taken the near-wreck to make him realize if he didn't do something, he would lose her for good. But what if she didn't feel the same way? She certainly hadn't said anything when he'd told her he missed their friendship.

What had he been expecting? Her to say she'd made a mistake ditching him years ago? That she still loved him? He stifled a sigh.

Yeah, sure, they got along fine . . . but what if she only thought of him as a friend? Nathan didn't think he could take that. It'd be better to wait and not risk outright rejection.

He turned into the drive that circled the house and kept to the right, pulling around to a side patio that gave Alexis direct access to her bedroom. Then he turned to her. "Are you going to stay here, at your grandparents', or get your own place?"

Alexis blew out a breath. "I hadn't thought that far ahead. For right now, I'll probably stay here so I can keep an eye on Gramps. Gram told me this morning he wanted to start driving again, and I don't think he should."

"Good luck with that," Nathan said and climbed out of the truck, scanning the area. The full moon was directly overhead now, making the shadowy interior of the woods adjacent to the Stone property even blacker.

Seeing nothing that alarmed him, he jogged around to the passenger door, surprised Alexis had actually waited until he opened the truck door for her. "Do you need the step?"

"I'm good. Thanks for bringing me home." Once her feet were on the ground, she shivered and pulled her jacket close. "When did it turn so chilly?"

On the way home, she'd taken off the body armor and the baseball cap and loosened her hair, letting it fall around her shoulders. Now one strand clung to her cheek, and he wanted to brush it back. Instead, he found his voice. "I, ah, think it's been chilly all along. I just don't think we were focused on the temps."

She glanced up at him, and the air charged between them. He certainly wasn't thinking about the chill in the air now.

"You're probably right."

Her voice was soft, taking him back to other evenings when he'd brought Alexis home, and the memory of kisses they'd shared speared his heart like a flaming arrow. Maybe he would risk—

The sharp report of a rifle followed by his passenger window shattering into a thousand pieces sent his heart into orbit.

"Get down!"

Alexis dropped to the ground and rolled under the pickup.

Two more bullets kicked up gravel as Nathan yanked his Glock from the holster and followed her.

They crawled out on the other side of the truck. Alexis had her phone out, calling 911 as they worked their way to the patio, where they knelt behind the brick half-wall. "Help is on the way," she said, keeping her voice low.

Nathan strained to hear anything . . . footsteps, a twig breaking, but silence surrounded them. From the next street over, a motor revved and tires screeched. He slipped his gun in the holster. "I think whoever it was is gone."

Alexis nodded and holstered her gun as she leaned against the side of the house. After a minute, she said, "I certainly hope it isn't past midnight."

"What do you mean?"

Sirens approached. "Just that I don't want this to be the first thing happening in a new day."

He stared at her, and they both burst out laughing and couldn't stop. Before the squad cars reached them, Nathan drew a deep breath and got control of himself.

Alexis did the same thing. "What is wrong with us?"

"Reaction to being shot at?"

"I couldn't stop laughing."

"Me either." He took another deep breath. "Did you get a sense of where the bullets were coming from?"

"The wooded area." She nodded to the property next door. "There's a street on the other side. That's probably where the shooter parked."

The next hour passed quickly as they filled in the two Russell County deputies and Nathan's night officer who came to the scene, as well as Sheriff Stone, who was awakened by the commotion. Half of the county CSI team in the form of Taylor showed up and dug a slug from Nathan's dashboard.

After Taylor packed up her evidence and the three officers

left, Nathan and Alexis sat with the sheriff. Carson rubbed his jaw with his thumb. "What if you'd been shot again . . . or worse? Maybe I shouldn't have made you chief deputy."

"Gramps! I can take care of myself. Besides, I don't think the shooter meant to hit us."

"Unless the shooter was a really bad shot," Nathan said.

Carson nodded slowly. "If they were that bad, they wouldn't have used a rifle to attack you. Maybe they were just trying to scare you."

Alexis shivered. "I think they were sending a message to let me know they can get to me whenever they want."

"I don't like it either way." Nathan stared toward the woods where the shots had come from. "Even a bad shooter gets lucky sometimes, and if the purpose is to scare you, it'll escalate."

Carson nodded his agreement and then turned to Alexis. "Have Chattanooga send me all your cases. While I'm sitting here doing nothing, I can comb through them and maybe find a connection."

"Good idea." Nathan studied Carson. It was good to see that he was getting stronger and told him so.

The sheriff grunted. "Doesn't seem like it to me. I don't like standing on the sidelines."

"No one does," Alexis said softly, then she leaned forward. "It would be great if you could take a look at the files—I trust you a whole lot more than I do Madden."

So did Nathan. He turned to her. "How about you? Are you okay?"

She nodded. "Shook up but alive."

"Thanks for having her back," Carson said.

"She'd do the same for me." Nathan tapped the body armor she'd put on right after her deputies arrived. "Don't take this off again until you're in the house."

"It's one thing to have my back and another to hover." She crossed her arms. "And you're hovering."

He shrugged. "I can't help it."

"That's your last get-out-of-jail-free card." Then she smiled. "But you don't have to worry about me taking my body armor off until I'm undressing for bed."

"Thank you."

Alexis looked toward the wooded area. "I can't believe I thought this job would be safer than the streets of Chattanooga. That I'd just be pushing papers. Tonight certainly changed my mindset."

"It's not every chief deputy who has someone gunning for them," Carson said. "Russell County is generally a safe place, or as safe as any place can be."

"I haven't been here long enough to make enemies, so are we all agreed the shooter was probably the Queen's Gambit Killer?"

"I think that's a good conclusion," Carson said.

She cocked her head. "How well do you know J. R.?"

"Who's J. R.?" Carson asked.

"J. R. Whittaker," Nathan said. "You should remember him. I arrested him when I was your deputy."

"You arrested a lot of people."

"We raided a drug party, and he offered to give up the dealer who arranged the party if we let him go, and you did." When he still looked puzzled, Nathan added, "He's Marilyn Whittaker's son."

"Oh, now I remember him. Lives in Chattanooga now."

"Right. Still visits his mom sometimes."

Alexis tilted her head. "So he's been your CI since you were Gramps's deputy?"

"I hadn't thought of it that way, but I guess he has. We went to Chatt State together before I transferred to UT, and then I ran into him occasionally when he came to Pearl Springs to visit his mother. Even back in school, J. R. liked to see how close he could get to the fire without getting burned. Why are you asking?"

"That night at the Lemon Tree when I was trying to lure the killer out, he was on my radar. Then he shows up here tonight . . ." She glanced toward the wooded area.

"You're looking in the wrong direction. Both times he was meeting with me. Besides, I don't think J. R. has the stomach for killing or scaring anyone, and he has helped me identify some of the drug dealers coming here from Chattanooga."

Carson's eyes narrowed. "They think that because we are a small town in a small county, we have a backwater sheriff and police department."

"Absolutely. They start with the high school kids, get them to dealing to their friends, then go wide open. Back when J. R. first cooperated with us, the dealer found out pretty quick we wouldn't tolerate dealers moving into our county."

32

Alex peeled off the right Velcro tab on her body armor and slipped off the vest, tossing it on her bed. Nathan was right. She shouldn't have taken it off until right now. It was a rookie mistake, one she wouldn't make again.

What a day. She checked her watch. Two a.m. Had it only been seventeen hours since she was sworn in as chief deputy? And someone had tried to kill her twice. And had killed Gina Norman. Her stomach churned. Not the kind of day she'd expected at all, and if she didn't get some rest, she wouldn't be worth anything tomorrow. Make that today. She climbed into bed and didn't fight the encroaching sleep.

At six, Alex's alarm woke her from a troubled dream. In it she was driving the hairpin turns on Monteagle Mountain and couldn't stop her car. Even though she was awake, her heart raced like she was still in the dream.

She sat on the side of her bed, trying to shake the dream, and looked up when there was a light tap at her door. "Come in."

Gram opened the door and entered the room with a cup in one hand. "I heard your alarm go off and thought you might need this."

"Bless you," Alex said as she took the steaming cup and

inhaled the aroma of fresh-brewed coffee. "Sorry if we woke you last night."

"Your grandfather is the light sleeper, not me." Gram chuckled. "I think a bomb could go off in the bed, and I wouldn't wake up until I got my seven hours of sleep."

"How is Gramps?"

"Fine. I told him to go back to sleep, that I'd wake him at seven."

"And he did?"

"Yep, but only because he wanted to be fresh in case you need to discuss anything with him before you go in today. I assume you'll have a briefing first thing?"

"At eight." Alex definitely wanted to talk to her grandfather before she left for her office. He was one of the best detectives she'd ever known, and last night had shown that neither a heart attack nor age had diminished that. Tapping in to his experience would be the smartest thing she could do.

Gram nodded toward the Bible on Alex's bedside table. "Be sure to take time there."

"I will." Yesterday she had been so slammed from the minute she woke that she'd skipped her morning devotions. Alex had found herself doing that more and more lately.

Lately? She'd struggled with believing God cared about her ever since her dad died. The only reason Alex attempted morning devotions was her promise to her grandmother just before she went off to college. She shuddered remembering why. She and Nathan had just broken up, and for some crazy reason, she thought alcohol would ease the pain. It hadn't.

Her grandmother had been waiting in her bedroom when she came stumbling in. Someone had called her grandmother and tattled that her car was parked in front of the local beer joint.

Alex had been so sick, she'd made the promise just to get

her grandmother out of the bedroom before she threw up. But once she gave her word, she wasn't breaking it and had read her Bible most days. Today's reading was in Isaiah.

As she hurried through the chapter, one verse stopped her. *"I am the Lord your God, who teaches you what is best for you, who directs you in the way you should go."* She could certainly use all the help she could get to stop this killer.

So why hadn't God helped her before now? Surely he didn't want this person to kill anyone else. That opened the door to more questions. Why had he allowed it in the first place? If God was going to help her, why hadn't he helped her before she came home to Pearl Springs? What was she missing?

Alex went in search of her grandmother and found her in the kitchen.

Gram held up the coffeepot. "More coffee?"

"Sure."

Gram refilled her cup and settled at the kitchen table.

"Why does God let bad things happen?" Alexis asked.

Gram didn't respond right away. Instead, she poured herself a cup of coffee and joined Alex at the table. "You're thinking about the girl who was killed yesterday?"

"And all the others. What I read this morning said that God would direct me, so why doesn't he show me who the killer is?"

Her grandmother stared down into her coffee, then she raised her gaze to Alex's. "Have you asked him for help?"

The question took Alex's breath. "No . . . but why would I have to? If he knows everything—"

Gram raised her hand. "I wish I had an answer to your question. It's a question that's been asked since Eve ate the apple. Job, David, Solomon . . . But there are a few things I do know. God hates it when someone is murdered. And he wants justice for that person. Next time you're looking at the evidence, ask him for his help. And then pay attention."

"It's what I always did." Her grandfather's walker bumped the door as he slowly entered the kitchen.

Gram stood. "I didn't hear you. Sit down, and I'll bring your coffee."

It surprised Alex that he was using the walker since he hadn't used it last night.

"I hate using this thing, but I woke up kind of dizzy."

"I hope it wasn't because of what happened last night."

He gripped the walker. "It would have been my fault if something had happened to you last night. Not once, but twice."

Alex froze. She hadn't told him about someone taking control of her SUV. "How—"

"Harvey called me when it happened."

She would have a talk with Harvey. Her grandfather didn't need to know every little thing that happened.

"Don't be too hard on him."

Alex had to work on her poker face. "I don't need him running to you every time something happens."

"That's neither here nor there. Right now we need to focus on catching whoever is responsible, not just for that, but yesterday's murder as well."

That she agreed with. "I don't know what I'm missing."

"It's obvious the killer has a grudge against you. Maybe I'll find something in one of your cases."

"I've never arrested anyone for something that would arouse this kind of anger."

She took a sip of coffee and made a face. Alex did not like cold coffee even when it was supposed to be cold. She took her mug to the microwave to nuke the liquid.

"I'll call Chattanooga PD this morning and ask them to email you the files on all my cases," she said when she returned to her seat across from her grandfather.

"Good." He tapped his finger on the table. "Before I went

to sleep, I thought about the man you shot and killed a couple of years ago."

"Phillip Denton? As far as I know, the detectives who handled the case never found any family connected to him, and that was true as of last night when I asked Madden about him." She checked her watch. "If I don't leave right now, I'll be late for my first briefing."

An hour later, Alex faced her deputies. It would be a full briefing with Gina Norman's murder, the issue with her SUV, and the shooting. She dispensed with the SUV issue by asking Dylan and Taylor to meet with her privately at one thirty to discuss what they'd learned. Alex started with the shooting at her grandfather's house, leaving Gina Norman's murder to last.

"Taylor, what do you have?" As soon as it was daylight, the CSI had returned to the house to search for more evidence.

Taylor gave her report, which consisted of digging a badly misshapen slug from the wooden column on the patio outside Alex's bedroom.

"Did you find any casings?"

Taylor nodded. "This morning I found three—.308 and probably fired from a Winchester rifle, which unfortunately around here is as common as pickup trucks. And you were right about the location where the shooter's vehicle had been parked," she said. "Fresh tire marks were laid down on the next street over. When I left, a couple of deputies were canvassing the neighborhood to talk to the people we missed last night."

One of the deputies who'd been at the house spoke up. "I went door-to-door last night, and one person said they looked out when the vehicle scratched off, but it was too dark to see what kind of car or truck it was. I'm going back to the neighborhood to knock on doors again."

"Get some rest first," she said. "Starting now." Alex turned to Harvey. "Thanks for taking over yesterday. What can you tell us about the murder?"

"Not a lot." He took out a notepad. "I assigned a couple of deputies to canvass the neighborhood alongside Jared Westbrook, Chief Landry's sergeant. They had to wait until late yesterday afternoon since almost everyone on that street works. I think they pretty well talked to everyone."

"What did you learn?"

Harvey shrugged, and then looked down at his notepad. "No one had talked to her since she rented the house. No one saw or heard anything because they all claimed to be at work."

"Do you have anything on the victim other than what we already know?"

Harvey shook his head. "We're still looking into it, although I think it's a waste of time—Tom Weaver isn't renting to anybody he can't check out."

"Verifying our information is never a waste of time. Let me know when you get something." Alex kept her tone even and didn't miss Harvey's frown as she turned to Mark Lassiter. The handwriting was on the wall—she was going to have trouble with Harvey.

"Mark," she said, and he looked up from his notes. The teenage girl who'd found Norman's body had given them a list of students who gathered at Tom Weaver's rental house to smoke pot, and she'd assigned him to interview them. She hoped her show of confidence would encourage him to keep the interviews strictly professional. "What do you have for us?"

"Not much. The students clammed up, claimed they only stopped by the house to chill and none of them smoked any pot. Ever." He rolled his eyes. "I told them if we ever so much as suspected they were doing something illegal, we'd contact their parents. As for the victim, none of them including Mary

Beth knew her. Claimed they didn't know Weaver had rented the house."

In other words, nothing. "Thank you. I need you to follow up with Weaver on Norman's rental agreement. I understand he requires two references from former rental agents as well as neighbors. Would you interview her references?"

"Sure."

"Good. And I'd like to have a strategy meeting with you and Harvey today at one."

The two exchanged looks, and she gritted her teeth.

"Do you expect us to have the information you requested by then?" Harvey grumbled.

"You should at least have a start on it. See you at one," she said evenly, dismissing them. They were not going to disrespect her in front of the other deputies.

Why had she let her grandfather talk her into taking this job?

33

The question of who wanted Alexis dead followed Nathan into the next morning, making it difficult to focus on the stack of paperwork he had in front of him. On his way into the police station, he'd dropped his pickup off at the glass company to get the window replaced.

Twice he took out his cell to call and remind Alexis to check out the undercarriage of the patrol car she was using until the SUV was released. Twice he put the phone back in the case on his waist, the call not made. Alexis would not appreciate the implication that she wasn't on top of this.

The next time he took out his phone, he scrolled to the CSI tech and called him. When Dylan answered, Nathan asked about the electronic device that had allowed someone to take over the Controller Area Network in her SUV.

"It's more than a device—the device I can get rid of," Dylan said. "It's the software someone downloaded into the CAN. I can't be sure I got rid of all of it. We're calling in an expert."

Good. "Where do you get software like that?"

"Dark web for sure, or maybe a hacker who has the software. The actual device we found is the same kind mechanics use to

173

hook up to the electrical system to diagnose a problem. So it could belong to someone in the automotive field."

"How familiar are you with the dark web?" he asked.

"I like to troll it, see what's going on. No law against it."

"Don't take offense, I was just curious," Nathan said. "I don't suppose there were any fingerprints on the controller or anywhere else?"

"No. Sorry."

"How will you prevent it from happening again?"

"That expert I talked to said he could install a warning system that will detect if any type of software is loaded onto the system."

That should take care of a repeat problem. "Thanks. I owe you one."

The news lightened the dark cloud hanging over Nathan enough that he actually dialed Alexis this time. When she answered, he said, "Good morning, Chief Deputy Stone. How's it going over at the sheriff's office?"

"I know you said there'd be paperwork, Mr. Police Chief, but this much?"

He glanced over his own stack of paperwork. "It's the part of the job I don't like, so I try to get it out of the way by noon." He checked his watch. Twelve ten. "Not having too much luck today."

"Me either." Her huff came through the phone. "It looks like no one has touched the paperwork around here since my grandfather's heart attack . . . maybe even the week before. It'll take me days to work through this mess, and I have other things to do—like catch a murderer."

"Remember how to eat the el—"

"This isn't an elephant."

He held the phone away from his ear. "Are we a bit touchy this morning, or technically, this afternoon?"

"I'm sorry. This isn't your fault. Gramps must have been

really unwell to let everything slide like he did." Seconds ticked off. "And that scares me."

"I know, Alexis, but he seemed more like himself last night."

"You're right. Did you get your window replaced?"

"The glass company is working on it." Nathan glanced at the stack of papers waiting for his signature. "Can Marge help with any of your paperwork?"

"She already has." Alexis sighed. "Look, I have less than an hour to make headway on this mess before Harvey and Mark arrive for an afternoon briefing on Gina Norman's murder."

"Sure. Maybe we can talk later?"

"Perfect."

Nathan had no sooner ended the call than his cell phone rang. Alexis. "Forget something?"

"Yeah. Do you want to sit in on the briefing?"

"Definitely. Do you mind if I bring my sergeant?"

"That's fine. The CSI team will be here as well. We're meeting at one, so give me half an hour to address administrative issues." She paused a second. "I'm assuming we're keeping what went down at the field house last night quiet."

"Yes." Which reminded him, he needed to speak to Kayla—he thought she was supposed to come in at noon. And he needed to check with J. R.

"I figured you would. See you at one thirty."

He called Jared and informed him of the meeting. His sergeant was at the Corner Diner eating lunch and said he'd meet him at the jail. Then Nathan skimmed through the papers on his desk, taking care of the ones that only needed his signature. He paused at a request for overtime pay for his sergeant. Nathan barely had enough funds to cover the monthly payroll. He would talk to him either before or after the briefing about using comp time instead of overtime pay.

Five minutes before he was supposed to be at the briefing,

Nathan borrowed a patrol car and drove slowly through Pearl Springs. It was a pretty town laid out on a square around the courthouse. He noted the checker players had moved inside at Jamison Hardware. Not surprising with the fifty-degree temp. Until spring they would congregate around the potbelly stove at the hardware store instead of the court square. On the next block he returned a wave from Mrs. Fields on her afternoon walk as she waited at the only stoplight in town.

The town might be missing the amenities Alexis was looking for, but it had so much more to offer. In a town the size of Pearl Springs, it didn't take long for others to know when someone was hurting and respond. Didn't matter whether the family lived in town or out in the country. Alexis wasn't going to find that kind of community in a big city. Or the ability to drive almost anywhere in town in two minutes, including the distance from the police station to the sheriff's department.

Jared pulled into a parking spot beside Nathan, and a cold breeze nipped at Nathan as he waited for his sergeant on the sidewalk. "Everything good at Pete's?"

He patted his stomach. "A little too good."

Nathan eyed Jared. The body armor he wore didn't hide the fat inching over his belt. Of all his officers, his sergeant was the one he had to keep after about exercising. "Don't forget the agility tests are coming up in January."

He groaned. "It's not fair having those so soon after the holidays."

Maybe not, but it gave his officers incentive to stay in shape since they all spent too many hours in a patrol vehicle. "That's why you may want to cut back on those cinnamon rolls and hamburgers the Corner Diner is famous for—unless you want to put in extra time at the gym."

"Yeah, I know."

"Oh," Nathan said, remembering Jared's pay request. "Are you interested in comp time instead of overtime pay?"

His sergeant tilted his head. "Can I carry it over into next year?"

"I don't see why not."

"Comp time is fine, then."

Jared yawned, and Nathan looked a little closer at him. His uniform could use a little pressing. "Did you work last night?"

"Filled in for Cobb—he has the flu."

Both of their phones dinged with texts, and he glanced at his. As a precaution, one of his officers was requesting backup for an out-of-town speeder he'd pulled over. Two of his officers were out and that left just Nathan and Jared.

"You want to take this?" Nathan asked.

"Sure."

"I'll be here if you run into any trouble." His sergeant nodded. Nathan waited until Jared pulled out of the parking lot before he pushed open the door to the sheriff's outer office.

Marge looked up from her computer. "Alex just texted me to ask if you would mind waiting a minute when you got here."

"Sure." Nathan wandered around the room. The walls were lined with photos and newspaper clippings of Carson Stone dating back to his first years in office. After ten minutes, he turned to Marge. "Should I come back?"

Before she could answer, the door to the sheriff's office opened and a red-faced Alexis stepped out. "You can come in now."

He tipped his head toward the secretary-and-sometimes-dispatcher and followed Alexis inside.

Mark was seated on the right side of the room with Gem at his feet. Harvey sat in the chair beside the K-9 officer, leaving a chair by the window. Nathan took it as she walked behind her grandfather's desk and sat down. "My crime scene investigators will be here momentarily," Alex said.

It would take a saw to cut the tension in the room, and from the scowl on Mark Lassiter's face, the problem lay with him. If Nathan were a betting man, he'd bet that Harvey Morgan had sided with the K-9 detective.

Alexis leaned forward and braced her arms on her desk and clasped her hands, but not before he noticed her fingers shaking. "I don't know what's taking Taylor and Dylan so long, but I don't want to start without them."

Nathan nodded, and within a minute, the two crime scene investigators entered the room, and Alexis stood and picked up a stack of papers. "Before we get to anything else, I want to hand out the preliminary autopsy report Dr. Williams forwarded me."

She handed each person a report, and the room fell quiet as everyone read over the information. Nathan noted Dr. Ralph Edwards, the Hamilton County medical examiner, had done the autopsy and then skipped over the introduction to the heart of the report.

He mentally translated the medical jargon into his own words as he read. Single gunshot wound to the chest with the bullet perforating the heart and lung. According to body temperature and stomach contents, the victim died about two hours prior to discovery at approximately eight o'clock, and there were no powder burns on the body, indicating the shooter had stood at least four feet from the victim.

At the bottom of the report, Dr. Edwards had stated the cause of death was a single gunshot wound, and the manner of death as being homicide. Nothing new there.

So why was Gina Norman targeted? Was it only because she had the misfortune to move to Pearl Springs just as Alexis took over as chief deputy?

34

Alex waited until everyone read the autopsy report, taking the time to get her emotions under control. If she'd learned one thing at the end of the earlier meeting, it was that Mark Lassiter was going to try to block her at every turn.

She couldn't believe he'd suggested that she should pull herself off the case since Alex clearly was the target of the killer. Or that Harvey would agree.

Yes, she could. Mark had couched the suggestion in terms of her safety, but the issue was dropped quick enough after she asked how they would feel in the same situation. Both knew any time an officer strapped on a gun, they were putting their life on the line. Granted this situation was a little more tense than everyday danger.

No. Either Mark was angry that she'd reprimanded him at the crime scene yesterday about his interview with the teenager or he resented not being picked as chief deputy while her grandfather was out. Same for Harvey. Either way, the two of them were going to be a rock in her shoe. No, they were going to be a boulder in her shoe.

Once this meeting was over, she planned to call them back in separately for a private talk. Her grandfather had not raised a girl who was afraid of confrontation when it was necessary. Mark Lassiter could either get on board or resign. And the same went for Harvey.

"When do you expect to get the full autopsy report on Gina Norman?" Nathan asked.

His question brought her back to the here and now. "Six weeks, if we're lucky. The Hamilton County Medical Examiner's office is backlogged, as is the lab where the body fluids were sent. I called and talked to the medical examiner who did the autopsy to ask if the victim had anything under her nails. Unfortunately, Dr. Edwards said she did not."

She turned to Mark. "What information did you get from Tom Weaver on the references?"

"None," Mark said, his tone clipped. "Turns out they don't exist."

Nathan frowned. "That doesn't sound like Tom Weaver."

Mark turned to him. "I know. When I asked him, his face got red and he stammered all over the place and finally said he hadn't gotten around to checking them out." Mark chuckled. "The Norman woman was nice-looking, and I figure she batted her eyelashes at him a time or two and he didn't care if she had references."

"Still doesn't sound like him," Nathan said.

"I heard Weaver and his wife were having problems," Harvey said. Until now, he'd been quiet.

While Alex had known Tom Weaver and his wife before she left Pearl Springs, she'd never paid them much attention, nor was she looking at either of them as the murderer. She turned to her CSI team. "What do you have to report?"

"Basically nothing," Dylan said. "The killer was like a ghost. Lots of fingerprints to identify. The ones I've processed belong to either Weaver or the kids who hung out there. I'm sure some of them will be the victim's."

"Any other prints? Shoe, palm . . ."

"No. Like I reported earlier, the victim had mopped the whole area so there wasn't any dust to leave shoe prints. We did find a few tiny clumps of dirt, but they matched the mud on Mary Beth Meyers's shoes."

"Gina Norman appeared to be in the process of cleaning inside the kitchen cabinets to stock them," Taylor said.

"No hairs or unusual fibers?" Nathan asked.

Taylor shook her head. "We vacuumed the whole house, and except for the little bit of mud on the porch and in the living room, nothing."

Alex shifted her gaze to Mark. "Did any of the neighbors see anything?"

"Sorry, but no. The house where the crime occurred is the last house on that side of the dead-end street. The house next door is vacant, and the people across the street were at work. We even interviewed Mrs. Holcomb. Thank goodness her sitter was there."

Alex looked from Mark to Nathan. "Who is Mrs. Holcomb?"

Mark grinned. "You can explain that one, Chief."

Nathan scratched his jaw. "She's a tiny little woman in her nineties who stays up most of the night watching for burglars. Most nights we get a call requesting we check out her house or the house next door or across the street. Never is anyone trying to break in, and once the officer assures Mrs. Holcomb of that, she always invites them in for hot tea and cookies and won't take no for an answer."

"And you send an officer every night?"

"Sure. Unless we have a hotspot somewhere. She's lonely, and it's good PR—she tells every person she knows how great we are, and that my officers are special."

Alex made sure her mouth didn't drop open again, but what Nathan just described would never happen in Chattanooga.

Or any other city she'd lived in. But what amazed her even more was how the story touched her heart. "Does that ever happen here, at the sheriff's department?"

Taylor laughed. "Oh yeah, we have our Mrs. Holcombs."

"Pete Wooley," Dylan chimed in.

"And don't forget about Ms. Esther. She usually calls around four thirty. That's when her husband normally came home from the hardware store every day," Harvey said.

"Esther Jamison?" Alex asked. When all three of them nodded, she frowned. "I didn't know her husband died. Who's running Jamison Hardware now?"

"Their grandson," Nathan said.

"Dickie Jamison?"

"You sound surprised." Nathan cleared his throat. "Oh, and he goes by Richard now."

Dickie, now Richard, was a classmate of theirs, and he'd been even more anxious to get out of Pearl Springs than Alex. "I just didn't think he'd hang around Russell County after he finished college. What brought him back?"

"A pretty girl named Tess."

"He married Tess?" Alex asked as a text buzzed on her phone. A quick glance told her it was Marge.

"And they have two little ones running around." Taylor stood. "If you don't need us, I have a report to write."

"Me too." Dylan rose as well. He stopped at the door. "This is a good place to raise a family."

Harvey and Mark said they had reports to work on as well, but before she dismissed them she requested a meeting later in the day. After everyone but Nathan left, Alex used the pretense of reading Marge's text to gather herself, but the message blurred. The conversation had stirred memories she'd thought buried for good. Memories of growing up in Pearl Springs where people looked after each other.

Maybe she wouldn't tell Nathan what she'd discovered just yet. Alex looked up to find him watching her. "What?"

"You've missed a lot, not coming home any more often than you have."

"I'm beginning to see that." She glanced at the message again. "Oh, Kayla is here."

She quickly texted for Marge to send her in. A few seconds later, Kayla slipped into the room, wearing a backpack like the ones high school kids used.

"Hey, boss. I was passing by the jail and saw your truck," she said. "I need a favor."

"What kind of favor?"

"I talked to my college advisor about taking a criminal justice class, and it's a really popular class. They have a max on the class, and students going for a criminal justice degree get priority. She said if you gave me a letter of recommendation, it would help me get in."

"Sure," Nathan said. "Tomorrow soon enough?"

"That's perfect." Then she turned to Alex. "And I wanted to make sure you're okay."

"I'm fine," Alex said. Kayla's thoughtfulness touched her. "I hope you'll seriously consider attending the police academy. We need smart people like you on our side."

"Thank you." She smiled. "That's all I wanted. I'll leave you to your police work and get to my job."

After Kayla left, Nathan was quiet a minute, then he tilted his head. "Want to tell me about the problem with Mark?"

Had it been that obvious? She stood and walked to the window and looked out over the half-mile walking trail employees often used. Beyond the trail was another of the many groves of trees scattered around Pearl Springs. Did she want to air the sheriff department's dirty linen? Not so much dirty linen as insubordination.

Alex felt Nathan's presence rather than heard him approach. The electricity between them was like an early warning system. For years she'd been able to bury her feelings for him because she never saw him, but being around Nathan this last month had cracked the barriers. If she was around him much more, he'd tear them down.

That couldn't happen. Why not? She liked the way Nathan had her back, and it went further than just being part of a team like in Chattanooga. But she had a plan for her life and it didn't include Russell County or Nathan Landry, or at least it hadn't until now.

"What happened?" he asked softly.

"Mark told me I should take myself off the Norman case. He thinks the killer is targeting me."

"He has a point," Nathan said. "I think you should back off and let your deputies handle the investigation."

He was siding with Mark? "No! We don't know for sure the killer is targeting me." She fisted her hands. "And I'm not going to let my grandfather down by tucking tail and running at the first sign of trouble."

"You wouldn't be letting him down." He placed his hands on her shoulders, gently massaging them.

She couldn't think straight with Nathan touching her like that. Alex resisted giving in to his touch but found herself leaning into his hands as he kneaded the tight muscles. *Move away.* Instead, she stood there.

Gently he turned her around and raised her face until she was staring into his sky-blue eyes. "I don't want to see anything happen to you."

Alex soaked in his husky words. Her gaze shifted to his lips that were so close. The years since the last time he'd kissed her melted away. Her heart swelled in her chest.

She almost quit breathing as he lowered his head, his lips

capturing hers. Nathan wrapped his arms around her, drawing her close, and she pressed into the kiss.

Banging came at the door, and Alex jumped back. What was she thinking? She had no time to formulate an answer before the pounding started again.

athan could not believe what he'd just done. Kissing Alexis was totally unprofessional. Not to mention totally unfair to take advantage of her when she was vulnerable.

Somehow he had to think of a way to salvage this. He turned toward the window and took a deep breath as Alexis told whoever was beating down the door to come in. She no sooner said the words when Marge burst into the room.

A flash of sunlight reflected on metal, jerking Nathan's attention to the wooded area on the other side of the walking trail. For a hundredth of a second he didn't breathe. Then he sprang into action.

"Get down!"

Alexis half turned toward him. "What—?"

Marge screamed when Nathan dove for Alexis. They crashed to the floor just as a bullet pierced the window and splintered a board on the bookcase.

Alexis shifted, trying to get up.

"Wait." Seconds passed, and when there were no more shots, he rolled away from her. "You okay?"

She sat up and craned her neck.

"I think so. At least I'm not bleeding." She shuddered. "I guess you saved my life. Again."

Alexis allowed him to help her to her feet, and they both stared at the hole. It was head-high. If she'd been standing . . . He shoved that thought out of his mind. *Marge.* Was she okay? She'd dropped to the floor when they did. He whirled around, looking for the secretary.

Marge sat on the floor, her eyes wide open.

"Are you all right?"

She pushed her glasses up on her nose and then, using the desk for support, pulled to her feet. "Yeah, but what happened?"

"Somebody took a shot at Alexis."

"Or you," Alexis said. "Marge, get Harvey and Dylan and Taylor back in here, and Mark and Gem as well. Have them search for the shooter's position."

"I can't."

Alexis stared at her secretary. "What do you mean?"

"That's what I was coming to tell you. There's been another murder."

"Where?" Alexis asked.

"Who is it?" He'd spoken at the same time as Alexis.

Marge shook her head. "I'm not sure."

"I don't understand," Alexis said.

Marge took a breath. "Ethan Kennedy called in the death—he and a couple boys found a man at the gravel pit. Pretty sure the other two will be Cole McNeil and Mason Garrett."

The same three boys at the school last night. Nathan dismissed them as the killer. Drug dealers, maybe, killers, no. Besides, if they'd shot the man, the boys would've run instead of calling it in.

"Did they see what happened?"

"Ethan claims they just found him and that he'd been shot in the chest. He said something else—something about him

187

having a chess piece in his hand." Marge stopped and took a deep breath. "You think it's the same person who killed that Norman girl yesterday?"

"Won't know until we get there." Alexis grabbed her body armor. "Is everyone on their way to the scene?"

"They are. Except for Harvey. After your meeting, he took the rest of the day off. Said he had a migraine."

"A migraine? He didn't say anything about a headache during the meeting." When Marge shrugged, Alexis said, "See who else is available."

Her secretary nodded and returned to the outer office, closing the door behind her.

"I'll get some of my officers over there as well since the gravel pit borders the city limits." This was another case they would share, and this time Alexis didn't protest.

She took a deep breath. "We need all hands on deck. You ready to roll?"

"First I want to apologize for—"

"If you're going to say you're sorry you kissed me, I just might kick you in the shins."

"Not sorry about that, just the timing. You're vulnerable right now, and I took advantage of that."

"We'll talk about it later." She slipped into her body armor on her way out the door.

Nathan called his office as he followed Alexis to the gravel pit, and Peggy answered. "Where's Kayla?" he asked. Answering the phone was her job.

"Just came in the door. And she's not late," Peggy added.

He was a little surprised it'd taken her that long to drive the short distance from the jail to his office. He shook his head. Kayla was the least of his worries. "I need you to dispatch all the officers to the quarry on the edge of town."

"What happened?"

"Another murder," he replied.

"You're kidding."

"I wish." He disconnected and a few minutes later pulled in behind Alexis at the gravel pit and parked.

They walked the quarter mile to the crime scene on a path that paralleled the road into the gravel quarry. Because of complaints about the dust the trucks kicked up, the company wet down the road each morning, and there appeared to be a clear set of tire prints in the sand that Dylan was examining.

From where Nathan stood, it didn't look like there were any tracks exiting the quarry, overlaying the victim's. He probably knew whoever killed him. The killer could've even ridden with him into the gravel pit.

Near what Nathan assumed was the victim's car, Mark Lassiter strung the last of the crime scene tape around the murder site. His dog, Gem, followed at his side.

Nathan inched closer to the body that was sprawled in front of the car, being careful not to disturb anything. It was Trevor Martin, the fourth man in the Escalade, and regret stabbed his heart. It was true Nathan wanted to put the drug dealer in jail, but he never wanted to see him dead.

"Phoned Doc Williams, and he called the medical examiner in Hamilton County. Dr. Edwards is on his way," Mark said when they approached.

"What can you tell me so far?" Alexis said.

Mark nodded toward the teenaged boys standing with three deputies on the far side of the crime scene tape. "The three stooges over there walked all over the crime scene. Doubt we'll get anything from it.

"And I'm not an ME, but it looks like he was facing the person who shot him and fell on his back. Can't know for sure, but it appears to be like the Norman murder—a single gunshot wound to the chest. There also appears to be a note in his shirt pocket and a chess piece in his hand."

Nathan needed to get a look at the note. "Did the boys see anything?"

"They say they didn't, but I'd have trouble believing them even if they said the sun came up in the east. I posted deputies with them to make sure they don't get together and make up a story about what happened or why they were here."

Alexis looked at Nathan. "Would you like to go with me to talk to them?"

Instead of Mark.

"Sounds good."

Nathan took a couple of steps and stopped, turning back to Mark. "Any witnesses? Maybe one of the drivers loading gravel this afternoon?"

"No. The boss shut the operation down at noon for his father's funeral—the father started the business."

Nathan had noticed the gravel yard was empty but figured it was because of the investigation. That did put a different face on the case. He turned and jogged to catch up with Alexis so he could tell her what the K-9 officer had said. "Martin probably knew that and had the boys meet him here instead of at the field house tonight."

"Sounds logical," she said. "I assume we don't let the boys know we're onto them."

"Right."

They approached the boys, who barely looked up from their phones as Alexis and Nathan neared. She dismissed the officers for the time being and turned to the boys. "I hope you're not putting what happened here on social media."

All motion ceased. Ethan Kennedy was the first to speak. "Give us some credit."

"Yeah," Cole and Mason echoed.

"Good. Because I will be looking at your TikTok pages." Alexis took out her notepad. "I understand you boys found the victim. Are you friends with him?"

Again, Ethan took the lead. "No way."

"Why not?" Nathan asked. In spite of their bravado, there were signs of anxiety—Cole flipped his phone front to back, and Mason tapped his fingers against his pant leg. Only Ethan gave no outward sign of unease.

The teen wrinkled his nose. "He's like, old."

Nathan wondered how the teen classified him and Alexis.

"So you three weren't meeting Trevor Martin? You just happened by the gravel pit and found him dead?" He kept his gaze on Ethan. If he hadn't, he would have missed the twitch in his left eye.

"Yeah, that's right." This time Cole spoke up. The way his pitch rose, he would've been better off keeping his mouth shut.

Alexis tapped her pen against the notepad. "How'd you get here?"

For a second none of them spoke, then Mason pointed toward the east side of the property. "Our car is on the other side of the quarry."

"I see." She nodded slowly, then tilted her head. "So, why were you here?"

"We, uh, hang out here sometimes when the trucks aren't rolling in and out—you know, like on Sundays," Ethan said.

"Why?" Alexis seemed genuinely perplexed.

All three boys stiffened. Mason and Cole shifted their gaze to Ethan, who lifted his chin. "No law against it, is there?" he asked.

"It would depend," Nathan said. "If anything went missing while you three were here, alone, you could be people of interest in the case."

Ethan shook his head. "We just come here to shoot my dad's rifle. He got permission from the owner."

"I don't see a gun," Nathan said.

"I don't like your questions," Ethan replied. "Are we under arrest or something?"

Nathan widened his eyes. "Should you be?"

"No." Ethan folded his arms across his chest. "And we're not answering any more questions until I talk to my dad. He's an attorney."

"I know who your dad is," Nathan replied. "And we're not accusing you of anything. So, do you have something to hide?"

"No!" Then Ethan froze as Gem trotted toward them, her head going from side to side, sniffing the air. Mark and another officer followed behind.

The boys shared uneasy glances as the dog neared. Ethan backed up. "Get the dog away from me. I don't like attack dogs."

"You don't have to worry. Gem is a drug dog," Alexis said as the dog sat down in front of the boys and barked. While Mark rewarded Gem with a tug toy, Alexis turned to the officer who accompanied Mark. "Search them for drugs."

"You can't do that!" Ethan yanked out his phone. "I'm calling my dad."

"Tell him to meet you down at the jail complex." Nathan would gladly give the county jurisdiction on this case. He touched Alexis's arm and pointed toward the white van that had just entered the quarry. "I think the ME has arrived."

Alexis nodded and closed her notepad. "Mark, could I have a word with you when you finish here? In private."

"Let's make it now," he said.

She motioned for Nathan to join them as they stepped away from the teens. Alexis squared her shoulders. "I need you to investigate a shooting at my office."

"What?" He frowned, but Nathan couldn't tell if it was from concern or surprise.

Alexis quickly filled her deputy in. "Take Dylan and Taylor when they finish here and see what you can find."

"Do you think it's the person who killed Gina Norman?"

She crossed her arms. "I'm hoping you can tell me."

So was Nathan. Someone was out to kill Alexis, and they had to find out who before the person succeeded.

lex strode toward the crime scene, recognizing the ME and glad Hamilton County had sent Dr. Edwards. Dylan and Taylor had joined him, and as she and Nathan approached, Dylan held open a clear plastic baggie. Edwards used tweezers to move a card from the victim's shirt pocket to the baggie.

"Afternoon, Doc," she said. "Thanks for coming so quickly."

He looked up from his work. "I hope this doesn't get to be a habit," he said dryly.

"Me too."

Dylan sealed the evidence bag and handed it to Alex. "It's another chess move, signed by Phame again."

She studied the chess notation. "I understand this move—it's an opening—but I don't understand the strategy or the point the killer is trying to make. The notes before were clear—one side or the other made a stupid blunder, and the killer was making fun of the police. But this one . . ." She held the note out to Nathan.

He took the baggie. "The move is the Queen's Gambit—White is trying to sacrifice a pawn early to get better winning chances later."

She pictured the moves she was looking at on the chessboard she'd memorized. "Okay . . . got it. So what's the point?"

"It depends on which color the killer is playing—White or Black."

"Why do you say that?"

"If the killer is playing White, it's great if Black takes the pawn because in the next move, White will take out Black's center pawns and that gives White a direct move on the king."

"What if the killer is playing Black?"

"If he takes the White pawn, he won't keep the advantage—he'll lose the center, and keeping the center is the pawn's most important job."

"Would that make Black lose the game?"

"Not necessarily, but it will make it harder for Black to win."

So why would Black take the White pawn? She stared at the ground, trying to make sense of the note. Alex didn't know a lot about the game, but she knew Black didn't have to take the White pawn. So why would he make a move that cost him the center and make defending his king harder? She looked up into Nathan's concerned eyes. "Maybe the challenge is what it's all about for this killer."

"Could be, but what if it has to do with the name the media has given the killer?" He pointed to the card with the chess notation. "That move is called the Queen's Gambit. Maybe it's a copycat killing and the killer thought that move would make it tie in with the other murders better."

"Hey, Alex," Dylan called. "There's another copy of that clipping about Phillip Denton in his pocket."

She half turned as the CSI approached and handed her another baggie with the clipping that she really didn't want to look at again.

"Someone is really trying to tie these last two murders to Phillip Denton," Nathan said.

"Which makes me suspicious that they have nothing to do with him. But why?"

"Could be the Norman murder is from the Queen's Gambit Killer," Nathan said and turned toward the crime scene. "And this is a copycat . . ."

"If that's the case, since the clipping hasn't made it into the media yet, it implicates someone familiar with yesterday's case, like one of our officers."

Both fell silent. Alex didn't want to think that was possible, but . . .

Nathan rubbed his jaw. "Either way, we need to revisit Phillip Denton's shooting."

"Yeah." Like she didn't revisit it every night in her dreams.

f Alexis got any paler, he would be picking her up off the rocky ground.

She took a breath. "Since I don't think the Norman murder is a copycat, it's the only thing that makes sense. We need to find Denton's relatives—if he has any."

"Or friends. Tell me again why the Chattanooga detectives didn't find anyone?"

"His ID, employment records, resume—all turned out to be false. Any inquiries went to a site he controlled."

"And they didn't keep looking?"

Alexis shook her head. "Maybe they didn't see any need after they hit a brick wall. Denton was dead, the bomb case was solved, they had fresh cases to investigate—take your pick." Alexis rested her hand on her holster. "But why kill the drug dealer?"

"I don't know. Serial killers don't have motives that always make sense—just not sure Martin's death is by the serial killer." Nathan reread the chess notation. "But even disregarding this note, I believe the killer is playing Black, and is basically saying we can't catch him, even though he's giving us the advantage. He's getting cocky."

"We keep saying 'he.' Why can't it be a woman?" Alexis asked.

"It could be, but not likely. Women make up a small percentage of serial killers."

"I still don't think we should rule out a woman," Alexis said.

"You don't think the Queen's Gambit Killer did this, then?"

"Not ruling it out completely, but no."

"Okay. That gives us two options. Either the killer followed Trevor Martin here or accompanied him to the quarry. But if the former, how did the killer get close enough to kill him?"

"And if he was meeting the boys here, why would he bring someone with him? We need to trace Martin's activities this morning. See who he met with, who he talked to."

"I need to notify the family of his death first."

Nathan winced. He'd known the Martin family all his life, and while her son was rotten to the core, Mrs. Martin wasn't. Widowed at a young age, she'd worked two jobs to keep food on the table for three boys. "You're right. We can do that on the way back to town."

Then he would get one of his officers to interview the Martin family and the drug dealer's friends as to his whereabouts this morning.

They both turned as Taylor approached, beaming.

"Find something?" Alexis asked.

"Yep. I followed a hunch and looked for signs that someone else had been here. Over near the entrance the rocky ground turns to sand." Taylor held up a branch with brown leaves. "I think someone used this to sweep where they'd walked, obliterating their tracks. It looks like a piece of leather snagged on one of the limbs."

Their first break.

"Tag it," Alexis said. "Then bag it."

While she conferred with her tech, Nathan approached Dr.

Edwards. "Find anything we need to know? Like when he may have died?"

"Livor mortis indicates he's been dead about two hours." He indicated to his assistant to help him turn the body over, and then the doctor lifted the victim's shirt, exposing the faint tinge of blue on the skin. "The blood has just started settling, and that doesn't normally start until two hours after death."

He pulled the shirt down. "But the ground is cold, and that could affect the timing. I won't know for sure until I get him to Chattanooga and conduct the autopsy."

That meant Martin had probably been killed no more than an hour before they arrived.

The attendant rolled a gurney to the front of the victim's car, and the doctor turned to Nathan. "You mind helping?"

"Of course not."

After they loaded the body and the ME drove away, Nathan joined Alexis. The tow truck had arrived to take the vehicle to the impound lot where Dylan and Taylor could conduct a thorough investigation.

"Before you get started on that," Alexis said, talking to her two crime scene investigators, "I need one of you to search the woods next to the walking track and the other to dig out a spent bullet from my bookcase."

Nathan spoke up. "And I think we can get the trajectory of the bullet from where it went through the window."

Dylan crossed his arms. "Something happen we don't know about?"

Alexis nodded grimly. "Someone took a shot at me . . . although it could've been meant for Nathan, but probably not."

"As soon as we get this to the impound lot, we'll start our search." Taylor glanced toward Mark Lassiter, who was helping put the three boys in separate squad cars. "Does Mark know?"

"Yes," Alexis replied. "I've asked him to bring Gem to search the area."

"That'll help," Dylan said.

"See you at the jail."

Nathan walked with her to their vehicles parked outside the gravel pit. "Okay, what're you thinking?"

She didn't immediately respond, instead kept her gaze on the rocky terrain until they were out of the quarry and at their vehicles. "I think with this last note and clipping, we need to sit down and figure out the killer's motive and if we're dealing with one killer or two."

Nathan agreed and opened her car door, not caring whether she liked it or not. Alexis looked as though she could use a little TLC. "I feel like we're in a cat and mouse game, especially if the killer killed Martin and then came to the jail to shoot you. Once your deputies process the crime scene, maybe they'll find something that will point us in the right direction."

"And in the meantime, I need to notify Mrs. Martin that her son is dead." Alexis pressed the start button on the car. "You following me?"

"I know where the Martins live. Why don't I take lead?"

"Because I called the hospital, and Mrs. Martin is at work. Her shift doesn't end until six. Thought I'd go by there and then see to it that she gets home all right."

An hour and a half later, they left a stoic Valerie Martin in her living room, planning a funeral. When they'd questioned her about her son, she claimed she hadn't seen him all day— that he'd been asleep when she left for work at five thirty. She did give them a list of friends to contact.

Nathan looked over the list while Alexis drove him back to the hospital to pick up his vehicle. He'd driven Mrs. Martin's car to her house while she rode with Alexis.

"Recognize any of the names?" Alexis asked.

"Unfortunately. I doubt any of them will be much help in finding his killer, since I doubt they'll give us so much as a 'howdy.'"

At the hospital, Nathan unfastened his seat belt and turned to Alexis. "Might be a good idea to use the sally port when you get to the jail." She opened her mouth, and he held up his hand. "Hear me out."

He figured she would protest driving into the covered pull-through entrance and exit normally used to transfer a prisoner from a vehicle to the jail. "It's a good safety precaution until we catch whoever is trying to kill you."

Her lips compressed into a firm line, then she took a breath. "I don't believe they're trying to kill me, just keep me off guard. Whoever took control of the SUV could've crashed it into a tree or bridge abutment, and either the person is a terrible shot, or they were purposefully missing us both last night and this morning."

"I'll grant you that this person could be toying with you, but you never know when they might decide it's time to get down to business. You'd be an easy target walking from your parking space to the building." He dipped his head toward Alexis. "It's not that much trouble to use the sally port."

She held his gaze, then slowly her shoulders relaxed. "Okay," she muttered. "I don't like it, but neither am I stupid enough to ignore a safety precaution."

"Thank you." Nathan blew out a breath, feeling like he'd fought an epic battle and won.

38

Alex parked in the sally port and texted Mark and the CSI team where to meet her.

"Did they find anything?" Nathan asked when he joined her.

"We'll find out in a minute—they're meeting me in my office."

Neither of them spoke as they walked down the hall to the administrative offices. "Go ahead," she said when they reached the outer office. Then she turned to her secretary. "Any messages?"

"A call from Todd Madden." Marge handed her a Post-it.

"Thank you. Would you call and tell him that I'll be in touch as soon as this meeting is over?" Marge nodded and Alex placed her keys on the desk. "My car is in the sally port. Would you find someone to park it out front?"

Marge picked up the keys. "After what happened earlier, that was wise."

"I suppose." Alex did not like being hovered over, and that's what Nathan's concern felt like. "It's a lot of trouble, though."

"No supposing—just using the good sense God gave you.

202

And getting your SUV moved is a small price to pay for your safety."

"You sound like my grandmother," Alex said with a grin. "I'll be in my office."

She closed the door and scanned the room. A board covered the window, and someone, probably Marge, had swept up the glass. Alex's stomach tightened. Only seconds before the shot was fired, she and Nathan had been standing in front of the window. She pushed the thought away and nodded at Mark. "What did you find?" she asked

"Pretty sure we found the fork in a small tree where the shooter rested his gun," Dylan said.

"Any shell casings?"

"No. We're going to take a metal detector out there and go over the ground again," Mark said as Gem stood and paced the floor by his handler's chair.

Alex had noticed that the dog seemed restless since she entered the room. Now she sniffed the air and trotted to the door and put her nose to the floor then stuck it in the air. "Gem?" Mark said.

The dog barked and pawed the door. "She's alerting to something." Mark opened the door and let Gem out, following her as she bounded to the outer office door and scratched.

Alex had read the reports on Gem. The German shepherd was trained to find people and alert to drugs, like she had at the Martin murder scene. She'd also been trained to detect bombs. But which one was she alerting to now? They followed the dog down the hall to a storage room where Gem lay down beside a box.

"That could be a bomb! I'll clear the building." Nathan ran to the nearest fire alarm and pulled it.

Alex sent Mark and Gem to search the wings holding the prisoners while she called the Chattanooga PD and requested their bomb squad. The dog had cleared the buildings by the time the bomb squad unit arrived.

"Are you going to evacuate the prisoner wings?" Nathan asked as the robot rolled out of the bomb squad van and the operator guided it to the front door of the jail.

"I asked the commander of the bomb squad if we should, and he said to wait. He'll let me know if we should evacuate as soon as the robot x-rays the box."

"You work with him before?"

She nodded as sweat dripped down the side of her face. "He's good."

The minutes ticked off with her mouth getting drier by the second. First the murders and now a bomb threat on her first week as chief deputy. Was it all connected?

"You okay?" Nathan asked.

"About as good as anyone expecting a bomb to explode." She managed a wry grin, then she sobered.

"Most cops never work a bomb investigation." He glanced toward the jail. "Does it seem strange that you've been involved in two cases that deal with bombs?"

Nathan had nailed the thoughts running through her mind. "I've been thinking about that. The newspaper clipping about Phillip Denton connects him with the murders—"

"And he was responsible for the bomb at the mall in Chattanooga. Is there any chance he had a partner?"

"Madden hasn't found any relatives, much less a partner."

Nathan rested his hand on his Glock. "Someone has to know something about him."

"Maybe tomorrow we can check out his neighbors—I never interviewed them, Madden did, and sometimes his attitude can turn people off."

"I scanned what he sent last night, and it didn't look like he got much out of the neighbors. Why don't we plan to talk to the people in Denton's condo complex tomorrow?"

"That sounds good to me."

A tense hour later, the bomb squad commander approached her. "The X-ray shows a detonator and what looks like a stick of dynamite eight inches long and an inch and a quarter in diameter. The robot will bring the box out to the parking lot where we'll disable it."

"Are you certain we don't need to evacuate the prisoners?" She didn't want to risk any lives.

"I'm certain—even if the bomb went off, the amount of explosives the X-ray shows is barely enough to uproot a twelve-inch tree stump."

She caught his gaze and held it. "You're absolutely certain?"

He nodded emphatically.

"Then, let's do it."

"Get everyone backed up at least a thousand feet."

Harvey worked his way toward her as they moved out of range of the blast. "I think we need to evacuate the prisoners," he said, crossing his arms.

Alex cocked her head toward him. Why had he started second-guessing her? And did he not know what a nightmare that would be? "I thought you went home with a migraine."

"I got to feeling better and came back to work."

"I'm glad you're feeling better, but the commander assured me that with the amount of dynamite shown on the X-ray, the prisoners are safe."

"I don't like it."

"It's my call, Harvey."

"Yeah. Well, that's not the way Sheriff Stone would call it."

"And I'm his chief deputy, calling the shots while he's out." Alex clamped her mouth shut and counted to ten to keep from saying more. She might need to count to twenty.

Nathan walked over and stood by Alex. "What's going on?" She shot a glare toward Harvey. "It appears he doesn't agree with me."

"Here it comes," someone yelled.

The robot tracked through the front door of the building with the container, and Alex released a tense breath. At least the building wouldn't be damaged.

Once the robot safely deposited the box in the empty parking lot, the operator remotely removed the top of the box in preparation of blasting it with a high-pressure water hose.

A red flag popped up. But no explosion.

Alex flexed her calves to keep her knees from buckling while a collective sigh went up from the crew gathered around. Then her face heated up. All of this for a fake bomb?

She squared her shoulders and strode to the bomb scene unit commander with Nathan on her heels. The red flag had "BANG" written on it. "Why did Gem alert to it if it's fake?"

The commander used a pen to inspect inside the box. "It's a real stick of dynamite, but the detonator wasn't connected." He handed the box to one of his men, and he bagged it.

Alex blew out a breath. "Thank you for coming."

"No problem. As bombs go, even if it'd been connected there wouldn't have been much damage." He looked past her and held out his hand. "Nathan Landry, I thought that was you."

"You know Nathan?"

"I sure do. Our traveling ball teams have played against each other a time or two."

The two men shook hands, and Nathan asked, "You playing next year?"

"Planning on it."

One of the officers jogged toward them. "What do you have?" the commander asked.

"A chess piece."

A stabbing pain hit Alex's stomach, and she swallowed hard. Another taunt from the killer. She turned slowly, making a 360-degree circle, scanning the area. Was he here now, watching the chaos he'd caused?

What if she wasn't up to catching the killer?

No! She clenched her jaw. This killer *would* make a mistake, and Alex would be there to catch it. It was time to go on the offensive. She stepped forward and held out her hand for the pawn. "Is there a note with it?"

"Didn't see one."

"Would you make sure?" Alex asked.

"I'll check it out and let you know," the commander said.

"He's laughing at us," she said to Nathan once they were alone.

"Yeah." He squeezed her hand. "Don't let him get to you."

"Don't worry, I won't."

"Do you know if Ethan Kennedy and the other two boys were booked for possession of drugs? If they were, I thought I'd see if they would talk to me, then—"

"They're home," Alex said. "Jonathan Kennedy posted bail for them."

His eyes narrowed. "I'm not surprised. I'm going to my office to comb through the Phillip Denton file again."

Her phone chimed with a text. Marge reminding her about the press conference. The time had come and gone while they were dealing with the fake bomb, but the reporters had hung around. She called her secretary. "Tell the reporters I'll meet with them in front of the CJC in five minutes."

Alex hung up and turned to Nathan. "You heard?"

"I was hoping they would leave."

"They didn't, and you wouldn't have either with two murders and a bomb threat. Hang around and back me up, please."

"Always."

In exactly five minutes they walked to the front steps of the jail complex, and first Nathan made a statement about how the city and county were working together to solve the cases, then Alex basically repeated what he'd said. Then she looked into the camera held by one of the Chattanooga reporters. "This is for the Queen's Gambit Killer. You're not as smart as you think. I'm coming after you." Then she turned to the reporters. "Make sure you include this numeric value in your story—0-0. Thank you."

They ignored questions shouted at them as they ducked back inside the building.

Nathan looked over his shoulder. "That wasn't so bad."

"Not much worse than a root canal."

He grunted. "I want to go into Chattanooga tomorrow to check out Phillip Denton's neighbors. Madden may have missed something."

"I'll go with you. Eight?"

"That's good. Don't let this get to you."

"I'm not."

When he left, she texted Harvey and Mark, requesting their presence in her office in half an hour. This was one thing she could take care of today.

A few minutes later the bomb squad commander returned empty-handed. "Sorry. No note."

Alex had almost forgotten he'd gone to look for a note. She wished Nathan had hung around a little longer to give his take on there not being a message. She'd call him.

"Thanks for checking, and thank you for your help," she said. "And when you get back to Chattanooga, would you check the Phillip Denton and mall bomb records and see if anything in this package matches what Denton used?"

"Will do."

"Thanks again, and if you don't need me, I have a meeting with my deputies to get ready for."

He gave her a thumbs-up and started to walk off, then turned around. "You look good," he said, giving her a rare smile. "Being sheriff seems to agree with you."

"You need glasses."

He grinned. "We miss you in Chattanooga, although I can understand why you'd want to stay in Pearl Springs."

"I'm committed here for the next six months. Who knows what will happen after that."

"Just keep something in mind," he said. "Pearl Springs is a nice place to live."

"Right now it's pretty chaotic."

Alex walked to her office and spoke to Marge, then closed the door and sat behind her desk. Alex debated with herself whether to meet with them together or separately and settled on together. She punched the intercom she'd yet to use. "Marge, when Harvey and Mark get here, send them both in."

"They're here."

"Good." They were early. She took a calming breath as the door opened and the two men entered. Harvey was swelled up like a bullfrog, as her grandfather would say. Mark's stance was relaxed, in command, but with a defiant lift of his chin. Alexis motioned to the two chairs she'd placed directly in front of her desk. "Have a seat."

She picked up a notepad and studied the list of topics she wanted to address. Harvey's chair creaked as he shifted.

"Look, Alex, I have work—"

"From here on out, Harvey, it will be Chief Deputy Stone."

"Wha—"

"'Alex' doesn't seem to be working. In fact, nothing about our relationship seems to be working." She kept her voice neutral but firm and then leaned forward. "Until my grandfather returns to this office, I'm in charge. Neither of you have shown me the respect the office demands, and I will not tolerate that. So, you have a choice. Either get on board or resign."

A stunned silence fell on the room.

"But—"

"No buts, Harvey. Even though you're chief of staff, if you remain in that position, you will no longer publicly question my decisions. If you have a problem with something I do, talk to me privately."

She turned to the K-9 officer. "Mark, I know you wanted to be chief deputy if Harvey ever retired, but Sheriff Stone gave that position to me. And while I may be his granddaughter, he believed I am more than qualified to handle the job or he never would have asked me to fill this position. If you want this job, take it up with him when he comes back, but until then, I'm running the show, not you. Or better still, run for sheriff in the next election."

For the first time, Mark spoke up. "Are you going to run for the office next year?"

"That has nothing to do with what we're discussing today." She wasn't about to tell these two her plans.

Alex stood and leveled a hard stare at each man. "If you need time to decide, that means you need to go, and don't let the door hit you on your way out." She let a moment of silence fill the room. "So what will it be, gentlemen?"

39

Nathan sat in his pickup for a minute. He'd passed by Harvey Morgan and Mark Lassiter leaving the jail. Both looked pretty smug. Would they be as smug once Alexis had her talk with them?

A thought popped into his head, one he didn't like and tried to dismiss as he started the motor, but it wouldn't go away. Could Harvey or Mark have planted the fake bomb? Maybe to scare Alexis back to Chattanooga?

Nathan pulled away from the jail, driving on autopilot as thoughts bombarded him. Crazy thoughts—he'd known both of these men all his life. They'd never been anything but upstanding men and pretty good officers.

It wasn't a secret that Mark thought Carson Stone should have picked him as chief deputy or that Harvey was upset that Carson had talked him into taking the chief of staff position that didn't have nearly the power of his old spot. But Harvey was too lazy and Mark needed seasoning. Nathan doubted that Carson explained his reasons for picking Alexis to either of the men. But maybe he should have.

These first two days had proven she was perfect for the job.

Alexis had handled everything thrown at her with the same strength Carson Stone possessed.

What if the killer wasn't the one making the attempts on Alexis's life? Nathan hated to think Harvey or Mark would be that underhanded, but he couldn't dismiss the fact that they both had motive, opportunity, and means.

He wasn't sure about Harvey, but Mark was a computer genius. He could've hacked into Alexis's operating system and taken control of her SUV. And both times they were fired at, the bullets had gone wide or high. That didn't sound like someone trying to kill her, especially an expert marksman like Mark. He'd been a sniper in the service before he became a deputy. And Harvey was no slouch when it came to firearm proficiency.

But would they go so far as to kill Trevor Martin? Or Gina Norman? They knew the details about the murders in Chattanooga, including the notes and pawns left behind, so they could easily copy the serial killer.

Was there a note with the bomb? He pulled into his parking space at the police station and took out his phone. His call went to voice mail, and he left a message for Alexis to call him.

Kayla looked up from her computer when Nathan walked into the lobby. "Peggy gone home?"

"About an hour ago."

She handed him a stack of yellow notes, all neatly squared up. "Those are all about the bomb scare. Is Alex okay?"

Nodding, he flipped through the messages, each stamped with their call time and arranged from first to last. Kayla's work, since Peggy never went to that trouble. He glanced around the office, noting the absence of clutter. In fact, he'd never seen it so neat. "You do this?" He swept his hand around the room.

"You don't like it?"

"Of course I like it. I'm just surprised. Thank you." He turned to enter his office and stopped cold. "My office . . . You didn't—"

She laughed. "Uh, no—I would never go into your office. Should I have?"

"No. Please." Nathan was neat, but nothing like this. And poor Peggy. It would drive her crazy. She wouldn't be able to find anything in the morning.

He stepped inside his office, relieved to find his desk the way he left it—the files from Chattanooga stacked on the right side, and the paperwork he hadn't gotten to before meeting with Alexis in the center.

Nathan settled behind the desk and tackled the paperwork that couldn't wait. When he finished, he sorted through the files until he found the one marked Phillip Denton. He'd just finished when his phone rang. Alexis.

"Everything okay over that way?"

She chuckled. "Better than it was."

"How'd your talk with Harvey and Mark go?"

"All right, I guess. They elected to stay and show me some respect."

"I'm not sure that's good."

"What do you mean?"

He relayed his suspicions to her.

"The same thoughts had crossed my mind, but I'd rather have both men where I can keep a check on their activities than not."

"Good plan. Was there a note with the fake bomb?"

"No. And I've been looking at the pawn the bomber placed in the box. It's like the others, but anyone trying to pull off a copycat would be able to find the same pawns online or at a store in Chattanooga. How about you? Did you learn anything from the files?"

"How good a detective is Todd Madden?"

"I don't know. I've never worked with him—he doesn't like working with women. Why do you ask?"

"The notes on interviews with the neighbors are skimpy. I'll ask him about it in the morning. You still going with me?" Maybe Denton's neighbors would remember something new since the original interviews.

"I'd like to, but after my talk with Harvey and Mark, I'm not sure that would be wise. Let me think about it." Weariness tinged her voice.

"Sure. Just give me a call." He glanced out his window, surprised at how dark it was. What time was it, anyway? Seven? His stomach growled, reminding him he hadn't eaten lunch. He needed to eat before he set up surveillance at the high school. Not that he expected anyone to show up tonight, but he wanted to be there in case they did.

"Hey, you want to grab a burger at Pete's? And then drop by the Kennedy house and see if we can talk to Ethan? Of the three, I figure he's the ringleader."

There was a hesitation on the line. "I don't think so. Gram is saving spaghetti for me, but you're welcome to join me. We can stop by the Kennedys' on the way."

"I thought you'd never ask. Are you leaving now?"

"Yep."

"Meet you at their house."

Nathan stopped by Kayla's desk on his way out to let her know he was leaving for the day. "How late will you be here?" Kayla and Peggy had worked out her schedule, and he didn't remember what it was for today.

"Another hour, then Kelsey is relieving me until midnight. Not sure who takes over after that."

"Call me if you need anything. I'll either be at Jonathan Kennedy's over on Oak Street or at the Stones."

She grinned. "Tell Alex hi for me."

Nathan quickly drove to Jonathan Kennedy's house and waited for Alexis to arrive before he followed her into the

214

circle drive lined with topiary hedges. He climbed out of his truck to find her staring at the two-story antique brick house that Nathan would call a mansion.

"I didn't know attorneys in Pearl Springs made the kind of money to afford a house like this."

"There are a few," he said. "And this is probably the most expensive one in town."

They walked to the front door and rang the bell. "Jonathan," he said, when the attorney opened the door. "Is Ethan here? We'd like to speak with him."

The attorney's lips tightened. "He's here, but you're not talking to him. I filed a motion with the judge to dismiss the drug charges due to unlawful search—you didn't have a search warrant."

Alexis stepped forward. "I don't believe we've met. I'm Alex Stone, Russell County's chief deputy, and there was nothing illegal about the search. Our drug dog alerted to drugs in a public area where your son and his friends had no expectancy of privacy."

Jonathan's eyes narrowed. "We'll see about that."

"We didn't come to discuss the drugs," Nathan said. "We're here to interview Ethan about Trevor Martin's murder."

"You should have called first."

Alexis lifted her chin. "Would you have agreed for us to come if we had?" When he didn't respond right away, she added, "I thought not. Look, we can do this in the privacy of your home or down at the jail. It's up to you. Unless you want to be charged with obstructing justice."

Jonathan Kennedy seemed to be weighing her words. After a minute, he gave them a curt nod and opened the door wider. "Come in, but understand I'll be overseeing the interview."

"Understood," she replied.

Nathan waited until Alexis stepped into the entry hall, and

then he fell in behind her. He'd never been to the attorney's home before and couldn't help but be impressed. The place looked like a spread right out of *Architectural Digest*. Not one thing was out of place. Did anyone even live here?

"Follow me to the den. And the other two boys are here. Their parents have hired me to represent them."

Good, on the one hand—now they wouldn't have to track them down. But bad on the other—the boys wouldn't feel as free to talk, and he'd wanted to interview them separately.

The den looked slightly more homey, with three teenage boys eating pizza and swigging Dr Pepper. While Ethan's plate was almost empty, Cole and Mason had barely touched their slices. Ethan almost choked on the bite he'd just taken when he saw them. His two friends exchanged nervous glances.

Ethan dropped the half-eaten slice of pizza on the plate. "W-what are they doing here?"

"They want to ask you questions about the murder."

"We don't know nothing about that."

His father shot him a sharp glance. "The word is 'anything.' You sound as though you were educated in a barn." He turned to Nathan and Alexis. "Proceed."

Nathan felt like he was in a courtroom, and judging from Alexis's expression, she did too. He sat in a wingback chair across from Ethan while Alexis took one nearer the other two boys. He nodded for her to take charge. He wanted to observe Jonathan, who'd picked up a file and seemed to be absorbed in it.

Alexis took out a notepad. "We're not looking at you as suspects. Neither of us believe you killed Trevor Martin, but you may have seen something that will help us catch his killer. So, I'd like to ask you again what you were doing at the gravel pit."

Tension in the room ratcheted down a notch. Alexis eyed

each teenager, letting her gaze linger long enough to make them uncomfortable. "Which one of you wants to tell me what you were doing at the quarry?"

Cole and Mason looked to Ethan, and he shrugged. "There's nothing to do around here, and we knew they wouldn't be hauling gravel today, so we decided to hang out there."

"How'd you know they weren't working today?"

The three boys exchanged looks, then Mason had a light bulb moment. "I heard my mom telling my dad he needed to go to Mr. Gray's funeral."

She made a note on the pad. "Why weren't you in school?"

Again silence. Nathan was beginning to believe it'd be easier to dig a hole in concrete than get information from the boys. He was about to prod them when Ethan cleared his throat.

"We, uh, skipped a couple of classes." He shot a pointed look at the other two boys before turning to his dad. "It was just study hall."

Alexis scribbled another note. "So you didn't know Trevor Martin would be there."

Ethan swallowed hard then shook his head. "Why would we know that? Barely knew the guy."

Nathan leaned toward the shorter boy. "Do you agree, Cole?"

The boy flinched. "Uh, yeah."

"How about you, Mason?" Nathan asked.

Mason rubbed his nose with the back of his hand and looked everywhere except at Nathan. "Everyone knows who Trevor is—" He winced. "I mean, who he was."

Alexis looked up from her writing. "Is that because he provided you with marijuana and even heroin?"

"No!" Mason's gaze darted toward Ethan with a help-me-out look.

"So you're not aware that he dealt drugs?" Alexis asked.

"And you didn't get those five bags of marijuana we found on each of you from Trevor?"

"No!" Ethan crossed his arms.

Jonathan leaned toward his son, his face turning a dangerous shade of red. "You said you only had a couple of joints on you. What's this about a bag?"

"Five bags," Nathan corrected him.

"I thought you were only going to ask about Trevor." Ethan jutted his chin. "Look, we were just fooling around at the gravel pit. It scared the living daylights out of us when we found him dead."

"I never want to see anything like that again," Cole said.

"Me either." Mason rubbed his hands on his jeans.

"Enough!" Ethan's father stood. "Did you or did you not buy five bags of marijuana from Trevor Martin?" No one jumped in with an answer, and he turned to his son. "I expect an answer."

Ethan rubbed the back of his neck. "We didn't exactly buy it."

"Are you saying he *gave* it to you?"

"No, Mr. Kennedy," Cole said. "We were supposed to deliver it for him but—"

"Shut up!" Ethan fisted his hands.

"You have to be kidding," Jonathan muttered. "Let me get this straight. You were running drugs for Trevor Martin?"

"No," Mason said. "Just marijuana."

Jonathan raised his eyes to the ceiling. "This interview is over."

40

A lex leaned back and took a deep breath. Somehow, they had to get the attorney to let the boys talk. "I would advise against shutting the interview down, Mr. Kennedy. If they help us catch Trevor Martin's killer, it'll go a long way with the judge."

"I want that in writing."

"You know we can't do that," Nathan shot back.

Cole jumped up. "I don't need it in writing. What if whoever killed Trevor saw us there? And . . . and thinks we can identify him? What if he comes after us?"

An uncomfortable silence followed Cole's outburst, and she let it lay in the room for a full minute. Alex turned to the boy she deemed the youngest. "How about you, Mason? How do you feel about this?"

The teen jiggled his knee and wiped his hands on his jeans again. Then he took a breath. "Okay, yeah, we know Trevor . . . or knew him—that's where we got our weed, but we didn't kill him."

Tension eased from Alex's shoulders. "I believe you."

Mason's gaze fastened on Alex like she was his best friend.

Then he slumped back in his chair. "I'll never forget how he looked."

"Did you see anyone when you got to the gravel pit?" Nathan asked.

All three boys shook their heads. "There wasn't nobody there but us," Ethan said. "Whoever killed him was long gone."

So far Alex hadn't mentioned what happened at the field house. Had it only been a day ago? Should've talked to Nathan about whether to bring it up or not. She flipped back through her notes and saw where Taylor had found the branch with a piece of leather glove on it. "Did any of you handle a piece of brush and wipe out your footprints?"

"What do you mean?" Cole asked.

From their blank stares, none of them had been the person who tried to cover up their prints. "It's not important. One more thing. Have any of you ever heard of anyone who goes by Phame—fame spelled with a p-h instead of an f?"

Ethan sucked in a breath, and Nathan said, "How do you know this person?"

The teen dropped his gaze to the floor. "Don't know what you're talking about."

"Look, Ethan, you recognized the name." Alex tapped the notebook. "Tell me what you know, and that information stays here in this room. Otherwise . . ."

"Son," his dad said, "if you have information that will help the police find a killer, tell them."

Ethan chewed his thumbnail.

"We're not making any promises." Nathan placed his hands on his thighs and leaned toward Ethan. "But the more you help us, the more we'll help you."

Ethan continued to stare at the floor, then he raised his head and lifted one shoulder in a small shrug. "I was curious. Kept hearing about the dark web."

Alex strained to hear his words. "Can you speak up?"

He cleared his throat. "I researched how to get on the dark web," he said, louder. "Downloaded Tor and got in. It's not all bad. But I found this site, really I just stumbled on it, and that name you said—Phame, it was on the site. There was one photo that you didn't have to pay for. It was this girl, and you could tell she was scared."

He scrubbed the side of his face. "I'll never forget the caption." Ethan shuddered. "It said, *Alive one minute. Dead the next. Watch the video.*' And it was signed Phame." He palmed his hands. "That's as far as I went. I got out of there and never went back."

For a second Alex focused so hard on wrapping her mind around someone doing something so depraved, she couldn't speak. Killing people and recording it to make money? Who could be so evil? And who would pay for videos like that? That was easy. The world was full of evil people.

She shook away the mental image Ethan had painted. "How do you get to the site?"

He shrugged. "I don't know—like I said, I just stumbled on it. And I promise, I never went back, not even to the dark web."

She had asked Dylan to research Phame's name, but it wouldn't hurt to go behind him. At this point, Alex wasn't sure she trusted anyone other than Nathan. She flipped her notepad to a clean sheet. "Tell me how to access it."

The teen scratched up and down his arm, leaving red marks. "You promise you're going to help us?"

"I'll do everything I can." She glanced toward the boy's father. He looked like someone had punched him in the gut.

Ethan took a deep breath. "First of all, you have to download Tor. I downloaded it to a USB drive instead of my computer. Once I had it opened, I went to the Hidden Wiki and just started scrolling. You can probably put Phame into the search engine and find the site."

She closed her notebook and exchanged glances with Nathan. He barely nodded and they both stood. "I think this will be enough for tonight." Alex held out her hand to Jonathan Kennedy. "Thank you for your help, and Ethan's as well."

"I hope you will pass that along to the judge."

"I will."

"And I will too," Nathan echoed.

Alex palmed her hand. "No need to go with us—I think we can find our way out."

"It's no problem."

He probably didn't trust them to not hang around and see what they could overhear.

At the door, she thanked the attorney again, and he glanced toward the den. "I had no idea . . ."

She'd like to tell him he had a bigger problem than he knew. They would need to sit down with the attorney at some point and explain the fire Ethan was playing with. "We'll talk later."

As they walked to their vehicles, Alex used her fob to unlock her car. "What do you think about their story?"

"I think they're telling the truth to a degree. I never felt like they killed Trevor Martin, and I don't believe they saw the person who did. What they're not telling the truth about is the drugs, and I think we should let Jonathan know what his son is into."

"I agree. I almost asked them about the field house meeting."

"Glad you didn't. It'll be better to save it for another time. Get more leverage that way. Right now, they're stewing about just how much we know, and that'll work in our favor."

She nodded. "Are we going to check out the field house later? I know you don't think they'll meet, but they could."

"I am, but you don't have to come."

"But I want to. After we eat some of Gram's spaghetti."

Her grandmother had kept the dish warm and had made a salad as well. While they were eating, her grandfather came into the kitchen.

"I hear you've had a little excitement today."

"Who told you?"

"A body'd have to be deaf not to hear all the sirens . . . but it was Harvey."

The spaghetti in her stomach turned to stone. She hadn't wanted to tell her grandfather about the meeting with Harvey and Mark just yet, but Harvey had probably mentioned it. "I gave Harvey and Mark an ultimatum after the bomb scare."

"Harvey mentioned something about it. I tried to explain why I wanted you in the chief deputy position, but he still didn't like it." He cocked his head toward her. "I hoped this wouldn't happen, but if he keeps giving you trouble, let him go. Mark too."

"Maybe it won't come to that."

"Tell me about the Martin case."

"Afraid there's not much to tell. No witnesses. A pawn and a chess move like the other Queen's Gambit victims."

Nathan stood and poured a cup of coffee. "Anyone else want more?" Alex shook her head, but Carson held up his cup. Nathan refilled it and sat back down. "Does it seem like something's off about this last murder?"

"What do you mean?" she asked.

"I don't know, just a feeling. Have you gotten a preliminary report from Dylan or Taylor about the note?"

"No. Let me check with them." She excused herself from the table as she took out her phone and punched in her CSI's contact as she walked to the window. When Dylan answered, he said, "I was just going to call you. We used a metal detector looking for shell casings around the tree where your shooter stood. We didn't find any. Evidently the shooter took them with him."

One dead end. "How about the note at the Martin crime scene? Have you processed it yet?"

"Yes. The paper is similar but not an exact match to Gina Norman's."

"Okay." That didn't necessarily mean it wasn't connected to the other murders. Alex had heard a "but" in his voice. "And?"

"While the handwriting does look to be the same, the ink doesn't. I'd feel better sending it to an expert. That's not to say Martin's killer isn't the Queen's Gambit Killer—he could've purposely used a different pen and different paper to mess with our minds."

If they were dealing with a copycat, it was someone who had access to the other notes.

41

Nathan tried to hear Alexis's response as she talked to Dylan, but she'd kept her back to them and her voice low. When she turned around, her frown indicated she didn't like whatever her CSI had to say. She pocketed her phone and walked back to the table.

"What time do you want to be at the high school?"

He checked his watch. Nine. "Anytime. Want to ride with me?"

"Sounds good."

"But you haven't had your dessert yet." Judith pointed to the lemon Bundt cake on the table.

"Maybe when we come back." Alexis kissed her grandmother on the cheek.

Nathan shook hands with Carson, then turned to Judith. "Thanks for dinner," he said. "It was wonderful."

"Anytime, son."

Alexis worried her lip and didn't seem to notice when he opened the passenger door for her. He kept quiet until they pulled out of the drive. "Okay, what did Dylan say?"

She related the details about the ink and paper on the short drive to the high school. Dylan's observations strengthened

Nathan's belief that Martin's shooter wasn't the serial killer but someone familiar to the case.

He didn't say anything until after he parked deep in the row of buses and far enough away from the overhead light to avoid detection. "What did he say about the handwriting?"

"That just looking at it, the note appeared to be written by the same person. He's sending a copy to a handwriting expert." Alexis pressed her fingertips against her closed eyes. "That wasn't all his news. They didn't find any shell casings when they used a metal detector outside my office."

"I didn't figure they would," Nathan said. "You're tired. You shouldn't have come."

"It gave me a chance to talk about the cases." She opened her eyes and gave him a tired smile. "Not something I want to do in front of my grandparents, especially since it's possible one of my grandfather's deputies might be my shooter."

"Do you have anyone in particular in mind?"

"Harvey . . . or Mark . . . or maybe they're working together to get rid of me."

"I have a hard time believing Mark is involved. From what I've gathered, Mark's a straight arrow. All he ever wanted to be was a cop, so I can't see him going against his values."

"Jealousy can make people do strange things. He is really upset that my grandfather didn't choose him to be chief deputy."

"I still don't believe he'd shoot at you." Nathan killed the motor. "Let's go see if our drug dealers come tonight."

An hour and a half later they trudged back to the parking lot. "Why do you suppose they didn't come?" Alexis said as they neared the pickup.

"Any number of reasons. Should've asked the boys to call us if the men from Memphis contacted then."

"I know." Her shoulders cracked as she rolled them.

He opened her door. "I need to get you home since we're going to Chattanooga early tomorrow morning."

"No argument there."

Nathan stilled as the skin on the back of his neck prickled. Someone was watching them.

He eased the door shut and scanned the area as he jogged to the other side of the truck. Nothing moved. The only thing he saw was the shadows of the buses. Was he seeing shooters behind every unidentified object? Didn't matter, he wouldn't rest easy until he got Alexis safely inside her grandparents' house.

Nathan's gaze shifted between the rearview mirror and the side mirror as he drove to the Stones' house. No one followed them, but he couldn't shake his unease. He pulled to the left this time in the circle drive that went around to the back so that the passenger door would be next to the entrance.

"Are you coming in?" she asked

"I didn't get my piece of lemon cake . . ."

That made her laugh. "No, I guess you didn't."

"Just for a minute, though, since we're going to Chattanooga early tomorrow morning." Nathan didn't relax until they were inside the house.

"I saw you watching your mirrors." Alexis cut a generous slice of cake and placed it on a saucer, then licked the icing she'd gotten on her fingers. "No one followed us, did they?"

"No. But they wouldn't have to—everyone knows where you live."

She grinned. "That should make for a restful night."

"Sorry. Will it help to know that Jared is patrolling tonight, and he's supposed to swing by every hour?"

"Yes." She set the piece of cake in front of him. "Would you like a cup of coffee? Or maybe a glass of milk?"

"Neither. In fact, if you have something to put this in, I'll take it with me and let you get to bed."

"You don't have to."

"If I don't, you're going to go to sleep right where you're standing."

"Sorry."

More than anything, he wanted this case to be over. Not knowing who was responsible for the murders and shootings made it impossible to protect her—even if Alexis didn't think she needed protecting.

A strand of her dark red hair had slipped out of the clasp, and he brushed it back. The past month her strength and courage had made him proud. Maybe she didn't need him to protect her, but that didn't keep him from wanting to.

Alexis closed her eyes and leaned into his touch, sending currents of electricity up his arm to his chest. He cupped her face in his hand and ran his thumb along her jaw. He wanted more than anything to take her in his arms and kiss her. It took every ounce of restraint he possessed to instead draw her to his chest. He'd never stopped loving her.

Alexis must have felt his heartbeat. She leaned back, and their gazes collided. Her eyes softened, inviting him to kiss her. Nathan lowered his head until their lips touched. With a moan, she pulled him closer, and he captured her lips, tasting lemon icing.

When he released her, she nestled her head against his chest. For a minute she didn't speak, and he simply held her.

"I'm sorry, I shouldn't have done that," she said softly.

He froze. "What do you mean? You care about me. I know you do."

"Oh yeah." She sighed. "And that's the problem."

"I don't see it as a problem."

"But I'm not staying in Pearl Springs, and falling in love certainly isn't in my plan."

"I don't understand."

She pulled away from him and retreated to the other side of

the kitchen, opening cabinet drawers and closing them. After the third one, she pulled out a pint baggie, put the slice of cake in it, and handed it to him. "You need to leave. I'm too tired to go there tonight."

"You weren't too tired to kiss me."

"That was a mistake." Alexis stared at the floor.

He walked around to where she stood and lifted her chin. Her blue eyes were bright with unshed tears. "Tell me you don't feel the same way I do."

She tried to pull away from him. "I don't know how you feel."

"Yes, you do."

"It won't work. We're too different."

"I don't believe we're that different."

She crossed her arms. "You're not in the plan for my life. I'm going back to Chattanooga and one day I'll become the police commissioner."

He stared at her. "And you wouldn't be happy being the sheriff of Russell County? 'Cause I'm pretty sure you'd get elected if you wanted it."

"Let's not talk about this tonight."

She was right. With everything that had happened the past two days, this wasn't the time to bring up the future. "Okay."

She nodded and held out the cake. "Don't forget this."

The cake was the last thing he wanted, but he took the baggie and walked to the back door. Before he opened it, he turned to Alexis. The tears that rimmed her eyes punched him in the gut. He hadn't intended to make her cry, but maybe her tears meant her heart struggled with that future she had planned out in her head. And that gave him hope.

"Would it make any difference if I said I wanted you to stay . . . for us?" he asked softly.

42

When Nathan left, he took all the air in the kitchen with him. Alex sagged against the table. She'd done the right thing. If she didn't at least try for the commissioner position, she would always yearn for it.

Except she couldn't get his question out of her head. Why did he have to ask her to stay?

It wasn't the first time he'd said she should stay and what a great place Russell County and Pearl Springs were, but this had been different. The words had come from his heart. He wanted her to stay "for us."

Like Alex, Nathan didn't commit lightly, and while he certainly hadn't proposed tonight, she knew him well enough to know a proposal could be a future possibility. A happily ever after. But to get it, why did she have to give up her dream? Did Nathan love her enough to move to Chattanooga?

She braced against the counter. It was more than her mind could handle tonight. And tomorrow?

Tomorrow she was riding into Chattanooga with him to interview Phillip Denton's neighbors. If he still wanted her to go . . . Alex groaned. She put the cover back on the cake plate and flipped off the light switch, knowing thoughts of Nathan would return. Not if she went to work. She could attempt to access the dark web.

In her room, Alex found a USB drive and searched for the Tor browser. As she waited for the results, fatigue wrapped around her like a woolen blanket. She stared at the computer screen as fog filled her brain like she'd just finished a three-hour college exam.

Alex was too tired to think straight tonight. Tomorrow would be soon enough to access the dark web. Still, she hated to give up . . . Maybe Dylan could find the game. She quickly texted him with the name Ethan had mentioned and asked him to research it. Seconds later he replied with "On it." Satisfied, she set her clock for six and crawled under the covers, letting sleep claim her.

When the alarm went off, she silenced it and climbed out of bed. Five hours of tossing and turning, reliving Nathan's kiss, his lips on hers. She knew Nathan—he wouldn't take a back seat to anyone or anything. Was she making a mistake to not even consider living in Pearl Springs? Or even explore the idea with Nathan of him moving to Chattanooga?

She grabbed her phone to check her messages and knocked off a book that hadn't been there yesterday. When she bent over to pick it up, she saw that it was a daily devotional. Her grandmother must have put it there yesterday. Of course it fell open to today's devotion, and Alex's eyes were drawn to the verse Gram had underlined.

Many plans are in a man's heart, but the purpose of the Lord will prevail.

Alex stared at the verse. *Not today.* She pushed the verse away. She had her own plans for her future. The verse didn't mean she was wrong in planning her future. It was her life, after all.

So why couldn't she shake the conviction weighing heavy

on her heart? Maybe because she'd made those plans without even bringing God into the mix? Did she even have to? God wouldn't put this desire to be Chattanooga's police commissioner in her heart if it was wrong. Alex got up and headed into the bathroom to turn on the shower.

Parts of another verse Gram liked to quote when Alex was a teenager popped in her mind. Something about the heart being deceitful. No. Her heart would not lead her astray, and she drowned the thought with the pulsating stream of water from the shower. By the time she had her hair dry and pulled up in a ponytail, she'd succeeded in convincing herself she was on the right track. And now Alex was desperate for coffee and hurried to the kitchen.

"Good mornin', sunshine," Gram said. "How are you this morning?"

That'd been the standard greeting from her grandmother all Alex's life. "I'm good. How about you?"

"I'm walking and talking, so I'm good. Coffee is ready. But as late as you got in, I figured you'd sleep in."

"No time for that. I'm going into Chattanooga with Nathan this morning, and I have a lot to do at the office before we leave." She hoped he still wanted her company.

Alex picked up the coffeepot and had barely gotten some coffee poured into her insulated cup when a text dinged. Her heart leaped into her throat when she saw Nathan's name. With a shaky finger, she opened the text and breathed a sigh of relief. He wanted to know if she was going with him into Chattanooga.

Alex quickly responded.

Yes. What time?

I'll pick you up at eight.

She sent back a thumbs-up emoji before taking her coffee to the table, where she took a tiny sip of the steaming liquid. "Oh, this is so good. I needed it."

"Didn't sleep well?"

Alex took another sip. "Not too well."

"I laid a devotional on your table. Did you get a chance to read any of it this morning?"

"A verse or two." No need to tell Gram it was only because she'd knocked the book off the table, and when she retrieved it, the very verse she didn't want to read stared her in the face. Alex didn't need anything that made her doubt her plan. Not when she was already questioning it herself.

"Which verses did you read?"

Let it go already. Not that she said the words aloud. "Only one, actually—the one about making plans."

"Is that what has you so quiet?"

"I just need a jolt of caffeine." Alex gulped her coffee. "Ow!" She'd forgotten how hot her cup kept liquid.

"How many times have I told you not—"

"—to swig my coffee," Alex finished for her grandmother. She sipped the cold water Gram handed her, soothing her burning throat.

Her grandmother sat in the chair across from her. "I was hoping you'd read that verse today."

Alex braced herself for whatever "advice" Gram was about to give her. "Why?"

The older woman clasped her gnarled hands. "I see you going down the wrong road."

They'd had this conversation before when Alex had dated a man her grandparents didn't approve of. "Don't worry. Nathan and I aren't—"

Gram shook her head. "I'm not talking about you and Nathan. Or at least not exactly."

"Then—"

"I worry that you're focusing too much on this plan of yours to climb the ladder in the police department in Chattanooga."

She'd never told her grandmother about the plan, only Nathan and Gramps, although Alex was pretty sure anyone she worked with in Chattanooga could see her end goal. Not that anyone had ever mentioned it to her.

"What's wrong with it? I'd make a good commissioner."

"Oh, honey, it's not that you wouldn't make a good one, but not if you continue in the direction you're going."

Alex gaped at her grandmother. Gram didn't believe in her?

"The way you're going, you won't make a good sheriff either ... or even chief deputy. You need to make some changes in your lifestyle."

Even though her grandmother's words were gently said, protest swelled inside Alex. Never in a million years would she think her grandmother wouldn't have her back. "What's wrong with my lifestyle? I don't drink or smoke or—"

"Hear me out before you get all upset." Her grandmother took a sip from the cup she'd brought to the table. "You've been so focused on this goal that you've ignored everyone else in your life, including me and your grandfather. You're living a one-dimensional life, and that's not good."

"But—"

"Think about it. Until you were shot and then your grandfather's heart attack, we were lucky to see you once a month." Gram gave her a pointed look. "And how about Nathan? You two were close once, and I think you could be again."

"I don't have time—"

"Are you hearing me? Or is this obsession you have with climbing to the top drowning out my words?"

"I hear you. You're saying I'm not good enough for the job."

"I'm not saying that at all." She gently took Alex's hand. "Not having time for a life outside of your job is what I'm talking about, not that you don't come by it honestly."

"What do you mean?"

Gram raised her brows. "Ask your grandfather what happened when he did that."

Alex frowned. When her grandfather had been filling her in on policy and procedures before she was sworn in, he'd pressed the issue of not making the chief deputy job her life, but he hadn't explained why. "You tell me."

Her grandmother stared down at their clasped hands for a long minute and then took a deep breath. "We almost divorced."

"No." Alex shook her head. They were an advertisement for long marriages. "That would've never happened."

"It could and almost did." Gram released her hand and stood. Then she refilled her coffee cup and held the pot up with a question in her eyes, and Alex shook her head.

"What happened?" She wasn't sure she wanted to know.

Her grandmother sat back down in the chair and sipped the steaming coffee before she set the cup on the table. "When your grandfather first became sheriff, he was so focused on the job, he didn't have time for me or your father. Sometimes I think he worked 24/7. I got tired of never seeing him and told him either find a way to be home more, or I was leaving, and I was taking your father with me."

Alex felt her mouth drop open. "You didn't."

Gram pressed her lips in a straight line and nodded. "I don't like seeing you do the same thing. Just like your grandfather didn't ask for God's input, I imagine you haven't discussed this goal of yours with God, either."

"I don't think I would have this goal if God hadn't given it to me."

"He may have given you the desire to be police commissioner, just like he gave your grandfather his desire to be sheriff, but God doesn't want you to let it consume your life. There has to be a balance, and there will be if you bring him into it."

Alex sighed. After her father died, she'd been cut adrift, wandering aimlessly. It wasn't until she came up with the goal of becoming police commissioner that she found her footing.

"I'd really like to see you and Nathan get together."

Alex jerked her head toward her grandmother. "What?"

"I didn't stutter, girl. Nathan is a good man, and I see the way he looks at you." Her grandmother grinned. "And the way you look at him when you think no one's looking."

"Nathan and I . . . that's not happening."

"Alexis, if you keep running from love, you'll end up all alone." Gram raised her eyebrows as she took a sip of coffee. "You're not still mad at him for beating you out as valedictorian back in high school, are you?"

Gram would remember that. " Of course not."

"You sure?"

"I'm sure." She ran her finger down the metal cup. "It's just . . . I really wanted to go to UC at Irvine, and I blamed him for a long time for not getting in."

"Maybe that wasn't where you were supposed to go to university. It would've been terribly difficult if you'd been in California when your grandfather had his bypass surgery."

As usual her grandmother was right. She also would have missed a couple of really good courses that Irvine didn't have. "Nathan is a good guy, but I don't have time to add a relationship to my life."

"You may want to rethink that, missy. If you don't, one day I fear you will greatly regret it."

43

A t eight fifteen, Nathan slowed and turned into the sheriff department's parking lot. He was running a little late. He'd almost decided to go into Chattanooga by himself to dig into Phillip Denton's background, but he realized that was a mistake—he wanted and needed Alexis with him.

Not only that, he wasn't going to throw away a friendship forged on the elementary school playground—they'd been friends that long.

She met him just inside the entrance. "You're late."

"Good morning to you too. Did someone get up grumpy this morning?"

"No. But *someone* has had a lecture from her grandmother . . . and maybe God."

He bit back a smile. A discussion from God *and* her grandmother could only be good, but now was not the time to ask what it'd been about.

"Can we go? Madden is expecting us in an hour, and we may hit heavy traffic."

"I'm ready whenever you are—my truck is parked in the sally port."

By the time they rolled out of town, the silence in the cab

had grown like an overinflated balloon that threatened to pop any second. Nathan wasn't driving to Chattanooga like this and pulled over on the side of the road.

"Look," he said, turning to Alex. "I'm not sorry about what happened last night, but you are, so I apolo—"

"Stop. I was as much to blame as you were." She blew out a breath and leaned her head against the back of the seat. "Do you think we can forget it ever happened?"

"I don't think so—that was some kiss." Nathan had his share of relationships, and he didn't remember any of the kisses from them. "But we have to go back to where we were before last night, so why don't we put 'us' on a shelf to deal with after we solve this case?"

She raised her head and looked at him. "Can you do that?"

"Sure." No, but neither could they work together with this bomb ticking between them. "Can you?"

"Of course."

Alexis probably could. "Good. It's settled then." After making sure no cars were coming, he pulled back onto the road. "So have you learned anything from Denton's file that Madden sent?"

She took out her iPad. "No. I've only read my report of what happened, but I plan to read the rest on the way."

"Will this be your first time to read the whole thing?"

"Yeah. Every time I asked for it, Madden blew me off. But at least he's getting us a search warrant for Denton's place."

Nathan frowned. "It's an apartment—why hasn't someone rented it?"

"It's actually a condominium, and while it's up for sale, there have been no takers. Something about the deed, or possibly the fact someone died in the condo."

They needed to look into the deed. It was possible they might find a lead to a relative of Denton's at the courthouse.

Might even be able to access their records online if the county had uploaded all their deeds.

"I meant to read Madden's report before now, but I wanted a time where I could process it. Should have looked it over last night."

"You were tired and probably had other things on your mind." He certainly had.

"Yeah . . ." She stared out the window. "Why have two men died from my bullets?"

Her question hung in the air. Nathan had never killed a man and prayed he'd be like most career cops who escaped that fate. "It's not like you had any choice in either situation."

"That's what I keep telling myself, and it can't be undone—I'll have to learn to live with it. Hard to do sometimes when you hear other cops calling you Wyatt Earp."

A slow burn worked its way through Nathan's chest. "Who would do something like that?"

"Madden and his cronies."

Nathan hadn't much liked the detective before this, and now he had even less use for him. "Sorry. I've never understood what makes some people that way. And you'd rather be commissioner over cops like that than be sheriff?"

"Maybe I could make a difference. Besides, I don't see a lot of difference between Madden and Mark and Harvey."

He'd walked into that one. "I'll concede the point. Why isn't Madden meeting us at the condo?"

"Because that would be too simple. And he likes to be in control," she said. "I need to get Denton's report read before we get there."

Nathan had never been around Madden, and from what he'd learned from Alexis, he didn't care to be. Neither of them spoke as the miles rolled away, and traffic picked up as they neared Chattanooga. Twenty minutes later, they pulled into the Chattanooga police headquarters and Alexis put away her iPad.

"You okay?" he said after glancing at her somber face. Reliving that day had to be hard.

"Sure. Let's go see Madden."

After they signed in and received visitor badges, the detective came downstairs and escorted them up to his office. "How do you like being sheriff?" Madden asked as they rode the elevator.

"I'm the chief deputy, not the sheriff."

"With your grandfather out of commission, it's the same thing."

"It's been interesting so far," she replied.

"So I've heard. Why didn't you ever tell us your grandfather was Sheriff Stone?"

"I don't remember 'us' ever having a conversation about anything."

Nathan didn't know how she kept her tone light in view of Madden's condescending air. The elevator stopped, and Madden held the open-door button until they stepped out. "You're not going to find any answers at Denton's condo."

"Won't hurt to see," Alexis said evenly. "You did get me a search warrant?"

"Yes, and you owe me one."

"Sure—if you ever need help from the sheriff's department in Russell County, I'm your person."

"You running for the office next election?"

Nathan had had enough of the detective. "You might want to hope she doesn't."

Madden frowned. "Why's that?"

"I heard a rumor that if she returns, your captain is moving her into homicide—your department can use a good detective like the chief deputy here."

The detective's eye twitched. "We already have a good department." Then he shrugged. "Not saying anything against you, Alex. You'd be a welcome addition."

"Thank you." Her flat tone indicated her skepticism. "What can you tell me about Phillip Denton that I don't already know?"

"There's not much to tell. You know more about him than I do, anyway—you're the one who traced the stolen detonators to him."

"That was a month after he was killed. The detonators had nothing to do with why I went to Denton's condo," she said. "The commander of the task force sent me there because one of Denton's neighbors had reported suspicious activity after the mall bombing."

Alexis's phone chimed. and she stepped away from them. Nathan turned to Madden. "Weren't you on the task force too?"

He nodded. "But we had no idea Phillip Denton was the bomber. Not until Alex investigated a burglary at the excavating company Denton worked for. She tied the missing computers and detonators to him."

According to the information Nathan had compiled in the various reports in Denton's file, the man had been dead a month before the company discovered computers, C-4, detonators, and wiring were missing. Alexis had returned to work after the shooting and was assigned to burglary. She'd made the connection between computers she'd seen at Denton's condo the day he'd been killed and the stolen ones. "Did you ever find the C-4 or detonators?"

Madden shook his head. "Except for the computers and a few wires, none of that stuff was at the condo, but the detonator on the bomb at the mall matched the ones missing from the excavating company."

"Perhaps you should've brought Alexis back on the case."

44

A lex bit back a smile as the three entered Madden's office. Even though she'd stepped away from the two men, she'd overheard their conversation. It warmed her heart for Nathan to defend her skills, but she'd learned when she first came to the Special Investigations Division, Madden's ego was the size of Texas—putting him down wouldn't help their cause.

"Homicide didn't have the information I did, but as soon as they got it, they acted on it," she said, keeping a conciliatory note in her voice. "Before we go to Denton's condo, I need a few minutes to go by and talk to the bomb squad commander—he just texted that the detonator from yesterday looked like the same make as the ones used in the mall bomb and the one that killed a homeless man."

Madden stiffened. "You're kidding."

"Wouldn't kid about something like that." For the first time, the homicide detective seemed interested in them. "If you find a friend or relative of Denton's, I'd appreciate it if you passed the name on to us."

"Of course. Mind if I tag along to the commander's office?"

There was no way to graciously say no. "Sure." She turned to Nathan. "It's on the next floor."

When Madden stopped at the elevator, Nathan said, "One floor? I'm taking the stairs."

Alex grinned at him. "I'll come with you."

When they were in the stairwell, Nathan shook his head. "Is Madden always like that?"

Alex led the way up the stairs. "Pretty much. I think his shoes are too tight," she said over her shoulder.

His chuckle warmed her heart. "That could account for it."

"Thanks for taking up for me back there."

"You did a pretty good job all by yourself."

"I try not to antagonize him too much—he wields a lot of power around here. He and the commissioner are like this." Alex crossed her first two fingers and held them up.

"Gotcha. I'll try to be more careful."

She shrugged. "It works better not to make enemies." They'd reached the next floor, and she smiled as he reached over her shoulder and pulled the door open. "Always the gentleman."

"I try."

"Commander's office is at the end of the hall."

When they arrived, Madden was already there. "Get your exercise?"

The way he said it wasn't a compliment, so she ignored it and hoped Nathan would too. She turned to the man who'd defused the fake bomb yesterday. "So, you think the detonator on the fake bomb was the same kind Denton used?"

"Personally, yes, but we won't know for sure until it's been analyzed." Carl leaned back in his chair. "I've sent it to a lab along with two others for comparison. One from the company that Denton stole his from and what was left of the detonator on the mall bomb after the robot detonated it. Probably won't have an answer for a month or more."

That was too long. With Carl's experience, she had as much confidence in him as a lab. "What's your guess?"

He thought a minute. "I'd be surprised if it's not the same brand as the other two. Do you have any idea where he may have made his bombs? There wasn't anything at the condo."

"Did you search the place yourself?" Nathan asked.

Carl shook his head. "We did a cursory search, but the task force handled the biggest part of the investigation."

Alex shifted her focus to the homicide detective. "Did you see a safe? Or any place he could've hidden his bomb-making material?"

"No."

"You searched for that?" Nathan asked.

Madden stood straighter, hooked his thumbs on his belt. "If there's a safe or anything hidden in that condo, I'll eat my badge."

Nathan turned toward Alex, his eyes twinkling. It was clear he'd love to see that, but then, so would she. "Do you have an explosive detection dog?" she asked abruptly.

Carl nodded. "A Belgian Malinois. We didn't use her yesterday because you have a good explosive detection dog."

"Any chance we could take her and her partner with us to check out the condo?" She turned to the detective. "Unless you used the dog when you searched it?"

Madden's mouth twitched. "That's a pretty good idea. We didn't have Mal then, and Belle, our first explosive dog, was retired."

"I'll call her handler and have him bring the dog to the condo," Carl said. "Probably come myself."

He would be a good buffer. "See you there."

A few minutes later they stepped out into the sunshine. For the first time since this case started, she had hope. Her euphoria lasted until they were a block from Denton's condo.

Nathan pulled into the same spot she and her partner had parked in the last time she was here. Alex climbed out of the truck, her insides cinched so tightly she had trouble breathing. She'd never returned to the site where she'd killed a man.

Alex turned as first Madden, then the K-9 officer pulled into the parking area, followed by Carl Wingate. Didn't any of these people travel together? Alex almost laughed out loud. She'd only been chief deputy three days and already she was thinking about budgets?

"You ready?" Madden asked as he approached.

"As I ever will be." She and Nathan fell in beside the detective as they approached the building that had once been a warehouse. Ten years ago, it'd been converted to expensive condos. "How did Denton afford this place on his salary?"

"Good question, and one we never found the answer to."

"Why not? Everyone leaves a paper trail," Nathan said.

"Not Phillip Denton. My personal theory is he was in WIT-SEC since his paperwork was fake and Phillip Denton didn't exist before five years ago."

"Wait," Alex said. "There's no mention of Denton being in the federal witness protection program in the report."

"I told you, it's my personal theory. I contacted the US Marshals, and they denied having any knowledge of him so I left it out."

"Surely they wouldn't protect a bomber," Alex said.

Madden snorted. "They might, since he was dead and his activities would reflect badly on the Marshals."

It wouldn't be the first time a federal agency covered its rear. Madden took out a key, and Alex stiffened. She'd been so busy talking she hadn't realized they'd reached the common entrance. Her stomach knotted again and a band tightened across her chest.

When she'd been here before, she'd admired the way the renovator kept the integrity of the building and had used part of the ground floor as a courtyard. Today she barely noticed as she followed Madden to the second floor and Denton's condo.

The detective used another key to enter the condo, transporting Alex back to the day she and her partner came to interview Denton . . .

"You don't really think anybody who can afford to live here is a mad bomber, do you?" he said.

She didn't, but one of Phillip Denton's neighbors had reported him for suspicious activity on the hotline created after the mall bombing. "Doesn't matter what we think, the captain told us to check him out."

The ground floor was beautiful, with a courtyard and pathways. They climbed the stairs rather than take the elevator. Denton's condo was the first one they came to.

A TV blared through the door, and Alex rang the bell.

"Go away!"

"Police, Mr. Denton. We need to speak with you."

Silence followed. She ran the bell again, then rapped on the door.

"Go away! Leave me alone!"

"Move out of the way," her partner said.

She waved him off. "Come on, Mr. Denton. We just want to ask you some questions."

Something crashed inside the condo, and she unsnapped the strap on her Glock and her partner kicked in the door. Alex rushed inside to the right. Phillip Denton stood with a gun pointed at the floor.

"Drop it!"

Instead he raised the gun and pointed it at her. She'd fired immediately, hitting him center mass . . .

"You okay?" Nathan asked.

She jumped. "I'm fine."

But every day since she discovered his gun had been unloaded, she'd questioned whether she could've handled the situation differently. Why didn't he drop the gun? Did he forget it wasn't loaded? Or was it like she'd come to believe after they discovered Denton was responsible for the mall bomb—he'd used her to commit suicide, believing she'd come to arrest him for the terrorist attack.

And a month later, Alex made the connection between the stolen items and the bomb found at the mall and Denton.

That's when the small coil of wire CSI had found under his bed became an important piece of evidence. Wire that matched the kind found in the mall bomb.

They never found any other bomb-making materials, making Alex wonder if Denton had a partner. Was that partner now out for revenge?

45

Phame flipped from one Chattanooga TV station to another to catch coverage of the bomb scare in Pearl Springs. A day later and it was still news. There was so much power in being one step ahead of Stone.

By now the newly minted chief deputy had figured out the reference to Phillip—or at least she thought she had. It was all about misdirection. Making everyone think the killings were in revenge for Phillip's death when that was only partially true. There was no way anyone could connect Phame to him. An image of Stone flashed on the TV screen, and Phame paused channel-surfing and leaned forward. When did Stone give a news conference?

"This is for the Queen's Gambit Killer. You're not as smart as you think. I'm coming after you."

Phame's hands curled into tight balls. Who did she think she was? It was time to get the final plan rolling after retrieving a few articles from Phillip's condo.

The chief deputy wouldn't know what hit her.

46

The entryway was dark just like it had been that morning, and Alex fought to not fall back into a flashback. She automatically reached for the light switch and was surprised when light flooded the room. The room looked just like it had the day Denton died. "His stuff is still here?" she said.

"Yeah. Since Denton had no heirs, the property belongs to the state, and no one has gotten around to packing it up. The state turned it over to a real estate company. They keep the power on," Madden said to no one in particular. He turned to Carl. "Why don't we first see what the dog finds?"

Carl had introduced them to the dog's handler when they first arrived, and now he gave the dog the signal to seek explosives. As the Belgian Malinois worked the room, Alex glanced at the bookshelves she remembered seeing while she waited for the CSI team and the medical examiner. Books that included titles written in Latin and French. A brilliant man, evidently. What could have gone so wrong with him? She scanned the titles. *Madame Bovary, Ultricem Angelus, Les Misérables, L'Étranger—*

Mal barked, jerking Alex's attention to the dog.

"Good girl," her handler said and turned to them. "Nothing in here."

He led the dog to the hallway and gave the command to seek. Mal trotted to the master bedroom. Madden shook his head when she didn't alert there. "I didn't think she'd find anything," he said as the dog moved to the other bedroom. "And be prepared when you go in here."

"Whoa!" Alex blinked when she entered the room.

"I told you."

The floor was covered in three-by-three squares of multicolored, geometric carpet that made her dizzy. "Who in the world buys something like this and puts it in a small bedroom?"

Mal barked once and scratched at a center square.

"Maybe someone who makes bombs," Nathan said.

Madden approached the square where Mal alerted.

"Wait! It may be booby-trapped," Carl said. "We have to evacuate the entire block."

The bomb squad commander yanked out his phone and dialed for his team and robot while Madden phoned for backup.

Alex and Nathan took the building they were in and went door-to-door evacuating residents. By the time they had everyone out, the entire block had been evacuated and cordoned off, and the area was swarming with police cars and officers.

While they waited for the robot to x-ray the floor, Alex pulled photos of Denton from her file, and she and Nathan interviewed his neighbors. The neighbors who recognized the photo said he was reclusive. A few said they got weird vibes from him. All in all, no one knew much about him.

Alex had about given up hope that she would come across anyone who had knowledge of Denton as she interviewed the last tenant on his floor of the building, a young woman with her six-month-old baby. Brooke Masters. "Thank you for your time," she said, closing her notebook.

"Sorry I couldn't tell you any more about him." The woman bent over her stroller to tuck in her baby's blanket. When she raised up again, she shivered. "It makes me so mad, just thinking about it. What was Denton thinking, anyway? Having that kind of stuff in the building. We could've all been blown up."

Alex frowned. "How did you know there were explosives?"

Brooke pointed toward the people gathered. "Someone said the bomb dog alerted to explosives in Denton's condo."

The media would take that and run with it. What they wouldn't tell is that C-4 by itself was harmless—it took extreme heat and a shock wave, like the detonators they'd found, but they had to be activated.

"Say, you ought to talk to Ms. Mattie," Brooke said. "She used to talk about him being alone, and sometimes she took him food."

"Ms. Mattie?" Alex said, opening the notebook again. "Do you know her last name?"

"No. I've just always called her Ms. Mattie." Brooke shrugged apologetically. "We're not much on last names around here—I only knew Phillip Denton's last name because . . . well, someone getting killed in your building—you'll remember their last name."

"Can you describe Ms. Mattie?"

"About my height, blue hair . . . old. She lives across from Denton's condo, been here forever, but she does go to visit her sister sometimes and may have been there when he died."

Alex could get her last name from the company that managed the building. "How long have you lived here?"

Brooke tilted her head. "I think I've been here maybe five years. No, my husband and I moved in right after we got married, and that's been six years." She shook her head, bouncing her blond curls. "I can't believe it's been that long."

Fearing Brooke would rattle on, Alex thanked her and scanned the crowd still gathered a safe distance from the building, but didn't see anyone who might fit that description. She turned back to the young mother. "Ms. Mattie—do you see her anywhere?"

"She isn't here. I saw someone pick her up earlier, probably for a doctor's appointment. She has a lot of those." The young mother chuckled. "She'll be so mad to miss all the excitement."

Alex thanked her again. If the older woman lived across from Denton, it wouldn't be any problem to come back and interview her tomorrow.

She caught up with Nathan near the command center talking to the bomb squad commander. "Looks like there was no booby trap in the floor where Mal alerted," he said. "The robot removed the carpeted square and found enough C-4 to take the building down if it had been detonated."

Even knowing it would have been all but impossible for the plastic explosive to go off on its own, Alex still wouldn't want to live in a building with a bunch of it lying around. She turned to Carl. "What do you suppose he was planning to do with all that explosive?"

He shook his head. "Your guess is as good as mine."

"Was there anything in the space that might give us a lead on Denton's family members?" she asked.

"No. But I found a sheet of notepaper that matched the one on yesterday's fake bomb. It was on the kitchen floor, like someone dropped it, and if they did, it had to have been no more than two weeks ago. That's when an agent last showed the condo, and the company assured me no one left paper lying about."

That meant someone had been in the condo recently. Phame? Carl rubbed the back of his neck. "I'm mostly worried that the box of detonators has some missing. What if this Phame person had access to the condo and took some of the C-4 and the detonators?"

The thought made Alex's head hurt. The fake bomb yesterday let them know this Phame knew how to make a bomb. "But whoever made the fake bomb used dynamite, not C-4."

"Not hard to substitute the two. Maybe we'll get lucky and our killer left fingerprints when he got the supplies to make that one."

"I wish." Alex turned as a car pulled to the curb. A silver-haired woman sat in the back. Maybe it was Ms. Mattie.

47

There was something off about this whole bomb deal. A piece of stationery left on the kitchen floor . . .

Nathan looked up. Madden walked toward him. It might be a good time for Nathan to question the detective about the Queen's Gambit victims in Chattanooga. It might help with the investigation in Pearl Springs. So far neither the Russell County deputies nor his detectives had found a connection between Gina Norman and the other victims other than she'd moved from Chattanooga to Pearl Springs and her resemblance to Alexis.

"Learn anything?" Nathan asked when the detective reached him.

"No one I've talked to knew Phillip Denton personally."

"That's been my experience too. What's your take on the explosives?"

Madden shook his head. "I didn't understand the bombing when it happened, and I certainly don't understand what we found today. Never have been able to discover Denton's motive for the bombings, and until we know that, there are no answers."

"Not likely to happen with him dead and no one to ask."

"You got that right. Denton was the reason the city came up with the funding for another explosive detection dog after they retired Belle. Sure would've been nice if we'd had Mal then. I understand there may be missing C-4 and detonators."

"Afraid so." Just what they needed. A serial killer on the loose with bomb material. Nathan scanned the crowd. He imagined Carl would release the building soon and the people could return to their homes.

"Do you think Denton and the Queen's Gambit murders are connected?" Madden asked.

"Alexis said the newspaper clippings found at the crime scenes were about Denton, so that makes me think this Phame we're getting notes from is related to him in some way."

Madden rested his hand on his service gun. "Phame. What kind of name is that?"

"Alexis's CSI thinks it might be a gamer name. Or a hacker," Nathan said. "Have you ever played one of those computer games?"

"Don't have the skills for them, but my kids play all the time," Madden said. "I have to keep after them or they'll spend all their free time on them."

"I don't doubt that. What can you tell me about the Chattanooga victims of the Queen's Gambit Killer?"

"Not a lot on the first three, except the one Alex knew, and not all that much on her. They would've been easy prey for the killer, on the streets like they were. I'm not sure the killer stalked them—could've just happened upon them." He shoved his hands in his jacket pockets. "But the other two . . . all their friends indicated they weren't the type to take up with just anyone. Career women with good jobs. There were witnesses who saw the women leave the Lemon Tree and they were alone. I think the killer followed them home and either forced

255

his way in or the victims recognized the killer and thought he was harmless."

"How about George Smith?" Nathan asked about the man Alexis had shot and killed, the one they'd originally thought was the Queen's Gambit Killer.

"I've written that one off as a copycat. Some of the people he hung around with said he talked about the Queen's Gambit murders all the time."

"Okay, thanks for filling me in."

"Most of it was in the report," he replied.

"But not all of it. I think I'll try and find Alexis."

His phone rang as he walked toward the building and he checked the call. His sergeant. Nathan pressed the answer button. "What do you have, Jared?"

"We got a hit on Gina Norman's prints."

"And?"

"She was arrested for prostitution in Chattanooga."

"You're kidding. Let me call you back." Nathan turned and jogged back to where he'd left Madden standing. When he reached the detective, he said, "Gina Norman is from Chattanooga, and you guys arrested her in the past for prostitution."

Madden frowned. "What are you talking about? Who is Gina Norman?"

"Our victim in Pearl Springs. Didn't you get the case notification? I emailed it to you Monday night."

"Haven't seen it, but I'm juggling five homicides right now, and I could have missed it. Send it again, and I'll check it out." He handed Nathan a card. "Email address is under my phone number."

"Thanks. I'll get my sergeant to send it right away." Nathan started to dial Jared.

Madden cleared his throat. "This Gina Norman. Did she look like Alex?"

Nathan stopped with his finger on the send button. For a second he was in Tom Weaver's rental house staring down at Alexis. No. Not Alexis—Gina. "They looked a lot alike, same build, same color hair, same shape face."

"Bingo. There was a strong resemblance to Alex with the other victims. Maybe not the total package, but in some way each victim reminded me of Alex. I've always believed she's at the core of this crime, and it's connected in some way to Phillip Denton."

"But the killer could've gotten to Alexis early on. Why drag it out?"

Madden scratched his jaw. "I'm not a psychologist, but even I can see the killer wants her to feel pain . . . and guilt. Maybe because he does?"

"What if Denton had a sibling or a child . . . and that relative wanted to get revenge for his death?"

"It's one theory."

"Did you request a DNA workup on Denton for familial matches?"

"I don't know—two and a half years ago it wasn't standard practice to conduct DNA searches like it is now, so it's possible we didn't. I'll have to check."

"Do that and give me a call."

Madden started to walk away and stopped. "You know, I'm certain we would have gotten Denton's DNA, but an analysis probably wasn't performed, budgets being stretched and all. After all, he was dead, and we didn't have enough detectives to cover our caseloads as it was. Still don't." He shrugged. "You know how it is—I had at least five new murder cases before he was even buried."

Nathan nodded sympathetically. He knew exactly what Madden meant even though Pearl Springs didn't have Chattanooga's crime rate. It was all about the lack of manpower.

"Tell you what. I'll submit a request to have that done . . ."

Madden tapped his jaw. "Or better still, I have a friend who owns a lab here in Chattanooga. He's been fooling around with finding relatives through DNA, and he's got a massive database. I could send him Denton's DNA and see if he has any hits for family members."

"That would be great. Any idea how much it would cost?"

"He's trying to build his business, so his prices are good. He might even do it pro bono."

"That'd be great."

There had to be a connection between Alexis, the murders, and Denton. Possibly a brother who wanted revenge? Or maybe there was a child who believed Alexis could have avoided killing Denton. But there was no way she could have known the gun he'd pointed at her wasn't loaded.

48

Alex unhooked her badge as she approached the petite woman who stared at the packages the driver had placed on her Rollator. "Ms. Mattie?" she asked as the car pulled away from the curb.

The silver-haired woman turned to her. "Yes?"

Alex identified herself. "I have a few questions I'd like to ask you."

The older woman stared gravely at her. "You're a police officer?"

"Yes, ma'am."

"Oh, good. You'll help me take my package in, won't you?"

"Yes, ma'am—when they let us in." She took the bags from the Rollator.

Ms. Mattie plopped in the seat. "I've never had a driver that didn't take my bags to the condo. And I didn't tip him, either." Ms. Mattie fanned herself and glanced around. "What did you mean about when they let us in? What's going on? Why is everyone outside the building?"

Alex explained, and the older woman's gray eyes widened again. "Oh my. Poor Phillip."

"So you knew him pretty well?"

"Such a sweet boy. And so misunderstood." Ms. Mattie shook her head. "But that's not what you were asking about. I'm sure I knew him better than anyone around here—no one knows anything about anyone nowadays, which I'm sure you've discovered if you've talked to anyone in the building."

She glanced down the street. When she turned her attention back to Alex, her eyes glistened. "It's not like it was when I was the age of most of these young people around here. Those days everyone helped each other out. Now they call it meddling or being nosy."

"Tell me about Phillip," Alex said, directing the conversation back to her subject.

"He'd had a hard life and had just moved to Chattanooga when I met him almost five years ago."

"Do you know where he came from?"

"He never would discuss that."

"Did he ever talk about his life before he moved here? Did he have family in the area?"

"He wouldn't discuss that either."

"Then how do you know he had a hard life?" Alex forced herself not to sound irritated.

"You could see it in his eyes." Ms. Mattie rubbed her arthritic fingers over the rubber handle grips, lost in thought. Then she took a quick breath. "You asked about family. I think he had a sister. I never saw her, but I know she came sometimes because he would tell me."

If he wasn't fabricating a sibling. "Have you seen or heard anyone at his condo recently?"

"The real estate company sends someone over every couple of weeks to check on the condo."

"Was anyone there this week?"

"Oh yes, and I thought it was odd that someone would come on Sunday," Ms. Mattie said. "I'd never seen this agent before, and when I asked if that's what she was doing in Phillip's condo, she said yes."

Now they were getting somewhere. "Could you describe her?"

The older woman's shoulders sagged. "I don't know . . . it was dark in the hallway, and I don't see as good as I used to."

"Was she tall? Skinny? Blond?" Alex tried not to sound impatient.

"Not tall. And not blond—I know that. It'd been raining, and I *think* she had on one of those . . . you know, a thing that covers you all over . . ."

"A poncho?"

"Yes." She smiled big like Alex had answered the $64,000 question. Then she palmed her hands. "So I couldn't tell if she was skinny or fat."

"Have you seen anyone else over there? Like maybe a man?" Alex thought they were most likely looking at a man being the serial killer or bomb maker.

Ms. Mattie scratched the back of her neck. "I think the last time the real estate company showed it was to a man." She wiggled her brows. "Good lookin' man too."

"Oh? How long ago was this?"

"Not last week, maybe the week before? The agent knocked on my door to ask what my utility bill usually runs. He and the prospective buyer came in while I looked for some of my old bills, and he was so nice. I hope whatever is going on doesn't stop him from buying it."

"Do you know what his name is? Or the real estate agent's?"

"Oh, honey, I don't remember my name half the time, much less someone's name from a week ago."

The real estate company should be able to give her the name. They both turned as Carl approached. "We're about to let everyone back in, if you'd like to get this young lady to her condo first."

"Thanks, I will." She turned to the older woman. "Ms. Mattie . . . what's your last name, anyway?"

"Proctor. Mattie Proctor, but most people call me by my first name."

"It's a pretty name. Let's get you upstairs before it gets crowded."

Alex had to almost jog to keep up with the older woman as she rolled her walker to the elevator. Once inside her condo, she took the packages from Alex and carefully placed them on a mahogany dining room table. The condo was a mirror to Denton's, except Ms. Mattie's was furnished with well-polished antique furniture. "Your place is lovely," Alex said.

"Thank you, dear. The furniture is old, like me, but you can't get pieces like this any longer."

Alex ran her hand over a dark green rocking chair. "This is a Windsor, isn't it?"

"You have a good eye."

"I should. My grandmother dragged me in and out of antique stores when I first went to live with them and would now if I had time." Her phone dinged a text. Nathan. She quickly messaged him where she was and told him to come up.

"Then you probably have an appreciation for old things."

She'd never thought about it, but Alex supposed she did. "I've asked a friend to meet me here. Do you mind?"

"Of course not. I'll put on a kettle and we'll have tea." She pulled out an electric kettle before Alex could tell her they didn't have time for tea.

Ms. Mattie smiled at her. "Phillip was an old soul like you. I guess that's why we clicked." She stared at the kettle, lost in thought. "I was so surprised to learn he was a magician."

"A magician?" The revelation made her forget that she was about to protest that Ms. Mattie wasn't old.

The doorbell rang, and they both turned toward the door. "That must be my friend. I'll get it."

After she let Nathan in, she made the introductions and said, "Ms. Mattie was friends with Phillip Denton. In fact, I think she was his only friend in Chattanooga."

"Oh, I don't know about that," the older woman said from the doorway. "He met someone for lunch almost every week. Never did say who it was, but they must've been friends. Have you talked to that person?"

"Unfortunately, no." Getting information from Ms. Mattie about Denton was like getting water from a rusty pump. It came in drips. "Anything else you can think of?"

Ms. Mattie shifted her eyes to the right. "Have you talked to the friend who dropped by late at night?"

"No. Did you ever see this person?"

"Just from the back." She shrugged. "I suppose it could've been one of his magician buddies."

"Magician?" Nathan looked from Ms. Mattie to Alex.

"Yes." She beamed at him. "My, you are one fine specimen of the male species."

Nathan turned three shades of red, and Alex ducked her head to keep from laughing. "I'm confused," he said. "What about magicians?"

"Oh, I'm sorry," Ms. Mattie said. "I bet you feel like you came in on the middle of a conversation."

This time Alex did laugh. "I think he did, Ms. Mattie."

The older woman frowned then shook it off. "Phillip was a magician. His best trick was sleight of hand. He'd misdirect my attention with his left hand so he could hide something in his right. Got me every time."

Alex's breath caught in her chest. Misdirection. The fake bomb yesterday. Spending today in Chattanooga chasing a ghost . . . While not exactly misdirection, it certainly tied up her time.

49

M isdirection," Nathan repeated, his voice echoing in the stairwell as he followed Alexis down the steps of the condo building.

"Maybe not misdirection, but a waste of time." Alexis hit the exit door, spilling them into the lobby.

"It's only three so not the whole day and not sure it was wasted, anyway." Nathan caught up with her and opened the entrance door. "We're down the street."

He'd moved his truck from the building parking lot after the evacuation. Five minutes later they were headed to I-24. "We got a lot of information today, and a couple of things Madden said gave me ideas."

"I'll take anything."

"We talked about video games, and I think we need to check out that video game on the dark web that Ethan Kennedy mentioned last night. Your CSI is familiar with the dark web, so have Dylan search and see how many sites Phame's name pops up on."

"Good idea. I meant to check it out this morning, but time got away from me. Let me call him." When she had her tech on the phone, she said, "Nathan's with me, so I'm putting you on speaker."

"Good with me," Dylan said.

"Have you had a chance to search the dark web for information on Phame?"

"I've been so busy with these investigations . . . but I have taken a stab or two at it. The problem is, with over a billion files, it's much slower than the regular web. I did look for Phame—you wouldn't believe how many sites came up when I entered the name in DuckDuckGo."

"What's a DuckDuckGo?"

"It's like Google for the dark web. Regular web too. But it's going to take time—a lot of time."

Dylan didn't sound very optimistic. At the US 27 split where traffic had slowed, Nathan took the north leg. He'd be glad to get off the interstate.

"Well, try anyway." Alexis tapped her fingers on her leg. "But wait until I get there—I've never been on that part of the web, and I want to see what it looks like. Meet me at the jail in about an hour."

"Good deal," Dylan said.

Alexis hung up and turned to him. "You said you and Madden talked about a couple of things?"

He nodded. "He's pretty sure they have Denton's DNA, and Madden is checking to see if Chattanooga PD ran a DNA profile on him. If not, he's going to request one, but that will take time we don't have. However, he knows a guy with a lab in Chattanooga with an enormous DNA database—they search out lost relatives through DNA analysis. It's a startup company and their fees are a fraction of the big names. The owner might even do it pro bono."

"In case he doesn't, how much money are we talking about?"

"I looked them up. Probably a couple hundred dollars."

"Do it," Alexis said. "I'll pay for it myself if I have to."

Nathan turned off US 27 onto Tennessee 302 that wound around the mountain to Pearl Springs. "I've been thinking... why did Denton put the bomb at the mall? Why not a concert?"

"I don't know," Alexis said. "And I've thought about it. Maybe he was mad at a particular retailer, or he hated Christians or Jews—it was the start of Passover and the weekend before Easter. Hamilton Place was crowded. The panic that ensued when the bomb was found and the bomb squad got there was bad enough—can you imagine what would have happened if it'd actually gone off?"

"But *why* did he do it?"

"Your guess is as good as mine, but it was probably his second bomb. The bomb squad commander is pretty sure the bomb that killed a homeless man was Denton's, but we'll never know the why since he left nothing behind. Or if he did, we haven't found it yet." She stared out the window a few minutes. "If there is a sibling, what are the chances they are both sociopaths?"

"It's not unheard of." They both fell silent until they rolled into Pearl Springs a little before four.

"Sure hope the killer didn't strike while we were gone," Alexis said softly.

"Me too." He drove through town to the jail and pulled into the sally port for Alexis to get out. Once she was safely inside, Nathan parked beside Dylan's vehicle in the parking lot and jogged to the front door.

He nodded at Marge. "Alexis in her office?"

"With Dylan. She's expecting you, so go on in."

"Thanks." Nathan knocked and entered the room without waiting for an invitation. Dylan sat at the desk in front of the laptop. Nathan had never been on the dark web and was interested in what was there, and what the lure was to so many.

"Do you need to use a different laptop to surf the dark web?" Alexis was asking.

"No. I have the Tor browser downloaded on this USB drive," he said, inserting the drive into a port on the computer. "That way if I need to get out of the browser in a hurry, all I have to do is pull the drive out, and bingo—there's no sign of me anywhere. It's not on my computer and a search engine can't track me."

"Then it sounds like it could be dangerous," Nathan said.

"Anything can be dangerous. That's why it's important to use a USB drive—there are no controls on the dark web—you *can* get hacked, or maybe someone is trying to track you, but if you get out quick enough, that ends the threat."

"You're saying if someone tries to track you on the dark web, they can't?" Nathan knew enough about computers to do his reports and a regular search for information, but he'd never gone beyond that.

"You got it. Tor is what's known as 'the onion router,' meaning information is routed through thousands of layers called relay points."

Alexis bit her bottom lip. "And that's what makes it almost impossible for someone to track you."

Dylan looked away from the computer screen toward them. "Right."

"Exactly what do you do on the dark web?" Alexis asked.

The look he gave her indicated it was none of her business.

"Let me rephrase that. What do most people who aren't looking to do something illegal do on the dark web?"

The CSI tech shrugged. "There are legitimate reasons to be on it. People in Russia, China, places where they monitor your email, that sort of stuff—they talk to people on the dark web and don't have to worry about payback.

"But a lot of people who access the dark web are like me

and play games. There are some great horror games that are 'homemade' that you can't find on the regular web. The ones I've played are fun. You never know what's going to pop up on one of them."

Alexis crossed her arms. "Ethan said he'd found a game that scared him. Something about it saying, 'Alive one minute. Dead the next.' And it had the name Phame attached to it. Do you think you can find that one?"

"After you called, I asked about it in a chat room, and this guy gave me a lead."

"Did you play the game?"

"No. I haven't even been there yet, mainly because he said it takes"—Dylan rubbed his thumb and fingers together—"money to play it. More money than I have."

"Like?"

"A hundred bucks just to get in, and then another hundred to get past the quarter mark. He'd paid the hundred dollars to get in and said it was so scary that he bailed before his time was up. Another person claimed the video showed a couple of photos—in one the person was scared but alive, and in the next one they were dead. And it didn't look like it was fake."

"What's the name of the site?" Nathan asked.

"Frankenstein–Dracula Gambit."

"You're kidding." Nathan turned to Alexis. "It's a famous chess move."

50

Nathan's words chilled Alex to the bone. Could the video game Dylan learned about be the same one Ethan played? Could it have photos of the Queen's Gambit victims? Alex's stomach clenched just thinking about how sick someone had to be to create a game based on real murders. Good thing they hadn't stopped to eat. "How do you pay?"

"The guy said Bitcoin. Another reason I can't play—don't have any."

"Take me to the site," Alexis said.

Dylan turned to look at her. "You sure?"

"I'm sure."

"If you're going to play the video game, you'll need crypto-currency," Nathan said.

Alex shook her head. "Let's look at the site first. See if we can get a lay of the land."

She moved so that Nathan could watch as Dylan accessed the dark web. With a few clicks, he was at the site.

The home page was dark with red and yellow flames across it. A figure stood to one side dressed in black and wearing a white Vendetta mask. A message appeared—the one Ethan had seen—*"Alive one minute. Dead the next."* The message was replaced with a photo that lasted only a blink, but it was long enough for Alex to see that it was a woman. She wasn't sure, but it looked like the third Chattanooga victim. Why hadn't Madden found this site? What else had he missed?

Across the top was a banner that appeared to be a link—*"Enter Phame's Dark Side."* What was below the banner made everything else click into place. *"Ultricem Angelus."*

"Avenging angel?" Nathan said. "Is it possible the killer is a woman?"

"I don't think I've met a woman as bloodthirsty as this killer—not to say they're not out there. But it confirms the Denton connection, and I still believe it's connected to me in some way."

"Why do you say that?" Nathan asked. "I mean, I get the connection to you—I've always said the killer is after you, but how—"

"Denton had several books in his condo, and the title of one was *Ultricem Angelus*. It's about an avenger's quest for justice."

Alex clenched her jaw. This was one sick killer—blaming her for Denton's death and then killing those women because they looked like her. She turned to Dylan. "See if you can get in."

He clicked on the link. *"One hundred dollars in cryptocurrency needed to access this site"* flashed across the screen.

"How do we know we'd get in if we pay the hundred?" Alex asked.

Dylan shrugged. "You don't, but it's probably legit simply because if a player gets in, Phame stands a chance of getting more money from them."

"How do I get cryptocurrency?"

"From sites that are like ATMs, where you can buy Bitcoin using a credit card or PayPal."

"Then get me a hundred dollars in Bitcoin. I'll use my credit card."

"You sure?"

She gave her deputy a curt nod. "I want to see what's on this site."

It was amazing how easy and quick it was to spend a hundred dollars. Dylan returned to Phame's site and paid the money. Immediately a grainy video started and a person's legs and feet appeared.

"Okay," Dylan said. "I see how you play this—it looks like it's story driven. And watch out for shooters—it's probably how the game is scored."

"What do you mean?"

"Some of the most popular video games are shooters—you know, like the shoot-no-shoot targets at the firing range, only these are on the computer, and when you make a mistake you lose points—you have to be fast. I wish I had my gamepad."

"What's that?" Alex asked.

"It's a controller. Makes it easier to play, but we can use your keyboard and track pad, just won't be as fast." He frowned. "That's weird."

"The whole thing is weird," Nathan said.

"That's not what I mean. The character onscreen looks like a real person instead of animated . . ." He shook his head. "Anyway, that person is basically you in the game, and I bet there's a crossroads ahead where you'll have to choose which way to go. Ready to start?"

"I guess."

Dylan clicked on the begin button and the video jumped to life, the steady, slow beat of drums playing as the character walked through fog. The music seemed to thrum in her chest. Sure enough, there was a crossroads and a question flashed on the screen. *"Left, right, or straight ahead?"*

"Which way?" Dylan's hand hovered above the keyboard.

"Does it matter?"

Before he could answer, the drumbeat intensified as a photo flashed on the left side of the screen and quickly faded with the drums. Alex stared at the screen. "Can"—she swallowed hard—"you bring that photo back?"

"I don't see an option for that. What was it? It was so fast I couldn't tell."

Nathan leaned in closer. "It was the first victim of the Queen's Gambit. Courtney Johnson." His voice held a quiver, and she raised her gaze. He was right, and Nathan looked as sick as she felt. This monster had made a video game of his kills.

The question flashed again. "Go left," Alex said.

The player turned and a masked player popped out of a side street with something in his hand. "Shoot!" Alex said.

Dylan pressed the shoot button, and the player dropped. A red message flashed on the screen. "*You killed a man armed with a cell phone. Minus one hundred points.*"

Alex regrouped. *This isn't real. Focus.* Her character traveled down a narrow street and approached a woman standing on the corner. Alex pressed her hand to her mouth. "Can you stop the game? I want a better look at the woman."

"There's no option for that other than to bail."

"Keep going, then." Not that she needed to see the image again. Alex would know the woman she'd mentored anywhere. The woman who was trying to get off the streets. The woman who had been the killer's second victim. Rebecca Daniels.

A cloaked figure jumped out from behind a tall cedar. Alex's reaction was automatic. "Fire!"

Another red message popped up. "*Too slow. Minus a hundred points.*"

What was wrong with her? Phame was playing with her mind. "Keep going."

"It's asking left or right."

"Left again." Her character turned left, and immediately fog filled the screen until the screen went black. A guitar blended in with the steady beat of drums, growing louder until Alex wanted to cover her ears. Suddenly, it stopped, and the screen jumped to life, revealing two doors.

"Which one?" Dylan asked.

"Right." The door opened. "Bail!" Alex closed her eyes, but she couldn't block the last image she had of Rebecca.

"No need," Dylan said. "It's asking for more cryptocurrency."

"I don't need to see more." She pulled off the tie that held her ponytail and shook out her hair. Anything to get a semblance of normal in her mind. "What kind of person is this?"

Dylan swung the chair around to face them. "A crazy person."

"Definitely a sociopath," Nathan said.

A blessed silence filled the room after the reverberating drumbeat. Dylan cleared his throat. "If you don't need me, I have work I need to finish."

"Go." Alex waved him toward the door, then after he left, she walked to the window that had been replaced, careful to stand to the side. Several people were using the walking trail. The sun hung low, sending golden beams through the trees. The scene was normal, the way things were supposed to be.

Not the dark world they'd just left. That world was satanic. Defeated wasn't in her vocabulary, but this . . . this person came close to adding it. *Dear Lord. You have to help us.*

There had to be a way to draw this person out, but for the life of her, she couldn't imagine how. She felt Nathan's presence behind her and leaned her head against his chest as his arms cradled her. Being held by him felt so right. Alex shook the thought away. She didn't have time to fall in love. Except, time or not, Alex feared she already had.

"We'll get him," Nathan whispered against her hair. "He's getting cocky, and he'll make a mistake."

"How do we flush him out? Up until now, he's called all the shots."

"If we had a way to challenge him . . ."

"Yeah," she said softly. "He thinks he can't be caught."

Alex closed her eyes and mentally rehearsed every chess note, then pictured the website and video. And then the name. Phame. The killer had a huge ego. And that was the way to draw him out. She took out her phone and dialed Dylan. "Can you come back for a few minutes? I need your help."

"What are you going to do?" Nathan didn't sound at all happy.

"I want to send a message to Phame and let him know he's not invincible. The best place to do that is either on that website or a forum where Phame hangs out. Dylan will know how to do that."

"I don't like it." He paced in front of her. "I don't like it at all. You're poking the bear, trying to lure Phame into coming after you when you don't have to—he's been after you all along."

"I'm tired of the killer calling the shots, attacking when and where *he* wants to. Up to now, he's faced no pressure, thinking no one knows anything about him. By leaving a message, I'm letting him know I found his website, and I'll find him."

"I still don't like it."

"Do you have a better idea?" She held his gaze. "I'm willing to listen if you do."

He palmed his hands. "You know I don't."

"That's the problem. This is the best idea we've come up with, and you'll just have to have my back."

He sighed. "I've always got your six and you know that," he said softly as Dylan reentered the room.

A warmth spread through her chest that she couldn't have

explained if she wanted to. Still basking in the feeling, she turned to Dylan and told him what she wanted.

Once Dylan was at Phame's site, he searched for a place to leave comments. "It's not an option."

"So how do you suggest that we contact Phame?"

The crime scene tech hesitated. "I've seen that name in a game forum. Not sure it's the same Phame we have here, but I can check."

Alexis crossed her arms. "Do it, and make a copy of the link to the site for me and text it to me."

A few clicks later, they were in what looked like a chat room. Dylan entered Phame into the search box, and messages started popping up. Alex and Nathan leaned in closer to read them. The overriding theme was the game and cryptocurrency.

"When did Phame post his last message?"

Dylan scrolled through the messages that were not in order. "Two days ago."

"So, he checks this site regularly," Alex said. "Can we respond to one of his messages?"

"Yeah—it's like any other chat room. Except here you don't have to give your ID, but you do have to check back for any responses."

"Okay," Alexis said. "Write this: 'You're not as smart as you think you are, and I'm hot on your trail. You're making mistakes, or I wouldn't be on this forum leaving you a message. I will say this for you—I've met a lot of cowards, but you top the list, hiding behind a silly name like Phame.' Sign it 'Alex Stone.'"

51

Once Dylan hit enter, Nathan's stomach clenched. This was a mistake. He felt it in his bones, but Alexis wasn't listening to him. She was so determined to catch this killer that she was willing to risk her own life.

And he understood that. If the roles were reversed, Nathan would do the same thing. He wished he could make that happen—get the killer to come after him. But he wasn't the target. Alexis was. He'd just have to do like he'd promised—watch her back.

"Thanks, Dylan," Alexis said. "I owe you one."

"I don't know. I'm with Nathan—not sure this is a good idea."

"It'll do until we come up with a better one."

He stood. "Do you need me for anything else?"

"No," they both said at the same time and then laughed.

"Oh, wait," Alexis said. "Leave me the bootup for Tor—I want to see if Phame responds to the message."

"Let me copy it to another USB drive." Dylan sat down again and made a copy of the Tor drive. "You remember how to get in?"

Her eyes narrowed and a thin smile played around her lips. "I do know a little bit about computers."

Dylan palmed his hands. "No offense intended."

"None taken, but I'm not as clueless as I look."

When Dylan closed the door behind him, Nathan turned to her. "What time are you leaving?" He warmed under her questioning look. "I'm following you home," he said.

"You don't—"

"Yes, I do. So don't argue with me."

"Then how about now?"

"Perfect." He jingled his keys while he waited for her to slip her computer into a bag, then he opened her door and followed her out.

"Are you going to the field house tonight?" she asked as they walked through Marge's empty office.

"I don't know yet."

"Which means yes, but you don't want me to go with you."

"I didn't say that."

"You didn't have to. You're worried I'll get hurt."

Nathan couldn't very well deny that. He let out an exasperated breath. "Okay. I'm going around ten, and you can tag along if you'd like, but I think it'll be a waste of your time. Mine too, probably, but I want to check it out just in case."

"If no one's there, it'll be perfectly safe."

Was anyplace safe for Alexis? He'd never felt this helpless while protecting someone. "If you're going to the field house with me, we might as well go in one vehicle now."

"Why?"

"It will make things simpler. We pass right by here on the way to the school, and once we're done at the field house, I can drop you off and then follow you home. Does that sound okay?"

"I—never mind. It's fine."

"Good." A few minutes later, he pulled out of the jail complex with Alexis silent in the passenger seat. After a couple of blocks of the silence, he said, "I don't know what you're mad about, and I'm not sure I even want to know. But someone is trying to kill you, and you just poked our number one suspect with a cattle prod. I'm just trying to keep you alive."

"Would you have wanted to follow my grandfather home if he was the one who was being threatened?"

He gripped the steering wheel. "Look, I think you're as capable as any police officer I've ever met, more capable than most, but that doesn't have anything to do with this situation. I can't change that I was raised to protect women. And you are definitely a woman . . . and not just any woman, but the woman I love."

Nathan clamped his mouth shut as his breath froze in his chest. Surely he didn't just say that. If only he had a rewind button. The Stones' drive was just ahead, and he turned on his blinker, the *tick, tick, tick* so loud in the dead silence.

He sneaked a peek at her as he slowed. *Dazed* was the only word he could think of for the way she looked. His phone dinged, breaking the silence. He handed his phone to Alexis.

"Would you please check that for me?" he asked as he turned into the drive and kept to the right.

She tapped the phone. "It's Kayla. You forgot to sign her reference letter, and she wants to email her application today. Said she was leaving, but if you're coming back to the jail right away, she'd wait."

Nathan groaned. He did not want to drive back downtown, but he'd probably blown his shot at dinner. "Tell her I'll swing—"

"Just have her bring it here and you can sign it."

"You sure?"

"Yeah. I'll text her to come, along with our address. That way you won't have to return to town."

Returning to town wasn't the problem. Nathan had been

278

hoping Judith would ask him to dinner again, giving him time with Alexis away from the investigation.

Wait. She'd said *our* address, not *my grandparents'*. That had to be a good thing. Maybe she was changing her mind about Pearl Springs. If that was true, maybe she would change her mind about him. His mood lifted as he parked by the back door, surprised when she didn't immediately open the door.

"Hold on and I'll get your door." Nathan didn't give her a chance to protest and hopped out. He jogged around to the passenger side and opened her door. "Do you mind if I pop in a second and say hi to your grandparents?" He practically ran the words together.

For a second, he thought she was going to roll her eyes. Instead, her mouth twitched. "You wouldn't be angling for an invite to dinner, would you?"

"Maybe."

She raised her head, and their gazes locked, kicking his heart into overdrive.

"Would you mind?"

The hollow in her throat deepened as she swallowed and then licked her lips. "Why did you say you loved me?"

"I didn't mean to say that."

"So, you don't love me?"

"No! I do . . ." Nathan searched for words that wouldn't make everything worse. "I don't want to scare you away or give you an excuse to run."

lex shifted her gaze, trying to regain her equilibrium. Nathan's declaration had not only taken her breath, it had rocked her. She didn't have to ask why he thought she'd run—he evidently had talked to her grandmother. *"If you keep running from love, you'll end up all alone."* Gram's words echoed in her heart.

Alex couldn't help it. At the first sign a relationship was getting serious, she found an excuse to end it, usually with an "It's not you, it's me" speech. Which was basically true.

Nathan cupped her chin, turning her to face him again. "You okay? I didn't mean to upset you."

"You didn't." She shivered, for once thankful for the bulky body armor. "It's just—" The phone chimed again, releasing the tension in her body. "You better see what that is."

He seemed as relieved as she was. "Kayla is stopping by here. ETA is five minutes."

"Tell her to come around to the back and come in. I'd like to introduce her to my grandparents." Alex led the way into the house through the mudroom and into the kitchen. "Lasagna smells good, and is that garlic bread I smell?"

Her grandmother turned from where she stood at the stove. "It is. Where's Nathan?"

"Should be right behind me. He had a text to answer first."

"I'm here," Nathan said as he entered the kitchen and took a deep breath. "Something smells good."

"You don't have to butter me up. I already have a plate set for you."

Nathan hugged Gram. "Thank you. I get tired of my own cooking."

Alex gaped at him. "You cook?"

"I'd starve if I didn't."

"I figured you were a regular at Pete's."

"Uh-uh. I want to live long enough to enjoy my old age," he said. "But if he ever has something besides hamburgers and country-fried steak and fried okra and everything else fried, I might reconsider."

Gram cackled. "Ethel's been trying to get him to do that for the last ten years. I'm worried about you if you seriously think Pete Harrel will ever have a healthy menu."

"He may. I heard him tell somebody he was going to have stent surgery next week."

"Doesn't surprise me—he's probably responsible for half the heart attacks in the county." She turned to Alex. "Would you get your grandfather? He's in his office."

"Yes, ma'am. Oh, and there's a young woman stopping by in a few minutes," she said.

"I'll set another plate."

"She may not have time to stay and eat." Although once Kayla smelled the lasagna, she might make the time.

Smiling, Alex walked down the dimly lit hallway to her grandfather's office. For a few minutes, she'd been able to put Phame's website and video out of her mind. But this home had always been her safe haven, probably because her grandparents had always encouraged her, even when Alex feared she'd fail. Gram always said a person learned more from their failures than successes.

She knocked on Gramps's door. "Dinner is ready."

He looked up from his desk stacked with papers, books, and what looked like junk. "Good. I'm tired of looking at this mess."

"What's going on? Your desk has always been super neat."

"Getting rid of case history files, notes, that sort of thing."

She detected sadness in his voice and searched for something to say. "Don't get rid of too much. I might need some of those case histories."

"Really?"

"You bet. If I were sheriff, I'd hire you as a consultant as soon as you were feeling up to it."

"There would be no money in your budget for that," he said dryly as he stood and slowly walked to the door.

"Then you can volunteer. Did you finish reading over the files on the Chattanooga murders that I printed out for you?"

He sighed. "Afraid not. I start reading and everything blurs. Just not up to much yet."

"You'll get there. Where's your walker?"

"Graduated."

"Really? Does Gram know?"

"She's my wife, not my warden."

Alex linked her arm in his, more to keep him steady than anything else. "It's your funeral."

"Hmph. That's hardly the thing to say to someone who had one foot in the grave and the other on a banana peel a month ago."

"You know what I mean."

He sighed. "Yeah. The walker is just inside our bedroom."

"Good. Hold on a sec and I'll get it." She stepped inside

the bedroom and rolled the walker out. It was similar to Ms. Mattie's only the handles were much higher. She handed it off to him. "When did you get this one?"

"They delivered Fancy Dancy yesterday. At least I don't have to bend over to push it."

"Fancy Dancy?"

"Got to call it something."

She laughed, contentment settling on her again. She'd been really worried about him, but anyone who could grumble like this and name his walker was going to be okay. Voices reached them as they neared the kitchen. Kayla had arrived.

Gramps turned to Alex. "Who's that?"

"A friend I want you to meet. She's the one who saved my life the night I was shot."

"Good. I want to thank her, then I have some questions for your rescuer."

She cocked her head. "I don't understand. Why?"

He smiled patiently. "From what I understand, this Kayla being there was a coincidence, and you know how I feel about that. There's—"

"No such thing as a coincidence," Alex finished for him. "But this time there is—her tire light came on. Come meet her and you'll see."

She pushed the kitchen door open and then stood to the side and let her grandfather roll his fancy walker in first.

"There you are," Gram said. "Carson, this is Kayla."

He rolled close enough to extend his hand. "I want to thank you for what you did."

A blush rose in Kayla's face as she took his hand. "I didn't do much."

"But you did. Most people would have run the other way. Where did you learn martial arts?"

A shadow briefly crossed Kayla's eyes, disappearing as her

face brightened. "I've been involved in it forever, it seems. I was taking Taekwondo lessons by the time I was four. It's almost second nature to me."

"Enough talk," Gram said. "Kayla's staying for dinner. So let's eat."

It didn't surprise Alex that Kayla accepted Gram's invitation to join them. Most people who dropped by around dinnertime ate with them. Nathan sat in the chair beside Alex, and Gram had Kayla sit to Gramps's right.

"Nathan tells me you're working for him now," Gramps said.

"Yes, and he's written me a letter of recommendation to get into a select criminal justice program. That's why I stopped by—he forgot to sign it. All I have to do now is scan it into my computer and send in the application."

Gram tilted her head toward the girl. "So you want to be a police officer?"

"I think so. This class should help me decide." She picked up the tall iced-tea glass and took a sip.

Alex forked a bite of lasagna. "Which school did you decide on?"

"Chatt State."

"And she'll have the same professor I had for that class," Nathan said. "He's really good."

Gramps leaned forward. "Where'd you grow up?"

Alex almost missed the slight stiffening of Kayla's shoulders. "Chattanooga."

"Really." He frowned. "I thought I detected a stronger Southern accent than most people who grow up around here."

She scratched her nose with the back of her hand, then shrugged. "Maybe it's because my mom grew up around Atlanta. How about you? Have you always lived in Pearl Springs?"

"We surely have," Gram said. "And Carson, I want you to

stop grilling this girl." She turned to Kayla with an apologetic shake of her head. "He's so used to interrogating people, he slips into that mode when he shouldn't."

What was going on with her grandfather? If Gram hadn't stepped in, Alex would have.

"No problem." Kayla took a bite of the lasagna. "This is so good. Do you have a recipe?"

"I'm afraid it's all up here." Gram tapped her temple. "A little bit of this and a little bit of that."

"Figures. Maybe I could come watch you the next time you make it."

"I'd love that."

Gramps cleared his throat. "At the risk of receiving my wife's ire, may I ask why you relocated to Pearl Springs?"

53

can answer that one," Alex said. "Nathan offered her a job."

When her grandfather shifted his gaze to Nathan, he shrugged. "I needed a part-time dispatcher when Jimmy Arnold left."

"Well, good. I'm glad it worked out. One more question and I'm done." He waved his fork between Alex and Kayla. "How did you two meet?"

She'd have to explain later to Kayla that her grandfather wasn't singling her out—he'd been this way ever since Alex could remember, even when she was a teenager. Especially when she was a teenager. "We met when I was on an undercover job. She was a waitress at the Lemon Tree."

"I quit right after that," Kayla said. "And decided to go back to college."

"Wise decision," Gramps said.

They all fell silent as they finished the salad and lasagna and then Gramps looked around. "Any more of that lemon cake left?"

Gram stood. "You can have one tiny piece."

"But—"

"No buts. Your doctor said your triglycerides were high and you had to cut back on your carbs."

"So that's why my portion of lasagna was so small," he grumbled.

"Yes. Now do you want a small piece of cake or not?" When he nodded, she turned to the others. "Anyone else?"

Kayla and Nathan took a piece, but Alex held up her hand. "I'm good. I just remembered I want to go over a file at my office. And then Nathan and I have a couple of things to check on. I won't be home until probably around eleven."

"It's cold out. Want to take a thermos of hot cocoa with you?" Gram asked.

She must really look tired for Gram to make cocoa—it was her "it will fix everything" remedy. Alex shook her head. "I may make some when we get back."

"I need to be going too," Kayla said. "But I want to help with the dishes."

Gramps waved her off. "I'll help with the dishes. You run along."

Alex stared at her grandfather. He had never willingly helped with the dishes before.

Alex followed Nathan out the back door to his pickup.

"Great dinner," he said.

"Kayla seemed to enjoy it too. I hope Gramps didn't offend her."

"He was just being Sheriff Stone."

"I'll have to let her know he wasn't singling her out," she said with a laugh as Nathan opened her door. She was getting used to his chivalry.

He turned to her as they pulled out of the drive. "Your office first?"

She nodded. "I want to check for a response on the dark web but not from home. And I was thinking about playing more of the video game, see if there are more photos of the victims."

"Good thinking."

287

Alex spoke to the night dispatcher as they entered the building. It was quiet and she hoped it stayed that way. It didn't take long to boot up the dark web, and not only was there no message in the chat room, but the website with the video game was gone. Alex leaned back in her chair and blew out a breath. "Phame has gone to ground."

At least Nathan didn't point out the obvious—it was her fault. "But probably not for long—he was making too much money on the game. He'll surface again." He stood. "Why don't we check out the field house, and then I'll take you home? You need a good night's rest."

"I won't argue with you there."

An hour later, Nathan pulled behind her grandparents' house. "I didn't figure anyone would be there tonight. You could've stayed home."

She ignored his comment. "Have you gotten any hits on the photos you took Monday night of those men in the Escalade?"

"Haven't heard from the Drug Enforcement Agency. The Hamilton County sheriff's department says they're not in their database, and I'm still waiting on the Chatt PD. Whoever they are, evidently they've been keeping a low profile."

She yawned and unbuckled her seat belt. "It's been a long day."

"Hold up a minute so I can clear your bedroom."

Alex half saluted. "Yes, sir. Be sure to enter the code for the alarm or one of your officers will end up on our doorstep."

"The code is your birthday, right?"

She nodded, surprised he'd remembered.

A minute later, he came back to the truck and opened her door and ushered her into the house. "All good—except I need to talk to Carson—the alarm wasn't set."

"You're kidding." She thought a minute. "Maybe because they knew we weren't going to be gone long."

"Do they always set it?"

"Not during the day—it's too much trouble for Gram since she's in and out the back door all the time."

He nodded. "She left a note in your room saying there's a cup of hot cocoa in the microwave for you to reheat."

"Gram only makes me cocoa when she thinks I'm really tired. I must have looked awful earlier."

"You never look awful," he teased. "But you do have raccoon eyes."

"Thanks. You're about as subtle as my grandfather."

He laughed. "Your grandfather isn't subtle."

"Bingo. He was terrible when I was a teenager."

"True, he did always vet your friends."

"I don't remember him ever treating you that way."

"That's because we've been friends since fifth grade. I was too young for him to put under the bright light."

Alex looked up at him. "We have been friends a long time, haven't we?" Then she yawned again.

"And I'm going. You're dead on your feet. See you in the morning? Maybe grab a cup of coffee after briefing our officers?"

"Sounds good. I'd like to go over some of what we learned yesterday."

"Be sure to set the alarm."

After Nathan left she did as he'd said as thoughts of the video and photos of the victims tensed her body again. Alex flipped on the shower, turning the handle as hot as she could stand, and let the hot streams from the jets pound her neck and shoulders.

Ten minutes later, she slipped on her leggings and pajama top and climbed into bed, almost knocking over the mug and Bible that hadn't been there earlier. Alex smiled. Gram must have warmed the cocoa and brought it to her bedroom while she was in the shower. And obviously placed the Bible there too as a hint.

She didn't need the warm drink to go to sleep, but her grandmother had gone to the trouble of making it—she'd be disappointed if Alex didn't drink it. And if she didn't read at least a chapter in the Bible . . .

She sat up in bed and sipped the hot liquid as she made out a schedule for the morning. Alex frowned. Her grandmother must've changed cocoa brands. It wasn't bad, but it certainly wasn't up to Gram's usual hot chocolate. She drank half of it and set the cup aside. In the morning Alex needed to tell Gram if she'd changed brands, to change back. Then she picked up the Bible and opened it where her grandmother had placed the bookmark.

Fifteen minutes later, Alex's eyes blurred, and she reached to turn off the lamp, fumbling with the button, when the floor outside her door creaked. Her grandmother? Maybe something was wrong with Gramps.

Alex threw back the covers and stumbled as she climbed out of bed. What was wrong with her? Fog filled her mind. She turned as her hall door opened. "Gram?"

54

A jackhammer pounded in Alex's head. Moldy air clogged her nose.

Where was she? Somewhere so dark she could feel the blackness. And the damp. The smell was vaguely familiar, like she'd smelled it before but a long time ago.

A memory broke through the mush in her brain. A cave. She was deep in the ground. *Why?* If only her head didn't feel like it was going to explode, she could pull it all together. Alex moved only to have something hard poke her back, and she squirmed away from it, immediately wishing she hadn't moved her head.

"Ah, you're awake. Good. I was afraid I'd have to leave without saying goodbye."

She peered into the darkness, searching for movement as her muddled brain processed the distorted words. "Who are you? What do you want?"

"Think about it."

Again the delay in figuring out the words. She'd heard speech like that before. A Halloween party. The DJ used a voice changer, and his voice sounded the same way. She took a deep breath, and her head settled down a little.

Phame. It couldn't be anyone else.

"You really shouldn't poke the bear."

Poke the bear. She'd heard someone say that recently . . . Her breath caught in her chest. Nathan. In her office. He'd warned her not to antagonize the serial killer. She hadn't listened. Now she was in this mess because of her pride. She'd just had to let Phame know she'd found the website.

Alex tried to sit up only to realize her hands were tied behind her back. Her heart thrashed in her chest.

"I have to leave now."

No! Being with a serial killer was better than being all alone in a cave with her hands tied. "At least give me a fighting chance. Untie my hands."

"If you're half as smart as you think you are, you can get out with your hands tied behind you. And if you're not, then you die here." Even through the voice changer, the words were matter of fact.

"Why are you doing this?"

"To let you know you'll never catch me. And to make you pay."

"Why? And pay for what?"

"Think about it."

The bomber. "Phillip Denton was a murderer." So stupid, taunting a serial killer.

"Just think—people died because of you. And someone you love is going to die."

Alex was still processing the words when light filled the cavern, blinding her. The pain in her head went off the charts. By the time her eyes refocused, her captor was gone, and so was the light.

Seconds later, the sound of someone scrambling over rocks faded, and quiet wrapped around her like a straitjacket. Even if she got her hands free, she had no light. She would be crawling blind. Alex had been in caves before, but never without a light. What if she got turned around and went deeper into the cave? Or went over a sheer drop-off into a pool of water thirty feet below? Or a drop-off with no water . . . Either way was a sure death.

A sense of loss filled her thoughts. She had so many regrets.

Nathan. Why hadn't she told him she loved him? Even worse, why had she told him she didn't have time to fall in love?

He loved her, had even said the words—not that he had to, she saw it in his eyes. Had he ever seen Alex's love for him in her eyes?

Pretty sure not—she was too careful to not show her feelings. And how stupid was that? He'd been her hero since he'd tackled the boy bullying her the first day she attended Pearl Springs Elementary.

And her grandparents. If she died, what would it do to them? What if Gramps had another heart attack?

Resolve filled her. Dying wasn't an option. Alex wiggled and kicked her feet, trying to get on her side. It wasn't working, and she fell back against the stony cave floor.

Angry, she kicked again, sending rocks skittering. In the dead silence that followed, the faint plop of the rocks hitting water below echoed in the cave.

Alex stilled. She was at the edge of a drop-off, maybe only inches away. Her heartbeat filled her chest, beating so fast she couldn't count it. And her breathing tried to match it until she was panting. A cold wind moaned through the cave, chilling Alex, or maybe it was fear making her cold. Shaking started in her legs and spread to her chest and arms.

"Stop it!" The scream echoed on and on, startling her out of the panic attack. She said it again. "Just stop it!"

She was not a quitter. Alex forced herself to breathe slower and deeper until her body calmed. *Take it one step at a time.*

How many times had she heard her grandmother say that? Alex needed to organize her thoughts. If only her head didn't hurt so much. She pushed past the pain.

First, she had to get her hands loose. They were so numb, she couldn't tell what the kidnapper used for binding. If it was rope, maybe she could use the sharp limestone rock that'd poked her in the back to cut it. Being careful to not move one way or the other, she found the rock, but it was useless against her restraints.

She didn't think her wrists were bound with wire, but maybe plastic . . . like a zip tie? She'd done exercises to get out of zip tie restraints, but to execute the move would require her to stand. Which at the present moment seemed impossible to do.

Was she going to die here? For once, had she met a problem she couldn't solve? *Lord, help me.*

Shame burned in her chest. Praying should've been the first thing she thought of, not the last. Why did she have to come to the end of herself to realize she wasn't God? Her plans might sound good, but right now they were futile.

Rest.

Alex stilled. She didn't want to rest. She wanted out of this cave. Besides, the thought could have come from anywhere. Like her tired body. Her mouth was so dry . . . Maybe she would rest just a minute.

Alex jerked awake. There'd been a noise. She strained in the quiet to hear, but only the deafening silence surrounded her. She didn't know how long she'd slept, but her head felt better. Maybe she could get into a sitting position.

With a grunt, she rolled over on her side and used her elbow to push herself up. Why hadn't she been able to do that earlier? Didn't matter. She was sitting now. "Thank you, Lord."

But could she stand? Once upon a time, Alex could stand

from a sitting position. But it'd been at least twenty years since those days.

She thanked God that her kidnapper hadn't tied her feet together and managed to get cross-legged. Then she rocked her body forward until her weight was over her feet. Sweat ran down the side of her face as she used the strength in her legs to slowly rise to a standing position.

Her legs trembled, and she feared they wouldn't hold her up. Alex took deep breaths and flexed her calves, sending blood to her lower extremities. She could do it. Alex kept telling herself that. After a few minutes, her legs grew stronger. Now to break the zip ties—if it was indeed the plastic binding.

If only she could see. This must be how it felt to be blind. Alex was afraid to move one way or the other—the drop-off could be inches away. *Focus on getting the ties off.*

At the police academy, they'd practiced breaking the zip ties during after-hours. At the time it'd been fun. Not at all today. Alex mentally rehearsed the move, and rehearsed it again. Then she bent over and took a breath and raised her arms as high as she could before she brought her wrists down against her hip.

Nothing except pain in her wrists. She forced her arms higher and then slammed her wrists against her body again. This time the restraints broke loose. She dropped to her knees on the cave floor, and pain shot all the way to her hip. When that pain eased, she was left with a throbbing wrist.

Alex curled her left hand, and pain shot up her arm. No doubt about it, she'd broken her wrist. Too late to worry about it now. Gingerly she felt the cave floor with her good hand, first to the right side, then the left where her fingers touched air. Alex jerked her hand back. She'd been right—the edge was mere inches away.

A strand of hair tickled her nose, and she tried to blow it

away. When that didn't work, she found it and tucked it behind her ear and then carefully explored the ground in front of her. Solid. Alex slowly crawled, feeling her way with each move.

What if it was the wrong direction? The thought froze her. Earlier there'd been wind, and it should come from the mouth of the cave. But which direction had it come from? Maybe if she raised up . . . She did, and pain rocked her head when it collided with rock.

Don't give up. Alex repeated the words and imagined other caves she'd been in. Often they'd crawled in through a narrow opening that sometimes opened into a cavern. Had to be what happened this time. If it was, how did Phame get her in here? He couldn't have carried her—not enough room.

Somehow, Alex had willingly come to the cave with him.

55

athan's phone broke into his deep sleep. He rolled over and glanced at the alarm clock. Six? He'd overslept. Still groggy, he grabbed the ringing phone. "Landry," he growled.

"Nathan, it's Carson Stone. I, uh, don't know how to ask this, but is Alex there?"

"What?" Nathan raked his fingers through his hair. Carson wasn't making sense. "Why would she be here?"

"She isn't home and she's not at the office. If she's not there . . ."

"I'm on my way." Nathan hopped out of bed and splashed cold water on his face. Where could Alexis be? After he pulled on khakis and a white shirt, he grabbed his phone and checked the app he'd put on her cell. It showed she was at her grandparents'.

Alex would not have willingly gone anywhere without her phone.

Ten minutes later he pulled into the Stones' drive, expecting to see deputies' vehicles, but the drive was empty. He pulled to the back of the house, and Carson met him at the back door using the fancy walker to lean on. Judith stood behind him.

The former sheriff's gray color worried Nathan. "Have you heard from her?"

Carson shook his head. "And I'm worried."

Nathan could see that. "Mind if I search her bedroom? I put an app on her phone and it shows it's here at the house."

"Look all you want."

The Stones followed him down the hallway to Alexis's suite. "Wait out here. Just in case this becomes a crime scene—you don't want to contaminate it."

Carson gave him a solemn nod. "How could anyone get in?"

"Was the alarm set?"

Judith pressed her hand to her neck. "I-I'm not sure I set it after Kayla left . . ."

"It wasn't set when we returned."

"All of this is my fault," she said with a moan.

He didn't want to scare them by saying a security system probably wouldn't stop Phame. He turned to Judith. "There was a note by her bed, saying you had a mug of hot cocoa in the microwave . . ."

Judith nodded. "I put the note there. I knew she'd be tired when she came in."

"Did she get the cocoa?"

"The mug wasn't in the microwave this morning, so I guess she did."

"I'll check and see if it's in her room."

"It's her favorite—she picked it up at a pottery shop in the Smokies—cobalt blue on the bottom with white at the top."

Nathan pulled on a pair of nitrile gloves and a set of shoe booties he'd grabbed from his truck.

The bedroom looked exactly as it had last night, except her bed had been turned down. It didn't look as though she'd slept in it. A blue wheel-thrown mug sat on the bedside table. He carefully picked it up by the edge of the handle. Empty with no ring in the bottom. Like it'd been rinsed out.

He took out his phone and dialed her number. A phone rang near the head of the bed, right beside her pillow. His heart stuttered. Beside it was a White chess pawn and a note.

Nathan backtracked to the hallway and faced Carson. "I need my kit. And get Dylan and Taylor over here."

He double-timed it to his truck, grabbed his evidence kit, and returned to the bedroom. Nathan would normally wait for the CSIs to get there, but time was ticking. He used his phone to snap a photo, then using a pair of tweezers, he picked up the folded note and used another pair of tweezers to open it. It was a picture of a chessboard.

Nathan studied the layout of the board. With almost all the pawns and other pieces still in play, it was early in the game, but the Black queen had the White king in check. Why would Black give up his queen? Seemed like a foolhardy move to Nathan. If he were playing White, all he had to do was capture Black's queen with his king. End of the threat.

There was a note and signature at the bottom of the page.

Check. Do you know where your queen is?
You poked the bear and now you reap its wrath even as the wind stirs the flame. If you're smart enough, you'll find where the bear took her. If not, she'll die and it'll be your fault.

Phame

Poke the bear. He'd said those words to Alexis in her office just yesterday. Somehow, Phame had planted a bug there.

Vehicles pulled up outside, and Nathan refolded the paper and returned it to where he'd found it.

"Dylan and Taylor are here," Carson said.

"Good. Send them in." He scanned the room, looking for more clues. It was soon obvious the only clue was in the note.

"Find anything?" Dylan asked as he and Taylor entered the bedroom.

"I found a White pawn and a note. Phame has Alexis." It would be a while before they got to the note, so he showed them his photo. "Does anything jump out at you?"

"Any report of a fire anywhere?" Taylor asked.

"No." Even though he had the words committed to memory, Nathan stared at the paper as though it might tell him where Alexis was. "Where would a bear take its prey?"

"It's lair?" Dylan said. "Like a cave?"

"Maybe. But how would Phame get Alexis in a cave? She'd fight like crazy."

"He drugged her," Taylor said.

"The cocoa." Nathan nodded toward the cup. "There's nothing inside."

"Someone rinsed it out."

Phame. He read the note again. Nathan closed his eyes and concentrated. *"If you're smart enough, you'll find where the bear took her."*

He looked up. "Bear Tail Cave."

"It's worth a shot." Dylan took out his phone. "I'll get Harvey to send deputies out there."

"I'm not waiting for them." He dashed to the door and stopped long enough to tell the Stones where he was going. A minute later he wheeled out of their drive and pointed his truck toward Eagle Ridge, where Bear Tail Cave was located.

Years ago he and Alexis had hiked the ridge and explored the cave. He gripped the steering wheel. A quarter of a mile inside the cave was a sheer drop-off of at least twenty feet. If Alexis fell—

Nathan's phone rang. The forestry service? "Landry," he barked.

"This is Steven Rogers with the Tennessee Forestry Association. Your sheriff's department ask me to call and advise you there's a fire on Eagle Ridge."

"Near Bear Tail Cave?"

"How'd you know?"

"Just a guess."

56

Pain radiated from Alex's knees to her hips. It seemed like she'd been crawling for hours in total darkness, but from her experience caving years ago, it'd probably only been half an hour at most. Once again, the wind had picked up, blowing over her. Since she was facing it, Alex was certain she was going in a direction that would lead her out of the cave. That again was from experience.

The whole time she'd been crawling, her thoughts were on her captor. She thought it was a large person, not so much from the deep voice—the speech modulator was responsible for that—but because it would take a pretty good-sized person to get her deep into the cave. Unless she'd been forced to crawl through this tunnel.

Was that even possible? Certainly, with some of the drugs out there, like GHB. Maybe her grandmother hadn't left the cocoa on her bedside table. Alex stopped crawling and rested her forehead on the cave floor.

"Someone you love is going to die." What if Phame had harmed her grandparents?

The thought spurred her to crawling again, and the wind brought a whiff of smoke to her nose. Surely her captor hadn't . . .

More smoke, and stronger. Yes. Phame must have started a

fire at the entrance to the cave. Alex coughed and kept crawl-ing.

Phame must have piled brush at the entrance and set it on fire. It should go out unless he'd hung around and fed brush to the flames.

A fit of coughing hit her again. Her knees throbbed, her head ached, her wrist burned all the way to her elbow. The desire to curl up in a ball hit her. If there was room, she might do it.

No! She hadn't come this far to give up. *Think!* "Lord, I need help."

Alex felt with her good hand to make sure she wasn't near a drop-off. Solid walls all around. Like a casket.

Wait. If there was a fire, the forestry service should see it and send someone to put it out. But they wouldn't know she was in the cave unless she crawled to the entrance.

Alex started crawling again. The mouth of the cave had to be close. So why couldn't she see light? Maybe the tunnel curved. Or went up. She didn't know if she had the strength to go much farther. So tired. She rested her head on the stone, feeling the cold seep into her bones.

"Alexis! Where are you?"

Was she dreaming? If she was, she didn't want to wake up.

"Alexis!" Her name echoed through the cavern.

Except for her grandparents, Nathan was the only person who called her that. "Nathan?"

He'd never hear her whisper. She tried again, raising her voice with the same result.

"She has to be here."

That *was* Nathan, and he was looking for her.

"Let's see if Gem can find her. Seek, Gem!"

In no time, something crawled toward her, panting. A bear? She steeled herself for the sharp teeth to rip into her.

Then a dog barked. "Gem's found her. Hang on, Alexis, I'm coming."

She still thought it was a dream until a wet tongue licked her face. "Gem?"

The dog barked again, and Alex reached out, her fingers finding fur. It wasn't a dream. "Thank you, Lord."

Shuffling and another thump, and then there was light. Alex blinked against it as arms wrapped around her. "You came," she whispered.

"Yes. Are you hurt?"

"My wrist. I think it's broken."

"Lie still until I get the rescue basket in here."

Half an hour later, Nathan, Mark and a ranger pulled Alex out of the cave and into the bright sunlight. Sunlight she hadn't been sure she'd ever see again. After being released from the litter, she stood on shaky legs and sucked in a deep breath of fresh air that still had a tinge of smoke to it. Her deputies stood all around. Alex took another breath, and a fit of coughing overtook her.

"There's an ambulance waiting at the road," Nathan said.

"No hospital." Pain shot through her wrist. Okay, that was unreasonable, but someone had kidnapped her and left her to die. Finding them was her top priority, and she did not want to waste hours at the hospital.

Nathan frowned. "You need to be checked out."

"Maybe the paramedics can—"

"They don't have the right equipment. Carson Stone will have my—"

She grabbed his arm. "My grandparents. Are they okay?"

"They will be now that we've found you."

Alex glanced back at the mouth of the cave littered with charred branches. "Why set the fire?"

"I think Phame wanted us to find you."

It didn't make sense. Unless— "This was just to show how easy it was to get to me."

"I think so."

"I still could've died—there's a drop-off in the room I was in." She shuddered thinking about how faint the rocks sounded, dropping into the water. "We need to talk."

"As soon as you get checked out."

"All right." As long as he didn't leave her. She reached for his hand, but Gem poked her nose against her palm and whined.

"I think she's looking for a thank-you," Nathan said with a chuckle. "She's the one that found you."

Alex bent over and scratched the dog's head. "Thank you, girl." She raised up and nodded at Mark. "Thank you too."

He gave her a thumbs-up and then called his dog. "Will we see you at the sheriff's department later?"

Nathan answered for her. "Not today. She's got to get her wrist checked out."

What time was it? Alex checked her watch, but she didn't have it on. Oh yeah . . . she'd taken it off to take a shower last night. At least some of her memory was coming back. "What time is it?"

"A little after noon." Nathan pointed at the litter. "You want us to carry you, or do you want to walk?"

"You're not carrying me." She took a few steps toward the path. "I may have to go slow."

"That'll be a first," Nathan said with a crooked smile. "Can I at least offer my arm?"

It was on the tip of her tongue to tell him she could manage. What was wrong with her? It wouldn't kill her to accept a little help. "Thank you."

The closer they got to the road, the more she leaned on Nathan. Her legs were like noodles, and by the time they reached the ambulance, her wrist was throbbing again. Maybe letting the ER doctor check her over wasn't a bad idea. Might even save time if her wrist was broken, and they could set it.

When the paramedic suggested she let them transport her to the hospital, she declined. "I'd rather Nathan take me." She laughed at the shock on his face. "That is, if you will."

"Uh . . ." For once he looked like he was at a loss for words. "Sure," he finally got out.

The paramedic slammed the bay door closed. "I'll call and let them know you're coming so you won't have to wait."

"Thank you." There were perks to being the chief deputy of Russell County.

"My truck is over here," Nathan said and helped her walk to it. After she was safely buckled in, he tilted his head at her. "You surprised me. I figured I'd have to hogtie and drag you to a doctor to get that wrist seen. But why not go in the ambulance?"

"First of all, riding in an ambulance is worse than riding a log wagon with no springs. And . . ."—she wasn't sure how to say this—"after being in the cave, I didn't want to be alone."

57

Nathan paced the small ER patient room. Alexis had taken at least five years off his life today. He stopped and looked out the door. She'd been gone over thirty minutes. It shouldn't take that long to x-ray her wrist.

Phame immediately popped into his mind, and he marched to the nurses' station. "Where's X-ray?"

The nurse who had taken Alexis's blood pressure glanced up from her computer. "What do you mean?"

He repeated his question. "I want to check on the patient."

"Chief Landry, the chief deputy is fine. There was probably a backlog and they had to wait for an available X-ray machine."

He crossed his arms. "I still want to check on her."

She peered at him over her half glasses and pointed. "Go down that hallway, take a left at the end. You should find her there."

He'd made it to the end of the hallway when the orderly rounded the corner with Alexis.

She did a double take. "What are you doing here?"

"Just checking on you." He eyed the orderly. "Why don't I push her back to the room?"

The kid looked as though he would refuse, and Nathan

said, "Please. I'll make it okay with your supervisor if you get in trouble."

"Well, okay." He relinquished the handles to the wheelchair. "She's all yours."

Nathan caught her gaze and held it. If nothing else, today had made him realize how badly he wanted to make those words true. Alexis looked away, shifting her gaze to her hand that twisted the thin cotton gown the nurse had given her. The kid's words must have flustered her. He wasn't losing this opportunity, not after today.

"Thank you." Nathan bowed but didn't move until Alexis looked up. "Is m'lady ready to go?" he asked, winking at her. Color flooded her face, and she ducked her head.

He didn't say anything until they got back to the small room, and he helped her onto the bed. "Alexis—"

"Don't say anything." She pressed the closed fist of her good hand to her lips. After a minute, she moved it and looked up at him. "I need time to process what happened today."

"I understand, but I'm not going to let you push me away. I—"

There was a sharp rap at the door, and they both turned toward it as the hospital's orthopedic doctor entered the room. "Nathan," he said, nodding, then turned to her. "Alexis, I'm Doctor Mabry."

"I think you set my arm when I was eleven," she said.

"I don't remember that, but I'm sure you do," he said with a chuckle.

"What's the verdict?" Nathan asked.

"Good news of a sort." Dr. Mabry punched a button, and the screen lit up with the X-rays of her wrist. "I don't see a fracture, so that leaves us with damaged ligaments."

"How will you treat it?"

"RICE."

She frowned. "What's that?"

"Rest, ice, compress, elevate," Nathan said.

Dr. Mabry smiled. "I see you remembered."

Nathan turned to Alexis. "I sprained my ankle playing softball a few years ago, and I'm here to tell you if it's like my ankle, your wrist will be very painful for a few days."

"Joy," she said dryly. "But it's better than a broken bone."

"Absolutely." The doctor turned the screen off and walked to the door. "You'll need to rest it for the next forty-eight hours. We'll wrap it before you leave, and that should help with the pain."

"If it doesn't?" Alexis asked.

"Take anti-inflammatories. It'll also help if you keep your wrist above your heart. The nurse will give you written instructions and make an appointment for a follow-up." He started out the door and turned around. "Oh, and the tox screen should be back in forty-eight hours."

"Forty-eight hours?" Nathan hoped it would be back sooner.

"We outsource tox screens to a lab in Chattanooga. I asked them to put a rush on it, but you know how that goes."

"Thanks, Doc," Alexis said.

An hour later, Nathan helped her out of the truck in spite of Alexis's protest that she didn't need his help. Carson and Judith were waiting for them at the back door. Judith rushed to her granddaughter and Alexis yelped when her grandmother wrapped her arms around her.

Judith jumped back. "I'm so sorry—Nathan told me about your wrist, and I forgot. And I'm sorry we didn't set the alarm after you and Nathan left. We've been so worried."

Alex hugged her with her good arm. "Stop worrying—I'm okay now."

"If you want to blame someone, blame me," he said. "I should've checked the whole house when we returned."

The hair on the back of his neck raised, and Nathan scanned the area behind the house. Everything looked normal, but he'd learned to never dismiss his spidey feelings. "We need to get inside."

Nathan didn't relax until they were safely in the kitchen and he had a cup of Judith's strong coffee in his hands. Before he left, he planned to make sure Jared continued patrolling the house on a regular basis.

He took another sip of the hot coffee. "I need to get your statement about what happened."

"I know. I'm still trying to pull my thoughts together, but maybe your questions will help me."

Carson stood and motioned to his wife. "You need privacy for that. We'll be in the den if you need us."

"Thanks." When they were alone, Nathan opened the record app on his phone, then he took out a notepad and pen. "Can you give me a description of the person?"

"I wish. It was so dark in the cave, I couldn't see anything."

"Anything before the cave?"

She thought a minute and shook her head.

"Okay, start with when I left you and take me through what you remember."

"I hopped in the shower, and I guess I was there longer than normal—after the day we had yesterday, the hot water felt so good. When I got out, the cocoa was sitting on the table. I thought Gram brought it."

He stopped writing. "The cup wasn't there when I cleared your bedroom. That means the person was in the house when you got home unless you didn't set the alarm after I left."

She shivered. "I'm 99 percent sure I set it."

Nathan tried to picture both scenarios. He leaned toward the kidnapper hiding in the house when they returned. Otherwise, he would've had to break in, read the note and warm the cocoa, and get it back to the bedside table by the time Alexis got out of the shower. "No, I think they were here, observed your grandmother making the cocoa, and then read the note she left. I wonder what time Kayla left." He texted Judith the question.

Alexis caught her breath. "You don't believe Kayla—"

"Right now, just about everyone is a suspect."

"That's ridiculous," Alexis said. "Why would she save my life and then do something like this?"

"Why would your kidnapper set a fire in the mouth of the cave? He had to know it wouldn't keep burning and would only alert the forest rangers." He tapped his lips with the pen. "It doesn't make sense."

"It does if Phame is trying to make me look ridiculous, or he's trying to weaken me, like a cat when it plays with a mouse."

Nathan looked around as Judith stuck her head in the door. "Can I come in?"

"Sure," he said motioned her inside the kitchen. "So, what time did she leave?"

"I didn't look at the clock, but she insisted on helping with the dishes while I made cocoa, and then we shared a cup, talked about her college classes and her dad dying. She's a sweet girl."

"Would you say she stayed about an hour after we left?"

"Probably."

"And you actually saw her leave?"

Judith nodded. "I remember I started to set the alarm then, but Carson called me to help him find his sleeping medicine. I keep it separate from his other medicines . . ." Tears formed in her eyes. "I never thought of the alarm again."

"Stop worrying about it," Alexis said and hugged Judith. "I'm fine."

She nodded. "I'll try. Anything else?"

311

"That's all," Nathan said. "Thanks."

After Judith left, Nathan said, "I'll talk to Kayla later today. See if her story matches your grandmother's."

Alexis ran her finger around the top of the cup. "Just because she was here last night doesn't mean she drugged and kidnapped me."

"I know. But think about it. She was around when Smith was killed, and she moved here just before Gina Norman and Trevor Martin were murdered."

"I know we have to look at everyone, but those are coincidences." She held up her hand. "I know—neither of us like coincidence, but sometimes, things like that happen."

That left them with an unknown intruder who was here long enough to see the note in the bedroom and set up the whole thing. That just didn't set right with him. But it was hard to believe Kayla was that intruder or the person who kidnapped Alexis.

Alexis frowned. "I'm just glad my grandparents didn't encounter my kidnapper."

A text chimed on his phone, and he checked it. "It's Madden. Chattanooga PD sent Denton's DNA profile to the company he told me about to see if they can find any family connections. He'll send the report as soon as he gets it."

312

58

Phame set up the chessboard with the White king surrounded by his bishops, knights, queen, and pawns. The king thought he was safe.

Except... the Black knight was closing in, leaving the White king in check. With nowhere to run, the White king was in checkmate.

Phame snapped several photos of the board and printed them out, then using a Sharpie, carefully wrote "I WON! You lose."

Time to end this game even though it meant another trip to the cave.

59

First thing Friday morning, Alex had her CSI deputies sweep her office for bugs, and they found one in the lamp by her desk. Then she'd made it through the morning briefing where she learned Mark was meeting Nathan in an hour at the cave to look for evidence.

As soon as the deputies dispersed, she had Nathan on the phone. "Why didn't you tell me you were going back to the cave today? And taking my deputy."

"Good morning to you too." When she didn't respond, he sighed. "It's Mark's day off and he volunteered to go. And I didn't tell you because I didn't want to argue with you about going with us."

"There wouldn't have been an argument."

"Really?"

"Nope. Because I'm going." Not that she *wanted* to go back into that dark hole. She had to do it or Phame would win. It was no more than getting back on a horse after being thrown.

"Mark and I can handle this. You have no business—"

"I know you can, and I know you won't miss anything. But I was the one who could've died there. I want to see where I was held."

"How do you plan to get there? Have you forgotten your wrist?"

"I'm sure the deputy who picked me up this morning will drive me. Besides, the pain is much better this morning." And it was as long as she held her wrist above her heart. Surely she could block the pain long enough to get in and out of the cave. "Come on, Nathan." She wasn't above begging.

"All right," he said with a sigh. "I don't suppose you have a helmet with a headlamp?"

Rats. She'd forgotten she would need a helmet. "Do you have an extra? Until last night it's been years since I was in a cave."

"Yes," he said reluctantly. "You may want to go home and change into old clothes and shoes."

She agreed, remembering her pajamas from yesterday. "Why don't you pick me up at the house?"

"Sounds good. See you in an hour."

True to his word, Nathan was at the house in sixty minutes, dressed in jeans and a sweatshirt. He stepped inside the kitchen. "I'm parked here at the back door."

"Good." After last night, Alex had no problem taking every precaution for her safety.

"Where are your grandparents?"

"Gramps had a doctor's appointment." Alex set the alarm and turned to him. "I'm ready."

Nathan was quiet on the drive to Eagle Ridge. They passed virgin forests of hardwoods turning vibrant fall colors without a comment from him. She turned to him. "You okay?"

"Just remembering yesterday's drive. I kept thinking about Phame's victims. I was afraid the search and rescue would turn into a recovery mission."

"I'm sorry." Alex had been so focused on her own feelings, she hadn't considered how her kidnapping might've affected Nathan.

They topped a ridge with a pullout, and he pulled over and killed his motor. Below them a carpet of red maples and golden hickories stretched as far as the eye could see.

Nathan turned to her. "You have to promise me you'll be more careful."

"Last night was not my fault."

"You baited a serial killer, Alexis."

She gritted her teeth. "Okay, maybe I shouldn't have done that, but he made me so mad."

"But that's not like you. You've always been in control, had a plan and worked it. You're letting this serial killer get inside your head."

She took a breath to tell Nathan he was wrong and released it without saying anything. The website and video game *had* consumed her, so much so, she wasn't thinking clearly. "You're right." It cost her dearly to say those words. "I underestimated this Phame character. It won't happen again."

"I hope it doesn't." He held her gaze. "I don't think I can go through what happened yesterday another time."

Her blood raced at the concern in his eyes. "Here's hoping you never have to," she said softly.

Just as he caressed her jaw, an SUV blew past them, horn blowing. Alex jumped back.

"Mark," Nathan muttered and started his motor. "Guess we don't want to keep him waiting."

"Good thinking," she said, covering her grin with her hand. He would have kissed her if Mark hadn't come along, and she would have welcomed it.

Mark had already climbed to the mouth of the cave when they pulled up to the spot where the ambulance had waited for her yesterday. "I wish I could get closer," Nathan said.

"I'm good." She unbuckled her seat belt. "Just have to remember not to put too much pressure on my left hand."

"You want me to bind it to your body?"

"I think it'll be fine." She didn't tell him her wrist had low-level pain already. Maybe a couple of ibuprofens would take care of it. Alex waited until Nathan was out of the truck and getting their gear from the bed to find the pain relievers and take them.

When she climbed out of the truck, Nathan handed her a helmet with a headlamp and a vest with a bottle of water and protein bars in the pockets. Before she thought, she shook out her ponytail to redo it lower and tried to wrap the band one-handed. Her shoulders drooped. Just how did she expect to put her hair back in a ponytail?

"Ready?" he asked.

She held out the black hair elastic. "Could you—" She pointed at her hair. "It was too high for the helmet."

"Sure." He gently pulled her hair back and secured it with the elastic tie. "Is that low enough?"

"We'll see." She plopped the helmet on her head. "It's good."

"Ready now?"

"Ready."

By the time they climbed up to the mouth of the cave, she didn't have to remind herself to keep the wrist above her heart—the pain was enough.

Mark wore jeans and a sweatshirt as well. "I didn't know you were coming."

"I wanted to see the place where I was held. Where's Gem?"

"Home. The only time I took her caving when it wasn't search and rescue, she whined the whole time."

Alex nodded toward his fancy caving helmet. "I didn't know you liked caving."

"Been doing it for years."

She hated the thought that popped in her mind—Mark would've had no trouble getting her to the cave. And if the drug she'd consumed in the cocoa was GHB, she would've been compliant and have no memory of it.

Alex shook the thought away. Mark had helped Nathan find her yesterday. She turned to Nathan, and he gave her a reassuring smile.

"Alexis and I will go in first," Nathan said. "You can bring up the rear. Do you have another light, in case that one goes out?"

First rule in caving was always carry plenty of flashlights.

"I have two."

He nodded and turned to Alex. "You ready?"

"Anytime." At least her voice didn't shake.

They flipped their headlamps on, and Nathan went in first. She followed, remembering the narrow passageway from yesterday. It was much better with light.

"You okay back there?" Nathan asked.

Mark answered in the affirmative first.

"Me too," Alex said. But crawling was much harder with only one good hand than she thought it would be, and she should have put on knee pads. More than once, it took everything in Alex to keep from groaning, but she was afraid if she did, Nathan would send her back. Not that she wouldn't almost welcome it. Even with the headlamp, the close passageway was claustrophobic.

Just when she didn't think she could stand it another second, the tunnel opened up.

"I think we're here," Nathan said and rose to his feet. "Ow!"

"You okay?" Alexis asked as she practically fell into the cavern.

"Hit my head." He turned toward Mark. "Be careful standing."

Alex used one of the flashlights Nathan had given her to shine around the small chamber, and her breath caught. The light bounced off stalactites hanging from the ceiling in one corner, and on the other side stalagmites rose up from a shelf above the cave floor. Under other circumstances, the room would be beautiful.

Next to the stalagmites, two passages that led out of the cavern were tall enough for them to stand upright and at least three feet wide—not nearly as claustrophobic as the way they came in. But the passages could lead deeper into the mountain instead of out.

"Oh, man," Mark said, shining his light toward the far wall. "Looks like this is a shelf."

He walked to the edge and traced it with his flashlight. "There's a twenty-foot drop at least."

"I know," Nathan said. He turned to Alex. "We were in this cave years ago, and I remembered the drop-off."

That's why the cave felt familiar, and she hadn't been wrong about the rocks splashing. Alex eased over to the edge, and her knees threatened to buckle. More than enough room for her to have rolled off into the water below.

Alex uncapped the bottle of water and guzzled it. Then she wiped her mouth with the back of her hand. "Let's see if my kidnapper left anything behind."

60

Nathan turned away from the drop-off. Just thinking about what could've happened if she'd gone over the edge sent chills through him. "Don't forget to put on your gloves." He waved his nitrile gloves before shoving his hands into a pair.

While Alexis and Mark pulled on theirs, Nathan swept his light back and forth over the cave floor. Even if they found something, it could have nothing to do with Alexis's kidnapping. Caving was a popular sport around Pearl Springs.

"Hey! What's this?" Mark said.

Alexis and Nathan swung their lights toward where he was bent over and then pinpointed the item he examined on the cave floor.

"A scrunchie?" Alex said. Her hair had gotten in her face when she'd crawled out yesterday, and she peered closer. "I don't have any like that."

Nathan bagged the elastic band. "It doesn't mean it belongs to your captor."

"True," Mark said. "The path to the cave is pretty well worn."

Alexis kicked at a rock. "I'm going to keep looking."

"Good idea." Nathan swung his light around the shelf and craggy walls while Alexis and Mark examined the cave floor.

Half an hour later by his watch, he was about to give up on finding anything. He swept the light over the walls one last time.

"What's that?" Alexis said, pointing at the space he'd just passed the beam over.

"Where?" He looked toward where she pointed.

"There." She pointed again.

Mark stepped closer to the wall. "I see it!"

Nathan moved closer to Alexis. "Shine your light on it."

It looked as though a bag had been wedged between two of the stalactites that hung from the cave ceiling. "Can you reach it?" Nathan asked.

"If I climb up on this ridge with the stalagmites."

"Wait," Nathan said. "The kidnapper probably did the same thing. We need to check for any evidence he might have left behind."

He shined a light on the area, not seeing anything unusual. "Go ahead."

Mark climbed up on the flat ridge and then braced against a stalagmite. "Got it!" He hopped down. "It's a note to Al—"

An explosion rocked the cave, knocking Nathan backward. He slammed against the cave wall, and pain jolted the back of his head as he slid to the rocky floor. When his head cleared, he looked around, thankful the light on his helmet still worked. A slab of limestone had slipped out of place. If it came down, they were all dead. Once again, they had underestimated Phame. Thank goodness he'd told his dispatcher and sergeant where he was going.

Another light cast an eerie glow in the dusty room. Alexis. Or Mark. Where were they? He called both their names, but he couldn't hear his voice for the ringing in his ears. And neither would they.

Nathan needed more light. He rolled over on his knees and

grabbed the light he'd dropped, flashing it around the room. Alexis lay faceup on the floor, unconscious. Mark sat beside the stalagmites, coughing and shaking his head. Neither of their helmet lights were working.

Nathan crawled to Alexis and felt for a pulse. When he found it—strong and steady—he almost lost it. *Thank God.*

Alexis fluttered her eyes open, and he turned her face toward him. "You're okay." He was pretty sure she couldn't hear what he said, but maybe she could read his lips.

She closed her eyes and took a deep breath. Coughing shook her body, and she rolled over and hugged her chest.

The cave floor trembled. They had to get out of here. But which way? The explosion had sounded as though it came from the mouth of the cave. It had happened right after Mark grabbed the bag, but they would have noticed C-4 and a cord if there'd been one attached. The alternative terrified him— someone must have followed them to the cave and triggered the explosion.

Nathan shifted his gaze to Mark and pointed at him before he put his hand to his ear. "Can you hear anything?"

The deputy shook his head. Nathan pointed toward the two passages and then toward the passage they'd used to get into the cavern and held his hands up in the universal question position.

Mark pointed toward the one they'd come in on and slapped his hands together like an explosion. That's where Nathan had thought the explosion originated, so they couldn't go back the way they'd come.

Then Mark pointed to the other two passages. "Which one?" he mouthed.

Good question. Either passage could take them deeper into the mountain instead of out. He pressed his palms together, then tapped his chest and pointed to Mark, who gave him a thumbs-up. The cave floor trembled again, and Nathan shut his eyes and sent up a flare prayer for direction. Literally.

He didn't know if it was God or his own feelings, but he was drawn to the passage on the left. When he opened his eyes and looked toward Mark, he indicated the left passage as well.

Nathan nodded and leaned over Alexis and shook her shoulder. Fear flashed in her eyes when they popped open, then their eyes connected, and she relaxed. He didn't know how he'd make her understand, but it didn't seem that the ringing in his ears was as bad. "Can you hear me?" he yelled.

She frowned. "W-what?"

No use. He stood and pointed at the passage.

Alexis shook her head.

"You have to!" He extended his arm. "Give me your hand."

She didn't move and just stared at him. Nathan would get her out of this room before it fell in, even if he had to carry her out fireman style. "Take my hand." He said it even though she couldn't hear him.

She looked from him to Mark and then took Nathan's hand. He pulled her to her feet then checked his watch. Ten forty-six? It seemed as though they'd been in the cave for hours.

"I'll go first." He tapped his chest, then pointed at her. "You're next, then Mark," he mouthed, pointing at the deputy, and they both nodded they understood.

Nathan glanced up at the ceiling to see if the slab had moved, and his helmet light flickered. No! It had fresh batteries—it should be good. He took the helmet off and shook it, and the light went dark. Must've been from the explosion.

Nathan put his helmet back on just as light came from Mark's direction. He'd gotten his helmet light to work. Nathan gave him a fist bump as Mark fished another flashlight from his vest and handed it to Alexis.

Nathan took a deep breath and pointed his flashlight toward the passage. He didn't know how far they'd have to hike to get out of the cave, but it started with one step.

After they'd been walking for a few minutes, he felt a jerk on his sleeve, and he wheeled around.

Wide-eyed, she gripped his arm. "Where's Mark?" she mouthed.

Nathan looked beyond her. The deputy had been right behind them and now he wasn't. Had he set the explosive and was now escaping out the other passage?

Surely he wouldn't have been in the cave if he intended to blow it up. Unless something went wrong and it went off before it was supposed to.

"Do you think he's hurt?" Alexis asked.

That was a more likely scenario. "Can you hear anything yet?"

She pinched her thumb and finger together.

A little. Good. That would make it easier to communicate. "We haven't gone far," he shouted. "I'm going back to find him."

She gripped his arm tighter.

Nathan was torn between Alexis waiting here or backtracking with him. If there was trouble, he didn't want her involved. But what if someone else was in the cave, and they'd attacked Mark? Regardless, he felt better having her with him. Finally he nodded.

She pressed against the wall, and he crept around her. They found Mark on the cave floor not far from the cavern where Alexis had been held. Nathan shined his light on him, wincing. The deputy lay unmoving.

He should've checked him out better before they left the chamber. Unless . . . someone could be hiding in the shadows. Nathan quickly bounced his light around the walls of the passage and then down the straight path they'd just traveled.

Nothing moved. He turned to Alexis. "Watch," he mouthed, then knelt and felt for a pulse. Nathan blew out a breath when he found a strong one.

He shook Mark by the shoulder. If the deputy made a sound, he couldn't hear it. "Mark!" He shook him again, and slowly Mark's eyes opened.

"What happened?"

At least that's what Nathan thought he said. "Can you hear me?"

"Barely." Mark struggled to sit up.

Nathan helped him and handed him a small bottle from his vest.

The deputy uncapped the bottle and drained it. Then he pulled out a plastic bag from inside his vest.

The note that'd been wedged between two stalactites. That's why he'd gone back. Nathan studied the note. There was a string attached, but strings didn't trigger explosive devices.

That meant someone else did. Was he out there now, waiting for them to emerge from the cave?

gnoring the pain the fall had ignited in her wrist, Alex stared at the plastic bag with the string that Nathan held. Pretty sure he was thinking the same thing she was. A string didn't carry electric current through it, but it was too coincidental that the bomb went off right after Mark pulled the package down. Maybe it was attached to a trip wire that set the bomb off when Mark moved it. She pointed to the string. "Trip wire?"

Nathan cupped his ear, and she repeated the question louder, then looked to each man for their reaction.

The skeptical look on Mark's face said he didn't think so, but a few of the worry lines faded on Nathan's face. "Maybe."

Alex ignored her throbbing wrist and flashed her light on the note. Nathan turned it where she could read it. *"I WON! You lose."* And beneath the words was a drawing of the White king on its side.

Nathan turned the bag where she could see another paper of a chess game. Alex studied the picture. Even as a newbie chess player, she could see that the White king was surrounded by his pawns, knights, and bishops, and even his queen. Black had the king in check with a knight. No. Not just in check. Black had the king in checkmate—the White king had nowhere to run. That's what the drawing with the White king on its side indicated—White had conceded the game.

Mark fished his phone from his pocket. Alex stared at him. There was no signal in the cave. Then he typed something and showed it to Nathan, then her. "Smothered mate," she read.

She and Nathan exchanged glances, and then Nathan typed, "You play chess?"

"Since I was a kid."

Alex stilled. Mark liked caving, he resented her grandfather giving Alex the job, and he knew how to play chess. *And* he and Gem "happened" to find the fake bomb.

No. She brushed the thoughts away. If Mark was the murderer, he wouldn't have let himself be caught in the explosion.

Alex dropped her injured wrist and helped Nathan get Mark to his feet. Even though her gut said Mark wasn't her stalker, a tiny seed of doubt crept into her mind. He would bear watching.

Nathan turned and pointed forward. She fell in behind him, hoping the passage would lead to the outside. There was no guarantee. A few minutes later Nathan stopped. Why was he searching his vest? When he pulled out a lighter, she understood.

When they were caving years ago, he always kept a lighter on him. He flicked it and held it higher when the flame appeared. It flickered and then leaned in the direction they were walking. *Yes!* Alex glanced down at the cave floor. And unless she was imagining it, the floor slanted upwards. They were headed in the right direction.

A half hour later, she almost ran into Nathan when he abruptly stopped. Alex looked around him and her stomach unknotted. It was dim, but there was light at the end of the tunnel.

When they emerged from the cave, it took a minute to

adjust to the sunlight as they all sucked in deep breaths of fresh air. Her ears still rang, but her hearing was returning. She could even hear Nathan and Mark as they took stock of their location. Both agreed it was about half a mile to the winding road in the valley below.

Going downhill was much harder than climbing up, and when they reached the bottom, Alex sat on the side of the road while the two men argued about which direction the vehicles were located.

She cocked her head. "Hey, you two, be quiet a minute."

Both men stopped and stared at her.

"I hear something. Siren, maybe?"

"I hear it too," Nathan said. He helped her to stand, and they walked in the direction of the sound.

A half mile later, they rounded a curve, and the hillside was covered with police vehicles.

"Reckon they're looking for us?" she asked.

Four hours later, Alex rocked back on her heels. They'd gotten the last of the debris cleared from the tunnel, but Nathan and Mark deemed it too unstable for anyone to enter. She agreed with their assessment but was still disappointed that they couldn't search for evidence. Although Phame wasn't careless enough to leave anything behind.

"Are you ready for me to take you home?" Nathan asked.

She glanced past him to where her K-9 officer stood by his truck. "Let me say something to Mark first."

Mark nodded as she approached. "You okay?"

"So-so. You?"

"I'm alive."

"Yeah. I want to thank you for everything you did yesterday and today."

"Just doing my job."

"Yeah, but you used your personal time to come out here today." She held out her hand. "I know we've had some differences, but I hope we're past that."

He studied her for a second, then grasped her hand. "I don't think we'll have any more trouble."

Tension eased from her shoulders. "Good. Because you're a good deputy."

He ducked his head. "You're not bad yourself."

She grinned. "Thank you. Why don't you take the weekend off?"

"I might just do that. Appreciate it."

Alex walked back to where Nathan waited. "Go all right?"

"Better than all right." She hooked her arm in his. "Got a text earlier and Gram said to bring you to supper."

"Sounds like a winner."

An hour later, Nathan held the Stones' back door open and Alex gratefully stepped inside. For the second day in a row, she hadn't been certain she'd see this kitchen again or her grandparents. After embracing them, Gram insisted they sit down and eat.

Alex hugged her again. "Not everything can be fixed with food."

"Maybe not, but food never hurts."

Alex laughed. "True, but let's get cleaned up first."

"Sounds good," Nathan said. "I have a change of clothes in my truck."

Halfway through the meal, her grandfather laid his fork down. "I had no idea I was getting you into anything like this. But I'm proud of you."

Gramps didn't hand out praise easily, and his words swelled her heart. "Just doing my job, Gramps. Like someone else I know."

"Yeah, well, Marge said neither one of you would leave until the rocks were cleared from the tunnel." He turned to Nathan. "You too, son. I'm proud of you."

"I was hoping for evidence," Nathan said. "A clue to whoever tried to blow up the entrance to the cave."

The older man leaned forward. "Don't you think it was the killer?"

"Probably," he replied. "But we never found a trip wire from the bag with the note to where the explosive was placed."

"We know the note came from the killer," Alex said. "Phame expected us to search the cave again. Could it have been some sort of laser beam that sent a message to the detonator when the note was moved?"

"I've requested the Bureau of Alcohol, Tobacco, Firearms, and Explosives to investigate. They have more resources than we do." Nathan leaned back in his chair and pinned his gaze on her. "You've had quite a first week on the job. You are planning on taking the weekend off, right?"

Gram slapped her hand on the table. "She certainly is."

Alex counted to ten and thought about counting to fifteen. "Let's see. We have drug dealers from Chattanooga running around, not to mention a killer." She pursed her lips and looked toward the ceiling, then leveled her gaze at her grandparents and Nathan. "Nope. I don't think I'll be taking the weekend off."

An uncomfortable quiet settled in the room.

"Wouldn't hurt to at least go to church Sunday," Gram said in a small voice.

Alex joined in the laughter around the table.

62

Monday, after the morning briefing, Alex's phone rang and warmth spread through her chest. Nathan. They'd spent a fair amount of time together over the weekend. "Hello?" She cringed, hating how breathy she sounded.

"Good morning. How's it going so far?"

"Eh, so-so. Harvey is puffed up like a puffer fish. Mark's okay, though. I think we may have worked through our problems. At least I hope so. What's on your list today?"

"Court, in about half an hour."

"Oh, that's right. You said that yesterday after church. Think you'll be free by lunch?"

"I'm not sure when I'll take the stand, so I don't know. We do get a two-hour lunch break. Want to grab a salad at Garden G's?"

Garden G's was a new restaurant in town that specialized in healthy soups and salads.

"Sounds good. Buzz me when lunch recess is called."

With a lighter heart, Alex went back to work on the stack of papers on her desk. An hour later, she looked up when someone knocked on her door. "Come in."

Dylan stuck his head in the door. "You busy?"

"I'm always ready to stop looking at this paperwork. What's up?"

"Phame's video game is up again."

Her breath hitched, and she swung around to her computer. "I want to see it."

Within minutes they were on the dark web and in the video game. It looked a little different. Same flames, but in the center of the flames a chess game was set up. The same one on the photo they'd found in the cave.

Phame had known Alex would be searching for the game. "How hard was it to find?"

"Very easy—it's like this Phame wanted to be found."

Not surprising. As she studied the site, a banner appeared. *"Coming Attraction."*

A photo flashed into place and Dylan grunted. "You see that? It's . . . you, right?"

The shock of seeing her photo on the website chilled Alex's insides. She rubbed her arms. "Take me to the site where I can buy cryptocurrency."

A few clicks later, Alex had another two hundred dollars in Bitcoin. Immediately a sign popped up. *"Welcome, Chief."*

She turned to Dylan. "Can Phame tell I'm in the game?"

"I don't see how . . . unless he hacked into your computer."

"Pull the drive!"

Once Dylan removed the USB drive, the screen blinked then returned to her normal desktop. She pushed away from the desk. "Can you check my computer to see if it's been hacked? Or do I need to get someone else?"

"I can do it."

"Then get to work on it. I want to access that site again later today." Alex wasn't going to let Phame beat her.

Dylan hadn't been gone five minutes when her phone chimed with a text, and she glanced at it. Kayla.

Help! Don't call—can't talk. He might hear.

For a few seconds Alex couldn't breathe. Kayla was in trouble. She quickly opened her phone and responded.

Who might hear? What's going on?

Kidnapped. Escaped but he's after me.

Where are you?

IDK

Do you see landmarks?

Kayla wasn't from around Russell County.

I c waterfall

Alex's stomach churned. There was a waterfall on Eagle Ridge near the cave. He must be planning to take her there, but she needed more of the location before she went tearing up to Eagle Ridge.

If you turn around, what can you see?

A minute passed. Alex grabbed her body armor and slipped it on while she dialed Nathan. It went straight to voice mail. He was still in court. If he was on the witness stand, he wouldn't check his messages until a break. She dashed off a text telling him Kayla was in trouble at the cave, and she was going to her.

Alex hurried out of the office, telling Marge to send every available deputy to Bear Tail Cave. Then she dialed Mark as she jogged to her SUV. "Where are you?"

"The south end of the county. Why?"

"Phame kidnapped Nathan's dispatcher, Kayla Jackson, and

I think he took her to the cave at Eagle Ridge. She managed to escape from him. I'm on my way and need backup."

"Roger that, but it'll take a good half hour to reach the cave from here. Call Nathan. He'll back you up."

"He's in court and not answering."

"I'll call the other deputies and head them that way."

A text from Kayla dinged, and she put him on speaker while she checked the text.

Stone bridge

"From her description, she's definitely at the cave. Meet me there. And have everyone come in silent with no flashing lights." Alex disconnected and texted Kayla.

Stay where you are. Be there soon.

She texted Nathan again to meet her at the cave when he got out of court.

Half an hour of nail-biting twists and turns and worry on the winding road. She gripped the steering wheel at ten and two. If Phame killed Kayla, it would be all Alex's fault.

She parked her SUV half a mile from the cave entrance and texted Kayla.

I'm here. Where are you?

No answer.

Alex silenced her phone and climbed out. She scanned the area, her senses on alert for anything that might indicate where she'd find Kayla.

Rain from the weekend left everything clean but earthy smelling. The sun quickly made her want to take off the body armor, but she discarded that thought as quickly as it came. Alex turned in a slow circle, looking for anything that might give her Kayla's location.

Birds twittered in the dense undergrowth. A shadow raced across the area, prickling her skin, and she looked up. A turkey vulture circled overhead. She shivered.

Alex checked her phone again. Nothing. Why didn't Kayla respond? What if Phame had captured her?

63

athan stepped out of the witness box, thankful to be finished early. He opened his phone to take off "Do Not Disturb" and frowned.

Alexis had called twice, left a voice mail, and texted. He listened to the message first, and his heart sank at the news that Kayla had been kidnapped and might be at the cave. But it made him even sicker that Alexis was on the way to rescue her. The text was a forward from Kayla, describing where she was.

He started to call Alexis and thought better of it, texting instead.

> Where are you?

> At the cave.

> On my way.

His phone rang before he could pocket it. Madden. "What do you have?"

"My friend at the DNA lab came through with a match for Denton's mother, a Mary Margaret Wilson."

"You got her number?"

"Better than that, I've already talked to her and had her send me a photo of her daughter and son, whose name, by the way, isn't Phillip Denton but Phillip Wilson."

"Madden . . ." Nathan growled as his phone alerted to a text coming in.

"He has a sister, Violet Wilson. I just sent you the photos."

"Hold on. Let me look." Nathan put the phone on speaker then opened Madden's message. His heart almost stopped.

Violet Wilson was Kayla? And Phame. He tried to take a breath, but his lungs wouldn't cooperate. Nathan looked again to be sure, but there was no mistaking—they were one and the same.

"I'll call you back." Without waiting for Madden to respond, he hit the end button and punched in Mark's number.

"Lassiter."

"Is Alexis with you?"

"No. She's at the cave and I'm almost there. Did she get ahold of you?"

"I got her text about Kayla. She's walking into a trap. Kayla Jackson hasn't been kidnapped. She's Phame."

"What?"

"You heard me right. I'm on my way."

"Other deputies are coming, but we were scattered all over the county so I called Jared, and he's sending all your available officers."

"Good deal." Nathan disconnected and dialed Jared to get an update. "What's going on?"

"I'm here at Eagle Ridge, but I haven't seen Alex or Kayla Jackson."

"Keep looking, but be careful—Kayla hasn't been kidnapped, and she may have Alexis." He explained what had happened. "I'm on my way."

He'd barely hung up when he felt a presence at his side. Nathan cut his eyes to the right, and his heart seized. *Kayla.*

"Keep walking and act normal if you ever want to see Alex again. Alive, that is."

He stopped in spite of her command, and something hard pressed into his side.

"Keep going."

"Where is she?"

"You'll see. My car is in front of the hardware store. Now walk."

He forced his feet to move. "Why, Kayla? Because she killed your brother?"

"One of the reasons."

"But Phillip Denton threatened to kill her."

"With an unloaded gun? Gimme a break." She stared at him, wide-eyed. "Wait. How did you know?"

"You gave us clues, and we're not stupid, Kayla. Alexis didn't want to kill your brother, but if someone pulls a gun on you, you have to assume they're going to kill you. She had no way of knowing his gun wasn't loaded."

"She could've handled it differently. And shut up. I don't want to hear anything else about it." She pointed toward a blue RAV4. "I'm parked there. Get in the driver's seat."

He'd hoped she would drive. That way he might get the drop on her once he knew where Alexis was.

"Give me your gun, butt first. And be slow."

He carefully took his Glock from the holster and handed it to her exactly like she said. He had no doubt she'd shoot him without even blinking. He still had a backup pistol in his boot, but getting to it would be a problem.

"I'm going to the passenger side. If you try to run, Alex is dead." Her cold eyes held him prisoner. "Got it?"

"Yes," he said through gritted teeth. She'd killed seven

people—one more wouldn't bother her. But what if she was bluffing and didn't have Alexis?

Once Kayla was in the SUV, she said, "Let's go."

He jutted his jaw. "I want to talk to Alexis."

"Not happening."

"Because you don't have her, do you?"

"Do you want to risk it?"

"Where is she?" he demanded.

Her lip curled in a sneer. "Somewhere you'll never find her if you don't get moving."

His gut said she didn't have Alexis, and if Nathan got a chance, he'd take Kayla down. He started the motor and backed out of the parking spot. "Which way, Kayla? Or should I call you Violet?"

Her eyes widened and the gun wavered. Nathan grabbed for the gun, and they struggled for it. The console kept him from getting a good hold on her hand, and she broke loose from his grip and chopped him a glancing blow in the throat.

Even though he'd deflected most of the punch, Nathan had never felt such pain. Choking, he grabbed his throat while she leveled the gun at him. "Try that again and you're dead. Just be glad I didn't shoot you. Now drive."

"Where to?" He choked the words out.

"Harper's Point."

"The lake, not the cave at Eagle Ridge?"

"Why would I go there? The place is probably swarming with cops by now."

He pulled away from the hardware store. His court date had been on the calendar all week, so Kayla had known he was testifying today. The kidnapping had been a ploy to get most of the Russell County deputies and his officers away from town so she could kidnap him, not Alexis. He was the bait.

She cocked her head. "Does she know who I am?"

"I didn't get a chance to tell her." He didn't tell Kayla he'd told Mark. Maybe if he could rattle her, he could get the upper hand. "So you're responsible for the bomb threat and taking over her car, but the failed attacks on Alexis—I would've thought you were a better shot than that."

"The bomb threat was a good one—made her look the incompetent cop that she is—and not everyone can take over a car like that." She frowned. "If I'd shot at Alex, I would've hit her."

"Or maybe you won't admit it because you missed."

Her jaw muscle worked furiously. "Just shut up."

He ignored her. "I don't understand how you forced your way into the victims' homes." She didn't answer, and he thought about how she'd wormed her way into Alexis's confidence. "You didn't have to, did you? Somehow, you knew the women and they trusted you."

He caught the tiny smile that tugged at her lips. Kayla wanted to brag about what she'd done.

"Nah, you weren't that smart."

"Really?" She glared at him, a sneer on her face. "Getting the trust of those women was easy, just like with Alex. They all fell for my sob story—that my dad had died, and I had to drop out of college, and I had nowhere to go. The hookers even let me crash at their places.

"I changed my story up a bit for them—they wouldn't care whether I went to college or not. So I told them my brother abused me. And that wasn't an easy lie to tell. My brother was my hero."

"I still don't understand why you killed them."

"Money." Her voice indicated it was obvious.

"The video game."

"Give the chief a gold star," she said. "As of today, I've banked a million dollars in cryptocurrency."

"How does Alexis fit into this?"

"She's part of the game."

"I don't understand."

"It's all a game and I'm the creator. I decide who lives and dies. And the money . . . You won't believe how many people will pay to be a killer."

"You killed people for a game?"

She shrugged. "It wasn't as hard as you'd think."

"So it had nothing to do with your brother?"

"Of course it did. Alex Stone needed to pay for shooting an unarmed man, but I couldn't very well kill a cop—"

Kayla lived in a fantasy world. "So you killed women who looked like her."

"Bingo."

Her nonchalance sent a chill through him. She had no conscience at all. Nathan swallowed down the nausea in his throat. "But I don't understand this game you're playing today."

"It should be obvious."

"Explain it to me."

"The media had it right with the Queen's Gambit, you know. I always play Black and accept the gambit—makes the game much more interesting, and when I win, it shows how much smarter I am. The whole world will find that out today."

She had completely broken from reality.

Ten minutes later, they arrived at the deserted lake, and she instructed him to drive down to Harper's Point, where there was a small, sandy beach near the pier. She held the gun on him as she climbed out of the SUV and walked around to the driver's side. "Get out. There's a chair in the back. Get it."

Nathan searched for a way to run, but the nearest tree was at least fifty yards away, and he couldn't outrun a bullet.

He had better try.

64

Y ou can't be serious!" Alex stared at Mark. "Kayla is Phame? And Phillip Denton's sister?" She turned toward the mouth of the cave where she'd been certain Phame had taken Kayla.

"That's what Nathan said."

Gem nuzzled her hand as Alex scanned the men who had come to help find Kayla. "Where's Harvey?"

"He left at lunch, something about a doctor's appointment."

Harvey always seemed to be missing when she needed him. She nodded to each man as they gathered nearby. Practically every deputy and all of Nathan's on-duty city officers were here. Why had Phame drawn most of the police force of Pearl Springs and Russell County out of town? Except for Nathan.

Her face turned cold as blood drained from it. She whipped out her phone and dialed his number.

"I'm afraid Chief Landry is unavailable."

Kayla! Alex's knees threatened to buckle. She had to keep it together. "What have you done to him?"

"He's nursing a leg wound, which is going to make it really hard to keep him alive until you get here."

"You shot him?"

"I told him not to run, but he didn't listen."

"I don't believe you."

"Answer your FaceTime call. And then I want you here, on the point facing Eagle Ridge."

Alex looked at the phone. Kayla was FaceTiming her. She accepted the call, and Nathan appeared on her screen standing on a metal folding chair with a noose and slack rope around his neck. His left pants leg had a dark stain on it.

Her world shifted, and she fought the lightheadedness that engulfed her brain.

"Don't come!" He yelled the words.

Kayla kicked the chair, tilting it. The rope tightened as Nathan grabbed the noose around his neck and scrambled to right the chair.

"I'm on my way."

"See to it you come alone. If I even suspect that anyone is with you, I'll kill him."

"I'll be alone."

"To make sure, stay on the phone."

"The call will drop when I get to the road."

"You better hope it doesn't, but if it does, you have ten minutes to get here."

It would drop. There was no service of any kind once she left the ridge. She had to trust that God would help her.

It dawned on her—Kayla wouldn't kill Nathan. Not until she had Alex.

She looked at the phone. The call was still live. "There's no way I can get to Harper's Point in ten minutes from here. You will not see my face until I know Nathan is all right. I'll call you once I get reception, and I expect to see him alive and well."

"You're not telling me what to do."

"That's the only way you're going to get me to the Point."
Alex ended the call and looked at Mark. "You heard?"

"Yes. What's the plan?"

"Get everyone to the point, a few at a time. I'll wait for
you to get in place before I confront Kayla. And no sirens, no
flashing lights. Radio silence—that goes for phones too. We
can text. Then set up with your rifle."

Something flashed in his eyes. Fear? Surely not.

"Do you have a problem with that? You were a sniper in
Afghanistan, right?"

Mark gave her a curt nod. "I don't have a problem."

He clearly did, but once again she felt that sense of peace.
She'd have to trust him. "Have the men surround the point
but hold back unless there's a need for them. I'll trust you to
know if that happens."

He stood a little taller. "I won't let you down."

"I know you won't."

Fifteen minutes later, Alex was glad she'd met only a handful
of vehicles on her mad dash to the point. She turned onto the
road leading to Harper's Point and waited for Mark. Once he
pulled in behind her, she got out, and he met her with Gem
at his side. The dog might come in handy.

"The others are parking farther back and will hike in closer
to the lake," he said, his posture tense.

"Good."

"You sure you want to do this?"

She lifted her chin. "Nathan's life depends on it."

"I know."

For the first time, Alex saw respect in Mark's eyes. She just
hoped she lived to enjoy a better relationship with him. "If
you see a chance to take Kayla out, take it."

He sucked in a breath. "I will."

"Can you kill a woman?"

"If I have to."

Alex hoped they could take her alive. But she would not let Kayla kill Nathan.

"I'm counting on you, Mark."

Still standing almost at attention, he dipped his head in acknowledgment. "Be careful. And I have your six."

She smiled. "I know."

Alex turned, and he followed close behind as she walked toward the lake. A quarter of a mile from the point, they slipped into the woods, and she was thankful for the weekend rain that made walking on the dead leaves quieter.

Mark veered off from her to find a spot where he'd have an unobstructed view of the area. The clearing came into view, and she fought the panic brought on by seeing Nathan standing on a chair with a rope around his neck.

Not only that, Kayla had pulled her vehicle between Nathan and the trees. It was going to be difficult for Mark to get a good shot from the direction he'd taken. He'd have to backtrack and come down on the other side of the road. Maybe Alex could lure her out into the open.

The metal chair wasn't stable enough for Nathan to put his full weight on it. If he did, the chair would topple over. His arms ached from gripping the noose to keep his body from sagging and tightening the rope around his neck. He didn't know how much longer he could hold on, but he had to do something to keep Kayla from killing Alexis.

His leg burned where she'd grazed him, but it didn't appear the bullet had caused any lasting damage. He'd have to live for that to mean anything. Running had been a fool thing to do, but he'd felt he had to try.

Kayla paced in front of him. Maybe if she came close enough, he could push off with the chair and use the rope to swing himself far enough out to kick the gun from her hand.

Almost as if she read his mind, she moved away and looked up the road. "Where is she?" she muttered.

"She's not coming."

"Oh, she'll be here. She's in love with you."

"Don't know why you think that."

"Any fool can see it."

Could Alexis really love him? Pain ripped through his biceps, and he tried resting his weight on the chair. It wobbled like a newborn foal.

Kayla's phone rang, and she answered it. "You're too late."

Kayla was taunting her. Alex could see Nathan, and she wasn't about to give away her position by contradicting her words. "I told you I couldn't get to the point in ten minutes."

"I want you here, at the beach."

"Not until I see that Nathan is all right." Alex was getting under Kayla's skin, but she wasn't sure if that was a good thing or bad. Her phone lit up with the FaceTime call. She answered, and a close-up of Nathan standing on the chair, the rope still around his neck, came into view. He looked tired, and the bloodstain on his pants had grown. "Get him down!"

"Nope, not until you're here with us."

"Looks like we're at an impasse."

Kayla swung around and aimed her gun at him. "I don't think so. If you're not where I can see you in five seconds, I'm shooting your boyfriend in the knee."

"He's not my boyfriend."

"Then you won't care." She took aim.

Kayla would do exactly what she promised.

"Wait!" With her heart in her throat, Alex jogged out of the woods and onto the road. "I'm here."

"About time. Lay your gun on the ground. Your backup too."

"I don't have a backup," she said, laying the larger Sig on the gravel road.

"I don't believe you." She turned and fired in Nathan's direction, then turned back. "Lay it on the ground or I won't miss the next time."

Reluctantly, Alex pulled the smaller Sig from her waistband and laid it beside the other one.

"Now, come forward. Slow and easy."

When Alex was ten yards away, Kayla whirled around and pulled the chair out from under Nathan's feet.

"No!" For a second Alex could do nothing but stare as Nathan struggled to keep the noose from tightening and cutting off his air. If he died . . . she couldn't bear it.

"Now you'll know what it's like to lose someone you love."

Like a fiery ball, a rage so powerful it almost blinded Alex roared through her body. She launched herself at Kayla, but the woman was ready for Alex and used her momentum to flip her on the ground. Alex rolled and bounded to her feet as Kayla came at her again.

Alex tackled her, grabbing for the gun, and they fought for it. Kayla was much stronger than she looked. Alex couldn't break her hold on the gun as Kayla pointed it at Alex's head.

Suddenly the air split with the sound of a rifle. Kayla jerked her head toward Nathan as he crumpled to the ground, the rope sliced by Mark's bullet.

"No!" Rage darkened Kayla's eyes.

With a growl, Gem raced toward them, her fangs bared. Kayla's eyes widened and she swung the gun toward the dog. Alex knocked her hand away as Gem latched onto Kayla's arm, and she dropped the gun.

Kayla screamed. "Call the dog off!"

Footsteps pounded toward them. "Donne, Gem!" Mark said. The dog dropped her arm. "Garde."

Gem guarded Kayla as Alex yanked the woman's arm behind her back. "You are under arrest."

"I want a lawyer," Kayla snarled.

"Cuff her and take her to jail." Alex turned to Mark as deputies overran the area. "I have to see about Nathan."

"An ambulance is almost here," Mark said.

Thank God. She rushed to where Nathan struggled to get on his hands and knees. "Wait, I'll help you."

His eyes brightened. "You're okay," he whispered.

"I am," she said softly. "How about you?"

"I've been better."

67

Two hours later Alex ground her molars as Nathan insisted on walking out of the emergency room under his own power.

She opened the passenger door to her SUV. "You're stubborn, you know."

"Pot calling the kettle black?"

Alex narrowed her eyes.

"The bullet just grazed me, and I didn't lose enough blood to require a transfusion. There was absolutely no reason for me to stay."

Once he had his seat belt secured, she walked around to the driver's side. She wasn't moving too swift herself, but she'd never admit it to him.

"Don't you need to check out Kayla's rental?" he asked once she pulled away from the hospital.

"Mark is taking care of it."

"I'm glad you two put your differences behind you."

"Me too. He's a good man."

Nathan's phone chimed with a text. "It's my CI."

They hadn't heard from J. R. in almost a week. "What does he say?"

He groaned. "The Russian drug dealers are coming to Pearl Springs tonight with a shipment of heroin. They'll be handing it off to the Pearl Springs contact."

"Where?"

"You'll never guess—Harper's Point."

This time she groaned. Any other time and place. "What time?"

"He'll let me know."

She glanced at him. "Why don't you sit this one out?"

"Same reason you won't."

He had her there. "When we get to my grandparents' house, come in and rest until it's time to go."

"No can do. I wouldn't be able to relax there. Drop me off at police headquarters. Once I take care of business, I'll go to my house and catch some rest."

"Okay." She didn't argue because she knew it wouldn't do any good. And she was hovering, something she'd hate if he were doing it. But she'd almost lost him this afternoon. She was still processing and was pretty sure he was as well. Had to be the reason they hadn't talked about what went down today.

"Or . . ." He opened his phone. "Why don't I call and see if there's anything I absolutely have to tend to right now? If there isn't, let's drive to Harper's Point and make a plan."

Her body tensed. "Now?" She shook her head. "That's the last place I want to go."

"I don't want to go there either, but that's where the drugs are coming in tonight. Until today I hadn't been there in years, and I figure you haven't either. We need to get the lay of the land to know how to position our officers."

She clenched her fist and rubbed her thumb against her finger. Finally she took a deep breath and nodded. "You're right."

Half an hour later they pulled onto the gravel road that

led to the lake. "The mayor plans to have this blacktopped," Alex said.

"I know, and an influx of visitors like the mayor expects is going to be problematic. I hope he plans to come up with additional money for my department."

"Same here. We're stretched thin over the county as it is." She pulled close to the lake and parked, and they climbed out of her SUV. They both were making small talk to avoid thinking about what happened earlier.

Alex refused to look toward the tree where Kayla had held Nathan prisoner, and instead faced west as the sun dipped over Eagle Ridge. It would be dark in another couple of hours, but with Indian summer temps, it was comfortable. And any other time she would've noticed the beauty of the area.

Sweat bloomed on her hands, and she wiped them on her pants. "Let's get this done and get out of here."

Nathan took her hand and squeezed it, then gently drew her into his arms.

"I thought you were going to die when I saw that rope around your neck."

His body tensed. "And I was afraid she would kill you."

Alex slipped her arm around him, and he relaxed into her touch. "I know. I thought . . ." Alex shivered.

He turned her to face him. "The worst thing was when I saw you coming down that road, and I was afraid one or both of us might die . . ." He gently cupped her face in his hands. "I prayed I'd have a chance to tell you how I felt."

"I . . ." Alex swallowed hard as his thumb caressed her jaw. "I can't do it."

His thumb stilled. "What do you mean?"

She stepped back, a band constricting her heart so tight she couldn't breathe. "I thought you were going to die. And . . . I just can't do it."

68

The finality in her voice was like a dagger to his heart. "You can't do what?" He had to make her say it.

Alex palmed her hands, as if to push him away, then pressed them together prayer style against her lips. Nathan pulled her hands away from her face. "Say it! Tell me you don't love me."

She turned her head. "That's just the problem. I do love you."

"I don't understand."

Alex wrapped her arms around her waist. "Didn't you ever wonder why I never had a pet?"

"What? What does not having a pet have to do with this?"

Her chest shook as she took a breath. "Everything. Think about it. What happens when you have pets?"

"You love them?"

"And then they die." She was practically shouting. "I can't . . . I just can't."

He had to make her see the risk was worth it. "Alexis, you can't"—a text on his cell phone dinged and he silenced it— "please—"

"You better check that."

Nathan stared at her, wanting to make her understand. "Not until we settle this."

Alex lifted her chin. "I'm sorry, but it's settled."

There was no getting through to her. Another text came in, vibrating on his belt. He grabbed his phone. "The drug dealers will be here by eight."

She frowned. "Is that enough time to pull everyone together?"

"It has to be."

"Then we better get back to town."

Nathan wasn't done with their earlier conversation, but this wasn't the time to have it.

At seven that night Nathan scanned the room in the Russell County Sheriff's Department where he and Alexis were holding a joint briefing. She stood behind the lectern, explaining their plan.

They'd limited the team to eight, counting Nathan and Alexis. He'd intended to bring Jared into the loop, but Nathan's call to him went to voice mail. He'd called Peggy and learned his sergeant had volunteered for the night patrolman's shift and had gone home to catch a nap.

The other six officers, four of them Russell County deputies and two of his officers, made up the rest of the team. Nine total if he counted Gem, who sat at Mark's feet, ears cocked and ready to go. Nathan turned his attention to Alexis, who was wrapping up.

"All right, everyone," she said. "We'll rendezvous at the lake. Get your vehicles out of sight and then get into position. We don't have a full moon, but there's still enough light to expose you, so be mindful of staying out of sight until you get the radio command to move forward. And no texts."

Nathan adjusted his earpiece, where he would receive radio communications. When the drug dealers handed off the drugs to their contact, it was the signal to execute the operation.

Alexis stepped away from the lectern. "Can I ride with you?"

He nodded. "I'll pick you up at the sally port."

"Why?" She frowned. "Kayla is in jail."

"I asked her about the attacks with a rifle, and she indicated if she'd shot at you, she would've hit you. Not sure that means anything, but what if she wasn't your shooter?" A strand of hair had fallen out of her ponytail clip. He clenched his jaw instead of hooking it behind her ear. "Let me pick you up."

The frown lines smoothed out. "If it'll keep you off my case. Go ahead while I grab a couple of magazines for my Sig."

Nathan double-timed it to his truck and then pulled into the sally port. Five minutes later, he texted Alexis.

Where are you?

69

A drenaline pumped through Alex's body as she slipped two magazines in her duty belt. Phame was in jail, and if they crushed this drug ring tonight, it would be the perfect ending to the day. *No. A perfect ending would be in Nathan's arms.*

A shadow crossed the door, and she looked up. Harvey stood in the doorway. "What's up?"

"I might ask you the same thing."

Alex shrugged. "Got an operation going down."

"And you left me out of it?"

"I thought you went to the doctor and then home." Harvey's mottled face didn't look good. "And from the looks of you, home is where you need to be now."

"I'm fine." His nostrils flared as he crossed his arms over his chest. "You should've kept me in the loop."

She frowned. He was getting much too worked up over being left out. "What's going on, Harvey?"

"Nothing! I just don't like people doing things behind my back. I gotta—" He grabbed his chest.

Alex rushed to his side. "Are you having chest pains?"

Harvey barely nodded before he pitched to the floor. She

yelled for help while dialing 911 for an ambulance. None of her deputies came, and she called Nathan. "I need your help."

Alex hung up before he could respond and felt her chief of staff's carotid artery. His heart was beating way too fast. "Hang on. An ambulance is on its way." She loosened Harvey's belt and then his collar. "Can you cough?"

"Got to tell . . ."

"Don't talk, just cough." It was the only thing she knew to do to help him before the ambulance arrived.

Footsteps ran down the hall, and then Nathan knelt beside them. "What happened?"

"Heart attack, I think."

He turned to Harvey. "Do you have nitroglycerin?"

"Pocket. But first . . . drugs. Tonight."

An approaching siren gave Alex hope. "Hang on, Harvey. Help is almost here."

"You don't understand—" He grabbed his chest again, and his eyes fluttered before he lost consciousness.

Paramedics burst into the room and took over. Nathan helped Alex stand. "I didn't think you were going to tell Harvey about the drug bust tonight."

Alex shook her head. "I didn't."

"Then how did he know?" Nathan frowned. "You think Harvey is the dealer's contact?"

"I don't believe that. Maybe one of the other deputies told him."

The paramedic yelled for everyone to stand back as he applied paddles to Harvey's chest. The screen on the paramedic's laptop caught Alex's attention. Nothing but squiggles.

Harvey's body jumped as the medic applied current. No change. Once more he applied the paddles. This time a more normal heartbeat appeared.

"We're taking him to the hospital here in Russell County,"

the lead paramedic said while the other two worked to get him ready. "Once he's stabilized, they'll probably airlift him to Erlanger in Chattanooga."

"Thank you." She gave him the phone number for Harvey's wife. "She can give you background information on him."

Alex took a deep breath to clear her head. How *had* Harvey known about the drug operation tonight? She'd only said there was an operation going down, not what kind.

Nathan touched her arm. "It's getting late. You ready?"

She glanced toward her chief of staff, wanting to accompany him to the hospital, but there was nothing she could do to help him. "I'm ready."

Once they were on the road, Alex called a couple of her off-duty deputies and asked them to go to the hospital and keep her informed of Harvey's condition.

Alex checked her watch. Seven thirty. What if the drug dealers came early—before she and Nathan could get in place? She radioed Mark. "Any sign of the dealers?"

"Not yet. Where are you?"

"Ten minutes out." She explained what happened to Harvey.

"Is he going to be okay?"

"I hope so. You think it would be safe for us to park a little closer to the lake?"

"Should be. I'll radio you if anyone arrives."

Nathan turned onto the gravel road and drove halfway down to the lake. He pointed to a trail in the woods. "I'm going to park in there."

Once he had the truck out of sight from the road, they climbed out and crept nearer to the lake. Alex adjusted her body armor as she scanned the area. A half moon gave barely enough light to make out the two deputies hiding near the pier. She looked to her right for Mark, but he was hidden in the shadows of the trees.

Eight o'clock came and went. No dealers. "You think they found out?" Alex whispered.

"Don't know."

"What's that?" She couldn't quite identify the sound, maybe a whine? It wasn't a vehicle. Alex cocked her head toward the road, but the whine came from the lake, and she turned in time to see a speedboat round the curve in the lake.

The deal was going down.

The boat docked at the old pier, and four men clambered onto the iron structure, one carrying a bag. Probably the drugs. But where was the contact?

Alex froze as lights flashed from the road. She poked Nathan, who stood beside her. He sucked in a breath when a Pearl Springs patrol car eased by them.

"Who is it?" she whispered.

"Not sure. Let's give it a minute."

Alex held her breath, and beside her Nathan tensed as the patrol car parked near the pier, blocking the men from view. The only one with a clear shot was Mark.

A shot came from the direction of the lake. One of the deputies they'd stationed near the pier pitched forward.

"Go! Go! Go!" Alex yelled into the mic.

Guns drawn, Nathan and Alex raced with their teams through the wooded area to the lake. The drug dealers were scattering. One hopped in the patrol car while two ran for the boat.

Alex searched for the other deputy who'd been staked out near the pier and found him. He was crouched behind the concrete picnic table, the wounded deputy beside him.

"You take whoever is in the patrol car. I'm going after those two," Alex yelled to Nathan. She dashed down the pier toward the men running for the boat. "Police! Stop!"

A bullet whizzed by her head.

"Get down!" Nathan yelled from behind her.

Alex dropped to the pier floor. The heat from the next bullet burned her ear. A couple inches to the right, and she'd be dead. Alex couldn't stay on the pier and rolled off into the waist-deep water, landing on her feet. Thank goodness it wasn't ten feet farther out where the lake dropped off.

The boat motor roared to life. No! She couldn't let them get away. She fired, dropping one of the men, then fired again, hitting the motor. It died midsputter. Two deputies splashed in the water toward the boat. They would take care of the escaping drug dealers.

Alex used the iron steps to pull herself out of the water. Halfway up, someone extended a hand. Jared. He held a gun in the other hand, and it was pointed at her. "What are you doing?"

"You're my ticket out of here."

She wasn't going anywhere with him. "You're the local connection."

"Shut up."

Was that all criminals knew to say? "You're the one who's been shooting at me. Why?"

"I said shut up. Now, get up here!"

Alex took a step down the ladder. Her vest should protect her from a chest shot. "No. I want to know why."

"It was Harvey's idea. He found out about my drug dealing and threatened to turn me in if I didn't help him." He waved the gun toward the boat. "He thought if you went back to Chattanooga, he'd get his old job back."

A slight motion behind Jared caught her eye. Nathan. "But you killed Trevor Martin."

"He got greedy. When you came to town with a serial killer on your trail, it seemed like a good time to get rid of him."

She'd never figured Jared for a cold-blooded killer. Alex's

teeth chattered. The water was so cold. She hated jumping back in it.

"Enough talk. Climb up on the pier."

"Sorry." Alex launched herself into the water, angling for a spot under the pier. Jared fired at her, the bullet slamming into her back. He fired again, and burning pain seared her head.

70

Nathan dashed toward Jared, hitting his sergeant just as he fired at Alexis.

Jared turned, his eyes wide, then he dropped his gun and crumpled to the pier floor. Nathan kicked the gun out of reach and searched the water. Where was Alexis? "I need a light!"

Two deputies raced to the end of the pier and shined their lights in the water. Even though the water wasn't deep, if she was unconscious, she could drown. If she wasn't already dead.

Nathan caught a glimpse of something dark in the water and dove in.

ater closed over Alex. So cold. *Swim.* Too cold. Regret washed over her. She didn't want to die. Not yet. Had to tell Nathan how she felt.

You rejected him.

Had to. Didn't want to go through the pain of losing him. She would be all alone then.

You are never alone.

Never?

I will never leave you nor forsake you.

Peace enveloped Alex. Rough hands lifted her head above water.

"Her lips are blue. She's going into shock!"

The voices sounded so far away. She didn't want to leave where she was, but then someone cradled her in his arms. Nathan. Alex relaxed into his embrace. *I'm sorry. I should have told you that I love you.*

"Hang on," Nathan whispered in her ear. "An ambulance is on the way."

72

A WEEK LATER

Alex leaned back in Nathan's pickup as he closed her door then jogged around to the driver's side.

He slid across the seat and pressed the start button. "Thanks for coming with me today. Is your headache better?"

Alex nodded. Jared's bullet had creased her skull, and she'd used the residual headache to keep from seeing Nathan. Not because she didn't want to, but because fear immobilized her. But she'd made up her mind to end the fear today.

"It's a beautiful day. How about a drive up on Walden Ridge?"

It *was* a beautiful day with the sky so blue it almost hurt her eyes to look at it. "Sounds good."

Her mind whirled in the silence as Nathan drove. *Tell him. Not while he's driving . . .*

"Jared will be released from the hospital today."

She jumped as he broke the silence. "I guess that means Russell County jail will be his next stop," she said, glad to talk about normal things. She still couldn't believe Jared and her chief of staff had hatched a plan to get rid of her. Harvey survived his heart attack long enough to confess the plan.

"Too bad about Harvey," Nathan said.

"Yeah." His funeral had been two days ago.

"Maybe now things will be tamer than the past two weeks with both Jared and Kayla in jail. The Hamilton County District Attorney wants to try her first, but our DA is digging in his heels—he wants first shot at her."

Soon, he pulled into a turnout and parked. Nathan helped her from the truck, and they walked to a picnic table where they had a view of the valley below and the mountains to the east. Even this late in the season, there were splotches of color, mostly yellow. Nathan took her hand and they stood letting the sun warm their faces.

"It's so peaceful here," she murmured.

"Yeah," he said softly.

Her heart thudded as he turned her to face him. *Now.* But before she could say anything, he withdrew a small box.

He held it out to her. "It's not much, moneywise . . ."

She carefully unwrapped the box and lifted the top. A necklace with a delicate chain and a gold heart lay nestled in the satin. She touched the writing on the heart. *I will never leave you nor forsake you.*

Alex lifted her hand to her mouth as tears threatened to spill from her eyes. The very words God had spoken to her heart when she was in the water. "I—I need t-to tell you something."

"Not yet." Nathan pulled her to her feet. "Let me fasten this around your neck." Once it was fastened, he turned her around to face him again. "I love you, and I hope one day you'll be able to return that love."

This is it. Tell him. A lump squeezed her throat, making it impossible for her to speak. She lifted her gaze, and the pain in his blue eyes loosened the chains around her heart. Alex pressed her lips together and touched his cheek. Then she took a deep breath. "Maybe today?"

His eyes widened. "Are you sure?"

She nodded, and her heart drummed against her ribs as his gaze traveled to her lips. Nathan drew her closer until he was only a heartbeat away. Longing like she'd never felt before washed over Alex, and she held her breath, waiting.

His kiss was tentative at first but as she responded, he pressed his lips against hers, capturing not only her lips but her heart as well. She lost herself in his embrace as her whole world exploded into fireworks.

When he released her, she lay her head on his chest, feeling his galloping heartbeat match her own.

He leaned back and tilted her face toward his. "Have I ever told you that I love you?"

His gentle words took what little breath his kiss had left. "Maybe," she whispered.

"Just didn't want to let another minute pass without telling you again."

The love in his eyes undid her, but she refused to cry. Not until she did what she came here for. "I . . . this is so hard for me." She looked down, then took a deep breath and lifted her gaze. "When I was in the water, my biggest regret was that I hadn't told you how I felt."

She swallowed hard and looked away from him toward the lake.

"And . . ."

She turned to face him again and almost lost herself in his blue eyes. Her heart beat so hard she could barely breathe. "I-I love you too."

Nathan picked her up and swung her around. "Thank you, God!" He set her down. "You'll stay here in Pearl Springs?"

Alex couldn't ask him to give up the town he loved. She gave him a tiny smile. "It's growing on me."

ACKNOWLEDGMENTS

Thanks to my daughter, Carole, for always encouraging me and telling me I can do it! And to the rest of my family and friends who encourage me on this writing journey.

To my editors, Rachel McRae and Kristin Kornoelje, thank you for making my stories so much better. I'd be lost without you!

To the art, editorial, marketing, and sales team at Revell, especially Michele Misiak and Karen Steele, who have to deal with me directly—thank you for all your hard work. And to the ones behind the scenes, you're awesome!

To Julie Gwinn, thank you for your direction and for working so tirelessly with me and for being my friend.

To the wonderful and friendly people I've met as I research the new setting in the Cumberland Plateau near Chattanooga. I look forward to returning soon for more research.

To Christopher A. Davis, thank you for helping me refresh my chess game! And for all the brainstorming on how to integrate the chess moves into the story. Any mistakes are totally on me.

To my readers . . . you are awesome! Thank you for reading my stories. Without you, my books wouldn't exist.

As always, to Jesus, who gives me the words.

Read on for more heart-pounding suspense from Patricia Bradley...

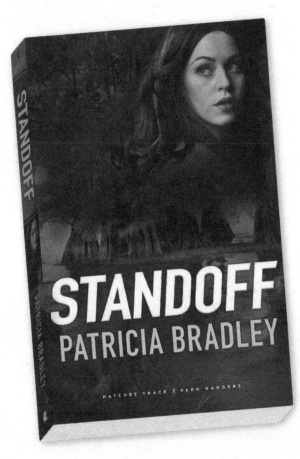

AVAILABLE NOW

1

NATCHEZ, MISSISSIPPI

Brooke Danvers checked her watch. Her dad had said six and it was almost that. She quickly twisted her hair into a ponytail and then buckled her Sig Sauer to her waist. While she hadn't been sworn in as a law enforcement ranger yet, Mississippi was an open-carry state, and her dad had okayed her wearing it.

She hadn't stopped smiling since he'd asked if she wanted to ride along with him tonight. It didn't even bother her that he'd chosen Sunday night because there wouldn't be many cars out and about.

Brooke glanced toward the flat-brimmed hat that she'd worn all day at Melrose, the almost two-hundred-year-old mansion where she'd led tours. At times it felt as though the August heat and humidity would cook her head. She wouldn't need the hat tonight, though, and left it sitting on her childhood bed.

Returning home after fifteen years while contractors finished the remodel on her water-damaged apartment was proving to be an experience. She'd always heard grown children shouldn't return to the nest, and now she knew why. At her

371

place, she came and went as she pleased without anyone asking questions. But now it was almost like she'd stepped back into her teenage years. Not that she wasn't thankful her parents had offered to let her move into her old room, but it would be good to get back in her own apartment in a couple of weeks. The chimes from the grandfather clock sent her hurrying down the hall to her dad's home office.

It was empty. He'd said he had work to do before they left . . . She quickly walked to her mom's studio.

"Where's Dad?" she asked.

Her mom turned from her easel. "He got a call and left. Said to tell you if you still wanted to do the ride along, text Gary to pick you up."

Disappointment was swift, and Brooke ground her teeth to keep from letting it show.

"He said something about you riding with him tomorrow night."

That brightened her mood slightly. Her phone dinged with a text. Gary, the retiring ranger she was replacing.

Are you riding with me?

She quickly texted him.

Yes. What time?

Give me an hour and I'll pick you up.

She sent him a thumbs-up emoji and hooked her phone on her belt.

"Come see what I'm working on," her mom said.

Brooke edged into the room. It wasn't often she got a chance to see an unfinished work by her mother. The painting was of her very pregnant sister. "Oh, wow," she said. "That's beautiful. She'll love it."

"I hope so. Meghan's feeling kind of . . ."

"Fat? That's what she told me the other day," Brooke said. "I tried to tell her that wasn't true, and maybe this will show her."

"I'm glad you like it. I should have it finished in time to take with the others to Knoxville next month."

The baby's due date was a couple of months away, just after her mom's gallery showing of her work ended. They both turned as the doorbell rang. It couldn't be Gary already, and besides, he would just honk. "I'll get it," Brooke said and hurried to open the front door.

"Jeremy?" she said, her stomach fluttering at the sight of one of Natchez's most eligible bachelors. Had she forgotten a date?

He looked behind him then turned back to Brooke with laughter in his eyes. "I think so."

Heat flushed her face, and it had more to do with the broad shoulders and lean body of the man on her doorstep than the temperature. "I wasn't expecting you. I don't have a lot of time, but do you want to come in?"

"Since it's a little hot and humid out here, coming in would be good," he teased. "And I apologize for dropping by without calling, but I was afraid you'd tell me you were busy."

Brooke steeled herself against the subtle citrus fragrance of his cologne as he walked past her. She'd had exactly two dates with Jeremy Steele and hadn't figured out why he was even interested in her. She was so not his type. The handsome widower tended to lean more toward blondes.

"Hello, Mrs. Danvers," Jeremy said to her mother, who had followed her to the living room.

"How many times have I told you to call me Vivian?"

"I'll try to remember that," he said with a thousand-watt smile.

"Good. A thirtysomething calling me Mrs. Danvers makes

me feel old," she replied. "And since I know you didn't come to see me, I'll go back to my painting."

"Good to see you . . . Vivian." Then he turned to Brooke and glanced at her uniform. "Are you working tonight?"

"Sort of," she said. "I was going to ride along with Dad on his patrol, but he canceled and turned me over to another ranger. Why?"

"I know it's last minute, but I was hoping you'd have time to join me at King's Tavern," he said. "I have a hankering for one of their flatbreads."

Her mouth watered at the thought. Brooke hadn't eaten since lunch, and she could do last minute, at least this time. But the question of why *her* kept bobbing to the surface. Ignoring it, she said, "That sounds good. I'll text Gary to pick me up later."

"Gary?"

She grinned at him, tempted to describe the aging ranger as a hunk but instead settled for the truth. "He's the ranger I'm replacing when he *retires.*"

Red crept into Jeremy's face. "Oh, that guy. Are you even sworn in yet?"

"No, that's next week. I talked my dad into letting me get a little early practice." It helped having a father who was the district ranger, even if he wasn't overjoyed about her becoming a law enforcement ranger. Then she looked down. "I need to change first."

"You're fine like you are," he said.

Maybe to him, but she was not about to go on a date wearing a National Park Service uniform and a Sig strapped to her waist. "Give me five minutes."

After Brooke changed into a lavender sundress and slipped into sandals, she gave herself a brief once-over. While the dress showed no cleavage, it accentuated curves the NPS uniform hid. She freed her hair from the ponytail and put the elastic holder in her purse. In this heat, she might have to put it up again.

Brooke checked her makeup. She rarely wore anything other than pink gloss. Thick lashes framed her eyes and the sun had deepened her olive skin to a nice tan. Brooke wasn't sure where she got her darker complexion and hair since her mom and sister, and even her dad, were fair and blond, but she wasn't complaining.

Tonight she wanted something more and added a shimmering gloss to her lips. Then she took a deep breath and slowly blew it out. Didn't do much good with her heart still thudding in her chest.

Why was Jeremy pursuing *her*? The women usually seen on his arm were ones who could mix and mingle with the rich and famous. Women who could further his career. Jeremy was a Mississippi state senator with his sights set on Washington like his daddy, while she was a National Park Service ranger who didn't care one thing about leaving Natchez.

Her heart kicked into high gear. Had the M-word just crossed her thoughts? Impossible. It wasn't only that she wasn't his type, he definitely wasn't hers. She was a simple girl with a simple lifestyle—nothing like the Steeles.

In the 1850s, half the millionaires in the United States lived in Natchez, and the Steeles were among them. A hundred and seventy years later, the family's holdings had increased substantially, not to mention the Steele men had a long history of public service.

Jeremy's dad was the retiring US senator and his son was poised to take his place in the next election. His photo appeared regularly in the *Natchez Democrat*, often with a beautiful woman on his arm. And never the same one.

She sighed. If they lived in England, he would be royalty,

and she would be the commoner who ended up with a broken heart.

Brooke chided herself about being melodramatic and hurried to her mom's studio. "Jeremy and I are grabbing something to eat," she said.

Her mom laid her brush down. "What about your ride along?"

"I'll catch up to Gary later," she said.

When she rejoined Jeremy, his eyes widened, and he whistled. "Nice," he said.

Jeremy Steele knew how to make a woman feel special. As they stepped out of the house, she immediately noticed the ten-degree drop in temperature from when Jeremy first arrived and nodded at the thunderheads that had rolled in. "Guess that means we won't leave the top down."

"I think we can make it to the tavern before it starts."

Ten minutes later Jeremy escorted her into King's Tavern, where the original brick walls and dark wooden beams added to the mystique of the inn that had been rumored to have a ghost. The tantalizing aroma of steak drew her gaze to the open grill, but she had her heart set on one of their wood-fired flatbreads.

"Inside or out?" Jeremy asked.

"The backyard, if you don't think it'll rain," she said.

"If it does, we'll simply come in." He gave the waitress their drink order, sweet tea for both of them, and let her know where to find them. They had their choice of picnic tables and chose the one on the hill. Once they were seated, Jeremy reached across, taking her hand. His touch and the intensity in his brown eyes almost took her breath away. "I'm glad you came."

"Me too," Brooke said, trying not to sound breathy. The question worrying around in her head wouldn't wait any longer. "Why me?"

"What do you mean?"

"Why are you interested in dating me? We don't travel in the same circles."

"But we do. We've gone to church together since we were kids."

"And you sit in your family's pew clear across the sanctuary."

His eyes twinkled. "We don't have a family pew."

She laughed. "I'd hate to be the one who sat in your mom's seat some Sunday."

"You're funny," he said. "That's one of the things I like about you."

"But I'm so different from the women you usually date." There. She'd said it.

He lightly stroked the heel of her palm. "That's what I like best. You're real . . . not saying anything bad about anyone I've dated, but honestly, sometimes I think the aura of the Steele name is the attraction. That and Dad's money." Then Jeremy smiled, popping dimples in his cheeks. "But you were never like that. Even in high school you were never afraid to tell it like it was."

Heat infused her cheeks. She'd been accused of that many times, usually by someone who didn't want to hear the truth. "I'm working on not being so blunt," she said. "I hope I never hurt your feelings."

"I won't say never," he said with a wink, "but you never said anything that didn't need saying."

Okay, she'd been rude and hadn't fallen all over him because of who he was . . . Before she could ask *why* again, the waitress approached with their drinks, and Brooke pulled her hand away from Jeremy's, missing his touch immediately. Maybe she should let go of her questions and let their relationship play out.

Once the waitress left with their orders, Jeremy took her hand again. "I've looked a long time for the right person."

His brown eyes held her gaze. He surely didn't mean her. Did he? "What about Molly? I'd hate for her to get attached to me and then we stop seeing each other."

"I don't plan for that to happen. And Molly is already crazy about you."

Brooke couldn't keep from smiling. His six-year-old daughter was a sweetheart.

"How about if we take it slow?" he asked. "Get to know one another?"

"No pressure?"

"No pressure."

Her phone dinged and she glanced at the screen. A text from Gary.

Pick you up in an hour?

Brooke hesitated, torn between wanting to spend more time with Jeremy and getting practical experience on her job. If the text had been from her dad, it wouldn't even be a question—she had so much to learn from him, but Gary, not so much. She'd known him all her life and he'd always been laid-back, never wanting to climb the ladder within the park service. But if her dad thought she should ride with him . . . With a sigh, she looked up from her phone. "Can you have me back to my house in forty-five minutes?"

"Do I want to? Nope," he said. "But I can."

She texted Gary an okay, wishing it was her dad she would be riding with. Then Brooke stared at her phone a second. What had been so important for her dad to stand her up?

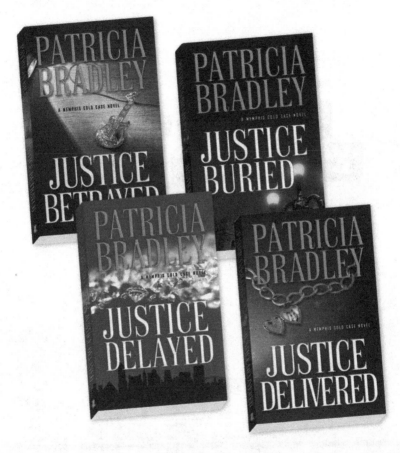

Meet

Patricia
BRADLEY

www.ptbradley.com

 PTBradley1

 Patricia Bradley Author